PRAISE F

"Fleet and fun, *The Fireballer* will appeal to fans of *The Natural* and Robert Coover's *The Universal Baseball Association*. Frank Ryder is a classic American hero—the phenom who has to overcome his own terrible past. Mark Stevens has done the impossible: He actually had me rooting for the Orioles."

—Stewart O'Nan, coauthor of *Faithful* and author of *Ocean State*

"Seldom do I read a book that knocks my socks off the way *The Fireballer* did. This is a feel-good baseball story with a hold on the vernacular, the heart, the soul, the big picture, and the subtleties of America's favorite summer pastime. The characters are beautifully etched, and pitcher Frank Ryder may be the most likeable hero since Gary Cooper gave life to Lou Gehrig on the big screen. I guarantee that you don't have to be a baseball fan to be swept up by this moving tale. With a full heart, I recommend—no, insist—that you read *The Fireballer*."

—William Kent Krueger, author of *Fox Creek* and *This Tender Land*

"Mark Stevens's *The Fireballer* is a timeless baseball story told with a love of the game and fast-moving prose that will leave you cheering and crying at the same time. Frank Ryder is the most appealing of heroes, taciturn and loyal, talented and haunted—truly haunted—and with a fastball that will change the game. With its authentic baseball scenes and its rich heart, *The Fireballer* is a novel that rests comfortably with other classics of the game."

—William Lashner, author of *The Barkeep*

"*The Fireballer* is not just a great baseball yarn that any fan of the game will enjoy—it is also a richly-layered exploration of character, regret, and redemption."

—Lou Berney, author of *November Road* and *The Long and Faraway Gone*

"The old game of baseball keeps coming up with new stories about the next twist or turn in the sport. In *The Fireballer*, Mark Stevens has invented a startling 'What if?' that stretches the limits of the game. More than a baseball book, the novel is a journey through the mind and heart of a gifted, but tragic, athlete who finds a road to redemption."

—Stephen Singular, *New York Times* bestselling author

"*The Fireballer* is a compelling story that I found hard to put down, rich with authentic baseball details and full of heart. Mark Stevens hits it out of the park with this intricate and moving tale of redemption."

—Robert Bailey, *Wall Street Journal* bestselling author of *The Golfer's Carol*

"Mark Stevens has crafted a powerful, heartfelt story—with a memorable baseball backdrop—that carves out a place alongside classics like *The Art of Fielding* and *The Natural*. Stevens knows the game—but it's his deft narrative and characters that help this book truly sing. I couldn't put it down."

—Alex Segura, bestselling author of *Secret Identity*

"You don't have to know baseball to love *The Fireballer*. At the center of this big-hearted book is Frank Ryder, a star pitcher tormented by a mistake in his past. Readers root for Frank not for his fastball, but because his redemption delivers us all."

—Stephanie Kane, award-winning mystery writer and author of *True Crime Redux*

NO LIE LASTS FOREVER

OTHER TITLES BY MARK STEVENS

Stand-Alone Fiction

The Fireballer

Allison Coil Mysteries

Antler Dust

Buried by the Roan

Trapline

Lake of Fire

The Melancholy Howl

NO LIE LASTS FOREVER

A THRILLER

MARK STEVENS

THOMAS & MERCER

This is a work of fiction. Names, characters, organizations, places, events, and incidents are either products of the author's imagination or are used fictitiously. Otherwise, any resemblance to actual persons, living or dead, is purely coincidental.

Text copyright © 2025 by Mark Stevens
All rights reserved.

No part of this book may be reproduced, or stored in a retrieval system, or transmitted in any form or by any means, electronic, mechanical, photocopying, recording, or otherwise, without express written permission of the publisher.

Published by Thomas & Mercer, Seattle

www.apub.com

Amazon, the Amazon logo, and Thomas & Mercer are trademarks of Amazon.com, Inc., or its affiliates.

EU product safety contact:
Amazon Media EU S. à r.l.
38, avenue John F. Kennedy, L-1855 Luxembourg
amazonpublishing-gpsr@amazon.com

ISBN-13: 9781662529597 (paperback)
ISBN-13: 9781662529603 (digital)

Cover design by Caroline Teagle Johnson
Cover image: © peeterv, © mikroman6 / Getty

Printed in the United States of America

For all the reporters who follow one fact to the next

CHAPTER 1
MONDAY

Flynn Martin balances on one foot, draws an X in the talcum-dry soil with the tip of her running shoe, and scolds herself for answering her phone. The signal, unfortunately, is solid. She can't fake a dropped call.

"You said this gunman dude has hostages?"

"Four. Big standoff with police."

Rick Goodman's voice calm like he runs a spa.

"And he wants a reporter as go-between?"

"He wanted Sara first."

Sara Cornette, longtime star anchor, currently lolling on a beach in Aruba.

"Naturally," says Flynn.

"The police have located the store manager. He was at a franchisee meeting out in Golden. He knows the 'gunman dude,' as you call him, is the estranged husband of one of his cashiers, a woman named Rosa. The gunman's name is Alfredo."

"I'm outside Brighton. Twenty minutes would be a miracle."

Two knife-blade clouds float next to a weak daytime moon above Longs Peak, forty-five miles to the northwest. It's a clear January day.

"The standoff is an hour old already," says Goodman.

"I'm second choice?"

"Number two ain't bad."

"Nobody remembers second anything."

"But you'll be back in your comfort zone," says Goodman. "So many cop cars it looks like they're giving out free doughnuts."

"Such a tired, cheap shot," says Flynn. "You want me there or not?"

Among all her station's reporters, Flynn has the best sources in the cop shop. First, due to her sheer number of years on the streets in the same city. Second, because her ex is a cop. But she has moved up to covering important issues and complicated subjects. Think pieces. Climate change. Groundwater abuse. Or the story today, about how global warming affects the vernalization period for wheat planted in October.

Flynn jerks a thumb at their news truck. Tamica Porter unsnaps the camera from its tripod. A seasoned videographer, Tamica prefers the meaty stories too. She is also good at spotting a lost cause.

"Am I reporting or playing a role?"

Goodman gives a protracted *hmm*. "Good question," he says. "Let's see how it goes."

A rogue lunatic with a gun . . .

A horde of cops . . .

And me in the middle . . .

"Okay. *Jesus*."

She shakes hands with the farmer, a string bean dressed in faded Carhartts. He has gray whiskers and a slew of angry comments for the water gods and government bureaucrats, so far all off camera.

"I'll be back," she tells him. "Maybe tomorrow."

Stories about climate change and the chronic water shortage make her feel worthwhile. Tamica Porter too. They are a team. They have won one regional Emmy, having traced the Big Thompson River from its headwaters to the South Platte, showing the variety of stresses on the water supply. Flynn has developed a new brand. Crime stories are a thing of the past. Crime stories remind her of her cigarette days. Now it's yoga once or twice a month. Now it's reporting about withered crops, Colorado's meager snowpack, wildfires, air pollution. She has graduated from crime.

They bomb down 85 from Brighton, Tamica behind the wheel. Yellow lights for mere mortals.

Goodman calls with a change of plans—the cops want her on the phone. She's to be patched in to the conversation from the station.

"Fine with me," says Flynn. "What's Alfredo's last name?"

"I don't think we've got it," says Goodman.

"It would be helpful."

Flynn thinks of the four hostages, imagines how they're feeling after a routine stop for gas or snacks turning into life and death.

Waiting. Wondering. Worried. Panicked.

The mayhem around the Pump 'N Go, hard by the highway where Park Avenue West ducks under I-25, puts the interstate in parking lot mode. All the ramps at the intersection are closed, and a trio of rubberneckers have compounded the problem with a three-way fender bender.

Flynn checks her phone for updates from her competitors and the cops. The stalemate is as stuck as the traffic.

What will she say to her son? Wyatt wants to one day run for president, for the sole purpose of saving the planet from its disastrous warming trend. Wyatt is the kind of fifth grader who dampens his toothbrush with three drops of water before brushing.

Flynn pictures the slow shake of Wyatt's head.

His conjured dismay matches her own.

The highway congestion makes Flynn feel stuck. *Useless. Behind. In the wrong place.* Like a bad dream where she shows up for the big college entrance test, only to discover she is hours late. Fate locked. Personal ineptness proved yet again! Does she want the traffic to get worse and make it impossible for her to get involved or clear up fast so she can try and help the cops and hostages? She isn't sure.

◆ ◆ ◆

Inside the station's control room, two green pinpoint lights flash on the desk telephone.

One, explains Goodman, is their cameraman at the scene, Danny Bell. The other, "the bozo."

"Did you get his last name?" says Flynn.

"Sanchez," says Goodman. "Alfredo Sanchez."

"Thanks."

"Bell's the left light. Those lines are both in your headset. I've got the cops on my cell phone, and I'll conference to your cell so you can hear what the cops want. Cops? I mean cop. The voice should be familiar."

Flynn sighs. "Seriously?"

"I thought you two made divorce look easy."

"I can't believe he has ever uttered the word 'negotiate.' Not his style."

Goodman ignores her. He's good at that. "The guy with the gun—Mr. Sanchez—wants to hear your voice on the phone by four p.m."

"A whole three minutes to come up with a game plan?"

On the only monitor that matters, a large sweaty man grips a prodigious black gun in one hand, a phone in the other. He towers over a rack of chips and Cheetos.

The image from Danny Bell's camera tracks the gunman as he paces between the front door and the inside of the shop. The video shudders from the long zoom.

Flynn accepts the patch-in call from Goodman.

"Max?"

Max McKenna. A cop's cop. Born cop. Her ex. Wyatt's father. A decent guy, but no longer her husband.

"Cutting it close," he says.

"You're welcome," she says. "We were standing in a wheat field on the far side of Brighton."

"He wants to negotiate through you," says Max.

"And I thought you worked vice," says Flynn.

"They thought, you know, that I could talk to you," says Max.

She pictures him standing, pacing. A tight black pullover shirt. Dark slacks. His cheeks sport an omnipresent five o'clock shadow. Nothing in his demeanor will project uncertainty.

"What? Do I require a special code? A handler?"

"Make sure he knows you don't have the power to make deals. You can listen, but don't lead him on. No coddling."

The accusatory zinger churns up gummy residue. Yes, she wants to let Wyatt be a child. Yes, she doesn't want him exposed to every one of his father's work-related horror stories.

But—*coddling?*

Four p.m.

Flynn needs time.

Doesn't have it.

Her station switches from the whimsical closing credits of a breezy afternoon talk show to a hard open of anchor Joel Dryden, looking deadpan and inscrutable. It's the same look he uses for drolly debriefing the weather forecasters, quizzing a celebrity chef, or interviewing the governor on set. Today, Dryden flies solo on the anchor desk while Sara Cornette orders another drink with a tiny umbrella somewhere in her sunburned oblivion.

"We've been monitoring a tense situation near downtown Denver that began unfolding earlier this afternoon," Dryden tells viewers. "This is earlier footage—the best images we have of the individual who has taken four hostages and drawn a huge police presence to this convenience store near I-25 at Park Avenue West. The gunman has asked to speak to one of our reporters, someone our viewers know well—Flynn Martin. They are due to begin talking any minute. For now, we'll switch to reporter Andrea Caulkins, who is live at the scene and as close as police are allowing. Andrea?"

A bass drum thumps straight from Flynn's heart. Two months ago, the station stayed with the live feed from the news helicopter as it tracked a carjacker racing at high speeds, at one point zipping the wrong way on I-25. The chase ended when the carjacker T-boned a minivan on South University, killing an innocent mother and her ten-year-old son.

Live . . .

Uncoddled . . .

No filter . . .

Andrea Caulkins wraps up her recap, which doesn't add much to Dryden's recap, even with the added flavor of having her feet on the ground out there in the real world. The station switches back to Dryden, who explains that they will "monitor the situation." He starts in on a new story—a house fire in Boulder.

Flynn's view is from Danny Bell's camera position, but her negotiations with Alfredo Sanchez won't be broadcast live.

Good.

A glance at the bank of monitors reveals that her station is the exception. All the others show tight shots of the store. Or live shots with their reporters. Or live shots from the one helicopter that all the stations share.

Flynn pushes the button.

"Mr. Sanchez?" she says. "Can you hear me okay? This is Flynn Martin."

"I didn't plan it this way."

Panicked . . .

Nervous . . .

"Don't make it worse," she says.

"Except I'll be fucked. And if all you're going to say is what the cops would say, I'll take a shot at your fucking truck."

The gun comes up. She hears the explosion in her ear. The picture wobbles.

Flynn pulls up Danny on speed dial.

"You okay?"

Five seconds feel like a week.

"Yeah," he says. "Mother*fuck*er."

Flynn's chest flashes with heat.

Danny: "Jesus Christ."

Flynn switches back.

"You want to start over?" Alfredo Sanchez glowers into the camera.

"What do you want?" she says.

Pulse up, mouth like chalk.

Sanchez turns. He takes five steps toward his hostages.

"I got no chance," says Sanchez. Poster ads on the floor-to-ceiling windows obscure the view. Soda. Chips. "My wife is screwing the manager. At my job? They dumped me. I got nothing. You know how hard it is to put together a life on eighteen fucking bucks an hour?"

"Where did you work?"

"What does it matter?"

"When did you stop working? Tell me a story."

"This ain't a fucking interview."

"You don't want to hurt anyone."

"I got nothing to lose."

"Flynn?"

It's Max on her cell. Flynn puts Sanchez on hold. "What?" she says.

"Keep him focused on what he wants."

She punches the phone to bring Sanchez back. "We can find you a job," she says. "You have to help us. Tell us what else you want so you can let these people get back to their lives."

"You ever been fired?" says Sanchez.

"No."

Never got the big promotion either . . .

"So you got no idea how it feels. Cheated on?"

"No."

But—she *wishes*. A clichéd case of straightforward cheating would have made the split a snap. Of course it would have been Max. She would never step out on anyone. Would she?

"There you go. *El número dos*. You've ever been told to your face that you are no longer worth anything?"

Except for all the times she's pushed for one of the anchor slots? And run into a series of dull dismissals?

"Not really."

"It's a yes or no."

He points his gun at the camera. At Danny.

At her.

"No."

"Lucky you."

Max on the cell: "Get him back to what he wants."

"Help us out," she says. "Tell us what you want. End this in a way you won't regret."

"One more regret don't bother me."

"Tell us," she says. "How do you get us all out of this? Why did you ask for me?"

She dreads the answer.

"Here's what I want."

In her ear: "Finally."

"No doubt I'm gonna die in a few minutes."

"Not if we all stay calm," she says.

Max: "Just listen."

"Maybe if the cops won't do it, I'll do it myself." He puts the gun to his temple, at too steep an angle. She flinches in anticipation. "Live TV don't get much better."

It's a good thing he hasn't taken hostages at a Best Buy—he'd know their negotiations aren't on *live* TV.

"I need a job."

"You need some help," says Flynn. "We can get you help. Let those four go. There's no need to make this worse. Those are innocent, innocent people."

Max: "Listen. Draw him out. Focus him on what he wants, not them."

"You don't want to hurt those people or yourself," says Flynn.

Sanchez: "You don't know them."

"They're honest, decent people. Why hurt someone else?"

Max: "No. Stay off the hostages. *Listen*—okay?"

She hears an internal whisper. A voice of calm and reason.

The camera changes everything.

Her father. Loud and clear.

The TV news camera alters the equation of gathering news.

The TV wants misery—live and in color.

It's like rubbernecking at a traffic accident, but you don't have to leave your couch.

Flynn doesn't need a new voice in her head. She doesn't need her father's print journalism purity.

Max: "Get him to focus. What he wants."

"These people?" Sanchez waves the gun in a loose circle. On the bank of monitors, Channel 4 has found a better angle. Their view lines up with the four huddled hostages. All women.

They sit on the floor. Flynn makes out a high heel. A small black purse. A leather jacket. A purple baseball cap. Blue jeans.

The woman closest to the window wears small round glasses. Her lips move as in prayer.

"These people were nothing to you before this. *Nothing.*"

"We care about all of you getting out of this safely. We care about them. We care about you, and we want to get out of this and let these women get back to their lives and for you to not make things worse."

Max: "Don't remind him of the hostages."

"You can do this," says Flynn. "Be as specific as you can. I'm sure the police will look favorably if you leave this with nobody hurt."

Max: "Don't make promises."

"Zeros!" shouts the gunman. "Nothing to you." He waves the gun at the four.

Channel 4's view widens. Behind a cage of propane tanks, a cop crouches in full riot gear. An assault rifle juts from his shoulder.

"Zeros!"

Max: "He's agitated."

The gunman steps to the door.

He stands in a shot of sunlight.

He holds the phone above his head, then sends it skittering across the asphalt like skipping a stone across a lake.

"No!" says Flynn.

Max: "Jesus. Fuck."

The gunman retreats inside the shop.

He turns.

He raises the gun.

His hand jerks.

The moment is eerily silent. A ghastly spritz of blood. The praying woman slumps where she sits. The screen fills with a swarm of cops. The gunman staggers back into the candy and snacks, racks toppling like dominoes, and disappears from view.

Max: "Jesus. Fuck."

A hot sensation surges from Flynn's scalp to toes. She stares at the live feeds.

Her disembodied father whispers: *Why did you get involved? You some kind of hero?*

Her phone buzzes.

It's a text from Wyatt.

What time will you be home?

CHAPTER 2

Vic Akin is thick chested and lumpy. The skin on his cheeks is like the medium setting on a dull cheese grater. His jaw hangs off kilter. He prefers, from what Robbie McGrath can tell, to never close his mouth. He wears a casual black shirt, good for cruising discos in the 1970s. Short sleeves showcase his Popeye forearms. The badge on his belt confirms his role as cop. So does the boisterous black gun.

Robbie McGrath booked the interview with Akin yesterday. Advance notice gave Akin time to bring in the police department's public relations honcho, Dwight Hatcher. Hatcher is a tall Black man with an attitude more suited to the corporate world. He's a touch debonair. Hatcher wears a crisp white shirt and a flashy blue tie.

Robbie's latest hand grenade question has landed with a clatter between them. Akin and Hatcher don't want to touch it. Hatcher asks if he and Akin might take "a moment."

Robbie rubs her forehead, sighs loud enough so they can hear it.

"A moment," says Hatcher. "That's all."

Don't bother! she thinks.

Robbie McGrath has Vic Akin and the Denver Police Department by the gonads. It's not a PR problem. It's a *problem* problem. And it's landing at the end of a rough afternoon for the DPD. All Robbie knows is that a hostage and the hostage-taker were killed at a convenience store standoff as television reporter Flynn Martin tried to negotiate a peaceful resolution. To McGrath, street mayhem is worrisome, but not something that will detour her insistence on getting Akin and Hatcher to respond.

McGrath, in fact, is starting to rough out the opening of her piece, focusing in particular on one greedy detective named John LaGrue, who reports to Vic Akin.

For this story, all she really needs is this one last interview to confirm the precise nature of the denial.

Large glass windows allow Robbie to study Akin and Hatcher, now chatting in the hall outside the conference room. Akin is hours from his last puff. DPD HQ is cigarette-free, but Akin fidgets like he needs something stronger than tobacco. Akin listens. One hand reaches high against the glass wall. The other rests on his oversize holster.

Hatcher's eyes sit inside deep sockets where a melon ball scooper might have gone to work. Hatcher spouts ninety words for every ten from Akin. Whatever sugarcoating Hatcher wants to sprinkle, there is no way that Akin can say "No comment" about the vastly improved financial standing of Detective LaGrue, one of the squad's investigators. Hatcher is known for his smooth style. But he is a cop. Cop first, PR flack second.

McGrath can only imagine how they view her. And her role. She doesn't look like much. She comes on so low key. She does all the background work first, then plays her cards. The mere fact that Akin and Hatcher are spending so much time in the hall, plotting their strategy, is golden. Or it could be a bit of preplanned theater, for her sake. To pretend they are worried.

Is that possible? She's always wary of traps.

Today Robbie McGrath has gone to extra lengths to appear a touch feminine, including a tight-fitting black turtleneck that confirms the presence of curves. Most days, she is good for loose-fitting tops, often with a military vibe. Always dark slacks or black jeans. She doesn't mind the semilesbian flavor. Let them all guess. She keeps her brown hair trim. She wears simple silver earrings and a pinprick stud in her left nostril.

McGrath brews cynicism in the marrow of her bones. She can't interview a politician without wondering about junkets and favors. She can't chat with a businessman—and they are usually men—without wondering what indulgence he has secured from government, what breaks and deals he enjoys under the table.

But she doesn't let it show. She maintains a matter-of-fact public face. She doesn't engage in long bitch sessions. She does her job. She follows one fact to the next.

It didn't take her long to develop a healthy sense of how the world works. Follow the lobbyists and lawyers and PR flack bozos back to their clients, and you'll know who is working an angle.

McGrath's reporting once caught a city councilwoman on the take from developers.

She also once uncovered a disturbing contract for an education consultant out of Texas. The consultant's business had won an award to work with underperforming school districts in Colorado. Among the investors in the business was a self-important policy adviser in the governor's office. The smug wonk had promoted the precise reading instruction curriculum the company supplied.

McGrath has followed lazy school district security guards running personal errands during the workday and stopping for beer siestas or girlfriend visits.

McGrath's head count of top-level resignations includes two state senators, one county commissioner, one school district chief operating officer, and one school board member with a loose sense of what to charge to taxpayers, such as champagne for the election-night party.

Akin and Hatcher return with an air of exasperation.

"On background?" says Akin.

McGrath gives it a second, to pretend she's considering it. "No thanks. We've done that dance."

Akin wheels his chair slightly away from his PR bodyguard. "Believe me when I say it's more complicated than it seems."

McGrath starts the recording app on her phone. She places it between them. Waveforms dance.

"Enlighten me," says McGrath.

Akin's chair blurts a squeak as he tips back, blows a smoke-free sigh at the ceiling. His six o'clock shadow turns the pockmarks on his cheeks crusty and dim.

Hatcher produces a yellow notepad, scratches something down.

"This is all part of a plan," says Akin. "Everything LaGrue is doing."

"Give me a break," says McGrath.

"True," says Akin. "And sure, that's on the record, since you wouldn't go off. But you use it, and you destroy years of work. We are close. And we are getting closer."

"And the things LaGrue is buying?" says McGrath.

"He has to spend it," says Hatcher. "He has to do something. He has to show off, you know?"

Undercover doesn't mean you start in with the over-the-top spending of under-the-table income. Did Detective John LaGrue think his fellow criminals would check that he was squandering his spoils?

"There are plans, of course, to liquidate and turn the cash back over to the city, sell the things he bought," says Akin. "But what LaGrue is doing is extremely dangerous."

"The chief knows?"

"He approved the plan."

The cops' response will make her editors wary. Something she does not need.

If they run the story, or a version of it, Akin and company could call a press conference and rip the newspaper for blowing up a carefully planned police investigation and for risking the life of an undercover officer.

If they're not bluffing.

McGrath sits up straight. "I need proof."

"Or?" says Akin.

"Or I'm going with it."

"With what?"

"With what I know."

"You can't. Not after what I told you."

"Of course I can," says McGrath.

"So your newspaper doesn't believe in community partnering?" says Akin.

"I can't say what *they* believe in. If you want, I can give you a chance to explain LaGrue's activities and his well-padded financial situation to an editor."

"My god," says Hatcher, jaw agape. He chews the scenery whenever he has the chance. Mock amazement, mock disbelief.

"You'd risk an officer's life—actually, several?" says Akin.

"LaGrue's partners—Arroyo and Vaca? Come on, even their mug shots make trouble."

Francisco Arroyo and Arturo Vaca are the names behind MVP Enterprises, d/b/a Mountain Views Property. The shell company, with a PO box on its corporate filings with the state, owns the house where LaGrue appears to conduct much of his "undercover" work.

"You don't really know what LaGrue's doing. Do you? Really?" says Akin.

"It's up to you. Give me proof," says McGrath.

Akin looks away, as if he's lost his favorite child. His lips purse in a tight line. "Give me two days," he says.

"No," says McGrath. "Tomorrow. Early. You can come up with your plan, whatever it is, overnight. I'll give you that."

"You want a rush job," says Akin.

"I want answers," says McGrath. "If there's something to show me, *show me*. Should be easy."

"Should we discuss this with your editor?"

"Help yourself. I told him before I came over you'd try something like what you're trying to pull, and he said, and I quote, 'Don't let them off the hook.'"

She says it like she means it, but Robbie McGrath never talks to any of her superiors about anything.

CHAPTER 3

Harry Kugel packs his briefcase at 5:15 p.m. The briefcase carries a sandwich-size Tupperware, two plastic baggies he reuses for a week or longer, and a copy of a newsmagazine he borrowed from the State Library.

The borrowing perk comes with his job in the human resources office at the Colorado Department of Education. This night, he packs a copy of a book called *Playing Dead*, a how-to about faking your own death, and a copy of Bach's Mass in B Minor, the John Eliot Gardiner version. Harry is steadily assembling the hundred best classical performances of all time, based on a list in *The New York Times*. He likes scrolling through the options, deciding what to play. Ultimately, he will purchase the best, but the library option helps him save money during the research phase.

He likes leaving work late, the same as his preference to already be working when others arrive. His office includes himself and two others. One is his boss, a woman named Jennifer Hills. The second is his secretary, Sandy Ingalls. They are a team. He treats them well. They take care of him. They click.

Tonight his trip home will require a detour to a market on Broadway to meet his friend Mary, who works in the state treasurer's office. They met at a statewide meeting of human resource officers. New procedures, new policies to be trained, et cetera. They sat next to each other, at a monstrous table in a windowless room, and she introduced herself while they waited for the presentation to start. She emailed him the next day and suggested a lunch. He preferred to eat lunch at his desk. So he suggested the after-hours option of a light supper.

This was now their routine. Of sorts. This was their fourth such sort-of date. Friends? More? She's changed the restaurant each time, "to explore." She is partial to organic food. She eats with care.

Mary has never been married. She belongs to the Denver Art Museum and the Museum of Contemporary Art. She's talked about an art show by the former lead singer of Devo. She has a gentle, appealing laugh. She asks questions. Some of the questions hit on dangerous territory. Harry has a sense she wants to talk about explicit things. Sexual things. Harry bluffs his way through, turns the tables back on her. He likes being friendly.

He likes *pretending* to be friendly, that is.

She offers no judgment on his status as a permanent single. He makes it clear, however, that he is heterosexual. At least, he looks for opportunities to do so. He conjures girlfriends from college days, postcollege days. He weaves a tale about one serious relationship and its four-year run. How can she check? She can't. He keeps no Facebook. He doesn't live online.

"Having a good week?" she says.

The market includes a café with a limited menu. Caesar salad for her. Greek salad with chicken for him. She has a glass of white wine with dinner—her second. He doesn't drink. If dating weren't a thing, would restaurants survive? It's all so silly. It's all a game.

"No complaints," he says. "Caught a guy today claiming he'd graduated from Howard University. I mean, terrific guy. Brand-new suit, you could tell. Smile a mile wide, and do they think we're not going to check? We need Black guys. Everyone needs Black. But he only finished two years."

"What did he say?"

"I'll call him tomorrow. Or email. We can't take a liar."

"Email is better," says Mary.

"Makes a better record," says Harry. "See what he wants to claim. I mean, it's a complete disqualifier. But the commissioner is after diversity."

Mary Belson's face is long. Clean lines, short hair. She looks like the type of woman who takes three minutes in the shower and doesn't need a hair dryer. Her eyes are bright and blue. They show no sign of dull bureaucracy. Year fifty is eighteen months away—one year closer than for Harry. About getting older, she says things like "bring it on." She takes care of herself, cares about fitness.

Harry tries not to say "Harry and Mary" out loud to himself. It sounds awful.

"What position?" says Mary.

"Assistant director of communications," says Harry. "You don't lie on your way to a job like that. Right? For a job where you're expected to tell the truth?"

"Communications people tell the truth?" says Mary.

"You know what I mean."

Harry laughs.

"He must have finished his degree somewhere else—that's what I'm betting. At Metro or some other place that doesn't look so, well, Howard."

"It was almost too easy," says Harry.

"Exactly. Candidates of a certain age have spilled their personal lives all over the stage for years, no respect for their own privacy, and then they don't think it matters. It matters."

Harry's whole story about the applicant is a fat fib—but what does it matter? He likes to have something to talk about, make it sound like he is a worthy soldier.

"Van Gogh opens next week," says Mary. They stand on the sidewalk, about to say goodbye. "The invitation stands. A weekend day, perhaps? Or evening?"

"Museums make me tired." Harry has a genuine desire to see her body. She plays tennis three times a week. But he can't imagine the complications of getting involved. He has taken care of his own sexual needs for a long time, and that is that. The last fifteen years have been all about not letting anyone get too close. He can leave Mary's secrets and all the rest to his imagination. For now.

He has a hunch about her, but he isn't ready to push that particular button. He will likely have to break off this "relationship." Soon. They should be sleeping together regularly by now. He knows she expects that. Wants that.

Seeing Mary for these social exchanges proves he isn't a typical loner. So do vague references to a divorce. He's never wanted to be *that* guy, the slowly aging hermit with a closed-in life.

"You ever take the audio tours?" she says. "It's a whole new experience."

"I've never seen the need to see art in person. I mean, it's all online. Isn't it?"

"It's not the same," says Mary. "The scale, the power of being right *there* where the artist stood. Your classical music, is it the same in your headphones as it is at a concert? Really?"

Harry grimaces. "I'm not a big fan of crowds. Sorry."

CHAPTER 4

They poke around for three hours across North Denver, back and forth across I-70 on the scruffy fringes of town.

Vic Akin drives a dark-blue squad car. It carries no DPD seals on the doors, but the car's cop darkness says it all. Akin explains the delicate nature of undercover work. He tells stories of infiltrators getting their covers blown. He sits hunched forward over the steering wheel as if nursing a tender back. The steering wheel rubs his massive thighs.

"That's the headquarters," says Akin. He points to a sad green stucco house with chocolate trim. The landscaping is laissez-sad. Plywood masks a front window.

"And that's where we saw LaGrue go inside," says Robbie. "Day after day. Like I said."

"We?"

"Me and a photographer," says Robbie.

"He's building trust," says Akin. "We're not after the first hit we come across."

"You sure he's in?" says Robbie. "The dude is so White."

"He's scrawny White, though. Street White. He's got those sunken cheeks like a junkie, and that hair is wild. Five days without shaving and *boom*, an undercover."

They head north on Federal past a scrappy assortment of blue-collar businesses, vacant lots, junkyards. They duck under I-76. She is wasting time, but so what? All she has to do is endure this ride, give them a chance.

Akin stares ahead. He drives with an edge.

"Step back and think of the big picture here." Akin wheels the car through a parking lot to a sleepy four-store strip mall. Robbie chats with Akin about the mess at the convenience store earlier today to change the subject. She takes a mild jab at how the television reporter handled it.

Akin doesn't bite.

"Buck or Less is where the street vendors come for their allotment," says Akin.

One red pickup sits off kilter in the faded paint of the parking grid. The store appears to be a dying concern. "What's the opposite of a beehive?" says Robbie.

"Tomorrow is pickup day," says Akin.

"I see an empty store."

This "story" feels so random.

"It's part of the network," says Akin.

Why is Akin showing her all of this? How does it help Detective John LaGrue?

"We're halfway to the heart of the matter," says Akin.

What is it like to know that your career, in the case of Vic Akin, has days left? Once her story runs, he will certainly have to hand in his badge.

"How do you know LaGrue hasn't flipped?" says Robbie.

"It's bullshit to even think like that," says Akin.

"Maybe he's stringing things out. Maybe he's firmly planted inside the organization but milking it to his benefit, pocketing what he can on the side." In the last six months, LaGrue has upgraded from a 1992 Nova to a new F-250. He has also built a composite deck half the size of his house. The deck features a gas grill worthy of the Food Network and a plumbed-in bar. No loan. He took a long weekend in New Orleans with his wife and another full week last fall to hunt elk with three buddies in the Medicine Bow Mountains of Wyoming, using out-of-state licenses and a trio of new Weatherby rifles purchased at Cabela's. Robbie made the drive to Saratoga to interview the outfitters, who remembered the shiny new gear and the Colorado trio.

Akin lets his engine idle. A downtrodden Dodge Dart, circa the Nixon administration, stops next to the red pickup. A Mexican mother steps out. She crosses her arms over her skinny frame. Her bushy black hair catches the breeze. Three young faces, two boys and a girl, press against the window. The woman takes three strides toward Buck or Less and glances over. Maybe she hears Akin's engine. She stops. She stands for a moment as if she's forgotten something and shuffles back to the Dart.

"We're bad for business," says Akin.

"You said you'd show me what was really going on. I've seen nothing."

"What would convince you?"

"All you've shown me is that you know your way around town."

Akin spins the car out of the lot, heads back south on Federal.

"You can drop me off at Thirty-Eighth," says Robbie.

She feels squirmy.

"What for?"

"Need to see somebody," says Robbie.

"I'm going back downtown, your way," says Akin. "I'd feel better if I left you where I got you. Who's your editor?"

"Call *the* editor. Cut through to the top."

Once you hate those involved, a scandal is easy to report. Robbie McGrath has broken her fair share of corruption stories. She trusts her nose. She smells the panic.

Akin gobbles up Federal Boulevard, turns off on Speer toward downtown Denver.

"You make some people look bad and you collect your paycheck," says Akin. "Your business—it's all about embarrassment, isn't it?"

"Call the editor. Get in your licks. Who knows? Maybe nothing ever runs."

They stop on Broadway by the newspaper. "Can I get out now?"
"When is it running?"
Akin releases the automatic locks with a metallic *thunk*.
"Not my call. Might be tomorrow, the next day. Any day."
Robbie climbs out, doesn't look back.
Akin doesn't need to know she hasn't written one word.

CHAPTER 5
TUESDAY

"They should never have put you in the middle in the first place."

"*They*, the cops, or *they*, my station?"

"It was lose-lose. Right down the line."

"Refusing to help the cops? How would that have looked?"

Coffees sit between them on the concrete picnic table in Cheesman Park, a short walk from Michael Martin's condo.

"Well, I mean, did *you* feel right about it?"

"I couldn't slow down the moment. There wasn't time to analyze all the ins and outs."

Michael Martin lets the statement hang in the air. He nods as if he understands. Flynn gets the look: *Listen to yourself.*

He was the first to call her—the first of hundreds of emails and messages. Reporters. PR pals. Media friends. She is awash in a flood of sympathy. Every message anticipates her need for forgiveness.

And confirms the fuckup.

Emails and phone calls to the station aren't so kind. Neither are the smackdowns on X. And all the online nooks and crannies where the public goes to vent. To the haters, the incident dangles like a hunk of bloody tenderloin. She is the number one trending topic. Her full name is the go-to hashtag, #FlynnMartin. With clever variations such as #FireFlynnMartin and #FlynnMartinSucks.

Followed closely by the ever-popular #reportergod.

Individual tweets often include the audio from the precise moments when Max told her what not to say, closely followed by her ignoring those directions.

None of the nastiness has come close to what she's saved for herself. Or the amount she's cried.

"The station should be taking the hit," says her father. "Not you. It was an ethical choice to get in the middle. They chose wrong."

The air is cool but not cold. Winter mist has lowered the ceiling to gray nothing. There is no view of downtown, let alone the mountains.

Her father's look penetrates like a hanging judge, but there is warmth inside. His way of comforting her is to spare her any commentary about TV news being an eternally hungry beast. He is retired, which only means he consumes more news than he did each day during his forty-four years in the newspaper business. He started his career during the Watergate scandal and timed his last day with the first inauguration of President Trump.

"I should have—"

"You can't go there."

"Everybody else is."

"Why are you reading the junk on social media?"

"Hard to miss," she says.

"You'll drive yourself crazy."

"All I know is I'm a scandal."

"You did your best."

"Tell that to, you know—"

Tears. The worst was the drive home, hours after the incident, alone. She could barely see the road. She'd cried telling Wyatt. She composed herself long enough to explain the events, all in the context of why the world was a generator of random pain. She made a connection to the polar bears and how they struggled against the forces of climate change. Wyatt loves polar bears. He frets over their dwindling ice. Her sadness for what happened to the hostage, she told him, was all the pain he felt for all the polar bears wrapped into one.

She barely slept.

The police released the ID of the victim this morning. Her name was Debbie Ernst, twenty-four. She was a religious studies student at Regis University, originally from Apple Valley, Minnesota.

Devout church person.

And *apples*.

Could it get any worse?

The number of times Flynn Martin has played back the sight of Debbie Ernst slumping over behind the wall of convenience store glass cannot be counted. Each mental replay leads to another new gush of anguish from a hidden spring deep inside. The number of times the brief clip has played on other news stations in Denver—and around the country—cannot be fathomed. Online? It's a joke. She has consumed plenty of reality-horror porn. Dashcam videos of violent traffic accidents. Security cam footage of carjackings. Flight 175 into the South Tower. War footage from Ukraine, tanks firing on sports cars. Rafah. Gaza. Suicide bombers from Brussels to Baghdad.

This one aches.

This one is *hers*.

"Are you reading about all this?" she asks.

"I read what was in the newspaper," says her father. "And then I glanced at a few things online."

Michael Martin is lying. He reads everything—and has made the shift to consuming the "newspapers" online. *Denver Post. Washington Post. New York Times. Colorado Sun*, which was only ever a digital effort.

"And?"

"And I'm not sure what else there is to say," he says. "I think there's ample room for criticism that the cops should have taken care of this, should never have pulled you in."

"They need someone to blame?"

"Not every bad thing can be assigned blame," he says.

"Maybe."

"You're taking a few days then?"

"A few," she says. "Unspecified. They said it's up to me. With or without the counselor they offered through the corporate mental health program."

"Start by avoiding all the opinionated junk out there."

"How do you avoid it?"

"You avoid it by avoiding it," he says. "You're the one who knows the truth of the moment, what was happening. Nobody else was in your shoes. Everybody who has an opinion on the matter doesn't know what the hell they're talking about."

"I was doing what I could to reach him," she says. "You know? I thought I was getting through."

"It's not like there is a road map for these things."

"I should have stayed in Brighton. I shouldn't have answered the phone when Goodman called."

"You're a team player. Like your mother."

"Random viewers have come to my defense. Four, I think."

"And what is your station saying?"

"You mean publicly?"

At age sixty-nine, her father has a gaze that holds a clear-eyed certainty. A minor, occasional tremble in his left hand is the lone outward indicator of his age. His once-thick hair has thinned, but he keeps it trim and neat. He doesn't let his eyebrows go unchecked. He shaves every day, he says, to make it feel like he's going to work. He puts on button-down shirts for the same reason, to create an atmosphere of caring. He hits the gym four times a week to work up a sweat on the treadmill, lift weights, and do chair yoga.

"Well, I read the corporate BS. What about behind the scenes?"

"You mean Goodman?"

"Him and the others."

"They say all the right things. They are supportive," she says. "In principle. To my face."

"But you're worried?"

"Every fresh face they hire makes me worried. And don't start talking about the vanity element of TV news."

"They won't put you out," he says.

"How can you be so sure?"

"That would look chickenshit," he says. "Too obvious."

"They're not indifferent to public opinion."

He waggles his head from side to side. "Maybe."

"And if they wait until the end of my contract and nonrenew, it's the same difference. Four months for them to wait."

"After all the time you've given them? The loyalty to one station?"

When there were two newspapers in town, reporters frequently hopped back and forth between employers. Not Michael Martin. And when there was only one newspaper, a dozen or so reporters "walked across the street" to join the victorious enemy. Michael Martin kept plugging away, doing his thing. There was one sports columnist who made more money and had more seniority. Nobody else had more experience as a reporter, and he declined all temptations to move to the editing ranks.

"Do you know how much cheaper it would be to replace me with a rookie?"

"They have to weigh the negatives too," he says. "You're a fixture."

"A week after I'm gone, nobody will remember my name or what I covered," she says. "Besides, the point isn't me. It's her. Debbie. What would she trade to be having this conversation? I should feel damn lucky to be here, even though I messed up."

"You didn't mess up."

"I don't think Debbie's family would agree."

Flynn stands. The images come rushing back. The video. She needs chest-deep gulps of air. She covers her face in her hands for a moment, expecting tears. Nothing. She's dry. She's all cried out. She walks a small circle, her head tipped back. She imagines the big picture, the long view. There is no long view. Yesterday morning she was riding out her routines. The arc of her career was practically a foregone conclusion. Now she'll be known for this one screwup. Again Flynn lashes herself for thinking about herself before the victim. She thought she'd never get over the stories of pain from Columbine or the Aurora theater. She's managed to put those in a drawer, only pulled out for anniversary stories about victims or heroes or first responders or all the ones left behind who mourn and ache and mourn some more.

How long will it take to find a drawer where she can neatly file Debbie Ernst? Certainly the ability to move on from witnessing horror—*instigating* horror—is an overlooked survival instinct of the human species. Somewhere deep down, she has to keep it together. She is required to strap on a brave face and plunge back into the fray. She needs the job. Wyatt, mortgage, stability.

Carry on, carry on, carry on.

And this is no fucking way to go out.

She returns to her spot. Sighs. "Sorry," she says.

"Don't be." He reaches out, puts a hand on her arm. "Please."

"Someday." A tardy tear bubbles on her eyelid. She wipes it away. "I'm not there yet. I want to go back and stand in the cornfield, take Goodman's call all over again. I'd write a better ending."

"How do you know?" Her father's eyes are steady and sure. "Maybe if you don't answer the call, the cops find their own way to get all four hostages killed. Did you ever think of that?"

CHAPTER 6

Robbie McGrath's desk sits in an odd-shaped corner. The interior walls of the newspaper jut in and out, leaving odd spots in the newsroom for loners like her.

She doesn't mind. She is untouchable. Editors with oddball whims hold no sway.

The newsroom doesn't buzz like it used to. Four-fifths of the cubicles are vacant. Each empty desk serves as a harbinger of her industry's grim fate. There used to be a team of three investigative reporters, plus an editor. Then, two reporters.

Now, one. And no direct editor.

For her work area, McGrath prefers a mess. Flotsam deflects casual snoops. She doesn't leave notes lying around. Notes are transcribed to computer, backed up via the cloud.

McGrath grabs her laptop and notes and heads for one of two small conference rooms off to the side of the newsroom. She sits where she can see out the glass wall to the newsroom, quieter than a cemetery in the pouring rain.

◆ ◆ ◆

"You're already weeks overdue."

Ted Withers's sweaty wire rims make his eyes extra beady. A Styrofoam cup dangles from his fingertips. The man sips coffee for oxygen.

"And where's your opening piece, the scene-setter?"
"I'm going through my notes now."
"Meaning?"
"I'm going to start."
"Start?"
"Start writing."
"What the hell?"

McGrath is lucky to have protection at the top—both Glenn Addison, the editor, and Withers, the managing editor.

"You'd run something half-assed?"
"You're so freaking slow," says Withers.
"'The two most powerful warriors are patience and time.' Leo Tolstoy, so you know. You want me to blog about my progress, tweet every interview?"

The beat reporters are under new production requirements to post more stories for the online edition, contribute to the social media feeds. All sorts of crap.

Withers scratches his neck hard enough to draw blood.

"Do you know we have to explain to new reporters and interns that you're not some vagrant we've taken in to help the city with its homeless problem?"

"I showered today," says McGrath. In fact, she hasn't. "And we're playing with cops, you know."

"We got a call. So I'm familiar with that fact."
"A call? You know that's a good sign, right?"
"So you've told me."
"Hatcher or higher?"

Withers jerks a thumb to the ceiling.

"And?"
"The usual threats. Choice words about our credibility."
"Make you worried?" says McGrath.
"More worried about getting words. Together, in full sentences and paragraphs. We can't edit thin air."

McGrath picks up a sausage and mushroom pizza from a neighborhood bar. Salty goodness. One slice for dinner. Maybe two.

She parks in her one-car garage off the alley behind her bungalow in North Denver, a house she can barely afford on one salary and a house she doesn't need, not with all the upkeep and nobody around to help with it. She's had boyfriends off and on. This is now an "off" time. She isn't opposed to life as a single. She has an aversion to the basic family structure. One boyfriend moved in for six months. When he wanted commitment, she showed him the door. Both at home and the office, lone-wolf status works for her psyche. It's a good thing to know about yourself.

McGrath promises herself to eat a slice and drink a beer before thinking again about Akin or LaGrue.

Or Withers. Or the newspaper's dwindling readership.

She kicks off her shoes in the breezeway, up two steps from the back door. She hangs her keys on a hook by the back door, drops the pizza box on the kitchen counter, and flops her coat over a chair at the small dining room table.

She needs two remotes to get MSNBC running, then flips on the lamp by her favorite television chair.

She sucks in a hard breath.

Prickles jab at her arms, skin to bone.

The man is statue still. He wears black, head to toe. He sits on a chair by the mail chute, where there is no light. Against the dark-red fabric, he is a fuzzy splotch.

A black nylon stocking pulled down over his head filters any detail except around his eyes, slightly lighter than the rest of his smudgy face.

He stares at her.

McGrath takes a step back, already thinking about her keys.

"Stay right there," says a voice.

CHAPTER 7
WEDNESDAY

Flynn wakes early. Makes coffee. Tosses the unread morning newspaper in recycling, streams NPR on her laptop. If she hears the word "Denver" anywhere in the national news, she is fully prepared to whack the off button with a closed fist.

She wakes Wyatt at six thirty. She makes him pancakes with fat frozen blueberries. No bacon. Wyatt is considering going vegetarian. He's already dropped red meat.

They usually walk to school. But Flynn wants as few random street interactions as possible.

"Waste of gas," says Wyatt.

She leases a new blue Chevy Malibu every three years. She hates dealing with car maintenance, and she adores the Malibu's ultra-generic look.

"I need to go straight to work," she lies.

"We could have walked."

"Life is full of little choices."

"The little ones lead to the big ones."

"I wish it was that simple."

Wyatt is trying to figure out when things will get back to normal. And how.

So is she.

At 9:45, a familiar figure appears on the porch of her house, an old Denver Square more than a hundred years old.

She isn't a big fan of surprise guests.

Flynn tries to recall if she has ever bumped into this person outside the newsroom. His lair.

Rick Goodman is a paunchy six-footer. He favors black slacks and gingham shirts. Today's shirt is green, open collar, under a light, unzipped jacket. Slate blue eyes sit like stones under thick dark eyebrows. A quick hug smells of sage.

She wears the same scent she's been wearing since yesterday morning. Morning funk. At least she is dressed, jeans and a purple V-neck pullover.

Goodman carries two large coffees and breakfast burritos, allaying her fears about the dark message he might be getting ready to deliver. Greasy chorizo zaps her mouth with a warm fire. She remains firmly unhungry.

Goodman's tone alternates between boss and friend. She doesn't expect too much from the "friend" side of things. Goodman is as unexcited as the ticktock of Greenwich Mean Time.

"You think I should have followed their script," says Flynn. They sit on the front porch. It's another one of those winter mornings when the light stays flat. Flynn grabs a thick taupe sweater, sits on her hands between bites.

"Well, that was the plan."

"There was no *plan*."

"The general idea. To follow their lead." Goodman seems oblivious to the determined chill.

"And they knew precisely what to do because cops can accurately predict all human behavior?"

Her fight isn't with Goodman, unless they are going to downgrade her rank. Or ask her to take a leave, paid or unpaid.

"By definition he was a nutcase. Everyone knows that."

"But what?"

"But imagine how much better we'd be if we had followed their lead."

"We?"

"The station is taking a hit too. You know that, don't you?"

"So, we are supposed to do everything we're told?" She says it with snap. The weight of her sadness doubles on the spot. Tears streak like shooting stars. She doesn't touch them. She hates the tears, needs them just as much. They're proof of something.

Goodman's gaze is distant. "I'm sorry."

"As if there will be a next time. Ever," says Flynn. "Anywhere."

"The cops need to share in the blame," says Goodman. "No question."

"Except I'm the face on every rehash. And the voice on the clip before it all goes to hell."

"You didn't pull the trigger."

Flynn wipes her cheeks on the sleeve of her sweater. "It feels like it."

Fellow reporters have left voicemails.

"I feel like I have to ask . . ."

"I know you may not want to talk, but . . ."

"Could you give us your account of what happened . . . ?"

Nobody has called with the magic combination of words to convince her brain to stop playing the Pump 'N Go tape over and over in her head with the final moments in the life of the religious twenty-four-year-old from Apple Valley.

"Wyatt?"

"At school."

"He's doing okay?"

"He's not used to seeing his mom hang around the house."

"I'm sure."

"Do I get to come back?" Flynn needs to know.

"What?" says Goodman. He looks surprised.

"You're not here for career counseling? Encourage me to take a mental health leave—or something worse?"

Goodman gives a smile. "Almost the opposite."

"What? Hustle back, pretend all is hunky-dory? Cover her funeral?"

"Sister station in Minneapolis will cover it for us," says Goodman.

"When is that?"

She clamps down another surge of sobbing. She needs to figure out why Deborah's death has jolted the illusion of time. It has sent her reeling to a place where she dwells hard on what minimal crap she's accomplished. She thinks about what time remains and what the hell kind of world she's leaving for Wyatt, especially with intractable gridlock at every level of government.

"Funeral details are pending," says Goodman. "And the parents don't blame you. They don't blame anyone. They were spiritual and thankful for what Deborah contributed to the world while she was here."

Great, thinks Flynn. *The parents of the dead girl have more perspective than you can muster for yourself.*

Or is it because they had a handy script at the ready? Lines they have rehearsed in church in preparation for such a moment?

Flynn is a nonchalant agnostic, carries no such scripts, and will not be ready when Wyatt starts asking about god and fate.

"You should do an interview," says Goodman. "You're bottling things up."

"Bottling things up?"

"Yes."

"And smack in front of a TV camera is *always* a great place to unbottle. This doesn't sound like *you*."

"It's—"

"No, let me guess. You brought in a consultant—a PR *consultant*—to discuss my situation?"

"The thought is to make sure people know you're willing to show how you feel about it."

"I hope that was worth your ten grand or whatever you paid. And what 'people'?"

"Our viewers. Your fans."

"I don't have any. Well, nothing compared to Sara Cornette or the young lookers fresh out of J-school."

Flynn's cute sharpness has softened. Around the eyes. Her chin. She was born with blond hair. Going gradually dirty blond didn't feel fake. She trims her hair back to shoulder length once a month. Her face is open, round. She leads her way, most days, with an easy smile. Her parents didn't spend a dime at the orthodontist, but her teeth came in as if by machine. The tall teeth sit in a big mouth with a carefree laugh. She is five five. She is one of the lucky ones when it comes to managing weight. A wrinkle here, a crease there. *Seasoning.* She'll never be mistaken for a newbie.

Goodman stands. Message delivered; mission accomplished. "I'm not listening to any self-loathing," he says. "Are you going to think about it?"

"I already have."

"You'd find it therapeutic, I do believe."

"I can't imagine how I'd get through an interview."

"One question at a time," says Goodman.

"And isn't it sort of self-important? Won't it draw more attention to the whole mess?"

"You put your mark on the story. And let folks know you're not running away from it."

"Who would do it?"

"Up to you," he says.

"Completely?"

"Within reason."

Flynn spins through the possibilities. Who should quiz her? A fresh face? A midcareer face? A chiseled veteran, like her? No matter who asks her questions, it will be impossible to describe what happened moment by moment. Or to relive it while the camera watches.

"What about Snelling?"

"What about him?"

The station's general manager has a nauseating sense of loyalty to the "community," a catch-all euphemism. The result is a weak spine when it comes to investigations or controversy. He wants viewers to feel good about their city through a warm, folksy presentation.

"He called me this morning," says Goodman.

"And?"

"You can imagine."

"Oh, so this is all his idea?"

"More than idea."

Flynn adopts a mock-Snelling voice, a slow-talking baritone. "We're supposed to cover news, not make it."

"You get the gist," says Goodman.

A long moment stretches itself out, curls up at their feet, and makes itself at home.

"I don't want anybody thinking I wanted it to end the way it did," says Flynn.

"That's why you do the interview," says Goodman. "Address it. Put the viewer in your shoes."

"And if they start asking about Deborah?"

"Show you care. Be yourself."

"*Yeccch*," says Flynn. "The media interviewing itself. Makes me gag."

"It won't take long. And then everyone moves the fuck along."

CHAPTER 8

Meeting up straight after work feels like there isn't any pressure. Neither of them has time to go home to shower or primp. This "date" is no different from one of their dinner get-togethers. However, in the email about the rendezvous logistics, Mary Belson announced her upbeat interest in a cocktail.

Primping wouldn't change much, except make him cleaner. Harry was a good-looking kid. He has sensitive, thoughtful eyes. He's heard the same description of his eyes from two sort-of girlfriends. He has started to believe it.

Part of what intrigues Harry about Mary Belson is the fact that he looks her right in the eye. He isn't sure he could deal with *taller*. He's never been with *taller*. He's also never been with Black or Hispanic or anything exotic, though he has a fantasy about a trip to Bangkok and exchanging a thousand dollars, say, for a week of study. He has nothing against Blacks or Hispanics—nothing at all. His various photograph collections, stashed here and there, do not discriminate. When and if he is ever discovered, and with each passing year the chances reduce considerably, the authorities will at least be forced to concede he was utterly agnostic about skin color. Tall Black women fascinate him. Especially tall, Black, fit women with long legs. Do they scare him? He will never admit it.

Harry doesn't know what to think about where things are going with Mary. *Things?* She's already mentioned she uses dating apps, practically a big red flag flapping in the breeze: *I sleep with strangers.* Why else mention it?

◆ ◆ ◆

They meet in front of the state capitol, at the top of the steps. A January day at 5:00 p.m. is as dark as midnight. They walk down the capitol steps and across Civic Center Park and around the Denver Art Museum. Mary has suggested a Cuban restaurant in the Golden Triangle, but first she wants to take him to a gallery called Rive Gauche. He is surprised when the door opens. The place looks lifeless.

"Twenty minutes," says the gallery attendant, a tall redhead. She peers out through oversize rectangular neon-blue frames. Cartoon glasses.

"The photographer is the daughter of a good friend. She's got a following," says Mary.

The photographs, to Harry's eye, are average. They feature textures like tree bark and grasses in extreme focus on one side of the picture and maybe a distant human figure completely out of focus on the other side. Mostly black and white. Some in highly muted colors and soft tones.

Wood plank floorboards of the old house creak as they make their way around. Harry feigns interest. Whatever trick or theme this photographer has developed, she has run it into the ground. All the human figures are a blur.

The photographs are mystical and evocative, but the prices are in sharp relief—$8,000 here, $10,000 there. The word "pretentious" comes to Harry's mind, but he keeps it to himself.

"New York exhibit next month," says Mary.

"Really?" says Harry.

"And she's like twenty-six."

"Crazy. Is this one of your routines?"

"I like the galleries. I like going to First Fridays, when all the people are out in the summer over on Santa Fe and there's free wine. Have you been?"

"No," says Harry. He can't imagine a worse scenario, all the bullshit amateur art commentary and all the crowds. "By the way, I'm not in the market tonight."

"They're all taken anyway," says Mary. She smells faintly tropical, a top note of coconut. Her ears glisten. They are shiny and clean like a baby's. They are, in fact, perfect ears, tight and efficient. And they match.

"Those green dots. It's a complete sellout," she says. "I heard she's scrambling to put together the pieces for the show next month in New York."

Harry drifts away from Mary and her soft breezy cloud.

He bends at the waist to study "About the Artist," no idea why the information is hung so low on the brick wall.

The photographer's name roils in his guts.

Emily Berns.

It's as if someone has folded up the decades and poked a hole in time so he can slip back and remember those weeks where he felt certain he'd be caught any day, any minute, any second. During that one particular dicey stretch, he had to think about each trip for groceries or to work, or the bars. It was a delicious time. Utter excitement and pure terror in a daily dogfight.

Emily Berns.

His last.

Could this one be her . . . *daughter?*

No.

The timing, the age . . .

Harry studies the photograph to see if he can spot a telltale something.

She stands by a fence in the mountains. It's a full-body shot, head to toe, so the face is hard to see. Long dark hair falls over a white sweater. She doesn't smile. Harry stares. Already he is thinking about the computer, but he can't investigate from home. The last thing he wants to do is pour out his curiosity about his own case, his own "situation," as he likes to call it, from the same IP address. Ping, ping, ping . . . *Why is one computer in Capitol Hill repeatedly querying about the victims of that long-ago killer, the guy who disappeared?*

You may as well go down to the police station and admit it all, lay it out. The cops at one point sniffed around Capitol Hill like bloodhounds, thinking they had something.

"Good looking, isn't she?" Mary has come up behind him. "Quite the figure. Mom's a looker too."

Harry sighs in relief.

Mary said she is a friend of Emily's mother.

Relief flushes his system. She's a different Emily Berns. He shoves every scrap of emotion down into a ball the size of a pea. He puts the pea in the leather pouch of a giant mental slingshot. He tugs back the bands and aims toward Pluto. And fires.

He'll never let Mary see.

Or anyone else, for that matter.

They eat camarones al coco and churrasco con chimichurri. One mojito with appetizers, another with dinner. Harry lets the second drink sit. Sociable sips only. The back room is raucous with conversation. There are so many people with money to burn. Harry leans over the table to show he is trying. He resists complaining. He doesn't want to appear small minded. The din of the joint drives him bonkers.

Mary suggests a serene bar for a final drink. She says it's three blocks away, and they will be able to hear each other. Harry is well outside his routines but glad he left the second mojito mostly untouched. It is 8:30 p.m. He hates to look like the short hitter.

Bookcases make up the bar back, floor to ceiling. All hardbacks. Bottles appear from a mysterious place down below. They sit at a long bar that appears to be poured concrete, sayings and quotes about reading and writing etched into the wet surface and allowed to dry. The result is a bumpy, uneven surface. Harry's Cuba libre doesn't sit flat. Harry hates the overwrought concept. Haydn's Symphony No. 22, *The Philosopher*, pours from invisible speakers. The sound is immaculate. Someone knows good sound. Harry recognizes the signature pair of cors anglais and the building debate among the musical themes. This is the fourth movement, a sonata. The room soaks up the stirring cellos and high-spirited violins.

"One of my best friends knew that woman who was killed in that awful hostage thing at the convenience store the other day." Mary says it out of the blue. A point of interest.

"Terrible," says Harry.

"My friend teaches at Regis, had her in her class. One of the nicest young women you'd ever want to meet, according to her."

"Deborah something," says Harry.

"Deborah Ernst," says Mary. "It's so hard to imagine what she was thinking, all those moments leading up to when things got out of control."

"I feel for that reporter," says Harry. "No, I really do. I mean, it was hardly fair to put her in a situation like that. And now, the guilt. Yeah, what's her name? She's been around the block."

"Flynn Martin," says Mary. "She did a story at our department a year or two back. Wouldn't wish that situation on anyone, but why the hell did she get in the middle? Ego flashing, if you ask me, you know, 'Reporter to the rescue.' She had no business being in the middle. None."

Mary props her elbow on the bar. She rests her head on her closed fist. She looks a bit tired, or maybe weary from all the rum.

"Let's do something together some weekend." Mary's eyes are pools of intrigue. "You know, go somewhere. By the way, where do you live?"

"Capitol Hill."

"House or—?"

"Condo. One of those big old mansions. Conversion job." Not hardly. She will never see it, so it doesn't matter. "Glad I bought when I did."

The state of the real estate market is a snoozeville topic. So what if Denver is catching up with San Francisco and other snobby cities?

"You?" says Harry.

"I've got a town house right here in Uptown." Mary plucks the lime slice out of her drink, gives it a squeeze. It's the third time she's tried to get more zing in her drink. "I thought you knew."

He could practically walk her home, run upstairs with her if the signals are right, and then walk to his place in Capitol Hill. He could be home sleeping by a reasonable hour, unless she expects a whole symphony of action. You can never really tell the women who are going to let it all out, the ones who don a new animal skin once the lights are low and the clothes are off.

He is expected to try, isn't he?

Maybe Lyft it to her place? He doesn't do the shared ride app thing, but maybe she can order one, and if she lets him climb in with her, there is no question he will press the issue. Walking would be seen as a safety precaution, not an invitation.

Haydn wraps with a flourish. Harry knows then it is Colorado Public Radio's classical station on the house system because of the telltale pause. The confident, stony silence.

And then a male announcer declares tomorrow's high temperature, not so high, and forecast for snow later in the week, "but only a dusting and not enough moisture, officials say, to even be measured against our record drought."

Another pause.

"Denver police and city officials have scheduled a morning news conference to discuss the apparent return of the PDQ Killer."

Harry gasps. He covers it by tapping his chest like his heart has fluttered of its own accord.

"A murder victim was found this morning in a North Denver home, and police believe this may be the work of the same killer who last terrorized Denver some fifteen years ago. The victim is a female, age forty-one, and lived alone. Police are withholding identity of the victim pending notification of her family."

Harry's cheeks flash heat. The room wobbles.

"Sorry," he says.

He coughs to clear a suddenly dry throat.

"You okay?" Mary reaches over, grips his shoulder.

"The rum, I suppose," says Harry. "Really, I'm fine."

The check comes, and Mary insists on paying for the drinks. "This stop was my idea," she says. They had gone dutch at dinner.

Harry needs to suck down some cold night air. He needs to not respond to Mr. CPR News. He doesn't need Mary to bring it up either.

"Give me your address," says Mary. "I'll get us an Uber, drop you off first."

"No," he says. "I can walk from here."

The night is much colder already. Something has blown through. A feisty wind scours the streets. The breeze is gritty. A white plastic grocery bag catches the wind and dances into the black night sky like a crazed ghost.

"You're not walking alone, not after hearing that." Mary's phone is out. "I don't mind an escort home. PDQ, I mean. Jesus *fuck*."

The Uber comes in a flash. A Prius. The inside smells like lemon. Harry feels his innards spin. And slosh. His lungs fight for air. The red light at Colfax takes forever. The red light at Seventeenth and Sherman takes longer.

Again with the pea and the slingshot and Pluto. He is in mixed company, he reminds himself.

She gives him a coconut hug when the Uber stops. He hugs back. He can see himself taking care of Mary. He can also see her hog-tied with a rubber ball gag and a chin strap. For fun. There doesn't have to be anything demeaning about it.

"I'll see you soon," she says. "You take care."

Harry watches Mary climb four steps to her town house. Her place is a faux brownstone à la Brooklyn. There is nothing original about anything anymore.

"You have an Uber account?"

The driver is Indian. Turban on top, graying beard jutting from his chin.

Harry doesn't answer. He climbs out, shuts the door.

He puts his head down into a stiff wind. He wonders how cold he'll be by the time he covers twenty blocks. He is now twice as far from his condo as when they left the bar.

Something is off. That Emily Berns holy-fuck moment at the gallery and then the CPR news announcer? The absolute last thing he needs is a wannabe copycat bullshit motherfucking monster out there trying to duplicate his scene and pretend he is back.

PDQ isn't back.

PDQ is long gone.

PDQ vanished.

Successfully fucking *vanished*.

Theories abounded and occasionally resurfaced. There are always the anniversaries for reporters to milk and for Harry to weather.

Five. Ten. And recently, eighteen years since the first.

But PDQ isn't fucking back.

A white tower crane leaps from a black hole in the ground to Harry's right. Its long white jib slashes the night sky like a wound. Leaves and trash blow at him down the sidewalk. The cold wind stings. Ahead, lit-up Colfax Avenue looks busy, as always. He thinks about flagging a cab if he sees one. Not as easy as it used to be.

"Anythinghelpsgodbless."

The homeless man sways on the sidewalk. An oversize parka covers his shoulders. The parka balloons out over layers of sweaters and god knows what. The man is short, looks old. Harry gets a stinging whiff of sour piss. He can't imagine the hygiene situation. Lack thereof.

"No thanks," says Harry.

Such a stupid thing to say.

"A quarter?"

Harry stops.

They stand in a dark spot on the street, dead houses to the east and the black construction hole to the west. Harry digs in his pocket as if he has a load of change and then brings his fist to the bum's cheek. The bum makes a horrible sound, surprise and pain balled into one. He loses his footing and stumble-staggers down.

Harry's heart races.

It feels good to release, to let go.

It has been a very, very long time.

CHAPTER 9
THURSDAY

A full platoon of uniforms flanks Police Chief Stan Wills. Grim faces, cement jaws. A blue curtain backdrop provides a soft touch in the cinder block room.

Chief Wills waits. The phalanx on each side of him, eight cops in all, stands rock steady. PR point man Dwight Hatcher whispers something in Wills's ear. Seeing Hatcher brings it all back home, the slosh of blood and guts she's covered, the never-ending variety of drive-bys and murder-suicides and drunken husbands with shotguns and stabbings and meth labs and bank robberies and more.

Flynn texts him: Can I catch you once this shindig is over?

No reply.

The room fills—council members and big shots of City Hall. Clustered in the back of the room, a dense thicket of tripods and cameras. Flynn hasn't seen a media scrum like this one in years.

Flynn stands in the rear of the buzzing throng, back to the wall. She scrolls through her cell phone, familiarizing herself with the major brushstrokes of the old cases. The first three killings all happened in a three-year window, the middle murder right at the eighteen-month mark. After the third, the killings stopped. The city held its breath after number three, but then a year passed and the homicides were carted out to the burying ground for collective memories, only to be visited on key anniversaries.

Maybe the killer died in a traffic accident.
Maybe he packed his bags and moved.
Maybe he got tired.
Maybe he got scared.

"You here—officially?"

Chris Casey, her station's crime reporter.

"Of course."

"Goodman knows?"

"I'll call him after. I know you'll need help. Well, not *you*, but the station. Everyone."

"No question. But if I were you, I'd call him now."

Showing up at the news conference is automatic. Reflex. Instinctive. This will be a story that will consume the town for days or weeks. All the stations are going live. The city will stop for this one, like the OJ verdict or after the first plane hit the North Tower.

"I heard Goodman mention your name," says Casey.

"He *did?*"

"Yeah."

Casey stands an inch taller than Flynn's five five. He is young and prone to overhyping his stories.

"Mention because?"

"Not sure. How are you feeling about this?"

"This?"

"Back on a crime story. You okay with it?"

Flynn feels she has graduated from crime, but PDQ isn't run-of-the-mill murder. Not hardly. The big question is whether PDQ's resurfacing will swamp the issues around the shooting at the Pump 'N Go, help Goodman move on. Help *her* move on. Or will the killing of Deborah Ernst be something others whisper about her for the rest of her career?

Other reporters.

Future interviewees.

The whole town.

And—does she want to forget?

Can she move on?

"Well?" says Casey.

"Not sure," says Flynn. "I'll let you know."

A quarter-hour behind schedule, Chief Wills does not appear rushed. Flynn knows why. Everyone knows why. The mayor walks through a side door. A trio of duckling aides scurry behind him. All mirror the grim bearing of their boss. Mayor Stewart Hollis is a short Black man. Most days, he works a room with a friendly smile and an affable demeanor, but Flynn has heard tales about his flashy temper behind closed doors.

The mayor takes a position near the podium. He stares out. Scans left. Right. He bows his head like he is about to pray, hands folded together.

"Ladies and gentlemen," says Chief Wills.

The chatter volume plummets from hurricane howl to dead calm like someone's flipped a switch.

"This morning, crime scene technicians and detectives are at the scene of a homicide in North Denver. The victim is female, forty-one years old. We are alerting the entire metro Denver community that we believe this is the work of the same individual responsible for three unsolved murders that began eighteen years ago. The FBI is making every resource available to us. The governor has offered all available talent from the state. We are following every single thread of evidence, and we will interview every potential witness."

He pauses. He leans over to whisper something to the mayor, comes back.

"I am not going to dignify the killer's nickname by uttering it here. I encourage the media to not reference the nickname either. That's what he wants. Certainly someone saw something. They may not think it amounted to anything, but somebody saw something. An unusual vehicle. Somebody on the street—coming or going."

The chief, typically glib, takes a moment.

"The victim." He pauses. "The victim is female, as I mentioned."

Wills struggles. His voice catches. He's rattled. The chief has made these kinds of announcements many times before.

"The victim is one of your colleagues." Long pause. "Robbie McGrath."

One of many gasps is Flynn's.

From time to time, Flynn would spot the elusive Robbie McGrath lurking at the rear of news conferences like this one. A Robbie McGrath byline was always page one, always led to investigations, and was always worth reading. Flynn didn't *know her* know her, but she feels a deep pull of sadness.

Questions shoot rapid fire.

Who found her?

"One of her editors went to her house yesterday morning after she didn't answer her phone."

Wills takes his time choosing his words.

Same method of killing?

"Our investigators have a long way to go. Everything points in that direction."

Where was she found?

"In her living room."

Any sign of forced entry?

"No."

Any sign of a struggle?

The chief thinks about this one. "There was a brief struggle."

Any message from the killer?

"We are not releasing that detail at this time."

So there was one?

"Next question."

Did Robbie McGrath live alone?

"Yes."

Flynn's cell phone vibrates with a text. Her father: They are going to need you back for sure.

Was Robbie McGrath threatened?

Chief Wills pauses, looks down. Hatcher steps to the podium, whispers something to his boss.

"We are pursuing all leads. Again, if anyone knows anything."

Flynn ponders the security at her house. She's grown lax. Windows need latching. She occasionally leaves the back door unlocked and Wyatt, alone, inside. On thirty-minute errands for a quick grocery run, he is fine. Isn't he?

"Are you developing a new psychological profile?" asks Flynn, surprised a bit to hear her own voice.

"We're reconnecting with our profilers," says Wills. "Definitely."

"So you think your previous profile may need updating?" says Flynn.

"There have been improvements in every aspect of profiling in the last fifteen years," says the chief. "Forensics too. Particularly DNA sensitivity. We are taking nothing for granted, and we assume nothing either."

Flynn runs through her options.

One, get to the crime scene and interview neighbors.

Two, get to the newspaper and interview Robbie's cohorts.

Three, find relatives and friends of the previous victims, though she's wary of revictimizing them. Some might want to talk.

Four, talk to psychologists, profilers, and experts.

Flynn: "Is there any advice you can give to somebody who is suspicious about a neighbor or has second thoughts about a coworker?"

"We're looking for somebody who blends in well. Someone you know. When we catch him, and we will, you will remember you had suspicions. So stop and think now."

"And what about reassurances, what message do you have for the people of Denver about their level of safety?"

"To be cautious," says Wills. "To be alert. Talk with and interact with people you know. Don't open your door to anybody you *don't* know. Ever."

"So to confirm," says Flynn, "there was no forced entry?"

"People should be extremely cautious about any individual they don't know," he says.

"So," says Flynn, "that's a yes?"

Her father texts: Good work.

"Everybody must be going a bit nutso," says Flynn.

Dwight Hatcher leans against a cinder block wall in a hall behind the media room. A toothpick rides in his mouth. "A bit," says Hatcher. "How are you doing?"

"I've been better," says Flynn. "What else can you tell me?"

"What *else*?"

"Is everybody sure it's him?" says Flynn. "Off the record if you want. I want to know if it's airtight."

"I'd love to help, and if I could break protocol and help one reporter, you know it would be you. And off the record wouldn't change a thing," says Hatcher. "There's nobody thinking otherwise."

"But why would this guy wait so long?" says Flynn. "Does that make sense to you?"

"You're looking for logic?" Hatcher folds his arms over his chest. "You know better."

"Were there any witnesses?"

"You think I'd tell you something the chief didn't tell all the others?"

"For old times' sake?"

"It's one big scramble now." Hatcher's brilliant white teeth contrast sharply with his smooth dark face. His eyes are inviting and warm. The toothpick stays put. "Don't forget, this guy is really good, right? Three victims and then *poof.* Gone. Maybe he misses the chase. Or he's bored. Lonely. Wants to be the center of attention. Again. But it ain't going to happen. New chief is pulling in every single offer of help. Every stone will be turned. Every grain of sand. You watch."

"It's weird, you know?" says Flynn. "How we move on, how we all go back to normal. Even with questions not answered."

"Glad you're back on the beat," says Hatcher. "You doing okay after the—you know. After what happened?"

"I've had better weeks. Years."

"Don't be hard on yourself."

"And now Robbie McGrath," says Flynn. "Same thing. I mean—"

Hatcher puts a hand on her shoulder, an old-school gesture from the Dark Ages. The touch is light, but it feels like an insult. Like she needs propping up. "Nobody knows for sure what to say in situations like the one you were in," he says. "Say or do. It's ninety-nine percent instinct, and you went with yours."

"Thanks, but you're the PR guy, and you're supposed to say nice stuff," says Flynn. "Don't worry, I know what you all are saying behind the scenes."

"No, really—"

"No spin, okay?" says Flynn. "Not this time."

CHAPTER 10

"You okay?"

Jennifer Hills, his boss.

"After watching that? I feel like everyone else around here, I'm sure."

"Makes you feel all creeped out. You look, I don't know, pale. Sorry to say."

Harry watched the police chief's news conference in a meeting room down the hall, a big dark assistant commissioner's chambers outfitted with a flat-screen TV. Half the building, it seemed, had huddled into the spiffy office, rich with leather and crammed with bookcases, all look-at-me hardbacks.

Harry wanted to worm his way out of the TV-viewing cluster, but he didn't dare call attention to himself.

Harry's mind buzzes with a thousand thoughts.

"Fine now," says Harry.

He sits in the chair in her office, the door shut. Hills keeps a mini fridge by her desk. Her office carries a faint whiff of tuna. She likes to blend it with red pepper hummus and call it lunch. Or a midmorning snack.

"Bit of a jolt for sure," says Harry.

"Worrisome. As in, very." Hills's brown hair is trim and boyish. Her green-brown eyes are large, but the left one is slightly off center. Harry wonders if anyone has ever told her, or if someone with strabismus is able to notice when they look in the mirror. Hills wears a thin gold chain around her well-shaped neck. She favors dark sleeveless dresses. She has shapely deltoids thanks to rowing. He pictures her having sex with her husband, and there's a seriousness to it. True desire.

"I have a touch of claustrophobia," says Harry. Out of sight from her, down behind the front of the desk by his folded-over leg, he clenches and unclenches his tender right hand. "Might be getting worse as I get older, but it was always there."

Hills looks puzzled. "Why do you mention that?"

"Oh, you know, all the people in that office. Crowds. Ugh."

"Oh," she says.

"In case, I don't know. In case I look flushed or something."

Once home the night before, he'd been angry with himself for not pushing the issue with Mary. He should have acted normally, not weird. He should have followed her inside. He should have done what single adults do when they're together.

He watched the late news at home, but it was a quick rehash of what he had heard in the bar from CPR. He scanned the newspaper website. Searching at a macro level posed no risk on a night when the whole town was googling PDQ, and he got the same general bullshit garbage. No details.

"I'm wondering what you think about some sort of safety alert," says Hills. "These are the darkest days of winter. And people have to walk clear out to Washington Street and beyond for cheaper parking. Long way. So maybe HR takes the initiative. You know, organizes a walking-buddy program. Long walk or short. Doesn't matter."

Hills floats "ideas." They aren't ideas. They are initiatives she wants to see in action.

"We've barred and banned the use of the building-wide email. How would people know when?"

"We lift the rule for these purposes only. Email subject line must say 'Need a Walking Buddy?' or some such. We can send around a memo, bring it up at next week's staff meeting, all of that. I mean, we need to do something to make folks feel safe about coming to work—and leaving for home."

The department is home to five floors of workers subdivided into dozens of separate offices and fiefdoms, hundreds of employees in all. Office space has expanded to nearby office towers, too, down the hill. All morning, the halls have buzzed with tense chatter. Alarm. Worry. Questions.

"Doable." Harry feels woozy.

"Why don't you draft the protocols. Maybe create a flyer? We'll post them in the elevators too."

"Easy enough." Harry nods. "Good idea."

Hills's eyes are pinched with accusation. "Sure you're okay? You look poorly, if you don't mind my saying so."

Harry bounces up. "I'm fine," he says. "I never want to be anything but the least of your worries."

At his desk, Harry puts in his wireless earbuds, the Bose QuietComforts. He is fussy about fit, sound, ease of use. He queues the Goldberg Variations from his cell phone. Always searching beyond Glenn Gould, today he chooses the German pianist Claudius Tanski. Harry owns a wide variety of recordings of the Goldberg Variations. Comfort food. He vastly prefers piano to the abrasive sting of the tinny harpsichord. Bach's sense of order appeals to him. The coolness.

He opens the program for tracking applications. There are fifty-seven files to review for an opening in the budget office.

His desk is not ideal. He sits in what was once an outer office, now converted into space for himself and the HR secretary. He's been given a three-sided cubicle with chest-high partitions, but the open side is exposed to anyone coming down the marble-floored hall. He can't fuck off *too* much.

He also can't focus on the applications. The rhythm in the building has changed, as if the water fountains are suddenly pumping Red Bull.

Nobody will mind if he spends more time looking at what the reporters are posting online. And Jennifer Hills won't expect work on the walking-buddy business for another day. Maybe he'll hit send on an email first thing tomorrow. He'll save it in his drafts and zap it to her when he arrives, always before her.

His boss has asked him to develop a safety memo, he tells himself, so he *needs* to go online to see what the Denver Police Department is recommending. There aren't prohibitions about online searching, but the tech department dudes monitor extraneous browsing. A guy in the testing office was fired for watching porn at work. A woman who worked in the federal programs office was let go because she spent all day shopping online for clothes.

Harry always enjoys the firings. He's sat in on his fair share. One juicy voyeuristic perk of the HR position involves watching the false-front images presented by job candidates at the hiring stage, then watching the posers squirm when it's time to go.

It's entertainment.

One hour after the news conference ended, #PDQ perches atop the trending topics on X. Harry scrolls through the hashtag stream, which covers the gamut from raw ripe fear to mocking cries about the weak-kneed citizens of metro Denver.

Everywhere, PDQ.

Every news site he checks has something. *The New York Times*: "Return of PDQ Puts Denver Back on Edge."

The Variations reach the fourth with its quick quaver rhythms, those dancing eighth notes. Too happy, too vivacious.

Channel 4 has already posted a link: "PDQ Safety Tips from the Denver Police Department."

A link next to it: "Watch Full News Conference."

Mid-Variation, Harry presses pause on his music app. He pulls out his earbuds and pulls on the old-school headphones connected to his computer. He clicks the link for the news conference video.

Harry steels himself for a second viewing. He didn't really see or hear much the first time around, standing in the cramped assistant commissioner's office.

There is no way anyone knows his mark.

Anyone.

The suggestion that someone has mimicked his brand sticks in his head like a knotty thrombosis.

He listens to the police chief make the announcement, and then he nearly chokes when he identifies the victim.

The chief's conviction is maddening. Harry's skin tingles. His neck flashes with heat.

What can the reporters do but take the chief's word for it?

They have no way of knowing.

The gall floors him. The giant leap.

And his imitator's gall? What else could it be but guesswork?

The biggest problem, of course, is stirring the old dormant pots. All the amateur theorists chattering and buzzing again, like cicadas wriggling awake, getting ready to rattle their tymbals after years of silence.

The so-called "experts" hired by DPD.

The so-called "experts" brought in by the cable crime shows.

The so-called "expert" retired dicks mucking around.

The grim-faced crime show pseudo-documentarians and their network-funded attempts to re-create everything and reconsider all the evidence, the way they did with JonBenét.

Oh, and surely a fresh wave of podcasts. Two have already revisited the old crimes and theorized to their podcasting hearts' content.

Jesus.

The reporters asked decent questions, but they ate it all up like starving helpless baby birds. Nobody asked for proof to match the new crime to the old. He recognized one voice off screen, the reporter he'd chatted about with Mary at the bar.

Flynn Martin.

She was around when Harry was active. She was all crime back then. She had a tough reporting style when he'd planned and carried out his "projects" with meticulous execution. She gave the cops a fair amount of grief back in the day.

How many years has she been a reporter? As long as Harry can remember, really. He has watched her age, from fresh and cute to mature and solid.

Harry wipes his brow on his shirtsleeve.

"I'm back."

The words touch a hot knife on his spine.

The tired voice is that of Sandy Ingalls, the office secretary, ever oblivious to the real issues of the world. She is near retirement, keeps her silver hair in a tight crop. Her cheeks are gaunt and lined from years of smoking, though she quit a decade ago. Ingalls tells a long saga about her parking woes, how the meter didn't take quarters and then she had to move her car. Harry pretends to listen. Shakes his head in commiseration as appropriate.

An idea blooms and it holds promise.

When Ingalls finishes her oral history of the great parking wars, Harry stands and stretches.

The "hall" outside their second-floor office doubles as a balcony overlooking the building's giant marble atrium.

Harry stands at the railing and watches his coworkers coming and going across the black-and-white diamond pattern in the floor below.

His idea takes shape.

He can see the risks, but the idea offers hope.

One thing for sure, he can't lie back and pretend he doesn't care.

CHAPTER 11

Flynn makes a show of cleaning her desk. It will take an hour to download and sort through all the emails. But sifting emails is low priority. She expects to be out the door with a PDQ-related assignment any minute.

Her cell phone chimes.

"Thanks for the text," she says. Her father isn't much for pleasantries and greetings.

"It was good to hear your voice in the fray."

"You could hear me that clearly?"

"Well, sure," he says. "Did it feel like the cops were a little too quick to announce on this one?"

Michael Martin, and she loves this about him, always reacts to the information and the way it's presented too.

How. Where. When.

What tone.

The number one thing she has learned from him is to think upstream, in the other direction from the way you are being led, to not get lulled into the dullness of believing what any institution or corporation wants you to believe.

"What do you mean?"

"They are so certain it's that same asshole."

He talks to her like a fellow reporter and a cop's ex-wife, not a daughter.

"Wouldn't they know?"

"Ask yourself if it makes sense for a killer to resurface after fifteen years."

"Seems out of the ordinary, but BTK did. Wichita." The reporters at the news conference chatted about the comparisons earlier. "Also fifteen years."

"Even that is too convenient," says her father. "And that led to BTK getting caught. PDQ would know about that too. He'd realize BTK's hubris got the best of him."

"Do we have much else to go on? Even when PDQ was around the first time, the cops held plenty back."

"Keep your chin up, kiddo. Glad to see you're back in the swing."

"Did you know her?" she says.

"Tragic. We overlapped, yes. Probably for a year or two. When it got to be that point in my career, the new reporters looked like high school kids to me, and I wasn't the best about being Mr. Gregarious Veteran Guy, you know? But I've been reading her stories, of course, for years. I mean, she was good. Slow, but really good. Had a knack."

◆ ◆ ◆

"I watched the feed," says Goodman.

"And?" says Flynn.

"And I heard your voice."

"Filling in the gaps," says Flynn. "Emphasizing a point or two."

In the open-concept newsroom, Goodman sits in his oversize cubicle one step beyond the fray. The newsroom flows outward from his middle-of-the-mayhem desk. Flynn expects mass rejiggering of the daily schedule, based on PDQ, and therefore all hands needed on deck.

Instead, routine reigns.

"You're not here," says Goodman.

Flynn cocks her head, looks at him sideways. She leans on Goodman's desk return.

Goodman crosses his legs from one direction to the other. "This isn't my call."

"Disappearing for a week isn't going to change anything," says Flynn. "I feel horrible. I'll always feel horrible. That will never change."

"Snelling wants that interview."

Flynn tips her head back, closes her eyes. "You're kidding."

"I'm afraid not."

"It's not in me."

"If you think you get to decide about your return to work, you're wrong."

It isn't the first time she has wondered if the office politics and interpersonal atmosphere at the station would be different if it weren't run by two veteran White guys. She can't begrudge them their experience because she wants her own brownie points for years of service, but the current paradigm is squarely unenlightened.

"So I'm on some sort of quasi-unofficial bullshit leave, even though I didn't know it," says Flynn.

"Paid leave," says Goodman.

"Open ended," says Flynn. "With fuzzy terms. When you need all the help you can get."

"You don't invite yourself to a news conference without checking in here."

"I didn't do anything."

"Again, this is not my call."

"Did you even fight for me?"

"Of course."

"I've got sources all over the cop shop," says Flynn. "No interest?"

"We'll take all the names and numbers you've got," says Goodman.

"These people trust *me*," says Flynn. "It's not names and numbers. You can't ask someone else to make those calls and expect the same results."

"You're welcome, of course, to provide any suggestions, but you're not back in the newsroom covering stories until Snelling changes his mind or you do the interview. You can try and wait him out, but I have yet to see that particular tactic work."

Flynn squelches a tantrum. Can she go through with the guts-spilling interview? With the city now riveted again on PDQ, why not get it over with? Contrasting the wrongs between a demented, purposeful, methodical killer and the loss of life based on her fuckup isn't a close call. Maybe she should do the interview and clear the decks.

Play along.

She can't imagine sitting at home while other reporters work on PDQ.

"Did you know Robbie?" says Goodman.

"Seen her off and on," says Flynn. "The answer is no. Elusive. Wasn't in it for friendships, that's for sure."

"Do you think the cops have it right?" says Goodman.

"Same thing my father said," says Flynn.

Goodman sighs. "Born skeptics make the best reporters. This town misses your dad."

"He writes. And blogs. And tweets or X's or whatever you call it now," says Flynn. "Seven thousand followers."

"He should be at the newspaper," says Goodman.

"And I should be doing my job."

"You're not getting the appearance issue, are you?"

"Appearance issue?"

"Credibility."

"I have decades of credibility. You're saying it's all down the tubes unless I do this bullshit penance?"

"Credibility covering the cops," says Goodman. "The organization you wouldn't listen to a few days ago?"

Flynn studies Goodman's hard expression for a crack. No such luck. "That is an extremely exaggerated way to describe a heat-of-the-moment judgment call."

"It was longer than that."

"Two moments. Quick ones. It was one person trying to connect with another, and I don't want to be defensive about it because I feel terrible about it, as I've already explained, but I was simply trying to reach him, get him to see the bigger picture. I'm downplaying the severity of the situation, but I felt the same as I did getting anyone to talk, on camera or off. I was trying to make a fucking *connection*."

"See?" says Goodman. "With the exception of that certain adjective, you could save your bacon and you could do that interview. Didn't sound hollow at all."

◆ ◆ ◆

"You gotta be joking."

Flynn catches Tamica outside by the news trucks. She is getting ready to head to the newspaper office with Valerie Sprague, a steady reporter with zero edge.

"I wasn't even supposed to have gone to the news conference. Guess I wasn't technically *there*."

"What the fuck?" Tamica is five ten, long and lanky. She is also fresh, perfect, and always looks ready to run another lap.

"My thoughts exactly," says Flynn. "They want the big fat confessional first."

"That's a crock."

"Those are the terms as dictated to me."

"Then get new ones."

"These come from the top."

"Snelling?" says Tamica.

"Like I said."

"Then let's shoot the darn thing and get it over with."

Tamica's skin is creamy smooth and dark as Italian roast. She keeps her hair stubble-length on one side and long on the other with a flip down over her brow. She has piercing eyes and button ears. Today, her fingernails are lacquered mango. She has a smile, when it flashes, that could quicken the polar ice melt. The hints about her carefree love life and the related action, the sheer variety of it, make Flynn's sex life sound like a G-rated romance novel plotted by nuns.

"It's a possibility," says Flynn.

"With all due respect—"

"I told you a hundred times about that phrase."

"And I mean it sincerely. I was in kindergarten when you started reporting."

"I thought we'd been through this. Treat me like an equal and I'll do the same. Spit out your youthful counsel and let's cut to the chase."

Tamica glares back. "Nobody gives a flying donkey about your interview. Plus, the towering white pillars of television know-how who run our station would be foolish to make a big splash out of it anyway. It's their way of running you through the gauntlet so they can whack your ass."

"I've gotta suck it up and fake it?"

"Whatever it takes," says Tamica. "Half the world thinks we stage the news to begin with."

"Let me ask you, then."

"Fire the fuck away."

"You saw the whole incident."

Tamica holds up her hand. "Whoa," she says. "I know where you're going with this, and the answer is you did nothing wrong. People could hear your heart, believe me."

"You're not just saying that. That's not some PR interpersonal keep-me-happy glossy thing to say?"

Tamica stares back. "Get over your damn self. There's only one story that matters now. So you gotta figure out a way to get back to covering it. Pronto."

CHAPTER 12

The key is separation.
If you take your time and if you plan well, you can delink one activity from the next.
It's like a story.
Detectives need narratives that fit with the natural order of how people move, like the time it takes to go from point A to point B. They look for smooth transitions from one chapter to the next. They need to piece together how a person arrives at the crime scene and how they leave.
But if you are willing to wait, you can mess with their thinking.
If you are willing to scope your next "project" for months and months, and make sure you have considered every possible wrinkle and complication, you can set yourself up for success.
If you don't fall into patterns and routines, it will become even harder for anyone to draw a bead on you as a potential "person of interest" or, worse, an actual fucking suspect.
They got close. Too close for comfort. They had traced PDQ, they believed, to a four-block area in Capitol Hill. It was all based on a wild theory and one minuscule scrap of potential evidence.
Potential.
They went house by house, apartment by apartment, condo by condo. But of course none of Harry's shoes matched, not even close. And the height was way off.

All that heart-pounding worry was two days after Project #3.

Two *years* after Project #3, Harry thought about moving.

But he pictured some cop with a database, watching the comings and goings. And in even two years, there were likely dozens and dozens of apartments and condos changing hands, but why help anyone narrow the pool?

And now all that time has passed, and he is glad.

Stay.

Do the unexpected.

Patience is more than a fucking virtue. It's the key.

Patience and separation.

◆ ◆ ◆

He has never lost track of his thought process. It hasn't gone away. It thrives in his downstairs brain. All he has to do is open the door and walk down the steps to the dark basement, where his other half lives. He opens the door once or twice a day. He walks down the steps to his downstairs brain, but only halfway. He never puts a foot on the floor down there, with its layers of muck and filth.

For years and years now he has been able to stop and stand there, generating images of himself getting beaten as a child, to watch his parents fight, watch his mother hide, watch her drown herself in beer and booze, feel the blood running from his ears.

He straddles two worlds. When he stands on the stairs halfway down to the downstairs brain, he straddles two halves of himself, a sort of twilight zone stasis of in-between. If he puts a foot on the basement floor, there is really no predicting.

Occasionally, he spends a minute remembering.

Maybe he'll feel the thrill, remember how good it felt.

Maybe his heart will race a bit.

He has the ability to imagine what would happen to certain women he encounters throughout the day. Lately, it has been Mary who is the star of these various raw and terribly human moments where the person, right before your eyes, goes from sentient being to desperate animal.

He will spend a few minutes halfway down the stairs, go back up and close the door, and go about his life with the rest of his upstairs brain.

◆ ◆ ◆

He needs to treat Flynn Martin as a project.

He needs to work as carefully and think as carefully and act as carefully as if he were conducting a project.

The risks are the same.

By reaching out to defend his honor and his brand, after all, he might expose himself.

Every project needs a working title. The titles mean you are starting to write a story.

Blank page, working title, chapter one, *go*.

Titles mean you are organizing all the details into one new compartment in your brain. Storing all the factoids. What you need. How it's going to work.

A title sets the theme and organizes his thinking.

If the title changes as the story progresses, that's okay.

He feels like a writer in control of scenes on a page.

Harry has access to the best materials through the State Library loaning system, but he also likes to visit the main branch of the Denver Public Library, to flip through the CDs, see what's new, maybe follow a cute something through the stacks for a floor or two.

Harry buttons his waterproof gabardine trench coat, a green so dark they call it "mountain moss." He slings his messenger bag over his shoulder like the millennial hipsters do. He plucks his gray felt fedora off the coatrack, precisely unlike the millennial hipsters.

Outside, a chill slaps Harry's face. He feels otherwise warm. Colfax Avenue traffic is at a standstill in both directions. He keeps his head down. He waits for crossing lights. The sidewalks are wet from a cold mist.

◆ ◆ ◆

Harry knows his purpose is clear. Like headphones that send the music to your inner ear via the cranial bone, he feels the purpose in a deep way. He can't sit still, not with his reputation on the line.

No way.

But there is a big problem he hasn't solved.

He hopes he can figure it out.

He will need to take his time.

He'll dabble. He'll poke around like any other user of the web.

He feels a burning urgency to start the cleanup process as soon as possible.

Still, he won't abandon his fundamental principles.

Separate.

Evaluate risks.

Be methodical.

He hears an oboe hanging in the air, a Mozart oboe. It is from the third movement of Serenade No. 10 for Winds. The delicate tune gathers itself in tantalizing fashion. It's quiet, unassertive.

It sets the precise mood he needs.

CHAPTER 13

Wyatt looks glum and worried. "So what are you going to do?"

"Keep thinking," says Flynn. "All I know how to do."

"They want you to say that you feel bad?"

"That's what it comes down to."

"But you do feel bad."

"Of course."

Wyatt picks at a plate of spaghetti and peas. He eats like a fashion model, which explains his slight physique. He twirls a knot of noodles, then nibbles on one dangling strand. He sits at the two-seat kitchen counter. Flynn sips a glass of cabernet.

"And you're not going to work tomorrow?"

"I haven't decided."

"But they said you aren't working."

"Doesn't mean I can't work on things," says Flynn. "You know, answer my own questions."

Tamica's offer, in fact, hangs in the air like a lingering odor.

What was it? Something like *Swallow hard, suck it up, get back to business.*

"What will I do tomorrow?" says Wyatt.

"We'll see," says Flynn.

◆ ◆ ◆

She watches MSNBC until it gets repetitive. When she gets tired of being told how to think, she watches the *PBS NewsHour*. She feels like a renegade, consuming the national news in real time. She skips watching her own station's evening news and all the other locals too.

Wyatt burrows himself in his room upstairs doing homework. Flynn cleans the kitchen. At least, a lick and a promise. She calls her father to fill him in. She pours another glass of wine and distracts herself by watching an edgy HBO series about high school kids doing drugs and having sex. The show is filled with gratuitous boobs and butts and heavy doses of ennui. It makes her feel clueless, but for a brief moment, she can gawk at the brash action and the lack of big-world problems. She knows she won't start work on PDQ until Wyatt is down for the count.

She hears Wyatt rustling in and out of his bathroom and heads upstairs to say good night. The old house is much too big for two people. The floorboards and stairsteps transmit every bit of movement with distinctive pops and squeaks, even from a flyweight like Wyatt.

Wyatt slips into bed, covered by a pile of comforters. At night, he likes to braise.

"They'll pay you even if you don't go to work?"

Wyatt lies on his back. Only his head pokes out.

"Yes."

"For how long?"

"Wish I knew."

"But not forever."

"Very doubtful," says Flynn. "Are you taking on all my problems?"

"I've heard of people who lose their houses when they don't have a job."

Flynn plants a quick kiss on his forehead. "Well, you have one job, and that's to be a happy young man who doesn't try to walk around with the weight of the world on his shoulders."

"But what are you going to *do*?"

"You mean, in general?"

"Yes."

"Clean, bake brownies, go for long walks, read a book or two, see friends. How's that?"

She might be able to follow the recipe on the back of a box. She can't imagine concentrating on a novel or caring about some random nonfiction topic, not with the state of her mind.

And *what friends?*

"You need one more thing in the picture." Wyatt opens his eyes wide.

"No," says Flynn. "We are not getting a puppy. But I'm glad you can look on the bright side. It's a good trait to have."

Flynn takes her laptop to the seldom-used dining room table. She puts a corner lamp on low. She makes rounds she wouldn't normally make, checking the downstairs window latches and the front door latch and lock. She lowers the shade over the window in the front living room.

It's a few minutes past 9:00 p.m.

The wine urges her to start a movie. Another voice screams *Be productive.*

Like Wyatt.

Wyatt focuses. He belongs to a tight peer group, one boy and two girls. They text and call each other for homework help, relying on each other's strengths. They meet at the library or each other's houses. They are serious about learning and also make it fun, goofing around and then getting down to work. Flynn has no idea how Wyatt ended up hanging with the academic crowd, but she feels lucky. At age six, he weathered the divorce. He went into a shell and teared up for a time. But he shook it off. He fell into the routines, going back and forth to stay with his father, the cop.

Flynn gives herself ninety minutes.

She checks X. PDQ remains a hot topic. But X adjusts the algorithm for location, doesn't it? On Google News, PDQ is tops. It is a national story.

A quick scan of the coverage gives Flynn the distinct feeling she hasn't missed any major developments since the morning briefing, the one she should not have attended without first getting hall passes from those guarding the station's so-called image at Checkpoint Public Relations, the most sacred gate of all.

Flynn pulls up the Wikipedia page on PDQ and scans it to refamiliarize herself with the basics, then skips over to her station's website, as if anyone but herself cares whether she gives them an extra click of ratings support. One click. Is her fucking pride *that* big a deal?

Her station's coverage is more of the same. None of the website writers and none of the reporters have obeyed the chief's request. It's "PDQ this" and "PDQ that." She watches interviews with Robbie McGrath's colleagues. She watches interviews with Robbie's neighbors. She has a burning need to find Robbie's house and see the scene for herself. She wants to find out what the FBI is thinking—and how heavily they're involved. They played a role in PDQ's first go-round. The FBI's Denver Field Office is right there. She wants to interview the lead investigator from homicide and all the crime scene experts gathering details.

Even without permission to fly, Flynn's reporter brain is on automatic pilot.

◆ ◆ ◆

Her station makes it easy. A link called "The First Three Killings" takes her to an entire page of thumbnail images and a list of headlines, in order.

She opens the top link.

And watches herself begin to speak.

Who was that reporter in the fuzzy frame? So earnest, so serious, so *young*. Her hair is bigger, her makeup more intense. Look! Once upon a time, Flynn's face had sharpness to the cheeks and definition to the chin. Ah, youth. She was a smoker, back when she was immortal and Max McKenna had sucked her into his worldview about the "low-lifes" and the no-goods.

The date on the first clip in the archive is January 2007. It was two years into her marriage to Max.

The first lonely murder, ghastly as it was, seemed like another one of those bizarre crimes for the shit-happens file. Of course, nobody knew at the time it was the "first murder."

It was one.

A singleton.

Intense coverage lasted a week, then faded. The victim was a woman named Karen Schultz. She had been a waitress at a loud tavern in South Denver called the Rusty Bucket. The bar featured live music Wednesday through Sunday. Way back in the 1980s, it was the scene of many cocaine busts. The parking lot included a special section for motorcycles.

Karen Schultz was twenty-nine when she was murdered. Professional career? None in sight. String of boyfriends behind her? Plenty. She had straight hair all the way down her back, prominent tattoos on her shoulders. Nose ring. In all the photos of Karen, she never smiled. She rented a tiny house in Bear Valley. She shared the expense with a friend who worked at a hospital. The roommate, a bit better looking, had a newish boyfriend and something of a life outside work, but Karen's life revolved around the tavern and making ends meet.

Karen Schultz was killed on her day off, a Monday. The roommate found Karen around 9:00 p.m., when she got home from an after-work movie with her boyfriend. The roommate, Sara Casner, needed two weeks to compose herself enough to talk to reporters. And Flynn, in fact, got the first opportunity to talk with her on camera. Even with all Flynn's patience and gentle prodding, however, the roommate was inconsolable.

She mustered coherence for one sentence and then, blubber and sobs. Flynn didn't blame her. Watching the footage, Flynn wells up.

Sara never again stepped foot in the house she shared with Karen. She'd seen too much. Once police cleared the crime scene, Sara sent family and professional movers to gather her belongings. All except a keepsake or two were donated to Goodwill. Sara couldn't imagine holding on to them, not knowing if the killer had touched them or handled them in any way.

Whatever horror Sara had seen, it was unspeakable. Her life changed forever. Her account would bring a tear to a glass eye.

The next link includes Flynn's reporting of a somber, gloomy day at an old stone church in Kiowa. There were so many people that the crowd spilled out onto the street. Karen had grown up modestly. She'd moved to the big city to make a go of it. She had managed a semester at Arapahoe Community College before being drawn into a more party-centric crowd. Karen's simple chestnut casket was buried under cold rain in a disheveled cemetery on the outskirts of town.

Flynn clicks through the coverage at the time, and it all comes back—the lack of evidence, the lack of suspects, the lack of motive, and the fruitless police search for a genuine lead. She watches Karen's parents plead for information. She watches interviews with the police—one week out, two weeks gone, a month, six months, and then one year, as if the calendar might prod loose a surprise witness or prompt a new piece of evidence to materialize like a bizarre magic trick that works only on grim anniversaries.

Slowly, the fate of Karen Schultz's case slipped down the priority list. And then it grew chilly. And then it grew cold.

◆ ◆ ◆

Until July 2008.

The second victim was Amy Pedigo, thirty-five years old. She was single and lived alone. Her body was found by police after anxious coworkers reported her missing on a Tuesday morning. She hadn't been seen or heard from since leaving work the previous Friday. At first, of course, it was once again "another murder." Like any big city, people get shot and stabbed. Many die, some do not.

Amy lived in a North Park Hill neighborhood. She rented a basement apartment from a retired couple upstairs. The murder happened in a fringy section of town. Given the location, a homicide could get twenty seconds of airtime and never be mentioned again, or it could be cause for steady coverage. It all depended on the circumstances and the rank, status, and income level of the victim.

Amy Pedigo might have gone down as another odd, unexplained homicide until three days later, when Police Chief Lewis Seaton, the guy who preceded Stan Wills, held a news conference to discuss the case and put out a plea for help. The request was not in the ordinary flow of postmurder routines, particularly since it had drawn attention from the top. A reporter from the *Post* wondered aloud if the Schultz case and the Pedigo case might be related. At the time, it seemed like an odd question to ask.

A reach.

Chief Seaton wasn't ready for the question. His slight bobble, the fact that he didn't immediately dismiss the question, told reporters what they needed to know. Chief Seaton sensed his mistake, conceding after a minute that they were looking into possible connections between the deaths of Karen Schultz and Amy Pedigo. Even after a week, the police did not say what connected the two crime scenes, but they finally allowed that there was "sufficient evidence" in the style and method of murder that they were "fairly certain" that they were the work of the same killer.

Pedigo worked as a driver for an auto parts distributor. She had moved from Plano, Texas, three years earlier. She had no family in Denver. She was slightly built and a bit of a loner. Amy Pedigo never looked the same in any two photos. She tested various guises. She kept the local tattoo shops busy.

One coworker managed to say some nice things, but the coworker who found Amy's body refused all requests for interviews. The owners of the house where Amy rented the apartment balked at an interview. Amy's body was quietly claimed by the family and shipped back to Texas.

The police refused to say how the two had been murdered, but the method involved some sort of sedation and then a lethal injection. But then what?

Amy Pedigo had lost her life eighteen months and one day after Karen Schultz. At the time, nobody thought much about the significance of the gap. Eighteen months plus one day? A random period of time.

It's as if the in-between years don't exist. Flynn wants to find Karen's roommate and find Amy's coworker.

What did you see? What did you see? What did you see?

An hour has gone *poof*.

She turns the light off on the front porch and stands in the night air, coolness a bracing smack on her cheeks. She lasts a minute, steps back inside.

The third victim lived in East Denver, among the modest one-story homes of a neighborhood called Goldsmith. If the city was a clock, PDQ had rotated from seven to one to four.

The victim was Emily Berns. She was thirty-four. She lived alone. She had been married for two years, divorced for four. She worked as a cashier at a chain drugstore. Her body was found by a neighbor who noticed the back door flopping open on a cold January day. Of all the PDQ killings, this was the least organized scene. He had been interrupted and forced to make a quick exit.

Within a day, police had connected Emily, Amy, and Karen.

The media made it easy for the public too. The headshot triptych became a staple of the coverage. It's odd, thinks Flynn, how the media settles on one image for each victim and how those photos become electronic tombstones.

Emily smiled. Amy brooded. Karen looked deep in thought, no smile.

Emily Berns was slight and dark. She cut a handsome, businesslike figure. After the divorce, she kept her married name. She was originally Emily Catteneo, as Italian as they come. No kids.

Emily died a day before the three-year anniversary of the murder of Karen Schultz. Now the city knew the killer's eighteen-month clock. The waiting time didn't alleviate the underlying note of fear in exchanges with strangers, random encounters. Gun sales soared. Security systems too. Self-defense classes filled. Experts and fake experts spouted their theories on the profile of the killer.

Even at the time, Flynn wondered how a man with white-hot rage could wait for the calendar to plod along before erupting again.

Emily's murder details led to the "PDQ" tag. An unnamed detective leaked a key detail to a newspaper reporter. Karen, Amy, and Emily had all been found with the block letters PDQ neatly centered over their sternums. The killer had used the DIY stick-and-poke tattooing method. The letters were about two inches high and precise, as if the work of a template.

The stories about Emily featured more and more quotes and commentary from Detective Joe Maze, a fairly forgettable cop with an unassuming style. One of the videos about Emily's murder started with a still photograph of Maze at the back door of Emily Berns's house. Maze was pointing to something invisible on the ground. Squatting in the background was Dwight Hatcher. Hatcher looked younger, naturally, and skinnier. Hatcher was staring at whatever Maze had found. Hatcher has been the PR face of DPD for so long that Flynn's forgotten he was a beat cop and then a detective, and only later the smooth-talking point person who feeds the media. What were Maze and Hatcher looking at? A footprint? A scrap of trash?

Flynn remembers that house. Was she standing there when the photo was snapped?

What was memory? What was not?

Maze put in forty years for the department. His biggest regret was not finding PDQ. Joe Maze's clearance rate for murders and nonnegligent manslaughter was 80 percent. He was given a plaque. But, before he retired a half dozen years or so ago, he'd never found PDQ.

PDQ's tattoo work, went the working theory, must have taken time. The tattoo was smeared with ointment and covered with a bandage, as if the recipient wanted to show it off—a living tattoo on a dead person. The tattoo work either meant the victim was semiconscious for a long period of time or dead for hours while PDQ set his stage, cleaned, and waited for the right moment to leave.

Ironically, however, at least with Karen and Amy, PDQ was not pretty damn quick. That is, if that's what "PDQ" stands for.

CHAPTER 14

He took his time.

Near Emily's body, PDQ left a note of disgust about the quality of the police work. PDQ asserted in the note that he was beyond help. The "urge" was something he had been grappling with since he was a young boy. It was something he could not overcome, even if he made a mistake and got caught.

PDQ said he had no intention of slipping up. He wrote that he hoped to avoid getting caught, but with each "urge" and each "project," he was making it easier for the police to do their work. PDQ offered to produce audio tapes the next time he "went to work" so everyone could hear what the moment entailed. "Suffering was at a minimum," he wrote. "Only enough for my enjoyment. To satisfy—"

But he hadn't finished the note—it ended midsentence.

At the eighteen-month mark following Emily's murder, the city braced itself. The media made sure of that.

But nothing.

And another eighteen months.

Nothing.

And then the police moved on. Fresh murders and new crimes didn't wait for the PDQ investigation to wrap up. Flynn recalled that a few cops weren't happy about the shift in priorities. How many times could a reporter write that the cops had never found their man?

Nobody closed a curtain. No end credits rolled. Nobody shrugged their shoulders in public and said, "We give up."

But the town knew.

Fade to quiet.

Fade to nothing.

Fade and keep fading.

◆ ◆ ◆

Flynn stares again at the three images.

Karen, Amy, Emily.

Did Robbie McGrath's fourth photo turn a triptych into a tetraptych? Something.

Which McGrath photo will be sealed in the minds of Denver? In future true crime books?

Something bothers Flynn.

PDQ's first cluster of victims was weak. Flynn hates herself for thinking the thought. At best, they were medium powered. Maybe they had aspirations and dreams, but they were working in routine situations. Maybe they were climbing all the virtual ladders out there, but something about their bios and their looks suggests frailty, and that makes Flynn think that PDQ knew what targets he was after in terms of size. And gestalt. And place in the world.

Robbie McGrath didn't fit. Investigative reporters need cojones. They live for the takedown, the resignations, the apologies. Even if they aren't public and showy types, investigative reporters need a certain backbone and fortitude to tackle an investigation that might last months or a year and cause all sorts of public relations nervousness on the part of the official, public or private, in the crosshairs. They belong to a breed that knows how to bite and then bite harder.

Has PDQ upped the ante?

Altered his targets?

Fatigue layers bricks on her shoulders. A throb pounds at her neck. The late hour. The wine. The emotions of those three horrific cases.

Please, please . . .

But.

One last thing.

Flynn logs in to her work email. A towering waterfall of boldface subject lines demands attention. The counter shows 247 unread emails.

She sends a quick text to Tamica.

I'm over it. I'm raring to go and get it done.

Then adds:

Let's figure out a time ASAP. Tomorrow would be terrific if you can squeeze it in.

Flynn glances at the time on her laptop. She changes "tomorrow" to "later today" and adds four snarky smiley faces, tongues out.

Pay no attention to the time this was sent, she writes. I'm fine.

She scans the subjects on the waiting emails:

You are pathetic.

Fuck YOU.

Reporters should report.

Where are you hiding?

Who do you think you are?

Or some variation.

On and on.

Some spam—dick enlargements (um, not an issue) and cheap airfares to Turks and Caicos (she loves saying the name). She scans the bargain travel for any space-bound jets with an empty shotgun seat headed to the dark side of the moon or Neptune or Alpha Centauri.

No such luck.

And then one near the top: "Tip for Flynn."

Every batch of emails brings a handful of "tips" and "story ideas" and "hot leads" or "must investigate." Or the ubiquitous "Hey Flynn" pretending to be a friend.

One more minute on the laptop, Flynn promises herself, and then she will stare at the dark and pray for sleep. She remembers to take a sleeping pill.

She opens "Tip for Flynn."

> They think I did this one. I didn't do this one. Somebody has ripped me off. Do you know how this feels? I have changed. I am still getting better. Let me know if you are interested in learning more. Simply leave a one-word reply like "Yes" or "More" and I will be in touch. Of course I won't be using this email again. But I know how to be in touch and you do not. I have details that will confirm I'm the guy. Couldn't you use a little help? To get back in their good graces?

Flynn reaches a finger for delete.

Fueled by wine and fatigue, the reply comes in a snap.

> Fuck you and your pea-sized brain. This is not a time for jokes or games. Go back to the slimy disgusting cave you crawled out of, pull the rock back in place,

and never come out again. And leave me alone. And everyone else, too.

Flynn hits send. She closes the lid on the laptop with a metallic smack. She is used to vile crap in the comments section of her stories. She is used to angry emails and pissed-off people, but this is a new low, even for the weirdos.

Her chest flutters.

I am still getting better.

WTF?

◆ ◆ ◆

Flynn fixes coffee so it is ready for the mindless morning press of a button. Pouring water and estimating Yuban scoops is always an easier task at night, even in her wobbly state. She checks the downstairs locks. She hasn't eaten in a long time. She heads upstairs without giving genuine sustenance another thought. With the hall light on, she cracks Wyatt's door. She makes out the general lump under the comforters and a dark thatch of hair like a muddy mop, barely visible. Flynn waits long enough to detect the gentle rise and fall of the covers, proof of life and lungs. Viability.

She hopes he is dreaming happy.

In the bathroom, she snaps the cap off her tub of sleeping pills. She shakes a powder blue capsule into her palm, hopes the generic grocery store variety packs the needed firepower. She contemplates doubling up.

No—only one.

She swallows the pill, brushes her teeth. Face wash, retinol cream, and a moisturizer. She waits the full two minutes for the electric toothbrush to finish its appointed rounds. She's got a weird inability to land the toothbrush back on its rocket launcher pad.

Flynn changes into her purple nightshirt, knowing full well she should have eaten something to go with all that wine. She stumbles to bed, thinking about probes and dicks and remembering drunken tumbles with her ex and all the times she had passed out happy after an enthusiastic romp. Dialed in correctly, alcohol and sex are a sparkling combination. Dialed in wrong, the mix can slant sloppy and mean.

No boyfriend waits in bed. No ex either. She has zero interest in sex, but an arm over her shoulder and a warm snuggle would be welcome.

Flynn snaps off the bedside lamp. A car hums by on the street outside. The square of light from the window flops and morphs like a kinetic Salvador Dalí as it sags from ceiling to wall and then races off and away. She grabs her phone to turn off her alarm.

She pulls the covers up, puts her head back on the pillow, and opens her messages.

"Tip for Flynn" is back.

Flynn clicks it.

> Got that off your chest? Okay then. You read me wrong. I am no prankster or some such. It's me. I can see, perhaps, why you don't believe me. But it's me. All for now. I will be in touch. And find a way to prove it. To you. In the meantime, ask them about the music. Yes, them. The cops. The music. Classical music. It's not just any old thing. Ask them about it.

Why *her?*

Is this . . . ?

Oh and don't worry, this email is entirely untraceable. And I won't be using it again anyway. And you will want to keep this all between us.

Just us.

If you don't, I can't make any promises.

But get ready.

We have work to do.

CHAPTER 15
FRIDAY

Every few weeks, Harry stops for breakfast at Charlie's Kitchen. He makes his way on two buses to East Colfax. He likes to sit at the counter in the haze of bacon smoke. He sits. And relaxes.

He doesn't read anything. He keeps to himself. He is polite. He avoids conversation. Nobody comes to breakfast to chat with a stranger. Going to restaurants makes him feel normal. A city guy doing city things.

Charlie's Kitchen is real-people territory. The restaurant sits on a corner across from a Walgreens. It draws the hangover crowd on weekends. Cheap carbs, greasy chow. It is, to say the least, unpretentious.

The morning after the email exchange with Flynn Martin, he arrives at six thirty, when the restaurant is shifting from lazy overnight hours to the morning grind.

Greta, the waitress behind the counter, takes his order. She is tall and older. Inscrutable. Harry feels oddly happy, but he senses a grim flavor from the others around him. Many stare at their phones. Spoons *tink* against coffee cups. Water and ice flow from carafe to glass with a sparkling *whoosh*. Eggs issue a gentle sizzle on the grill. But mostly, Harry hears quiet. The occasional low chatter.

There's a weight to the room.

And city.

And he knows why.

◆ ◆ ◆

And then comes the decision to press play.

And watch the movies in his head.

There are three movies. The one titled *Emily* is his favorite. Not his smoothest work, no. But, in the end, the one that left him with the biggest thrill. And the one that suggested, well, that three was enough, that if he wanted to go down in history, he would have to wrap it up, call it good. Sure, he got scared. There was a week or two of touch-and-go. In the end, however, he knew not to let arrogance trump survival.

The movie titled *Emily* starts a few weeks after the movie titled *Amy* wraps. All the mental movies begin the same way, and they are all riveting material. There's no need to skip ahead to his favorite parts because they are all his favorite parts. The planning time is as exhilarating as the last breath.

The projects start with choosing the neighborhood. The neighborhood is always blandsville generic, full of working stiffs who toil way too hard and will go through life with miserable dreams and wistful, unrealized fantasies. It's tragic, really.

First he finds the neighborhood, then he zeroes in on a block, and finally he picks his house with a single woman or at most two roommates with distinct, separate schedules.

For Emily, he spent weeks traveling around Denver by bus at night. He'd leave his phone at home, of course, and venture out. He had four neighborhood candidates before settling on Goldsmith. Overlooked, unspectacular, vanilla. Nowhere. Postwar, built when the United Fucking States of America dispensed promises like cheap candy, and look at it now. A springboard to Dullsville. A place where hope goes to die or get ground to dust in the daily pulverization of unproductive routines that amount to sideways, sideways, sideways. He will be doing one of the females a favor, really. They can stop pretending they are going anywhere. They can stop pretending they have to look fetching and if he gets to see them naked for a few minutes after he dispatches them to the other side, well, it would only be for the sake of his private mental movie because he draws the line at fucking something that isn't alive and right up until the minute when he says goodbye and eases their pain he offers them hope. Hope is the key to keeping them calm. If they have hope, they obey. Acquiesce. And no, he isn't there for nonconsensual sex. Again, maybe he'd study their anatomy for a few minutes once they're gone, record those moments for his movie, but he draws the line. He is there to watch the long slow slide to the end.

They don't know that.

But he does.

Neighborhood, block, house.

Lottery, lottery, lottery.

You had to win three lotteries to win PDQ's danse macabre, and he wanted to make it memorable for them and he wanted to make it memorable for him.

It was a bargain.

He felt sad for the people who lived there, and the hours he spent at night walking its streets reminded him of his own anger and sadness, and when he first spotted Emily and the three days in a row she arrived home at the same precise time, he knew she was the one.

He had picked Goldsmith in the late summer, chosen the block by Christmas, and had Emily dialed in the following April. He watched her for nine months before easing her pain. He knew where she worked because once he had picked the house, he checked the mail in her porch mailbox and had a name and then off to the races with social media and there was a selfie of Emily getting a pathetically small ten-cent pin at work for her one-year anniversary at the chain drugstore up on Evans Avenue. He shopped there too. Once a month. He looked her in the eye. Deodorant, toothpaste, a tube of disinfectant wipes. She couldn't possibly know she was making change for the man who carried her fate in his pocket. He watched her outside, smoking and reading fat paperbacks on her breaks.

The block became his own movie set, and he started adding dawn trips to shake things up. He started assigning names to the characters in his movie. Milkman, Harvey; postal delivery dude, Dick; neighbor #1, Charlotte the grandma; neighbor #2, Dean with the fastidious front yard and Instagram-ready decorations for the next holiday mounted days after the last; UPS driver; Rachel the lesbian.

So on the day when it finally happens, on the day he brings all his supplies in a tight little case and he steps up on Emily's meek little porch, he belongs. He fits in. He knows the rhythms of the block. He has a serene, serious melody dancing in his head. Dusk flips to full dark as he bounds up the stairs. She answers the door quickly. Maybe a little too quickly? Maybe she is expecting a package from Rachel the lesbian but she sees a man with his winter coat and collar way up and wool hat way down low but there's a clipboard and he starts to say how he hates to interrupt her and he knows it's late but he's taking a poll and midsentence he catches her off guard and pushes his way inside and the first few seconds are so critical, keeping the screams and shrill blurts of panic to a minimum, getting the door closed, and ripping the prepared lengths of duct tape waiting on the inside of his coat around and around her mouth. He had four three-foot lengths of duct tape ready, and winter makes it much easier because the heavy coats give you an easy place to prep your tools. A chef's mise en place. Next, zip ties around the wrists and around the ankles, keeping everything low below the windows so snoopy Grandma or snoopy Dean can't see a thing but he already knows that Emily keeps her shades drawn because how many times has he walked past her house at all times of day? A hundred? More?

Next, turn down the wretched laugh track from a sitcom but leave the TV on so the lack of a flickering glow doesn't draw attention because Emily is a devout TV watcher, and he wants the light from her small sad living room to be right even as he drags her into her tiny bedroom that smells of that fake fucking floral spray. Then make sure all the windows are covered and immediately begin telling her it's all going to be okay.

Endless reassurance, like comforting a wounded animal. He lets things calm down. He lets her calm down. He waits for her to ease down all the way to tranquil. An hour? It doesn't matter. Steady reassurance. All will be okay. There is trust in the room. Trust vanquishes dread, at least on the surface.

Trust takes much less energy. Requires less squirming.

Finally, he shows her the round liner needle and he cleans a patch on her sternum with the wipes he bought at her store but he spares her that detail because she might realize all the planning that's gone into this moment. He asks her if she would like to listen to one of his favorite pieces of music of all time and she says neither yes nor no but he takes it as a yes and shows her the iPod Nano and pushes the buds into her ears.

Gently.

Presses play.

He begins his tattoo with the three letters he adopted. They mean nothing. The cops can try and figure it out, but they mean squat to him. They are his stamp, that is all. India ink. The pricks sting, no doubt, but he doesn't go super deep.

And, next, while she's sighing in relief that the tattoo is done, the fatal prick in her arm probably feels like almost nothing and then the short quick ride to oblivion.

Done.

It's 12:03 a.m.

Next, he finds a piece of blank paper in the kitchen and composes a note telling the police and all the detectives how much they suck at their jobs and he's really starting to lay into them, knowing perfectly well that his handwriting will give them no clues or evidence unless he's caught and he's never getting caught and he's enjoying the afterglow when there's a knock at the door.

Firm.

Purposeful.

Serious.

The high deflates.

He's already packed but now he can't exactly move around in the living room and double-check and he stays low down the back hall but there's a crash behind him and he needs to double back because somehow his leg bumped a table and there's a vase in pieces and he can't decide whether to leave it or try to clean it up, in the dark, and goes for the latter for some really stupid reason that will never make sense. His hands have been wrapped in soft nitrile gloves since he appeared on her doorstep, but who would care about a busted vase? He flees out the back door and down the alley. He finds a random dumpster and unburdens himself, only to realize blocks later that the pieces would have given a perfect chance to mislead the dumb cops if he had headed in the opposite direction first because no doubt they will find the shards and think they indicate, maybe, his direction home. He hopes to hell he's got everything and wonders who the fuck had come around.

And why.

But it doesn't matter.

Harry eats his breakfast and pays his bill plus a 20 percent tip. Outside, the first scrap of dawn.

He puts his earbuds in. He presses play on Mozart's Piano Concerto No. 23, performed by Murray Perahia and the English Chamber Orchestra. He crosses Colfax and walks two blocks in the wrong direction to catch the speedier 15 Limited, which only makes four stops on the way downtown. Who needs a car in the city? He stands in the windowless articulated middle section, and it bobs on the bumps like a surfboard under his feet. Again, the grimness.

Mozart adds lightness to his thinking.

Of course it was a huge risk to send the late-night email to Flynn Martin.

To respond, in fact, in any way.

He uses an online service based in Switzerland. Harry has done as much research as he can. He has read reviews, studied his options. The site promises "end-to-end encryption." All IP addresses are stripped from each message, the service claims, "by default."

Proton Mail.

He sent the first email from the computer room on the top floor of the main branch of the Denver Public Library after waiting for a computer station to open up. He studied the others in the queue. He studied the ones who were "working." Watching videos. Playing games. Distracting themselves from their nothing lives.

He used two Purell wipes, single packets, to clean up before he touched anything in the station. He spent most of his allotted time making sure those around him weren't paying attention. He logged in to Proton Mail, where he had an account. He had already practiced—sending tests between the two email accounts he keeps as well as one to his work email, which wasn't the smartest thing to do. For the email to Flynn, he created a new anonymous account in Proton and sent it off.

After sending the first email, he walked home. He waited four full hours before checking to see if there was a response. After all, even dialing into Proton Mail alone leaves a track, right? Of course, Switzerland guards its secrets. What about the NSA? The NSA has *reach*. Based on what's been gathered at the Colorado Department of Education about all the kiddos and all the employees of school districts, nothing would surprise him about the NSA and what it sucks down into its big data gullet.

What about intergovernmental police agreements—with Switzerland? Who knows for sure if IP addresses are stripped? They arrive as metadata with the message. So where does the IP address go? When? What scrap heap keeps them? Stores them? These days, it seems as if every trash has another trash. Or a purgatory trash. And putting Proton Mail in his URL bar leaves a trace, right?

The real PDQ can't be too careful.

Harry needs to wrap himself in his old head with its much younger brain. Harry feels age has sapped him a bit. At work, he has been a bit forgetful of late. He wonders, with each error, whether this is the beginning of some form of dementia, the same one that took down his grandfather. He hopes it nails his father, though dementia would be too good, too easy. Right below the surface of every waking thought, Harry watches for signs.

Forgetting to zip up, say. Good grief!

Leaving his computer running with employee applications, personal data, sitting there for anyone to walk in and read. *Horrible.*

And the strangest one, really needing to concentrate to figure out the day of the week. There used to be a flavor to each day of the week, an essence to it. No longer. There are times he has to concentrate to conjure the month. Is it spring or fall?

Not good.

Sending the first email gave him a delicious feeling, almost one of *those* feelings. It felt damn good to be doing something about the alleged return of PDQ.

CHAPTER 16
SATURDAY

"Glad you changed your mind."

"You helped."

"What tipped you over?"

Tamica Porter lives in the bottom floor of a renovated Victorian near trendy Five Points. Rents have soared with gentrification and the speedy transformation of the nearby RiNo district from warehouses to brewpubs and from industrial to residential use.

"I hate missing out," says Flynn.

"Don't I know."

"This is my ticket back."

"Then let's get it punched."

On the short drive over from her home in Congress Park, Flynn mulled telling Tamica about the creepy emails.

Flynn hates being played. She hates missing out. But what idiot sent the emails? Flynn has done plenty of stories on cybersecurity. Every online activity leaves a trail. Should she march her laptop down to the cops? She is sure it is someone's idea of a not-funny joke. Or a trap to make her look foolish.

A small camera waits on a tripod. The coffee table sits cockeyed. A dining room chair stands like an outlier in the mod living room. The hot seat.

Tamica loves framing and lighting as much as she loves a good story. The overcast morning mutes the geometric greens and reds from a strip of stained glass at the top of the tall front window.

Flynn hands Tamica a black coffee and a toasted sesame bagel with a smear of almond butter. As always, Tamica appears both eager and laid back at the same time. She is fit, ready for anything. She wears black jeans, hyper-turquoise running shoes, and a formfitting gray sweater with a funnel neck. Flynn wonders if, even for a minute, she has ever looked so sharp or with it. Flynn wears a navy blazer, a greige blouse, a simple silver necklace, and black slacks. Maybe she is dressed for her own funeral.

Tamica adjusts the tripod for height and angle, tweaks the placement of three landscape photos propped on the bookcase in the background of the shot, and sits down in front of the camera to play inquisitor.

"Let's get this done and get you to work," she says.

"Wait," says Flynn. Should she tell Tamica about the alleged PDQ emails?

"You can't change your mind now."

Certainly Tamica will think she is crazy. Maybe, thinks Flynn, she should let her hangover clear before making things complicated. One mountain at a time.

"Never mind," says Flynn. "Fire away."

"You don't really need my questions."

"It will make it seem more natural," says Flynn. "And you know Goodman will watch the whole thing. So ask as if you were Yamiche Alcindor."

One of Tamica's many favorites, a hardworking PBS reporter who happens to be Black.

And whip smart.

"Okay then," says Tamica. "Maybe I'll use this grilling on my audition reel."

"Audition for *what*?"

"You never know."

CHAPTER 17
MONDAY

Goodman sighs.

"Sincere," he says. "But it's got to pass the Snell Test."

The pseudo "interview" is ten minutes long. Tamica edited it over the weekend. Flynn showed emotion, but she didn't chew the scenery. After years of interviewing public officials following disasters, Flynn knew what tone to strike. *Keep it simple. Keep it simple.* It wasn't hard.

Flynn feels terrible, and that feeling isn't going anywhere for a long, long time.

"How many takes?" says Goodman.

"That's an insult," says Flynn. "Tamica?"

Tamica leans over the partition. "One take, boss," she says. "That's raw, first-time everything."

"I do care," says Flynn. "And by the way, where's Snelling?"

"I know you're chomping at the bit," says Goodman, "but Snelling has to get you green-lighted."

"Is he here?"

"If he is, then it shouldn't take long. And don't make it sound like I'm the one holding you up."

"I've got some ideas on PDQ."

Goodman: "We don't discourage ideas."

"No. You only discourage experienced reporters." Flynn says it with a fat grimace.

Goodman doesn't blink. Or smile.

"I'm leaving." Tamica pulls on a baseball cap. "Let you two duke it out."

"You have someone talking to a profiler?" Flynn asks.

"Why?"

"Because the Robbie McGrath killing doesn't fit."

"How so?"

"The first three were so, well, ordinary. Regular people. All three were undersized. McGrath wasn't a basketball player or a volleyball player, but still. She was a full five nine. Her role in the community was more substantial too."

Goodman cocks an eyebrow. "You want to tell the families of the first three that PDQ's victims were ordinary?"

"Under the radar."

"Whose radar? Not their friends. Not where they worked."

"You know what I mean," says Flynn.

"You mean the media radar."

"I mean, look at Robbie McGrath and think of all the people who must have known, and feared, her name. And then think of the other three from fifteen years ago. They lived and worked in much smaller circles. You know, unassuming."

"Maybe PDQ has changed his targets," says Goodman. "Fifteen years and all."

"We don't sit around and study criminals all day," says Flynn. "Let's find a reputable forensic profiler, bounce these ideas off of him."

"Or her."

"Or her," says Flynn. "Of course. Him or her."

"And some of them will say anything you want to hear. Look at JonBenét."

"From everything I know, the cops are a heck of a lot better now. Let me work the phones, at least." Goodman's reply doesn't matter. She will make all the calls she wants to make. "What harm can that do?"

Flynn revs her computer, keeps her head down. No office mingling. No use of the bathroom. Until February. Or summer. She will work the phones. She will make it obvious she is being productive, even if all she hears is a goddamn dial tone.

Max answers. Thank *god*. He says he is glad to hear her voice. They chat briefly about Wyatt. Logistics, hand-offs, drop-offs, weekend plans. He makes the little things easy. But he can't discuss an issue. He can't take a topic deep. His worldview is set. There is no need for fresh data or fresh ideas. That was always infuriating.

"Do you want to clear the air?" says Flynn.

"Over what?"

"Over what happened."

"It's not going to change anything."

"You think there's nothing to sort through?"

She pictures his solid cheekbones, his strong nose, his closely cropped hair that never goes two weeks without seeing a barber. Max is six feet tall with a natural power to his body, though he happily hits the gym three times a week. His looks turn heads of all persuasions.

"I don't think a rehash is going to lead anywhere good. Or be productive in any way."

"I want you to know I feel terrible," says Flynn.

"I never questioned that."

"But you are questioning something. And you don't need to say it to know what that 'something' is."

"What?"

"About going my own way."

"Describe it however you like," says Max. "And weren't you suspended? I heard you showed up at the chief's news conference? Something?"

"Jesus," says Flynn. "Really?"

Despite its sprawl, Denver is a small town. Word spreads like a bad virus agitated by the notorious Chinook winds.

"You're not an unknown quantity," says Max. "You realize that, right?"

"Okay," says Flynn. "I can see this isn't going anywhere."

Max asks about the status of the locks on her doors and windows. "They've got the best of the best crawling all over PDQ," he says. "They aren't holding back."

Flynn quizzes Max about profilers outside of DPD. He gives her a lead to an old friend at Metro State, a professor who attends all the forensic research and technology conferences and stays in touch with the profiling community. The tip comes with the professor's email address, work and home number too.

"They know what they're looking for." Max is assigned to vice, but no doubt the whole building buzzes with information. "A White guy. Probably educated. Late twenties or early thirties fifteen years ago, so he's mid-to-late forties now. Acts and looks normal, like the BTK guy in Wichita, who was an officer in the church. Our guy had some issues as a kid, maybe out of favor with others, with the bigger group. Maybe had an issue with one parent or both. Probably bullied. Outcast. Maybe abused. Trouble with girls, but not necessarily. His killings prove to him he's an ill motherfucker, and he knows he's sick but doesn't know how to ask for help. Which is—"

Max pauses.

"Which is what?"

"Which is odd because . . ." Max takes a moment. "Because here *you* are. Asking for help."

This is an accusation, a festering scab from a belabored charge during their marriage. Variations included *Flynn Martin keeps everything to herself; Flynn Martin never asks for help; Flynn Martin is pretty sure she always knows what's best.*

"I'm not going to bite," says Flynn. "That was long ago. I wouldn't have called if I didn't need help. You sure it's PDQ?"

Max hesitates. "Well, yeah."

"Did you see it?"

"The crime scene?"

"Yes."

"Not my turf," says Max. "And I thought you didn't do crime stories anymore? Didn't care? Or at least have moved on?"

"It's one of those times," says Flynn. "This is the only story that matters right now. Did you see any photos?"

"I'm not a nosy type."

"How about in general, what do you think?" says Flynn.

"The details look correct."

"What details in particular?"

"All the PDQ details."

"And what are those, exactly?"

They rarely talk about work. Max's overactive vigilance about crimes and bad actors is like an ever-present angry rash. His alarmist worldview drags her down. The divorce brought fresh air to her thinking. After they split, she cleaned up. She paid more attention to diet, took up yoga, thought about exercise (*thinking* counted, right?). She chucked the cigarettes. She'd never been a heavy smoker, but a smoke after dinner always felt good. Like she'd earned it. But she had quit "cold chicken," as Wyatt liked to say.

"You think I'm a leak?" says Max.

"I thought you might know."

"You know there's things they held back, on purpose."

"So Robbie was found naked?"

"Where is this going?"

Max's patience is fading.

"So she was *exactly* like the others?"

"From what I gather."

"No blood?"

"Just enough."

"No sign of a struggle?"

"The chief answered that one."

Emily Berns, PDQ's last victim before Robbie McGrath, put up a fight. Detectives found pinprick dots of broken glass on the floor. Three blocks away, detectives found a plastic grocery bag with the shards from the broken vase in a dumpster. The line from Emily Berns's house to the dumpster suggested PDQ's direction home, to the heart of the city.

And cops had one witness from the Karen Schultz murder who claimed she saw a stranger walking in the neighborhood the same morning Karen's body was found. The witness lived two blocks north and one block east of Karen Schultz. She claimed she knew every person who belonged and could spot the ones who did not. She did not want to go on camera, but she had convinced a reporter to talk to her without showing her face, and she gave a very blah, very ordinary description of the man she had seen.

Karen Schultz's house and the house where PDQ might have been spotted also suggested a direction home, to the heart of the city.

And the lines from the Berns murder and the Schultz murder would have crossed in Capitol Hill, which narrowed the search if you bought these data points as being valid.

Police spent days looking for witnesses. There were a few weeks when detectives seemed to be zeroing in on a few densely populated blocks on the western flanks of Capitol Hill, around Governor's Park. Detectives went door to door, scouring for brittle alibis and close-enough profile matches. The increased activity lasted a few days. Between the way PDQ left his crime scenes and taking the time to sweep up broken glass, it didn't take a profiler to know: The killer was a neatnik. But the Berns situation had required him to abort his full plan. What the hell happened?

"Does it all fit? Are they going back to Governor's Park? Checking alibis?"

"You know it doesn't work like that."

"What?"

"Me . . . being your source."

Flynn stands at a big fat fork in the road. One sign points down a road called "Where Fools Tread." The other, "Safe Way Out."

She chooses WFT.

"Can you find out what music has to do with the PDQ case?"

Max clears his throat. "Excuse me, did you say 'music'?"

"Yes."

"What kind of music?"

"Does it matter?" says Flynn.

"Jesus H.," says Max. "Who is feeding you stuff?"

"Can you find out?"

She pictures Max squeezing the bridge of his hawk nose with thumb and forefinger. "You want me to walk into a room full of homicide detectives and ask about PDQ and music and see if anyone reacts?"

"In a subtle way," says Flynn.

"Because you might know something that nobody else in the whole city knows? Recently exiled Flynn Martin returns from Elba, and the second she gets back her sources come through?"

"The Mediterranean might have been nice, but I was only at home and my sources happen to like me, whether the station does or not."

"Jesus," says Max.

"Can you find out for me if anybody in the crew thinks maybe Robbie McGrath's murder doesn't fit the pattern?"

"And bring up music?"

"Yes."

"Not if you're going to turn around and report it."

"You need to do it without raising any suspicions. I might have something. I think it's in the one percent range that it's anything, but this is a way for me to check."

"Oh, really?"

"Maybe," says Flynn.

"Then you should share what you've got. A trade."

"Mine is—" Flynn pauses. "Most likely nothing. But if I got some corroboration from the inside, or even if one or two detectives were scratching their heads a bit, it might support this other tiny piece of information."

"Wow, that was a lot of words to say not very much."

"Thank you," says Flynn.

"Are you coming up with a story to get me to spill information I shouldn't be giving you?"

"Come on, Max," says Flynn. "No."

Max says goodbye and hangs up.

Flynn hates her nothing-status limbo. Why the hell should she have to endure some public relations gauntlet to get her job back?

Her email cascade refreshes with an all-too-familiar soft *boop*, a mini gong demanding attention.

> You are wanted...
>
> Your attention is needed...
>
> The news never stops...

The top subject line reads "Tip for Flynn."
The message is short:

> You find out about the music? Did you get somebody's attention? You better get fucking cracking. There are other reporters out there who would be able to move on this—and move quickly.
>
> Yours, PDQ.

CHAPTER 18

He did it from Sandy Ingalls's computer. He waited one minute after Sandy left for lunch, before her computer went to sleep. He opened a new browser window in incognito mode, hit control-shift-N, pulled up Proton Mail, logged in, wrote the message, hit send, logged out, closed the browser window, sent the computer to sleep, and slipped back to his desk.

Faster than if he'd needed to borrow a Post-it Note from the purple cube of stickies on her desk.

His heart pounded like the timpani in Mahler's Second Symphony.

It felt sort of good.

Sandy Ingalls was at lunch. Jennifer Hills was at lunch. He always ate at his desk, manned the fort. Sliced turkey sandwich today, with Dijon, on seven-grain bread.

Would one exchange to Flynn's work email cost him? In the end?

Hell, no.

It feels good to be back in cat-and-mouse mode, his system on fire and alert for every possible slipup, but also not too afraid to push matters because the cops are truly, truly, *truly* inept. There is no way someone else could have pulled off a perfect PDQ copycat killing.

If you don't understand the underlying motivation, how can you mimic the act?

He feels the warmth in his chest. He senses the telltale surge in the corpora cavernosa. Out of nowhere! The body's response system is truly a marvel. It has a mind of its own. It is nothing he can control. It's chemistry at work. The formula bubbles gently within him. The formula, perhaps, went into a kind of suspended animation during all the years he was away.

Harry eats his sandwich. He lets the feeling linger. The feeling is a physical swell, a sustained sense of the delicious preliminaries. The moment is every bit as good as being in full bloom. Perhaps it's even better, in some ways. This moment is all about anticipation.

Harry puts on his headphones, as he always does over lunch. He works on his crossword, clipped from the morning paper. He hates the online versions. He uses ink.

Eleven-letter word for "fear," beginning with *T*? The universe sending him a message.

"Trepidation." Comes like a snap. Of course. His hands shake, rattled by adrenaline.

Harry learns something.

In order to prove that the latest murder is not his handiwork, he'll have to slip back into his old self.

To do what he needs to do, to uncover whoever the hell is imitating his work, he will need to go slightly, ever so slightly, into PDQ mode.

The downstairs brain gives a little smile.

CHAPTER 19
TUESDAY

Goodman will call and say Snelling watched the tape and a reporter will package it—she can start in the morning.

Goodman will call and say it doesn't matter if Snelling has watched the tape; he needs her back.

Goodman will call and say Snelling won't be back in the office for three days and he won't watch the tape until then because he isn't in a rush to get her tired old face back on the news.

Imaginary scenarios do no good. Flynn needs her phone to chime. She needs to hear Goodman's "All clear, come on back."

In these situations, there is only one person she wants to see. Flynn drives to her favorite fancy-ass grocery store. She gathers meat loaf, mashed potatoes, gravy, and a salad with a sesame Asian dressing. She stops at the indie coffee shop near her house, now on its third owner and fourth clever name in two years.

Has Beans.

Suddenly the name holds new meaning.

Two giant black coffees in hand, she heads back to Cheesman Park, gets herself buzzed in at her father's sleek condo building, and rides the elevator to the eighth floor.

The latest "Tip for Flynn" email throbs in her head like a mean migraine.

Should she have replied?

With what?

> Dear PDQ,
>
> Thank you so much for taking the time to write. Please tell me more.

Or...

> If you send me one more email, I will be forced to call the police and they will track you down because I hope you know that every single thing that happens on the internet can be traced and tracked and you will be found and arrested and embarrassed for trying to mess around in a situation where you don't belong. And if you are PDQ, then so much the better because it will all be over.

Or...

> I'm right here. Tell me more. It's funny, but I've been looking over your history from fifteen years ago and I happen to think that Robbie McGrath does not fit the pattern of your victims. I'm open to any suggestions but, yes, I'm afraid you must first prove that it's you.

◆ ◆ ◆

"You spoil me rotten." Flynn's father pushes his plate aside. "I could skip dinner, but now I'm going to have to pretend I'm hungry later because

I have a date. I can't sit there and eat like a bird, or she'll think there's something wrong."

"You *what*?"

"And you should be dating, too, young lady."

"Who says I'm not?"

"I can see it in your face."

"I have an 'I'm dating' face? And an 'I'm not dating' face?"

"I would have heard something."

"You sound like Mom."

"Someone has to pick up the slack."

Frances "Franny" Barley, who never stopped using her surname after she married Michael Martin, died of cervical cancer a year before Wyatt was born. Flynn has covered random deaths for years. Is a medical takedown any different from a stray bullet or a deadly rockslide on the highway? It's her least favorite topic to ponder. "Who's the lucky girl?"

"I know her name and that's all."

"And the name is?"

"Rhonda. She prefers Ronnie."

"And you met her how?"

Empty plates sit between them on the small table. The view of Cheesman Park grows fuzzy and washed out. A midday front threatens to plunk its frozen butt down like an unwelcome relative who can't take a hint.

"Bumble," says Michael. "Match for oldsters."

"You've got a profile?"

"Why not? No commitment. No guarantees. No need to know anything more than remember the name Ronnie—and not to forget it all the way to Niko's. What can really happen at Niko's, anyway?"

A joint that offers Greek and American food, and even Mexican options, in a generic booths-and-tables setting. Despite the mishmash, it rarely disappoints.

"You should try it."

"You mean online dating?" says Flynn.

"Yes, sure."

"Unneeded. I have guys lingering around."

A lie.

"And?"

"And I'm busy enough, you know."

"And?"

"No sparks so far. Meaningless flames that will probably stay that way." Or she can kick dirt on them if they get serious. "What does this Ronnie do?"

"Retired teacher and then school administrator. We exchanged a bunch of messages, and the main thing is she's a reader—you know, meaty fiction. Contemporary or classics, either one. Goes to the theater."

Flynn hasn't decided whether to bring her father in on Mr. Poser PDQ.

"If I was a single woman," says Flynn, "I might be looking for dependable companionship."

"Yes, I'm sure she will think of me like a bodyguard." He taps his bicep. "Pure muscle. And by the way, you *are* a single woman."

"Not like single-single, all lonely, sitting-around-the-house-all-day kind of woman."

"Just because you're busy, have an ex, and have two or three guys hovering around doesn't mean you're not single."

"I suppose technically I'm single."

"It's not a blurry line." Michael Martin is not a big believer in gray zones. "In fact, without Wyatt coming and going all the time, I'm sorry to say you'd fit what PDQ is looking for. Almost to a T."

◆ ◆ ◆

All of PDQ's victims were childless.

All of PDQ's victims were dogless, catless, petless in any way, shape, or form.

Flynn can't imagine dealing with a dog. Her schedule isn't dog friendly. Wyatt's ping-pong schedule to Max's and back isn't dog friendly either.

A cat? Would a cat deter PDQ? Cats are amusing and might add some life around the house, but would they do the trick? Give her immunity? What if one turns into eight?

If that happens, she'll be single forever.

CHAPTER 20

Harry doesn't use incognito mode on his work browser. It might draw attention. It isn't part of his routine. But it isn't unusual for a human resources staff member to be digging around online. The tech boys in IT don't care about his searches or the pings off his computer to Facebook and X or TikTok. And it isn't like he types "PDQ" into Google eighty-five times a day.

The first thing is a basic Google search. Of course "Flynn Martin" generates all sorts of hits.

An old profile in *The Denver Post* shows she was once married to a cop. A cop!

Max McKenna.

So her real name is Flynn Martin. He thought he was hunting for a maiden name.

One of the Google hits leads to Flynn's Instagram feed. He is disappointed to see she has a son. A son poses a challenge. *Potentially.* The son appears to be ten or older and on the slight side, perhaps short as well.

There are pictures of the kid, very infrequent, but no sign of the husband.

Not one.

Harry goes to Facebook, searches "Max McKenna Denver."

He posts once or twice a month. Max with a restored Ford Mustang. Max standing atop Quandary Peak. Max in a Denver Broncos jersey. Max grilling hamburgers.

And Max with the same boy. The boy's name is Wyatt. They spent the day at an amusement park the previous August. They survived a ride on a new roller coaster. The postride shot shows them with goofy looks, tongues out in mock fear. Along with the Wyatt pics are shots of Max with a young woman, Amy Beekler. Amy's Facebook page posts her status as "in a relationship." Her profile picture includes Max McKenna. Her mouth is open and her eyes are wide and Max plants a kiss on her cheek while she stares at the camera.

Flynn Martin is . . . *divorced.*

Scrolling through Flynn's Facebook photos, Harry spots Wyatt at school, standing out front with a fat gold ribbon for his entry in the science fair. The next shot shows his display board, all about the plight of the polar bears. Not even the gold ribbon seems capable of cheering Wyatt up. He looks thoughtful and serious. In the background stands Wyatt's school.

Teller Elementary.

The name of the kid's school doesn't necessarily narrow it down. What if Wyatt opted into Teller from another part of the city? If Teller is his neighborhood school, that could help, unless this is his dad's neighborhood school and not Flynn's.

But the area doesn't seem like cop country. In fact, Congress Park and some city blocks between Congress Park and Cheesman Park, liberal neighborhoods to the core, seem about right for a television reporter.

But where?

Harry's state job allows access to a powerful online database to confirm applicant claims about previous employers. The state could not and should not rely on the creative fiction and overblown self-promotion of LinkedIn or any bullshit résumé compiled by applicants. But each time he logs in and queries the database, the state is charged. He is supposed to get approval.

The query might raise an eyebrow from his boss. And then?

No.

Patience.

Care.

Discipline.

Harry goes back to the photos. First, Facebook. Then Instagram. Five minutes here, five minutes there.

It doesn't take long.

From last April, Flynn sits on her front steps. The steps lead to a wide, beautiful porch on the front of a classic Denver Square.

In the shot, Flynn Martin is one of three on the porch. Wyatt, with a warm smile, sits in a tight hug under Flynn's left arm. And she tagged them both, so when Harry hovers over the shot, the unknown man is announced.

Michael Martin.

The caption reads: "My boys."

Her *father*.

Then who is behind the camera?

Michael looks reserved, indifferent. Flynn's right arm flops over her father's left shoulder. She beams like a cheerleader.

Straight back under the overhanging porch, in simple block numbers, black against white paint, are four numbers: 1339.

The house looks like perfect Congress Park material. There are hundreds with the same look and feel. Maybe thousands. The neighborhood covers everything from Josephine Street clear east to Colorado Boulevard, about twenty blocks east to west and about as many running north to south.

But 1339 takes care of the north-south question.

Harry clicks on Google Maps and switches over to Street View. All he requires is a match.

Harry picks Josephine Street and starts working his way east.

Five minutes here, five minutes there.

CHAPTER 21

At home, Flynn checks the windows on the lower floor.

Again.

The kitchen side window facing the narrow gap between houses is painted shut. It's five feet above the side walkway leading to the gate to her backyard. The gate is waist high and easily hurdled. What good would a padlock do? Should she get a taller gate? Something opaque?

The back windows on a newish sunroom addition are snug in their twenty-first-century hardware. The bond feels immutable. The latches on the original windows on the south side of the house, off the dining room, aren't so reassuring. Two front windows, one on each side of the front door, are accessible from her house-wide porch. Coming in this way would require some degree of boldness on the part of any would-be intruder. PDQ would have to navigate a windowsill full of paraphernalia. Knickknacks and vases that would create a ruckus.

She pictures him *ordinary*. Cheeks slick from oily skin. Clean shaven. Reddish-blond eyebrows to go with light freckles. Heavy jaw. Deep-set, beady eyes. She pictures him with no affect. Never smiling. Always looking around. The kind of guy who sits on the bus and clutches his briefcase to his chest with both arms, as if he holds a bomb.

The safety inspection finds a half dozen spots needing attention for spiderwebs and smudge marks. She sets about the issues with a broom, a spray bottle filled with an organic orangey spritzing cleanser selected by Wyatt for its least-harmful ingredients, and a rag. Having found some satisfaction from the quick wave of spot cleaning, she decides to attack the living room and the sitting room, now a salon de television, with a bit more of an organized assault.

Flynn checks her phone for messages, calls Max.

"Anything?"

"Anything what?"

"About the music."

"Those guys are busier than a one-arm taxi driver with a case of the crabs."

"And?"

"There's a guy I know on the team who might help. I'm waiting."

"Bug him," says Flynn. "Whatever it takes."

"You said not to raise suspicions."

"Right. So what are you two doing tonight?"

"Three," says Max. "We're taking Wyatt out for pizza, and then Amy's going to help him with his math homework."

"Sounds exciting."

"It's not meant to be," says Max. "Amy has brought Wyatt a long way with math, and he's starting to enjoy it. I think."

Flynn flips on MSNBC for background.

The foggy fuzzy fucked-up job situation, coupled with no Wyatt, multiplied by her insecurity about her home security, makes her feel alone.

And then she sprouts an idea that could be her temporary ticket out of her big rambling house and its questionable security.

At least for an hour.

Or two.

CHAPTER 22

How many times has Flynn covered weird stuff in RiNo? The area was once underilluminated, full of shadows on the brightest summer day. Murders of the homeless, train derailments, chemical leaks.

The South Platte River is the waterway that gives River North its geographical identifier. The only things flowing now, in this brewpub artsy millennial expensive hipster haven, are young people and their money. Sex, of course, goes right along with the hip factor and the money factor, but the hungry side of getting laid is subsumed behind inscrutable, uber-serious beards and the women attracted to them. Besides, now, with Tinder and Match, it's easy to take care of the getting-laid part. At least, from what she's heard. The idea of posting a profile on Tinder or Match or Bumble or One-Night-Stand-dot-com or One-Night-Stand-dot-*come* scares the crap out of Flynn.

Now River North is the scene of an invasion of actual people who call it home. They eat kale and roasted brussels sprouts. They bike and paddleboard and toast each other with hoppy IPAs. They take everything seriously, from the artsy factor of their Instagram shots to baking bread and their weekend nonprofit volunteerism. They dig murals and brag about how many jobs they've held since college. They reject corporate America and the long-haul view of a career. They don't care about stepping stones or career ladders or glass ceilings. And only a few of them read the news on a regular basis, and that means glancing at a headline on their phones, or some twisted dark variation of the headline via *The Onion*.

Flynn wishes she could take an injection of millennial juice. She would shrug off years of yearning for anchor chair stability. Swallow one big chill pill, and she'd relax into the comfort of knowing she is privileged to use her brain for a living. Maybe she should sip fussy tequila or dial in a specific strain of cannabis to erase her old-school career desires.

Flynn finds a spot in the forlorn frozen dirt parking lot at a renovated old ironworks building and former warehouse. The RiNo mecca is home to an eclectic mix of brewers, butchers, bakers, and restaurants, including this trendy spot and its dynamite tacos.

Tamica waits. She pats the empty seat next to her. The only empty seat. The bar buzzes. The stools are full-blown seats, with backs. A gorgeous golden margarita sits in front of Tamica, its crusty rim of salt all chunky and jagged. When the bartender comes around, Flynn doesn't feel like shouting. She points at Tamica's drink, then puts the same hand on the bar and then raises it to eye level. The bartender, thank god, is good at charades.

A tight black turtleneck covers Tamica's swan neck. She wears military-green pants with a plethora of pockets. She looks sleek and ready. Tamica Porter never needs a wing girl, but Flynn would require a full makeover, and shed fifteen years, to play the role in credible fashion. Flynn's tired jeans and her red hoodie, studded with an overpromoted designer's logo, are decent guy repellant.

The first drink evaporates. Chips and guac. Another marg. Even the "large" drinks are like oversize thimbles.

They only have an hour. She is Tamica's predate, pregame.

"Okay," says Flynn. She might order a fourth thimble. "A what-if."

"Fire away."

"Let's say you got some information from an anonymous email."

It feels strange to put words around it all. She is giving her emailer credence.

"For instance, yeah," says Tamica. "Doesn't it happen all the time?"

"That's part of my scenario. The recipient of this information, ahem, is familiar with all the junk that floats around out there on the worldwide interwebs. Fake news, clickbait crap, and trollish idiots who sit home all day and write mean shit on comment blogs and hound celebrities on X."

"You're talking about the ocean, I do believe, in which we swim."

"Correct," says Flynn. "And let's say you're working on a major story, a story that's got the whole city's attention. And let's also say that it was a story that gripped the city fifteen years ago and is now back in the public's eye."

Tamica pops an eyebrow, gives Flynn a sideways look. "Continue? I think?"

"The information is so good that it surely would be something the police could use," says Flynn.

"As I like to tell my partners, keep going."

Flynn rolls her eyes.

"When he's pouring drinks." Tamica gives a naughty smile.

"He?" says Flynn.

"I'm open to bartenders of all persuasions," says Tamica. "How much detail do you want?"

"None."

"Okay."

"Is it a woman—tonight?"

"Does it matter?"

"Not in the least."

"Then?"

"Know I admire your poise and wish I had half your cool."

"Give me a break," says Tamica. "You're Flynn Martin. You know everyone in this town, and you can open doors with those two words. 'Flynn' and 'Martin.' Don't tell me about cool. You'll get your mojo back. Let's return to the hypothetical."

"Okay, even though the guy claims he sent the email by some untraceable encryption device from the dark side of the moon and that he isn't using his personal computer."

"Still," says Tamica.

"What?"

"It might be useful to the cops—the message you may have received."

"Correct."

"And you know for a fact there is no way the police have it?"

"Yes."

"Okay. And what does the message say?"

Flynn takes a long sip of limey salty sourness. She lets the liquid swirl in her mouth, searches for its sting.

She digs her phone out of her pocket. "There are three."

"Three?"

"I think I pissed him off. I wasn't too friendly at first."

Tamica reads, scrolling through the thread.

"Holy crap, that scares the bejeebers out of me. Show it to the cops. Or even your ex. He'll know. The last thing you want is to—"

Tamica catches herself.

"Yes?"

"Nothing."

"I know what you were going to say," says Flynn.

"No way you don't."

"Yes, I for sure know what you were going to say."

"Okay," says Tamica. "What?"

"You were going to say the last thing I want to do is to make another mistake."

Tamica's elevator eyebrows go to the top floor. "Maybe."

"Which implies I made a mistake the first time."

"I know," says Tamica. "And I didn't mean it."

"No difference," says Flynn. "The question is the email. You don't think it's a joke? A prankster?"

"If I was a short-haired Weimaraner, my hackles would brush the treetops."

"You serious?"

"Dead. And what the hell is up with the music stuff?"

"That's enough for you?"

"There's conviction in those words. Anger. Do you know what the music refers to?"

"I'm trying to check."

"Whoever wrote that shit is angry."

"Could be an attention-seeking, you know, troglodyte."

"So let him prove it's him and then decide. But you'll have to pull the cops in, right? At some point?"

"If I want to stay on the straight and narrow," says Flynn. "And not make another *mistake*."

"Sorry again," says Tamica.

"Don't be," says Flynn. "I got myself here. But why would the cops be so certain, hold a big news conference, put a jolt of fear in the city, if they weren't sure it was PDQ?"

"You gotta find an investigator who is having second thoughts."

"If it's real."

"And if it's not, your worries are over."

"Even if keeping it quiet might mean more people get hurt?"

"Get your ex's take? Let him decide? I mean, if there is one shred of evidence in the email, something in the metadata, something that would give the cops a lead, you'd be a hero for letting the cops do their work."

"But if it's him, he's damn good and knows what he's doing, given that he got away with it all fifteen years ago. So he's not going to be dumb enough to let his world crumble by sending a few easily tracked emails."

"So take your dance with this dude to the next level," says Tamica. "You know, so to speak. See what he's got. For now, you think he's a flake. Make him come out of his slimy black hole of cobwebs and bullshit and prove it, one way or the other."

"Now *I* got the willies."

"You'll know when," says Tamica. "Trust yourself."

"Easier said than done."

"And don't let Snelling and Goodman get under your skin."

"I wasn't even supposed to ask *you*. Anyone."

"You didn't," says Tamica. "This was all hypothetical."

Flynn parks her Malibu in the brick garage off the alley. The door to her porch issues its traditional greeting, a baritone squawk. She tosses her coat on the table in the sunroom, dumps her purse and phone on the kitchen counter. She finds a half-full bottle of white wine in the refrigerator and pours four fingers to fuel her buzz.

In her current state, mulling Tamica's advice and imagining a thousand different ways to argue with Goodman, or better yet Snelling, she might require more than half a bottle to reach the golden-glow state of oblivion she desires.

Flynn needs to avoid thinking about the fun Tamica is having, the carefree sex she'll soon be enjoying.

But there are worse things than falling asleep in the front television room downstairs, especially if she can slip from reality to sleep without thinking again about the emails from the crackpot.

CHAPTER 23

The ticks and clicks of a strange house.

The smell of boy. Youthful sweat. Sweet-stinky gym socks in the hamper, moist and youthful.

Harry likes the smell of boyishness, so much less staid than the closet of a grown woman.

A whiff of innocence.

◆ ◆ ◆

He likes waiting.

He likes listening.

He expected to have more time to sit and compose himself before he heard her rattle through the door downstairs.

Compose. There's a good one.

Gustav Holst in his head.

"Jupiter, the Bringer of Jollity," such an awkward title for such a classic piece. It is the same tune his mother played in the mental movie clips Harry has generated of when young Harry was getting whacked around. Harry later studied all the recordings and landed, without question, on Adrian Boult conducting the London Philharmonic.

That version. On EMI Records.

Perfection!

Harry's mother kept an old-school CD player on the kitchen table, and she played a tinny version from CBS Masterworks. His mother's version was dreck. His mother loved Mozart and Brahms, and whenever his father had the strap out and came after Harry, in the strobe-like images from the mental movie he's written and produced, she went to "Jupiter, the Bringer of Jollity."

And turned it up.

Way up.

So she didn't have to listen.

◆ ◆ ◆

A good thing about old houses, how the sound travels.

A bad thing about old houses, how the floorboards talk when you move.

He waits.

◆ ◆ ◆

Discipline.

Patience.

Flynn will—*what?*

Call someone?

Flee?

He had planned to be gone by the time she came home.

But this is good practice too. A bit of nostalgia.

◆ ◆ ◆

He has learned to wait in closets. They have always been his thing.

Harry pulled off his first good hide when he was ten. It taught him everything he needed to know about patience. About finding tranquility. If you're in the corner and if you don't jump when the door flies open, they won't see you.

If you pull a chair inside and sit with your legs and feet crossed and your head and torso buried in the clothes, you disappear.

He's always liked these moments as much as the actual act.

The prolonged tease.

He likes to listen to himself not breathe.

He likes to listen to himself *not make a sound.*

In his head, he loops Holst's pentatonic scales, the folksy happy melody when the horns and violas and cellos pass the tune to the clarinets, bassoons, and low brass.

During these moments, he can see both life and death. He can feel the thrill bubbling inside.

But now he has the power to whack it down.

If it gets out of control.

Right?

Jupiter.

"The Bringer of Jollity" . . .

It should have been "joviality," anyway.

By Jove . . .

CHAPTER 24

Flynn finds a station with reruns of *ER* and kicks off her shoes. Dr. Doug Ross makes for a friendly pal. Her wineglass makes its circuit, coffee table to lips. And back. And forth. She should take it easy. Go slow. Or not.

She can think about George Clooney and all his well-chiseled charisma and not think about Tamica and her beautiful Black boyfriend. She pictures him Black, but Flynn has no idea and scolds herself a bit for the assumption.

She will not think about her weird waiting-for-Snelling suspension.

She will not think about "Tip for Flynn."

She will not think about Tamica, Snelling, "Tip for Flynn," or Deborah Ernst. The Deborah Ernst is a particularly grim crater of misery, the number one must-avoid.

She wraps herself in a quilt like a semidrunk burrito. She reclines, feet on an antique ottoman.

The junior-size drinks with Tamica didn't put a dent in where she wants to go.

Not blotto.

Away.

CHAPTER 25

Harry needs a break.

    His butt is tired. If only he could stand and stretch.

    In his head, he flips tracks to the trilling piccolos from *Swan Lake*.

    He inhales the stuffy sour-boy BO from the hamper.

    The trilling piccolos, he is sure, remind nobody else of death.

    Harry feels a connection to Pyotr Tchaikovsky. Audiences can go ahead and think about the poor trapped swan. Harry feels Tchaikovsky's repression, his sensitivity. His frustration. In a way, Harry always feels like he spent part of his life like the year Tchaikovsky spent after his disastrous, two-month marriage.

    Harry doesn't have the luxury of being able to head off for "years of wandering."

    Instead, he needs to wander—even if in his head—every day.

    For release.

    What's the harm?

Tchaikovsky never blamed his wife for the busted coupling. It wasn't like him. Instead, Pyotr Tchaikovsky stewed. Uncertainty ripped at his soul.

    Harry knew the questions Tchaikovsky asked of himself.

Who was he? Why did he have these feelings? Was he put together the wrong way?

Tchaikovsky had his art. He could pour his rage into his art. He might have accidentally sipped cholera-tainted water, but Tchaikovsky took his own life. In Harry's mind, there is no controversy.

Please.

Harry feels the boiling rage in the music, the essence of the human struggle.

Harry hears her down there, rustling around. The tinny clatter of the silverware drawer. The sharp short hello of a cork being popped. The yammering television. He can't make out one word.

Harry sits.

And waits.

And inhales the scent of boy.

And rank socks.

She'll come up soon.

And then?

And then?

What if she freaks?

Given the gift he's prepared for her, freaking out is guaranteed.

If she runs from the house, he'll have time to slip down and out the back.

Tonight is all off script.

He didn't bring extra nylons. He didn't bring fentanyl. Or a syringe.

He feels every bit like he could do all those things again. But he doesn't want to. He really doesn't want to. Those urges are gone, aren't they? The all-the-way urges?

His heartbeat is fine. His keenness is fine. He is centered, calm, relaxed.

He has a sudden urge to see Mary. He pictures himself with her. He pictures opening her up, peeling her back, looking inside. He pictures himself pounding away and flipping her around. He pictures her enthusiasm mixed, maybe, with a bit of fear.

Sometimes they dig it.

See? He can have normal fantasies. His fantasies live in the G-rated section of pornography. Nothing extreme.

However, he feels the surge.

For now, he keeps the surge in check.

This moment is delicious.

Anticipation.

The piccolos trill.

CHAPTER 26

Flynn wakes. She thinks she heard something off. A shift. A strange noise. She listens.

Her hand grips the stem of the empty wineglass on her stomach. She listens harder.

Nothing.

What the hell was that?

Something...

Something...

She stands.

Slowly.

Listening.

The key is to stagger to bed without the brain cells working or worrying or waking the fuck up.

She leaves the bottle, bottle number two, for the morning cleanup. She snaps off the TV with the remote.

Flynn lurches on the stairs. She brushes her teeth like a good girl. She stares back at the tired face in the mirror. She drinks a glass of water to prove she understands the principles of hangover prevention. She knocks back one sleeping pill to get herself low, then bites another in half and pops it as insurance.

She opens the door to check on Wyatt's sleeping form. She is greeted by the sight of his empty bed, like a cold plank.

Kidnap races through her brain. Her whole system springs awake. And then, of course, she remembers Wyatt is with Max.

Pizza. Math homework. *Amy.*

It takes a moment for Flynn to stop wrestling with how to respond to the imagined crime. And why has she come home all selfish and not checked on him earlier, even if he wasn't there?

There is something strange about the cold room. Too neat? Something. The room belongs to no busy boy, especially Wyatt and his room of many projects, where the floor is usually a place for walking only if guided by a minefield sweeper.

Flynn spots the out-of-sorts thing. The closet door is pushed shut.

That never happens.

Had Wyatt shoveled his crap inside as a gesture to his mom while he was gone? She can't picture him doing it, but at least there's a decent assortment of junk on the floor.

Her brain percolates.

Just. Say. No.

She turns off the light in Wyatt's room and walks to her bedroom down the short hall. Flynn needs to flop into bed pronto or face the prospect of starting the George Clooney process all over again.

Flynn unbuttons her jeans, pulls them off. She slips out of her hoodie and pulls on her soft flannel sleep shirt, determined to not wake up any further.

Jesus, too much already—

Flynn gasps.

A naked girl doll lies on her back. American Girl.

The doll's head and brunette locks rest on Flynn's pillow.

Green ribbon holds the pigtails together. The doll stares at the ceiling. Stuck in the doll's ears are a pair of purple earbuds, the wires connecting down to an old-school iPod Nano, flat on the bed next to the doll's thigh.

The doll's legs are spread. The doll's arms are propped in the up position.

A white envelope rests in the slots of her tiny fingers.

Three words are printed on the outside of the envelope.

TIP FOR FLYNN

A shudder rips at Flynn's chest. She is instantly sober. Her mouth goes dry.

She steps quietly to the top of the stairs and listens. For what? Her arms prickle cold.

She opens Wyatt's door again to check on the nonkidnapping. She studies the lifeless bed again.

She listens. Her heart melts. She gets a strange feeling that her next move will be her last.

How is this possible?

Flynn steps back to her room.

She leans over to pluck the envelope from the doll's hands. Something orchestral leaks from the doll's earbuds. Faint. Tinny. Flynn stares at the screen of the iPod Nano, a silver oblong with a square screen at the top.

"Jupiter, the Bringer of Jollity."

The envelope . . .

Unsealed.

Slides a sheet of paper out.

Her hands tremble, not 100 percent on board with the plan.

> Miss Flynn,
>
> Nice house.
>
> This paper is recycled from Office Depot.
>
> This was printed on a Hewlett-Packard laser printer.
>
> I hope that narrows down your search.

The doll was purchased many years ago. It's been in my possession ever since. Its origin will be of no use.

You can tell the cops they won't find any DNA anywhere in the house.

But, in fact, you better not tell the cops a fucking thing.

If you go to the cops there will be hell to pay. Going to the cops won't do any good. They couldn't catch me then and there is no NEED to catch me now.

I got better on my own.

But I still know how to do what I need to do.

As should be obvious by now.

Why WON'T you go to the cops?

I know Wyatt's bedroom. I know it quite well, in fact.

I also know where he goes to school.

And I know where your father lives.

A better plan is for us to work together.

Robbie McGrath's murder was not the work of PDQ.

You asked for proof.

You got proof.

Stop fucking around and let's work together.

Wyatt? Her *father*?

A loud click from the radiator is answered by a soft tick from the ever-shifting old house.

And Flynn realizes the tick wasn't the first.

It was the second or third.

On the stairs.

One more.

Louder.

Heavier.

She stares at her open bedroom door, as helpless as the doll.

Are the ticks going down?

Or are the ticks coming up?

Tick . . .

Tears bubble on her eyelids. Flynn inhales, holds it.

Flynn scans the room for weapons and things to throw, and the downstairs back door whacks shut, followed a moment later by the squawk from the porch door, and she knows if she races to Wyatt's bedroom overlooking the backyard she could watch a shadow scurry across.

But she can't move.

She doesn't want to see.

CHAPTER 27

Harry finds a shadow by the back gate.

He soaks in the delicious tension.

He has screwed up.

The stocking over his face, the blue nitrile examination gloves, black sweatshirt, black jeans, black boat shoes—if it had come to a blow, she wouldn't have gotten much detail other than, say, height.

He hadn't been sure of the timing. He couldn't tell where she was, of course, and what she was doing. Luck had helped. He'd seen the light in Wyatt's room flip on the first time. The light had stayed on too long. And then the second time, shorter.

She isn't going to call the cops.

She won't call anyone, in fact, unless she also has a landline. Harry cups Flynn Martin's cell phone in his jacket pocket. Harry left the key, the one he found "hidden" under a wintering flowerpot on the back deck, in exchange for the phone.

A car comes down the alley. A garage door thrums on its motorized chain. A grating thumping rap song blasts from the interior of the car, a girl singer with a foul mouth. Harry slips off the stocking and the gloves. He balls them in a fat wad and jams them in his pants pocket.

He waits for the neighbor's car to park. The garage door's clanking return is perfect cover to unlatch the back gate. He flips the lever with his hand inside the pocket of his jacket.

Harry steps out into the alley. He adopts the carefree attitude of a man walking home from a date. Nothing to hide. Carefree. Maybe just-got-laid carefree. At the end of the block he pushes his baseball cap up a bit higher so it looks more boyish, less sinister. A man walks his Great Dane on the opposite side of the street past a small strip of shops. The dog is so big it could double as a pony. Why so late?

Snow floats like mist through a wedge of streetlight. Shoe prints will find more purchase in sandy spots, but they'll soon be covered up.

Even if he walks home in wet cement, it doesn't matter.

They are burner shoes, plucked from a stash. They will soon go in a random dumpster.

Harry is overthinking everything.

And it's a good, good feeling.

Two blocks from Flynn's house, heading west, Harry sits down for a moment on a bench at a bus stop. Without reaching in and touching the phone, he grabs the jacket pocket from the outside and expels the device with his thumbs. It tumbles out on the metal bench with a soft clang. With his hand pulled back under the sleeve of his jacket, he shoves it into a scruffy patch of snow-dusted scrub.

No cops are coming. No detectives. Flynn won't.

If it weren't so late, he would have walked all the way through the cool night to knock on Mary's door and show her the meaning of the word "arousal."

What a night.

Now, he hopes, he'll finally have some help.

CHAPTER 28

Flynn stares at the key.

She'd spent five minutes scrambling around for her phone, but then spotted the key with its powder blue plastic key tag on the kitchen counter. It's the key she hid outside, years ago.

And rarely uses.

And forgot about.

Her phone is gone.

She stopped paying for a landline years ago. She is an all-cell-phone girl.

Flynn kills the lights in the kitchen. She steps through the blackness to the back door and snaps the dead bolt shut from the inside.

She stares across the backyard. A slash of yellow light from the alley catches a first bit of falling snow.

Nothing moves.

Flynn cranks the blinds tight. She goes to the French doors that lead from her dining room to the back deck and pulls the curtain across. She closes the blinds on the front windows, tries not to think she was drinking wine and watching George Clooney and falling asleep while PDQ sat upstairs in Wyatt's closet.

She's been attacked. Violated. Until she has the nerve to move the doll and has the guts to look where he hid in Wyatt's closet, the feeling will not change.

Maybe never.

Every minute, however, counts.

Even if she had a phone, who would she call?

She once downloaded a finder app to the phone in case she ever misplaced it—a feature online or in the cloud or something if she can steady her nerves long enough to log on and find it.

In fact . . .

What if he was walking with it? Driving with it? Right now?

What if he doesn't realize he should power it down, and what if he carries it all the way . . .

Home?

Flynn grabs her laptop from the dining room table. She settles into the darkest corner of her living room. She plunks herself down on the cold wood floor.

Flynn feels the wet wreck of tears and smudged makeup on her cheeks. She can't stop thinking about the doll.

The whole staged *scene*.

She has never used the finding-app feature. But she knows there is an instructional video on YouTube for everything except how to build a working relationship with an allegedly reformed serial killer who wants your help.

She types in "find your phone" and listens to the droll narrator demonstrate how to log in to your iCloud account and click the icon. She opens her password spreadsheet, tries to remember the last time she refreshed it, and logs in at iCloud. A moment later she is staring at the "find your phone" icon, a green glass eye. Another sad reminder she is always being watched. She clicks it.

A pulsing red dot appears on a map. She clicks on the map, zooms in.

The dot blinks on Twelfth Avenue, two blocks away on the other side of Josephine Street. The dot doesn't move.

She pictures the spot in her mind.

A bus stop.

Is he out there *now*—waiting for a bus?

Are buses running this late? Not being a bus-riding type, over Wyatt's protestations, she has no clue.

Flynn opens a new browser window and types in "Denver RTD bus hours." She clicks on the local bus route option and then Route 10: East Twelfth Avenue. She's spent enough time at lights and stop signs behind the 10.

The last bus stops at York Street at 12:20 a.m.

Her computer says 12:29 a.m.

The dot doesn't move.

Flynn drives past the spot no faster than a slow jogger, her heart letting her know she has precisely no idea what she'll do if she spots a figure waiting on the bench.

The bench is empty.

She circles the block, comes at it again. She parks, leaves her car running, and walks across the lifeless street.

She grips her flashlight like a club.

The beam from Flynn's flashlight sweeps the dead metal bench, gathering snow. She shudders. He was right *here*. Maybe he caught the last bus west or maybe he is walking and if she gets in her car and drives maybe she'll find the cocky asswipe motherfucker shuffling along the sidewalk pretending to be nobody and she can yank him into her car, beat the shit out of him, extract a confession, and drag him to the cops and explain in the morning news conference how she knew it was him.

And how eager she is to get back to work.

Flynn shoves aside the fantasies, the product of the toxic elixir of adrenaline and utter fatigue. She walks a tight circle around the bench. Her flashlight beam glints off a red plastic rectangle.

Fucking technology.

Jesus.

Now what?

CHAPTER 29
WEDNESDAY

Harry slips off his shoes. He places them in a medium-size paper sack. He pinches the top closed and rolls the paper down into a scrunched-up handle. He leaves the sack by the door to his apartment. He'll find a dumpster on his way to work.

It's 1:24 a.m.

He needs Flynn's work on the impostor PDQ to get rolling. Proving himself to Flynn Martin required a risk. Maybe too big a risk. He'd miscalculated. She came home so early! He'd felt the long-ago thrill of breaking in and hiding, but he'd nearly wrecked it all.

The walk home across Cheesman Park and across Capitol Hill took forty minutes. During the last few blocks, his footprints landed in a smooth film of white snow sifted from a dead-calm sky, like powdered sugar sprinkled from a dusting wand.

The tracks couldn't be avoided, but it doesn't matter.

Harry lives in a top-floor apartment in an old building two blocks south and one block east of the Governor's Mansion, the state-maintained official residence with its two-story Ionic columns and gabled dormers. He likes knowing the state is right *there*. Of course he works for the state, draws a paycheck from the state, and does his best to help the state. He has protected it, in fact, from many miserable fakey-fake liars.

He needs stable employment. The longer he keeps working and doing good things, the better his claim he is fixed and reformed. He doesn't require rehabilitation. He hasn't hurt a soul in fifteen years.

Having the Governor's Mansion up the hill on the corner reminds him there are real people who are "the state" and that real people tried to find PDQ way back when. A whole big task force had been assembled, and now those people, or new people in those old positions, are gathering.

Again.

They are digging for evidence. Even if reassembled because of a phony crime scene, the regathered war room of investigators will churn through old evidence, whatever it is they thought they had back then, and look at it with fancy new gear and fresh eyes.

Does it matter?

Hell yes.

Flynn Martin needs to get busy and focus hard.

Doesn't she see now that he can help her?

Doesn't she know by now that he is, in fact, *harmless*?

Harry empties his pockets of the gloves and stocking. He stuffs them in a lunch-size paper sack. He shoves the first bag into a bag from the grocery store, yanks the plastic handles into a hard knot, and puts the whole wad into the trash under the kitchen sink. He reminds himself to take out the trash and toss the burner shoes too.

But it doesn't matter.

Nobody is looking for him.

Flynn won't call the cops.

Harry pours himself an E&J XO, sipping purposes only. He doesn't drink, not like that anyway. He needs a shower and a few more minutes to think.

Mark Stevens

◆ ◆ ◆

He likes a sharp apartment, showroom ready. Being neat makes him feel well off. He has upgraded his entire living room set to a chocolate brown leather model from Room & Board. Matching armchair too. The set shows refinement. Each piece cost a month's salary. He owns a high-end stereo from ListenUp, one of the best systems off the shelf. No installers came to his place, thank you very much. The television is unpretentious in size but as sharp as they come. The sound connects through his stereo gear with one click of the remote. Living room, kitchen, bedroom, bathroom. What else does he need? He is a civilized bachelor living down the street from the Governor's Mansion.

And he has good taste.

The counter from the galley kitchen extends in front of his window to the west. He could sit there, five floors above the street, and watch the comings and goings while he listens to, say, Mahler's Adagietto or Mozart's *Eine kleine Nachtmusik*.

Tonight he is fatigued. But routine helps. Harry decides on one spin of Mahler and maybe Mozart to calm his busy head. He sips brandy from a tumbler. He peers down from the darkness of his perch on the top floor. He watches the snow drift down through the streetlights below, flakes materializing out of the blackness. Parallel black snakes wriggle behind cars as they cut a path in the snowy streets. An underprepared pedestrian in a short skirt and bare legs scurries across Seventh Avenue, coming from a fancy new restaurant on the corner. The woman struggles to clear her windshield without a brush. An ambulance races north on Logan Street, flashing blues and reds like a child's whirligig sparkler. No siren.

Both the Mahler and Mozart are clichés, given their popularity. Playing them feels like a drug in his veins, something mystical and reassuring. Soothing. Mahler's and Mozart's melodies will always be there, long after Harry is gone. He hopes Flynn understands the importance of Holst's "Jupiter, the Bringer of Jollity," playing on repeat on the iPod Nano.

Both Mahler and Mozart are immortal, and, of course, so is Holst. How many ballets have been composed to Mahler's Adagietto? Twenty? More? And Mozart can thank movies, an idea 150 years in the future when he died, for sticking *Eine kleine Nachtmusik* in millions and millions of memory banks, as familiar as a jingle from a TV commercial. The "Little Serenade" wasn't even published until after Mozart's death. What would Mozart know about immortality, about the nature of his exquisite contributions?

Harry wants immortality. It is within reach. He studies the mistakes of others, like BTK in Wichita, and the successes, too, like the Highway of Tears. He is no Zodiac Killer (five known kills, twenty-plus presumed). He is more like the Alphabet Killer (three). Small potatoes.

There is a drink called the Boston Strangler (vodka, gin, tequila, rum, triple sec) and a joint in New York City called Jack the Ribber. He wants proof of his status along those lines. When the fear is gone, the mythmaking will begin. BTK made so many mistakes. The big one was coming back after all those years. BTK liked taunting the cops as much as he liked the killing. The dicey dance with law enforcement, enjoyable as it must have been, did him in.

Harry walked away.

He got better.

I make no mistakes.

Immortality is in his grasp.

Harry feels a powerful urge to push the agenda with Mary.

How does he know she isn't lying in bed right this minute after a hearty romp with a relative stranger?

He might call her or email her in the morning and see what's what.

◆ ◆ ◆

Harry sloshes the last gulp of brandy like mouthwash. He loves the nutty tingle on his gums. He reminds himself: Harry does not drink. Not like *that*, at least.

He turns off the stereo, checks the door lock, and gets out his laptop. He logs in to Proton Mail.

Come on now. Time is wasting. Are you ready?

In the subject line he puts "Tip for Flynn."

CHAPTER 30

Flynn lies in the dark. Her mind sprints from the propped-up doll to Wyatt's closet to the sight of her phone in the shadow of the bench. And back. And around.

How did she get here?

How, *exactly*?

She curls in a tight ball on the TV room couch under a blanket so heavy it weighs on her like chain mail. No armor can protect her head and its busy ways.

She has no idea where she stands in terms of sleeping pill intake, so she opts for nothing more. No alcohol either.

PDQ could have *easily* killed her.

Which means her emailer was him.

Or maybe *this* was the ultimate test for a killer like PDQ. Wait fifteen years, pull off another one, then figure out a way to prove it isn't your work.

The ultimate self-challenge for a serial killer. The ultimate *fuck you* to the cops.

Flynn can't imagine the work required to stage the doll and the whole scene.

How he'd found her address in the first place, got lucky with the not-so-hidden key in the second place. And then, clearly, he watched. And waited.

The margarita with Tamica was impromptu.

She'd come home early.
What if she had come home *earlier*? Or even *earlier* than that?
He was watching the house.
He was watching her.
Doll.
Closet.
She had pondered opening the closet door . . .
Phone.
Around and around.
Wyatt . . .
Her father . . .
How?
How did he learn so much so fast?
And how is she going to protect them? Keep Wyatt and her father clear?
By figuring this out, that's how.
But how?
Red digits on her cable box scream the passing of each mean minute.
It's 2:41 a.m.

CHAPTER 31

In the morning after coffee, Flynn heads upstairs. She takes pictures with her phone. Her hands shake. The doll's face. A wide view of the room from each side of the bed. One from the door. The envelope. The note.

She's got a burning desire to rearrange the furniture. Or swap rooms with Wyatt.

Or move.

She stuffs the envelope and the note in her back pocket. She yanks up the corners of her bedspread. She smothers the doll in a ball of bedding. Flynn feared all night the doll was programmed to blurt out something accusatory about the state of Flynn's so-called career, but the doll said nothing.

No booby trap bomb either.

Flynn carries the plump bundle to the basement laundry room. Her burden is so large and unwieldy she can't see her feet. She descends like a two-year-old. The last thing she needs to do is fall on her face and break an arm. Or her neck. She clears a space on a shelf near the washing machine, compacts the wad there. Wyatt will notice she is missing her favorite bedspread. She'll have to come up with something.

Back upstairs in Wyatt's room, Flynn opens Wyatt's closet door. She is as casual and matter of fact as any housecleaning mom. The motion is the same as a thousand times before. Right?

Wrong. Her pounding heart won't go along with the attempted ruse.

The chair is tucked into a back corner of the closet. Flynn grabs it with the same unsteady hand she might use to pick up a loaded mousetrap. She returns it to its rightful spot, glad she remembered this detail. Had she failed to look, Wyatt would have been curious. He would have brooded over a hundred different theories. It would have bugged him for days.

Flynn runs a thorough inspection of her house.

She pulls her things together. She checks her email. She knows one will be there.

She reads the latest message, sent at 1:52 a.m.

She writes back:

> If I'm in your shoes, I'm thinking "who wanted Robbie McGrath dead?" Start there, yes? If you have anything specific, let me know. I'm ready. And what the hell is the music all about? Holst? Jupiter? I would love to know.

Casual, friendly.

Flynn does not mention he scared the living crap out of her or that she found her phone.

◆ ◆ ◆

First, a phone call.

She gets Dwight Hatcher's voicemail, but he calls back close to noon.

"Is this official business?"

Dwight Hatcher always skips the pleasantries.

"Why wouldn't it be?"

"Heard you were, I don't know, taking a break."

"Your sources need to be reevaluated," says Flynn. "The rumor mill's reliability, you know, is pretty low."

"What's this about?"

"The only story that matters."

"On these questions, I'm working with Chris Casey from your station on anything to do with PDQ," says Hatcher. "You two talk?"

"Different angle," says Flynn.

"Same answer," says Hatcher.

"You haven't heard my question."

"Don't need to. The answer goes something like this: 'The investigation is ongoing.'"

"I want to talk with the lead investigator," says Flynn.

"See my comment from three point five seconds ago."

"I need five minutes on the phone with your lead guy."

"He's busy," says Hatcher. "All media coordination goes through me. And you're on the clock? For real? So you're calling me in an official capacity?"

"Yes."

"You wouldn't want to misrepresent yourself, would you?" says Hatcher. "I mean, I'm just trying to help."

"I appreciate that," says Flynn.

"Given, you know, what happened."

"I'm not on air, but I can ask questions."

"Why don't you and your cohort Casey coordinate so I'm not getting pounded from all corners. Okay? I got national. Calls from the BBC. Even Australia. Can your station get its ducks in a row?"

"I'm protecting a source," says Flynn. "You know how this goes."

Silence is Hatcher thinking. He's always been even keeled. And, when time allows, helpful.

"What questions do you have for the lead investigator?"

"Many, but I'd prefer not to pass them through channels."

"What if 'channels' are your only choice?"

Flynn anticipated being left on the far side of the moat, drawbridge in the up position.

"I need to know if the scene at Robbie's murder included music," says Flynn. "Classical."

"Really?" he says. "Music? Like PDQ leaves the stereo on or something, tuned to a certain station?"

"Something," says Flynn.

No need to be specific.

"Anything else?"

"I'd like to talk with him. Or her. In fact, I'd like the name of the lead investigator and the size of the task force being assembled. Who has the lead? City, state? Feds?"

"The task force is pulling on its collective pants," says Hatcher. "Getting organized."

"As soon as possible," says Flynn.

"Chris Casey asked about the interagency cooperation," says Hatcher.

"Good," says Flynn. "I need it too."

◆ ◆ ◆

"You're in one of your states," says her father.

"What does that mean?" says Flynn.

"You're being circumspect."

Her father sets a pace north of a regular walk and south of outright jogging. He wears a simple gray puffer jacket, blue jeans, and well-worn brown running shoes. His eyes hide behind sleek dark sunglasses under a Colorado Rockies baseball cap.

Michael Martin typically completes two circuits of Cheesman Park. Nearly three miles. He is known to put the pedal down on the second loop. Flynn wants to keep up but doesn't think she can make it. Her oomph has gone pffft.

"I need to run something by you."

She realized during the morning's evidence destruction that she could ask her father for advice without revealing every creepy, freaked-out way she has come across the information.

"A tip a day," says her father. "Better than an apple. But you can't do anything with it because you're not working in an official capacity?"

"Nobody said I can't ask questions," says Flynn. Their path is covered in a quick shot of overnight snow, slick underfoot. Traction is iffy. "But I can't do it under the station's banner."

"Well, you're still Flynn Martin everywhere you go. You can't shrug off your public identity."

"I'm not that big a deal," says Flynn. "Believe me. And the average age of our viewers is people who voted for Kennedy or Nixon."

Flynn takes a moment. Yoga has taught her that agony, like the growing fire in her lungs, is one sensation in the whole fabric of life. She must not obsess over it or let it take over her whole being. She needs to shrug off the feeling of pure violation she's carried around all night and morning. She feels icky and despoiled and yet she hasn't been touched. Flynn needs to lay out the tip for her father without the information coming across as emotionally charged, though it is.

"Anytime." Her father pumps his arms. He is a shadowboxing speed walker who doesn't give a lick about his public image.

"I know," says Flynn. "And it's not even that complicated."

"Who's it from?"

"That's irrelevant."

"That's your first mistake," says Michael. "The source is everything. Every source has an agenda. That means self-interest, means creating a whole narrative you get behind."

"Of course," says Flynn. "But it's irrelevant for us now. The source is bona fide. Trust me on that."

"Neutral?"

"No."

"Has a stake?"

"Like a thick T-bone."

"Very funny," says Michael. "You may have heard these same three words sometime in your distant past. Spit it out."

"Robbie McGrath's death was not the work of PDQ."

Michael stops.

"What?" The look on his face is pure puzzlement.

"You heard me."

"The cops are wrong?"

"They're being fooled."

"A copycat? After all these years? Why?"

"I don't know."

News flash absorbed, her father walks. "Your tip is from a dissenter in the cop shop? One of your ex's friends who sees the evidence in a different light?"

"I can't tell you the source," says Flynn. "But no."

"You can tell me the perch, if you will, the point of view." The strong timbre of her father's voice never falters. "Is the tip based on assumptions or close-in analysis of the evidence?"

"Yes, maybe, both, everything," says Flynn.

They round the southeast corner of the park and start up a gentle grade.

"So why are you telling me this?"

"Because I want your help." Flynn clears her throat. She stops. He stops. "I thought we could work together."

"What have you got to go on?"

"You mean, what have *we* got to go on?"

"Crime was never my bag. Give me draft legislation about tax increment financing or the school finance formula's negative factor and I'm there."

"This is PDQ, for crying out loud."

"What do you need from me?"

A pack of four female runners, fleshy flashes of thighs and shins in a blur, glide out of the trees at a speed worthy of Olympic trials, sprints or marathons, it doesn't matter. They are Flynn's age. They chat as easily as if they're sitting around on the front porch. They don't look over or acknowledge their cleared path as Flynn steps off the trail in one direction and her father takes the other. Four sets of shoes crunch a beat as one. Their collective motion leaves a goddamn wake, the breeze in Flynn's face.

"Ah, youth," says her father.

"Ah, habits," says Flynn. "Must get in your system. Did you spot an ounce of fat between them?"

"No. And I looked." Her father regains his pace. "You're suggesting you need help?"

"It would be good to work together." Stopping felt good, but Flynn catches back up to her father's stride. "Since I'm out and on the loose."

"I didn't think you'd need help."

How the hell does she know they aren't being watched right now? One of the trailing walkers? Or someone in a car? Even if she meets the request of Mr. Tip for Flynn to not run to the cops, she needs to get her father and Wyatt out of harm's way.

"Call it a project, something to do."

"Okay." They reach a cluster of trees. Under the dense canopy, the cool air carries a bite. "Where are you going to start? Wouldn't your sources inside the cop shop be able to tell you if there's an internal dispute about the analysis of the Robbie McGrath crime scene?"

"You mean Max?"

"Don't overlook the shortcuts," says Michael.

"He's in vice."

"But he can poke around. Be your mole."

"Much too loyal to the badge," says Flynn.

And not enough to me . . .

"So where are you going to start?"

"So if it's not PDQ," says Flynn, "then you have to begin as if it was any other murder."

"By Denver standards, Robbie McGrath had more enemies than Woodward and Bernstein combined. Those were print reporters, by the way. Pretty famous too."

"Oh do tell, my newspaper purist father. Tell me about the days of type pressed from hot lead and boys hawking papers in the street."

"The real nostalgia is when newspapers had readers," says Michael. "Them were the good old days. So what was Robbie working on?"

Her father veers off the path. He cuts a beeline to the empty cold pavilion with its view over the park's battered lawn and the cluster of downtown skyscrapers to the west.

"That's the big question right there," says Flynn. "Want to go down to the paper with me and nose around?"

CHAPTER 32
FRIDAY

Flynn never puts her finger on "it."

"It" isn't something she can touch. Or point to. "There it is—see?" Some PR shorthand would be handy, a few catchphrases to sum up the reason Max McKenna no longer keeps her bed warm and now lives with girlfriend Amy clear across town in Bear Valley.

Has she been shortsighted? Was she too quick to strap on a parachute and bail?

Flynn listens to Max's phone ring.

She pictures his house and spit-shined cars. Max likes his couch square on the rug, the television a notch or two above normal, his movies action-adventure. He has, it turned out, no real use for the news. He harbors a slow-burn hate for the media. Once they were married, it became so much easier for Flynn to realize Max McKenna's jabs about the state of journalism were the voice of all *copdom*.

Why didn't she stay? Why didn't she tough it out for Wyatt's sake?

◆ ◆ ◆

"Uh-oh," says Max.

"Finally," says Flynn.

"I was in the basement with Wyatt. Cell's no good down there."

"Model trains?"

"What does it matter?"

"I guess it doesn't."

Flynn stands at her father's kitchen table. She's only gone home to sleep and shower, deciding the living room sofa will provide sufficient comfort for the time being. Flynn watches the earnest exercisers on the Cheesman Park trails below. If one of them so much as glances at the condo tower or in her direction, she can run down and poke out his eyeballs.

"What's up?" says Max.

She is glad Max doesn't mind the intrusion. Again.

"Did you find out anything?"

"You cut right to the chase, don't you?"

"Well, I do have another question too. Did you?"

"On your music." He says the word like he's spitting at the same time.

"I'm assuming you got a good leak from inside the homicide squad—someone who believes he's not being heard in the war room."

"Maybe," says Flynn.

"You want me to press hard for this? Really?"

"Poke around. I need details. What kind of music, you know, and if it was the same song each time?"

"There is no innocent poking around," says Max. "It doesn't happen. And if they think there's a leak, you don't think they won't put me together with you? You want that—a bunch of cops darkening your door?"

"Maybe not. Isn't there another way? Can you ask to read the file?"

"On what freaking basis would I have a right to do that?"

"Okay," says Flynn. "I get it. Also, I need some extra help with Wyatt."

"You mean like homework? I thought he was doing good."

"Help like time," says Flynn. "Wondering if he could stay with you."

"For how long?"

"Few days. I'm not sure."

"Clear over here? How's he supposed to get to school way over by you on Monday? The city bus would take half the morning?"

"I need time on a story."

"I thought you were on the bench."

"I'm not sure if my status is even that official."

"In my humble opinion," says Max, "they are taking this whole thing way too far."

Her father wanders out from his bedroom, hair damp and a fresh plaid shirt splotched from his unsuccessful speed-towel action. Michael Martin holds an old-school reporter's notebook by its spiral binder. He waves it in the air. He grins. Raring to go.

"It is what it is," says Flynn.

"How's Wyatt going to get to school then? Today, for instance?"

"I'll pick him up. And drop him off."

"It's forty-five minutes each way."

But Wyatt would be staying at a home with an armed cop. Worth every stoplight. "I know," she says.

"I don't see how that buys you time."

"There might be some night stuff."

It's a giant fib.

"Sounds heavy. What are you *not* telling me?"

"It's a tip," says Flynn. "That's all."

"That narrows it down. Are the icebergs melting? Look on the bright side—fewer shipwrecks. Now there's a story."

"Amusing. This is a solid tip; I just can't say."

"Well, I happen to have the day off," says Max. "Didn't plan on spending it driving all over town. Twice. But—"

Flynn realizes she has been focused hard on a man who is standing on the running trail far below. He wears workday tan slacks, black sneakers, and a light-gray jacket. A scally cap sits on his head as if he is watching for his roadster to be driven around from the livery. The man talks on a cell phone. He keeps his elbow high in the air like a flag, but Flynn wonders if the phone isn't a prop for this bit of high school theater. From what Flynn can see, he has short reddish-brown hair and appears shorter than average height. Her high perch doesn't help with details. He is the only person out there who isn't moving. He turns and puts his back to the building, then makes a big show of ending his call and shoving the phone in his pocket.

He doesn't move.

He . . . *stands there.*

Flynn rises from the table and steps back from the window, cutting off the angle if he happens to look up. The man tips his head around like it's time for neck therapy.

"Let's go." Her father does the thumb-and-pinkie thing. Ear and mouth. "Yack yack yack."

"Wyatt may not love this." Max in her ear. She snaps herself back to the issue at hand. If she accuses every Average Joe White Guy of being PDQ, each day will last a month.

"I can explain it to Wyatt," says Flynn.

"So you're going to tell him more than you're telling me?" says Max. "Hardly seems fair."

"At least he appreciates what I do."

"Ouch," says Max.

"Sorry," says Flynn. "The truth pours out of me sometimes."

"I'm on your *side*," says Max. "Get your a-hole bosses on the line, and I'll rip them a new one."

"Like I said—sorry."

"Well, I'd love a full week with my boy around—of course."

"And Amy?"

Flouncy hair, blue eyes, a can of Miller Lite nearby that she'll sip for an hour. Demure. Amy is fascinated by cop stuff, admires the power.

No girlfriend of Max McKenna's gives impatient mocking mimes like the thumb-and-pinkie "you talk too much" look.

In fact, her father has his jacket on. And a scally cap she didn't know he owned. And tan slacks.

Jesus.

"We broke up," says Max. "Last night, in fact. If you ever want to get together for old times' sake, let me know."

CHAPTER 33

Sunshine. Brightness. A buoyant kind of giddiness. A bump in the old income from a lottery ticket. A perfect concerto. A fine old sipping brandy.

The morning clouds have dissipated. The quick smudge of snow drained into the gutters. Morning drivers need windshield wipers to clear street spritz splattered by the cars they follow.

By noon, the streets are dry.

At lunch, Harry walks. He needs to move. He rarely splurges on big dinners out but he has already emailed Mary in hopes she is free.

What is that thing, exactly, that makes you feel happy? Clear-through happy? Bone-happy happy? Where is it located? How does one simple idea in your head make all the other parts feel so good?

It's like he wants to sing, for fuck's sake.

Harry doesn't sing.

Harry stops at the market café on Broadway where he had eaten dinner with Mary. He eats a cheeseburger with barbecue sauce. The meal comes with an obscene mound of french fries. Harry imagines all the grease inside him if he devoured the tangled stack. No. He wants to feel this good forever. He wants to live like this now—*forever*. Harry eats three french fries. He savors the salt and the way the hot potato smacks around in his mouth. Three is his magic number.

Discipline.

He eats a fourth fry, calls it good.

The café is staffed by a tiny Black girl with a big smile. Patrons order at a counter, and she delivers food when it's ready and whisks dishes away when you are done. Harry pushes his plate to the table's edge and puts a ten-dollar bill next to it. She flashes her white-white teeth. Her eyes smile. Harry likes her hustle and sense of purpose.

Harry rides the skinny escalators at the library. The escalator isn't running from the third floor to the fourth. Harry disdains the feeling of walking on steps that are supposed to be moving, so he wanders past vast empty stacks of books to the staircase in the corner. He glances down each neat row. He thinks about the work invested in each book. He strolls the sciences—biology, physiology, biochemistry.

He walks down one empty row. Moving on durable carpet, he makes no sound. He glances at titles and imagines the writers, organizers and assemblers of information. How they must believe in their work. In the next to last row, a young boy sits cross-legged on the floor. His mouth puckers like an old trout's. A book sits in his lap. A full-page drawing of a perfect vagina peers back at the boy. The boy reminds Harry of himself at that age—so curious about things he didn't understand.

Harry was never scared of girls. He wasn't a cliché. He was fearless when it came to those kinds of issues. Man and woman had been copulating for millennia, he figured, so how could it be that big a deal? All you had to do was focus on the girl or the woman. You had to befriend the female human being first and not make it so obvious you wanted to see how she was put together.

Women open up, quite literally, when trust is there.

When you come across as experienced, in control.

It's death that fixates him. It's death that his scientist self likes to study.

As a kid, he developed detailed hypotheses about how animals would react. First, it was the barn mice out in Snyder. Then rabbits. Then a neighbor's cat. Harry had helped search for the dead cat. Hours of pretending. He was despondent when the cat's body was found. He put on a good show. He had watched the life go out of the cat's eyes. That moment. The cat was angry and confused. It was a farm cat. It must have known its status among all the creatures. How many mice had *it* killed? Hundreds. What was the difference?

Harry is fate coming around, that is all.

Harry waits his turn for a computer in the Community Technology Center on the fourth floor. The computer stations are doled out from a central desk like air traffic control. Harry has the urge to coax the ten-year-old boy up here and show him a few things on the internet. Show him how female parts work.

Flesh has a mind of its own.

Harry logs in remotely to his regular email. Mary's email reply shows enthusiasm.

> Sure! I'm open. Name place and time. Will meet you there. No snails, sill vous plait. All else good.

Harry replies: Make tracks to Pearl St. Diner. 7 p.m.

The joint serves glorified diner fare. It's noisy and semihip. He might suggest a place for an after-dinner drink.

And then . . .

Who knows?

Well, how long does it take?

Harry logs in to Proton. He reads Flynn's reply.
And writes.

> Exactly. Just know your work will bear fruit. You ask the right people the right questions and you will see I'm telling the truth. By the way, the password I gave you to reply here is only for five total replies. Then I will need and I will get another account. And keep on switching. Be judicious and thoughtful in your communication. I may be watching more closely than you think. It's a big city. People all around.

"Judicious."
He likes the word, the way it sounds.

> As you must realize by now, I will know if you are working with anyone, if you have shared what you have learned. That would be a terrible idea.
>
> Yes, Holst. Yes, Jupiter. My mother's favorite tune. Was Robbie McGrath wearing headphones when they found her?
>
> Was she?

CHAPTER 34

Flynn wonders if they have the right place. Perhaps it's a diorama from a future museum in the twenty-third century.

A *newsroom*. How quaint! The same as watching polymer clay men discover fire during the Pleistocene epoch in a history museum today.

Nobody lives here. Nobody works here. A neutron bomb has wiped out every human-journalist.

"Holy shit."

Her father says what she was thinking.

Michael hasn't been to the newsroom since the offices moved from downtown to a warehouse with cheaper rent on the northern edge of town. Her father exited the journalistic stage before the great meltdown of readership and advertising. He missed round after round of buyouts and layoffs.

Managing editor Ted Withers greets Michael with an overabundance of good cheer. Flynn wonders what there is to manage beyond the faint hum of the fluorescent lights.

Withers leads them to a small, windowless conference room. One woman waits at the hexagonal Formica table. Her face is weighed down by heavy-rimmed black glasses. Her hair is spiky and short. She might believe in self-barbering. Her handshake is rough and perfunctory. The charm factor is zilch.

Flynn has never laid eyes on the woman, but no introduction is necessary. For decades, a Judy Hayes byline was a daily fixture of *The*

Denver Post. She lorded over the cops and crime beat like no other. She owns a legendary Rolodex—never uploaded as data to any computer file she has no reason to trust—that is fat with statewide law enforcement contacts.

She always was a combative, competitive reporter who worked and acted as if there was another paper in town ready to duke it out on deadline. But there's no competition. Now that the town is down to one newspaper, all she's doing is shadowboxing ghosts.

As a crime reporter starting out, way back when, there was at least one day each week when Flynn Martin chased a Judy Hayes story. In the good old days when Denver was a robust journalistic town, the paper hit the streets around 3:00 a.m., and too often Flynn felt as if she was a half day behind come dawn.

Hayes likes her crime stories funky and gruesome. She revels in weird. Judy Hayes is no press conference reporter. She gathers all her quotes and information by phone. Her chalky pallor, and body built for carrying her brain around from one meeting to the next, is proof.

And here she sits, looking every bit as ready to talk as to smack someone in the teeth.

Hayes gives Michael the good-old-buddy routine, her voice as feminine and pleasant as present-day Bob Dylan.

Flynn doesn't misunderstand. She is here thanks to her father's reputation and credentials.

After the pleasantries, her father straps on sincerity like a trusted pastor giving a eulogy. He offers heartfelt condolences about Robbie McGrath. Her father's brief speech is so earnest Flynn finds herself tearing up. Judy Hayes, on the other hand, remains an unmovable force, facial features with all the emotion of cold marble.

"It's good to see you and all," says Withers. Gold wire rims. Dead eyes. Bald. Overdone aftershave. Fake smile. "But explain again what it is you want to do?"

Her father takes a moment. How to navigate this conundrum? Michael Martin is negotiating on the basis of a partial truth but needs to gain access to a reporter's raw notes without seeming too eager or in any way suggesting the newspaper might be sitting on the answer to Robbie McGrath's demise.

"And before you explain." Withers turns to Flynn. He gives her the full once-over. "On what basis are *you* here?"

"I'm not here in an official capacity," says Flynn. "If that's what you're getting at."

"You're on leave?" says Hayes.

Is there a sign on her back?

"I'm off air. That's all."

"But you might be put back on any day?" says Withers. "I mean, theoretically."

"I hope so." Wrong answer. "It's killing me. I mean, right now, of all times."

"Well," says Withers, "I guess it won't hurt to hear your pitch, but we are not letting you sift through Robbie's notes and files as outsiders."

Outsiders like *vermin*, given the tone.

"Outsiders?" Her father stabs his elbow on the table and holds up one finger. "First, I'm a recent retiree. And I believe I left here with an honorable discharge."

"And you're out there blogging and Substacking or whatever it is these days?"

"Writing about obscure corners of the state budget and weird unintended consequences of new laws," says Michael. "I'm not covering breaking news."

"Not a big distinguishing difference," says Withers.

"And two."

Michael's second finger joins the first.

V for *victory*.

"One of the most dogged reporters you'll ever meet, someone who happens to have been screwed over by her station and, because of her longtime work in this city, happens to have received a tip from a quality source."

"Nice speech," says Hayes. "What else would a father say? These notes belong to the paper."

"Without question," says Michael. "Thus, my proposal."

"Slim chance but I will listen. As a courtesy."

"Whatever we find—you get the first crack at anything we put together. Anything we write."

Withers's bushy eyebrows are stuck in an up position above his greasy wire rims. Hayes rubs her forehead.

"Extra labor—no charge," says Michael. "The paper will come off looking like heroes."

"Waste of time," says Hayes. "Cops are sure this is PDQ. You know, BTK came back. He couldn't bear to stay away. PDQ is in the same mode—determined to make a game of it. He needs attention. Craves it."

"I know." Flynn smiles, to see if her positive facial language might prove contagious. It doesn't.

"The cops on the first three cases?" says Hayes. "They held back key details of the murder scene for exactly this reason. So they would know if he ever resurfaced. I mean, they didn't go out and publish a Wikipedia page on PDQ's precise methodology."

"I get it," says Flynn. "And I'm hearing the same thing."

Hayes remains unmoved by the professional companionship. She turns to Withers. "We'd be setting all sorts of precedents."

Withers puts his glasses on the table. He rubs his raw red eyes. "We are understaffed," he says to Hayes. "And these two are hardly strangers to our line of work."

Hayes is ready. "Robbie McGrath will roll over in her grave. Well, it will be the first thing she does as soon as she gets there."

Her father knows.

Flynn knows.

As soon as the judge says things in your favor, zip it.

"Scary times call for tough choices," says Withers. "Robbie McGrath might not have been crazy about someone else digging through her notes, but you can bet your ass she's happy someone aboveground is asking questions about why she's not here."

◆ ◆ ◆

The sea of confusion on Robbie McGrath's desk sloshes to all four shores.

They make two stacks of notebooks, papers, mail, news releases, spreadsheets, newspaper clippings, and dog-eared magazines. Her father takes one pile, Flynn takes the other.

Her father moves his pile to an empty desk. He has about twenty choices. How can a newspaper office feel so inactive? Even the occasional ringing phone sounds like it belongs in an elite research library, soft and unobtrusive.

Her father separates his pile into like-minded subpiles.

Flynn picks up the first notebook and feels her heart sink. Robbie McGrath's handwriting is a cross between a five-year-old's first attempt at cursive and the green horizontal line on an EKG screen of a dead person. The scribbles look like worms on a page with the occasional bump of an *h* or sag of a *g* or *y*.

Flynn studies the note-taking striations for a pattern. It seems clear, at least, when Robbie is conducting an interview. Why does she bother? How does she decipher the scratches? Interviews last a few pages. One goes to five.

One with someone named ROJAS—or *about* ROJAS?—runs to six. An hour slips by.

Two.

◆ ◆ ◆

Ted Withers appears like a vision with a cardboard tray stuffed with goodies—two giant hot coffees and toasted bagels with plastic mini tubs of peanut butter.

"Question," says Flynn. "When was the last time Robbie published a story?"

"Months," he says. "Months and months."

"Any idea of a general ballpark?" says Michael.

"She didn't share much until it was time to write. And she was way, way overdue with this latest project."

"Did she say anything about issues with past projects—you know, someone who felt wronged?"

"That's a long list," says Withers. "And it's full of people with grudges."

"Lawsuits?" says Michael.

"Plenty filed," says Withers. "Most didn't make it past the first round. Our lawyers always go through everything before her stuff is printed. *Was* printed."

Flynn goes back to the ROJAS notes. She thinks she's made out the words "ranch," "cattle," "big family." Definitely the word "translator," as if Robbie McGrath had to remind herself to mention it.

Who is ROJAS? Of all the notebooks, Flynn picks this one as the freshest. It's like thumping a cantaloupe. Or so she's been told. A certain feel to it. The pages seem alive, the ink not so dull.

On the next page, "Damphouse No. 2." Damphouse isn't worthy of all-capital letters. And where is "Damphouse No. 1"?

Did Robbie McGrath use a tape recorder or, like many reporters, record on her phone? If she used her phone, it would have been with her when she was killed and the phone would have been gathered by police as evidence.

Maybe.

Flynn spots the spiky hair of Judy Hayes bobbing above a cubicle wall across the vast ocean of empty desks.

With the backing of Judge Withers's ruling puffing up her confidence, Flynn decides to face the lion. And her roar.

"Did Robbie use a tape recorder—do you know?"

Flynn dials up a tone like they are old friends.

"Fuck off," says Hayes.

"The notes—there's not enough here if she planned on using any kind of meaningful quotes," says Flynn.

"Beats me," says Hayes. "She worked alone. A rogue. The last of the independents. You know that, don't you?"

"Not really," says Flynn.

"She was special. No quotas, no nothing. No requirement to produce, if you know what I mean."

"Was she, you know, not liked?"

"It isn't a matter of not like. It was professional jealousy, not having to worry about deadlines on a regular basis. Robbie McGrath floated above it all."

"But did good work."

"The best," says Hayes. "What are you finding?"

Is Judy Hayes *engaging? Helping?*

"Nothing yet," says Flynn. "Does the name Rojas mean anything to you?"

Hayes thinks. "Why?"

"She's got notes. Recent ones."

"Robbie wanted to interview the detectives who worked the case. You remember Rojas."

Flynn says nothing.

"You should," says Hayes. "Or do you wipe the memory clean when you turn in each night?"

"Amusing," says Flynn.

And probably true.

"Two words for you," says Hayes. "Railroad tracks."

"Enrique Rojas."

The name rolls off Flynn's tongue without any conjuring. Or thinking.

Of course.

One of the saddest stories of the past few months. A young guy found dead in the back alleys of RiNo, where the art galleries and brewpubs and artisan cheese shops are nearly finished with their campaign of complete hegemony over the warehouse district. He'd been brutally murdered.

"He was nobody," says Flynn. "Why was Robbie McGrath working that one?"

"She tucked things away," says Hayes. "She could have been thinking ahead to the next project. Or she could have gotten a tip. Or maybe it was something that looked innocuous to you and me but had more to it."

◆ ◆ ◆

Back at Robbie's desk, Flynn puts aside the ROJAS notebook and the Damphouse No. 2 notebook. She slides open Robbie's desk drawer. Pens, Post-it Notes, paper clips, packets of soy sauce, packets of red pepper flakes, packets of Parmesan cheese, a half-eaten sleeve of RITZ crackers, surprisingly no mice, and, way back behind all the detritus, four microcassettes.

"They still make these things?" Flynn holds a plastic cartridge between her thumb and finger.

"I remember when those were all the rage," says her father. "But, yes, I think they do. And I've got an old machine at my place. Needs a battery, but it should work."

Flynn slips the cassettes into her handbag, no different from if she'd run out of soy sauce at home.

◆ ◆ ◆

With a password supplied by Withers, Flynn logs in to Robbie's computer.

"Excuse me, Miss Martin?"

The reporter is young, college fresh, long limbed. Dazzling eyes. She has short blond hair, bright-orange running shoes, and sleek blue workout attire. She might be popping out for a quick marathon over lunch.

"Everybody knows you're here," she says.

Who is *everybody*? Flynn doesn't ask it.

"So I gather."

"And nobody has sat in Robbie's chair since, well, since—"

"Of course."

Is Flynn supposed to work standing up? Out of respect?

"And Judy Hayes emailed the whole newsroom."

"Really?" says Flynn.

The woman spins Robbie's computer, pokes a few keys. A boldfaced message sits at the top of the screen:

> To All: You may have seen me with Flynn Martin, the sullied television reporter. Yes, that one. Apparently we're under orders to assist. Her presence here is problematic. She claims to have a lead or something. Please be alert to her movements and questions. She is here with her father who, of course, is a longtime friend of the newspaper. But they have no status here, no standing. And I don't believe it's appropriate that we are aiding and abetting their work in any way. Over and out.

"Red carpet," says Flynn. "I can feel the love."

"I know. And it's not right."

The woman introduces herself as Charlie "short for Charlotte" Laswell.

"You don't remember this," says Laswell, "but you came to speak to my class at CU Boulder about five years ago. You helped me, you know? With how to approach the whole business."

"Really?" says Flynn, a vague image in her head of doing something along those lines.

"Yes," says Laswell. "At the time, I was thinking television news but wound up here with an internship, and then they hired me on. But I don't see a big difference. It's all questions and answers until it comes time to tell the story."

Sensing the presence of a comrade, Flynn's father stands from the scene of his excavations and drifts over. Flynn introduces him. Charlie Laswell blushes. "Oh, I know *you*," she says. "I follow your blog. I mean, citizen journalism at its best. It's a pleasure to meet you in person."

"Likewise."

"I don't see a problem myself," says Laswell. "Information is information. The city is standing on its ear anyway. Anything you can do, I mean, it's gotta help."

"Did Robbie tell you anything?" says Flynn. "About what she was working on? Did you know her?"

"No," says Laswell. "She didn't socialize much. She didn't travel in the same circles as the rest of us. She had a whole different way of viewing stories and finding ways to get at them. I wanted to show you something."

Laswell looks around like she's being watched. "Screw them," she says. "Anyone helping to figure out what's going on with PDQ, I'm in."

Laswell leans over in front of Flynn. She fiddles with a few function buttons above the main keyboard.

"All reporters have two baskets," she says. "The first is the edited versions of what has run. As you can see, Robbie's is empty. Because she doesn't publish much. Or often. The second one is this right here, PERS."

This is under a long list of options on the main menu. Laswell clicks it. A list of items fills the screen. "You can sort alpha or sort by date," she says.

Flynn's eyes land on a one-word file title at the top of the screen: *Damphouse*.

"And how does one access stories from your own archives?"

"Give me a keyword—and a name or a date," says Laswell.

"Enrique Rojas," says Flynn. She knows *that* name, at least, has appeared in the paper.

"Easy." Laswell taps a few keys. "Last few months, yeah?"

"Please," says Flynn.

Headlines flash on the screen.

"Will copies work?" says Laswell.

Michael nods. Laswell disappears around a corner, returns a moment later with a small stack of printouts. She points across the vast void. "My desk is that way if you need me again," she says.

And leaves.

CHAPTER 35

The first clip is dated November 5:

> Denver police reported the discovery of a man found dead in northwest Denver early Friday morning. A man walking his dog near the railroad tracks found the body, believed to be that of a Hispanic man in his mid-30s. Homicide investigators are working on the case.

The second clip is dated November 10:

> Police identified the body of a man found early Friday morning in northwest Denver as that of 33-year-old Enrique Rojas. Rojas lived in the Sun Valley neighborhood of west Denver. Police have asked anyone with information about Enrique Rojas or who may have encountered Rojas before he was last seen on Nov. 3 to contact Denver police.

The third clip is from an article about Robbie McGrath, published as an extended obit two days after her death.

> Robbie McGrath mostly concentrated on investigations, which could last months. Or more. But occasionally,

> her reporter's eye was captured by something that some may have overlooked. Recently, she went out of her way to ask questions about the death of a man who lived in the shadows of the city. Nobody seemed to know Enrique Rojas and nobody seemed to know how he died, although it was in quite violent fashion. Robbie never finished her profile of Enrique Rojas.

Back on Robbie's computer, Flynn digs out the ROJAS notes and raw quotes from families and friends.

The quotes are various combinations of uncertainty. Rojas was a day laborer. He lived with a wife and two children in Sun Valley, a Denver Housing Authority complex of subsidized units south of the football stadium. Lots of people said nice things about Enrique Rojas. Lots of people thought it was a shame he had been killed. Lots of people had no idea why it happened.

It isn't much, but Flynn Martin feels as if she has a place to start.

Enrique Rojas.

And somebody Damphouse.

Flynn thanks Withers, says they might be back.

Flynn thanks Judy Hayes, says they might be back.

She thanks Charlie Laswell, asks her to call if she runs across anything. She gives Charlie her number and her father's too.

Back at her father's apartment, they huddle at the dining room table over his chipped and well-dinged microcassette recorder.

They are greeted with a sound like the inside of an irritated seashell.

They skip ahead, stop. Skip ahead, stop. "White noise" is too genteel a term for the screeches and squawks. Flynn speeds the tape along, listening for the telltale squeak of a voice, some change in pitch.

One side, two sides. New tape, both sides. Halfway through the third cassette, a spurt of squeals.

Flynn rewinds the tape.

"This intr bout lade."

Flynn rewinds it again, puts her head down, and cranks the volume. Muffled, but the words are discernible this time: *"This interview is about the old lady."*

By comparison, the next voice booms from a PA system.

"Why didn't you secure the scene that day?"

Robbie McGrath, back to life.

A long pause follows. A soft cough. Background hum. It's the same yawning gap from many of her own interviews, the subject deciding whether to go Mount Saint Helens or lazy river.

First voice: "This interview is over."

Robbie McGrath: "Last spring. You were the first officer on scene? Arrived solo?"

Damphouse—a cop?

Damphouse: "We're done."

McGrath: "A few questions." Her voice normal, steady, cool.

Damphouse: "This was a trap."

McGrath: "How long did it take you to find her body in the flower bed?"

Damphouse mumbles something.

Her father goes wide eyed.

McGrath: "Margaret Stack told the dispatcher she went out on the roof. And she told the dispatcher there were burglars in the house. But they were gone by the time you got there?"

Damphouse: "What are you getting at?"

McGrath: "There are about fifteen minutes, maybe twenty, between when you arrived and when you said you found the body."

Damphouse: "And?"

A car whooshes by. The interview is outside.

McGrath: "You already know items have been taken, you know the owner is dead."

Damphouse: "I called for backup. Yeah, I found her. But if you'll check the records, there was a high-speed chase that afternoon."

McGrath: "In southeast Denver."

Preparation. Impressive.

McGrath: "Your precinct sent two squad cars over to assist. Detectives had partial footprints in the tulips outside the living room. But they were overlaid by a size eleven boot that matched yours."

"Christ," says Damphouse, his voice rising. "You reporters fuck people every chance you get."

The tape reverts to its mean hiss.

Flynn clicks the recorder off.

"She had him," says her father. "At least, sounded like she had something pretty solid."

Flynn flips her laptop around. She navigates through the "McGrath's Best" collection, a recent archive on the front page of the newspaper's website. She scans down the list, but there is nothing about a police officer or a burglary.

Next, she does a byline search in the newspaper archives.

"Good thinking," says her father.

Nothing.

Flynn flips over to her station's website, which offers a mother lode archive that's free. And searchable. She searches "flower bed Denver death," already remembering something about tulips, but maybe Judy Hayes was right. Perhaps each day's story is relegated to the scrap heap to make room for the next.

The screen fills with a list of hits. The first is "Margaret Stack."

Seeing the name brings it all back. Last spring, Margaret Stack had crept out on her roof in Park Hill to hide from burglars. She called 911 and left the line open, scared out of her mind. She slipped and fell. She snapped her neck in the garden below. She was sixty-eight. The burglars cleaned out jewelry, cash, two laptops, a stash of oxycodone. The next day, Flynn's colleague Chris Casey had interviewed the inconsolable daughter, Barbara.

Did Robbie McGrath have a line on crooked cops? Cops who add a five-finger discount of their own when the situation permits? Dead homeowner, burglars gone. Anything the cop swipes can be blamed on the thieves.

Max had stories about dirty cops. As much as Max toed the line, he knew there were bad apples.

"Was Robbie McGrath planning something more?"

Flynn's father opens two bottles of chilled Fat Tire. They sit at his kitchen table. Flynn lets the day's details marinate in her bones. Light fades over Cheesman Park.

"Must have been a good gotcha," says her father.

"She had something," says Flynn. "How do we know if she had more?"

"We don't."

"You feel up to reconfronting a troubled cop?" she says.

"Not right this second."

"Didn't think so."

"You know what I say."

"Michael Martin 101, if I'm not mistaken."

"Start with the lesser-knowns."

"And work your way up," says Flynn. "And that means?"

"Figure out the Enrique Rojas stuff first."

"We don't know if they connect," says Flynn. "Do we?"

"Of course not."

"By the way, do you mind if I crash on your couch tonight?"

"But your place is only—"

Her father likes his alone time.

"I know." She doesn't know how long it will be until she sleeps in her room again. Paint the room? New bed? New layout? New house? New city? New planet? "But I'm kind of enjoying this father-daughter time. Aren't you?"

CHAPTER 36

Harry can't hear a goddamn thing. Mary could be talking behind a green sheet of glass. She seems to be enjoying the packed hubbub and mingling with the carefree crowd.

Harry bobs his head like a dashboard bobblehead puppy. He turns up the volume when it's his turn to talk. He sips his martini like a man alone on a raft in the roiling South Pacific, down to his last swallow of liquid. He is going to press matters with Mary tonight. But not as a slobby sloppy drunk. Of course, he doesn't drink. He sips. He wants to urge things along as a disciplined, civilized member of society.

Mary drinks white wine. She races to the bottom of her first glass. Maybe she senses where Harry is heading. For some women, at times, don't you have to brace yourself for sex? As a woman, it must be a bit of a gamble not knowing how forceful the guy is going to be. There are all sorts of possibilities, right? The first tangle is always a bit of a risk. How much throwing around are you willing to endure? Or will your new partner be *active* enough? *Enthusiastic* enough?

Mary orders a second wine. The restaurant doesn't rush the food. "Farm to table" means "You'll wait a long time while we pluck the chickens, okay?" Food prepared fresh *blah-buh-dee-blah*. They want you to order more booze.

Mary eats meat loaf with a side of newfangled macaroni and cheese. What is there to fangle up with macaroni and cheese? The dish reminds him of his mother. She made double batches of the box stuff with real butter all throughout his grade school days in Snyder. The stovetop was often dusted in the orange powder from the "cheese" packets. The leftovers were congealed junk. The whole experience was disgusting.

Harry works on a plain hamburger, no cheese or overpriced sides.

Being here and making these kinds of plans to move on Mary, Harry thinks, is what he is supposed to be doing. Hiding out or holing up will work if he is a cliché. He is not a cliché. He isn't on the run. He is an active member of society. And he's doing what normal men do. Pursue women. This part is like going to the gym or going to the symphony. Routines demonstrate your interests. You need to stay active if you are to stay sharp. It must be like playing the piano or being a true athlete. You can't take years off without paying the price.

And, besides, if he doesn't ask or suggest or nudge matters along, it isn't going to happen. He has a hard time imagining a platonic relationship at this stage of his life. He isn't asexual. The Plato bit is a myth. Plato never talked about asexual heterosexual love. It was Socrates who talked about the vulgar kind of love and the kind of love and lovemaking when you think of divinity.

Good try, Plato and Socrates. More public relations bullshit.

Justify, justify, justify.

Stories help.

Harry, in fact, is the opposite of a cliché. He is a prototype. He knows what he did, back then, was wrong. He knows right from wrong. But he has urges nobody else can explain. He has urges that make so little sense they cannot be uttered aloud. There are things you do not discuss.

Crazy people are crazy because they keep doing what they're doing. They have no ability to stop. They have no ability to analyze their situation and back away. Harry has done both.

He has analyzed.

He has backed away.

Three isn't a big number. He is no Ted Bundy. He wasn't even the guy behind the Redhead Murders—six or more.

Three? In the grand scheme of things, from random cancers to random drunk driving fatalities to random highway accidents, he is a minor deal. In the big sweep of earthquakes and tornadoes and war and time, he is small potatoes.

And he's fixed himself! He straightened up, figured it out. Now, he pays taxes and buys tickets to the symphony.

He works hard.

He isn't *that* guilty.

◆ ◆ ◆

Harry pays the bill. He waves off Mary's attempt to go Dutch. She is the one who had two drinks, she asserts, and the bigger meal. Harry is having none of it, but he worries she assumes the eighty-five dollars plus tip is transactional. A ticket.

Hipsters rule on Seventeenth Avenue. The restaurants are jammed and buzzing on Nineteenth, too, as Harry walks Mary home. He puts a hand on her back as a large group passes. She says nothing. She doesn't flinch either. Or act surprised.

"Come up for coffee?" she says. "Or a nightcap? I mean, did you even finish the martini?"

"Don't think so." There is a chance she wants some too. It isn't a logical "thing" you want. It is another one of those urges. "What have you got?"

"Cognac," she says. "And amari. Some grappa too. We can take a look."

"Sounds like a regular bar." Harry laughs. It doesn't sound genuine.

She hangs her coat in a front closet, passes him a hanger. He loves the sight of the closet door closing. The door does not imply *quick*.

Mary unsnaps the buckles on her brown suede ankle boots, balances like a calm stork on the opposite foot each time. In the golden light of the front hall, she looks trim and spry. A dark-purple turtleneck clings to her curves.

Boots off, she stands an inch lower. "House rules," she says. Harry prefers not to take off his shoes, at least not yet. Walking around in socks makes him feel juvenile. But the smile on her face says it all, and so does the spot on the carpet where a blue mat sits as a home for guest shoes, as if the town house is some sort of goddamn Japanese Shinto shrine.

Harry complies.

"Maybe we could find a movie," says Mary, leading the way down a hall in her tight gray slacks. "It's not too late. So many streaming options these days."

Bottles clank as Mary pulls a selection of booze down from a high cupboard. Harry catches a whiff of lavender. He admires the spiffy style of her home, magazines in a neat row on the sideboard, mail waiting in a simple wooden holder. The broad kitchen counter is clutter-free.

"I like this," she says. "Aperol. It's orangey. Maybe an Aperol and splash of soda? The soda cuts it a bit, you know—"

He desires an E&J XO but doesn't want to sound fussy.

"I'll try it," says Harry. His black socks slide on the clean kitchen floor as he leans against the counter by the stove. He stands straight to improve the quality of his perch. "A 'wee dram,' as the Brits might say."

"Here I'm looking like the lush. Not usually the case."

Usually?

"I don't know how you do it." She fetches ice from the refrigerator's dispenser, searches for a bottle of soda in a closet-like pantry next to the fridge, plucks an orange from a wire basket near the sink, slices wedges with a paring knife. "I mean, this day and age and all that. Don't you want to cut loose sometimes, now and then? I mean, I'm not saying get smashed or out of control, but anyway, you show so much restraint."

If there is one thing Harry dislikes, and he has a long list, it is talking about how drunk you are, how drunk you *once* were, how drunk you want to get. It is those kinds of people who climb behind the wheel of a car blowing a 0.15, not giving a shit about the lives of anyone else. Why can't Colorado go to 0.02 like Norway or Sweden and yank licenses on the spot for drunk driving?

Harry smiles. Smiling is supposed to improve blood pressure—your own and that of others around you.

"What have you seen on Netflix?"

"Not much, actually."

"Do you *only* listen to music?" she says.

"I do watch a bit of television." Not really, but he doesn't want to admit it.

"I've seen those headphones." Mary stirs the cocktail, all orange and bold, in a fat broad-bottom tumbler with a sticky-wet slice of fruit for garnish. The drink looks neon and extroverted in Mary's white-gray kitchen.

"And when did you see me that I was wearing headphones?"

"I saw you walking through the park one day. I was down on Broadway going in the opposite direction. Perhaps you were coming from the library. Those headphones look serious."

"The music *is* serious. The work that went into some of these compositions. I mean, two years for Beethoven's Ninth, as one example. It's not a pop song, you know. And those wireless earbud things? I don't care how much they try, they aren't the same. And they never will be."

"Not playful?"

"Not playful what?"

"Is the music ever playful?"

Mary smiles. Harry's blood pressure does not ease. In fact, something has tilted in her favor. She gives a head-bob "follow me" gesture and walks back behind the kitchen to a sitting area with a couch and television so large it reminds Harry of a drive-in theater.

Mary sits on a brown leather couch. She tucks her ankles under her. She cradles her orange orb in two hands like an offering. Harry sits next to her, not too close, and sips. The first taste is orange, the second is rhubarb. He fights the urge to wince.

"You picture the story the composer is trying to paint," says Harry. "You go a hundred different directions. You feel what the composer was feeling. That's why each conductor's approach makes it interesting. Walter Susskind. Adrian Boult, you know. Toscanini. Don't you like saying 'Toscanini'?"

"Shall we cut to the chase?" says Mary.

When did he lose the upper hand? Her place. Her drinks. No shoes. "As in?"

"We're not here to watch *movies*."

"Okay." A chill flashes across Harry's shoulders.

"In fact, we're not here to talk about our interests either. We share a common goal, Harry. We share the interest in getting laid." She takes a healthy swallow of the Aperol, keeps her eyes on his. He wonders if this is how hookups happen on the apps, all this frank talk once you're alone. "We can draw this out for another hour or two if you'd like, or we can get to it. We won't know if we're any good at it until we give it a go, and that might also depend on how you like it. Beneath all that Chopin and Mozart, I have a hunch there might be someone a bit more aggressive underneath."

Harry's mouth goes dry. "There's not two of me, if that's what you mean."

"Another side, then. A side you can only show at certain times, Harry."

"On the contrary. What you see is what you get. Very much so."

"And we're adults here, so it's not like we have to pretend we're virginal teenagers with no experience. I accept the fact that you may have been with dozens of other women. Same goes for me and men. And, maybe, women. You know, the old college lesbian experiment. Right? Well, I'll confess to that too. A few times. It didn't *move* me, okay? I've found over time that you have a higher percentage of getting what you want if you come right out and ask for it, in a nice way of course. Ever try the dating apps?"

Harry studies his drink. "No."

"It's refreshing," says Mary. "It's to the point. It cuts away the bullshit. It's about compatibility. Let me tell you, it's not boring, and the questionnaire makes mincemeat out of what used to be six or seven dates to get to know the other person. But we're right here in person, and we're going to skip the Netflix pretext and see what happens."

"Rough?"

The word escapes his mouth without any screening or forethought.

"Was that a question or a statement?" says Mary.

"A question."

"Do I like it rough?"

"I didn't mean to ask."

"That's the point. You *can* ask. In fact, you *should* ask. All the advice out there, the enlightened advice, is about knowing ahead of time what you're getting into. It's all about permissions and consent. Consent is critical. And 'rough' has different meanings to different people—"

Harry puts his drink on the coffee table. A circular labyrinth is inlaid on a surface beneath the broad expanse of glass. The perimeter of the table is a snake about to eat its own tail. Harry's head spins. He thinks about the long walk home.

"Not tonight." Harry stands. "That's not what I had—"

"Oh, Harry," she says. "Come on now. Let's talk it through."

"No, really."

She stays seated as he moves back down the hall to his shoes, his gait more slippery than he'd like. No goddamn traction. He should have brought the fentanyl and shown her a thing or two.

"I guess." Mary comes up behind him. "I'm sorry if I—"

Harry plunks himself down on the pint-size bench in the front hall. He yanks on his shoes. He goes to the door and fumbles with the lock. Mary is suddenly there, and she has to reach around him to undo it, some sort of twice-around backward weird-ass spin on the dead bolt and then the latch. *Jesus.* Maybe her town house doubles as some sort of dungeon.

He doesn't hear the door close behind him. He doesn't look back. In a block or two, he will stop to tie his shoes.

Cold air slaps his face. It feels as good as sunshine.

CHAPTER 37
SATURDAY

Everybody knows nobody.

At least, that's what they tell the outsider, the one who claims to be a reporter.

Shrug.

No sé.

Headshake.

No sé.

The Sun Valley neighborhood stretches south of the football stadium. Somewhere in the blur of the last few days, Flynn has paid enough attention to know that the beloved Broncos are playing a playoff game soon. Does football matter? Compared to everything else? In a thousand years, will the people look back on this age and view it like the people of today viewed the Middle Ages?

They did *what* with their time?

What is the difference between a monk's vow of poverty and chastity versus a Denver Broncos fan who maintains a good beer buzz all weekend to get ready for the Big Game?

Blind loyalty, both.

◆ ◆ ◆

Sun Valley's public housing structures are two-level affairs. Flynn has done more than a few stories in the neighborhood. She finds the design relaxing, the indoor and outdoor spaces generous and humane. The Sun Valley development is a stepping stone neighborhood, heavily Hispanic.

The idea of finding the trail to Enrique Rojas is intimidating, but Flynn is not alone. Tamica Porter, donating a weekend day to the cause, has headed to the north end of the neighborhood. Flynn works in the middle. Her father takes the south. They have a group text running to keep tabs on each other.

She approaches everyone who moves on foot. It's late morning. It's late enough, she hopes, to not be considered disrespectful. But she's an outsider. Through and through. A White outsider. And, once self-identified, a White reporter outsider. The old triple whammy. And for those who track such things, a disgraced White reporter outsider. When doors open, she offers a low-key, professional smile. She stands in her blue station jacket. It's the uniform she shouldn't be wearing. Flynn asks everyone if the name Enrique Rojas means anything—anything at all.

The man who died.

She hands over a photo of Enrique. The photo was taken from the paper, then enlarged and copied at an office supply store.

He had two children.

They found him by the railroad tracks.

Did you know him?

Does his name sound familiar?

A few take the photo, stare at it, hand it back. She isn't sure who speaks English. One woman, with two children clinging to her full-length skirt, says she recognizes the name. But she has no clue as to the whereabouts of Enrique's family. She doesn't know he died. Her English is solid. "The manager might know," she says. She points around to the back of her own building.

The manager is small and barrel round. He wears a bright baggy orange Broncos jersey with MANNING across the back. The shirt could double as a muumuu. He has creamy brown skin and a heavy dark brow. He wears white pants like a housepainter's with red flip-flops like he is heading for the beach. He steps outside, a wary look. Glum. He shoves his hands in his pockets as his sole defense against the morning chill. His name is Diego Luna.

"I have seen you on television."

"I am looking for somebody who knew Enrique Rojas," says Flynn. She hands him a photo.

"You could have come in here a long time ago and saved yourself the trouble. Everyone you asked has texted me or stopped here to tell me you were asking. We watch out for each other, you know?"

Luna sounds like a native-born American, no accent.

"And?"

"His family is long gone."

"How long?"

"However long since they found his body. He was the one earning the money, so they left."

"How soon after?"

"A week. If that."

"Where to?"

"We don't ask."

"Wife?" says Flynn.

"And one daughter, one son."

"How old were his children?"

"Grade school," says Luna. "Kids, you know?"

"Did he have friends? A neighbor that knew him? Or them?"

"Do you know what the turnover is like around here? We may as well have revolving doors. These people don't stay in one place for long. They wonder why their children don't do so well in school, and they pull them out for long trips to Mexico—special holidays, labor needs, family needs. Frustrating. Why do you care about Enrique and his family? You'd be the first."

"I'm wondering what happened. What led to Enrique's murder? If someone might know why he was beaten. And left to die."

"And the police?"

"They have no leads." It isn't a lie, but close. She assumes the police let the case move to the scrap heap too. Enrique's second-class status in the community means his death has drawn second-class attention.

"What do you think happened?"

"I don't know," says Flynn.

"And why does this matter now?"

"It's part of another story, a bigger one."

"So it's not Enrique who really matters?"

"I didn't say that."

Luna says nothing, waits. "That's all you can say?"

"I'm not even sure myself. But if I can find his wife or a friend, I might be able to figure out if I have something or not."

Luna points in the general direction of Lakewood Gulch. "They lived on Clay Way. The renters who took their place in 968 wouldn't know them, but there is a guy next door in 972 who has been around a long time. The kind of guy who keeps track of the news in our little pueblo."

Flynn texts Tamica and her father.

> Found apartment where family lived. Heading there now. Neighbor knew them.

She texts the address too.

Then, Join me.

She starts walking.

Flynn checks her email.

The subject on the freshest message is "Tip for Flynn."

> I hope you have a good game plan for the coming week. My patience, so you know, is in very short supply.

Replies:

>Okay, yes, on the music. The music is a big deal.

Waits. Stares. Waits.

>Not just "music." WHAT MUSIC?

>Jupiter and all that. Holst. Got that. I'm working it.

>You need to be specific.

>Okay.

>Very specific!

>Okay.

>Well, what about Robbie?

She can't be precise.

>Waiting confirmation.

>WAITING?? FOR WHAT??

◆ ◆ ◆

"And my sources suggest you are not supposed to be making this call," says Hatcher.

It isn't hard to imagine Chris Casey, innocently or maliciously, giving her up.

"I'm not on air," says Flynn. "That's all."

"Really?" says Hatcher, stretching out the word. "That contradicts my sources."

She ignores him.

"Find anything for me?"

"No," says Hatcher. "Tracking down a long list of questions from a variety of your cohorts. You are in the queue. Music, right? Classical music, right?"

"Yes," says Flynn.

"Got it," says Hatcher. "Miss Unofficial Flynn Martin will be treated the same as any other journalist working on this story."

"I owe you."

Tamica strolls up, long black jeans and green running shoes under her puffy blue parka. She says nothing, waits.

Her father appears, moving with the gait of a man two decades younger than his age. His bearing hasn't sagged. He wears black hiker pants, a gray down puffy jacket.

Flynn and her erstwhile posse have attracted a flock of children, wary and curious. The kids watch intently. A laugh. A pointed finger. Two of the boys toss a football.

At 972 Clay Way, a man with a stiff limp and a cane answers the door.

Flynn introduces herself. The man's face is broad and open, but his eyes carry weariness. He shakes hands with limp indifference. His skin is rough, his fingers are thick. He is at least sixty. His posture suggests decades of worry and weight. Behind him, the interior of his apartment looks cavernous and dark. It smells of salty bacon. Tamica and her father stand back off the front stoop behind her, a natural attempt to lower the intensity.

"Did you know your neighbors, Enrique Rojas and his family?"

"¿Qué?"

"*¿Habla inglés?*" With two words, Flynn is at the limits of her Spanish. Flynn turns, gives Tamica the high sign.

"*Buenos días,*" says Tamica.

Flynn stands to the side of the front stoop. She does the thing she always does whenever Tamica gets a chance to go full bore with her second language, developed as one of her two minor degrees in college and during six months of work on a documentary about human rights in Honduras. Flynn's best bet at this point is to recognize a word or phrase, no different from identifying the shape of a piece of shrapnel from an exploding hand grenade. *Oh, there goes a hexagon.*

The man's name is Tomas Hernandez. He has lived in Sun Valley for *dos años.*

And, yes, he knew Enrique Rojas. And family.

With a sigh, Hernandez begins a long story. Tamica interjects now and then to clarify or confirm she is tracking.

Hernandez leans against the doorjamb. He seems to care. Flynn hears *May-hee-co.* Twice.

And then—Ciudad Juárez, *May-hee-co.*

Her father's eyes go wide. "How did you find her?" He says it in a whisper.

"She's a gift," Flynn whispers back. "And underrated."

They listen some more. Now the give-and-take is more balanced.

"*Momentito,*" says Tamica when Tomas finishes a long paragraph.

"Tomas said Enrique and his family came here about nine months ago," says Tamica. "They were sending money back to the family, parents, in Juárez. Tomas says Enrique was content. He loved his wife and children. He believed in the United States. He worked hard. He seemed to be getting ahead."

"Terrible," says Tomas in accented English. He waggles a finger in the air like he's scolding a naughty child. Maybe the whole country. "Terrible."

"Did Enrique say he was in trouble? Dealing with a problem?"

Tamica translates, but Hernandez holds up his hand. He understands. The wait says everything.

"*Sí*," says Hernandez. "I think so."

"Why does he say that?" says Flynn. "Ask him how he knew Enrique was dealing with something?"

Tamica launches into another round of questions. "*Claro*," says Tamica as Hernandez talks. "*Claro, claro.*"

"Enrique told him if anything happened, Señor Hernandez was to make sure his family got on a bus as soon as possible. And Enrique gave him money to cover the fares."

"And how long after that conversation was Enrique's body found?" says her father.

Tamica knows the answer: "Three days."

"And is that what happened?" says Flynn. "He brought them to the bus?"

Tamica exchanges rapid-fire words again with Hernandez.

"No," says Tamica. "When he first heard Enrique was missing, before the report of Enrique's body being found, he went to the apartment. He helped them finish packing. They got a ride."

"Then why would Enrique have given them money for the bus?" says Flynn.

Tamica relays the question to Tomas and translates his answer: "I had the same question."

Robbie McGrath connection or not, Enrique Rojas paid a price. For something. No matter how tenuous his official connection to his new country, Enrique Rojas was a citizen of the community. His murder requires prosecution. If the community lowers its standards for victims who live in the shadows, the law is meaningless.

Robbie McGrath had found something.

But what?

"Does Señor Hernandez know where the family lived in Juárez?"

The translated question is met with a headshake and heavy eyes.

"Ask him to think," says Flynn. "Is there anything Enrique said? Anything? And what was his wife's name?"

After a minute of back-and-forth, "The wife's name is Laura." Tamica rolls the *r* hard so it comes out like *Loud-uh*. "Enrique's wife worked in a maquiladora. She hated the job, doing the same thing every day, making no money. It was one of those big companies that makes printers. For computers."

"Does he remember the name of the company?"

Tamica asks in Spanish. Hernandez waves them inside. He leads them through a tidy living room with bright-colored furniture, the bacon smell digging its way into Flynn's bones. One of two back bedrooms serves as an office. Hooked to a desktop computer and sitting on a shelf is a shiny black wedge. Hernandez points to the logo and says something to Tamica in Spanish.

"They joked about the fact that Laura might have worked on the parts in his printer," says Tamica. "Apparently the largest printer manufacturer in the world."

Flynn knows the name. So does anyone with a computer and the need to print.

Swintex.

◆ ◆ ◆

"Who's game?" says Flynn. They huddle on the street.

Michael and Tamica both immediately catch her drift.

"I've got a boatload of comp time," says Tamica. "I could burn a few days."

"You don't need me," says Michael.

"I do need you," says Flynn. "The more eyes, the better."

"Three of us," says Michael. "Too much."

"You know what we're getting into, don't you?" says Flynn. "Ciudad Juárez?"

Michael nods.

Tamica shrugs. "*No sé*," she says.

"Murder capital," says Flynn. "They say it's gotten better in the last year or two, but for a while it was called the most dangerous city in the world."

CHAPTER 38
SUNDAY

There is no avoiding her house. Clothes, for one. Routine, for another. Appearances, for another.

Tamica arrives last, toting a large brown paper sack with a stash of foil-wrapped tamales. Rice and beans too. The air in the house fills with the spice and activity, chasing demons. Her coworker and father don't know it, but Flynn feels the air change inside the house.

Tamica sets about making coffee, squelching her disdain for Flynn's national brand from a grocery store tin.

Her father uses Flynn's laptop at the dining room table to check flights. Flynn kisses the money goodbye. What does it matter? Full fare, a good hotel, a roomy rental car for her father's long legs. She needs her team. It will be worth every nickel.

There are three or four calls to make.

First, Goodman. She catches him at a noisy gathering, some sort of community reception. She pleads her case. The only message she wants him to hear is the one welcoming her back.

"I'm talking to Snelling tomorrow," Goodman shouts over all the clanking and ruckus. "This is getting ridiculous."

◆ ◆ ◆

Second, Max.

"What the heck?" says Max. "For how many days?"

"I hope it's quick. One night if all goes well. Two nights at the most," says Flynn.

Max grumbles about his shifts and how the timing doesn't line up with school schedules.

What does she have to offer in return? "You said something about catching up sometime soon? Coffee or a beer?" She wouldn't mind an armed guard, twenty-four seven. "Dinner and?"

How desperate is she? Not very. Sex can go fuck itself. She can't imagine what it would take to get her interested.

Sex is the last thing on her mind. It is the first thing on Max's. He might be desperate to fill the gap until he replaces Miller Lite Amy with Coors Light Sharon or Bud Light Karen.

On the other hand, Max is giving Wyatt protection. And cab service. Does she owe him? Something? Isn't it part of what you do, even if he's The Ex?

"Sure." Max sounds unexcited. "Dinner and something. What the hell is in El Paso?"

"A thread," says Flynn. "It's across the border."

"This same tip?"

"Same one."

"Why there?"

"It's where the questions lead."

"And a phone call or email doesn't get it done."

Tension ripples through his words.

"Can you do me one favor?" she says.

Tamica puts a plate down in front of her. Steam rises from two plump tamales swimming in a pool of glistening green chili with fat hunks of pork.

"You mean another."

"Can you find out for me the status of the investigation into the murder of a guy named Enrique Rojas?"

"Did you try the pro team?"

She already has Dwight Hatcher working for her. At least, in theory. And making such a call would be about as useful as dropping a brick on your toe. Call number four, in fact, will be her way of going around the bureaucracy.

"I've contacted the official channels." It's true about PDQ, but not Enrique Rojas.

"And haven't heard anything back?"

"Nothing."

"Must mean there are no updates," says Max.

"Do you have a friend who can double-check?"

"Maybe," says Max. "Name again?"

She repeats "Enrique Rojas," spells it. She gets the distinct impression he is writing it down, not blowing her off.

"Can you see if there is anything cooking? Or find out the general status? If there is an investigation, even?"

"Was he legal?"

"Probably not," says Flynn. "But it doesn't matter to me if it doesn't matter to you. I'll call you tomorrow to let you know how we're doing. Tell Wyatt I'll see him soon. When I get back, let's find a night."

Third, Fred Sturm. Metro State University School of Criminology and Criminal Justice. Flynn explains that Max passed along Sturm's home number and apologizes for the Sunday interruption.

"Happy to help if I can," says Sturm.

But he can't. Sturm is chatty, friendly, passes along regards to Max, and has no fresh info or insights. He explains that he's usually able to tap friends at the FBI for insights, but they've all "clammed up."

"And are you seeing something that the rest of us are not?" says Flynn. "Any questions you think I should ask?"

"I mean, not really," says Sturm. "The big question is why would you resurface and risk it all? You know? Like BTK. The thirst for attention is unquenchable."

◆ ◆ ◆

Fourth, Chris Casey.

He sounds happy to hear from her. At least, for a minute.

"Did you call the PR shop?"

"Jesus, of course not," says Flynn. "And if I did, you know the odds better than anyone of getting a return phone call."

"Hatcher?"

"He says one reporter per station. First time I ever heard that."

"So you tried?" says Casey.

"Of course."

"And you do know it's the weekend?"

"You think homicide is taking days off? Really? Or anyone in DPD leadership?"

"The homicide boys hate questions about open murders. More like loathe. Abhor. And I quote." He clears his throat, speaks with a deep register. "'Every case is active. No case is too old when it comes to murder.'"

"I'm looking for a source outside of the PR channels, someone who worked the case or is working the case and can give me a rough idea of where it stands."

"It's only been two months with Rojas, so I guarantee they won't say what they've got or what they don't," says Casey. "It's not their style, no matter how good the source."

"Can you find out if they have any leads at all? And, one thing in particular, whether the police found and talked to his wife?"

Flynn doesn't want him to run a pro forma check. She wants him to dig. But she has zero leverage.

"And you can't mention my name," says Flynn. "I'm to remain reporter non grata."

"When are you back on board?"

"Soon," says Flynn. "The frost might be thawing."

"So if Snelling relents, you might be able to make this call yourself?"

"I'm going out of town," says Flynn. "And I don't have the connections you have."

"First, they have phones most everywhere in the world now," says Casey. "And your attempt at flattery is utter bullshit."

"Please?" she says.

"I'll see what I can do. Everyone is so focused on the Broncos game."

Flynn doesn't care for professional sports. She can't think of one good thing about it, except the general conviviality.

Except . . . there is one thing.

A Broncos win will make the town a happier place.

Including Max, Goodman, and Snelling.

She needs everyone happier.

And less on guard.

CHAPTER 39

On the first circuit past Flynn's house, Harry makes out a flicker of movement. From across the street, he sees in the living room window to the dining room.

The glance alone inside brings back the sharp tangy whiff of Wyatt's closet.

He catches a shadow of someone moving. The shadow is too tall to be Flynn Martin.

Harry is another guy walking down the street. He plays Felix Mendelssohn's solo piano pieces *Songs Without Words* through his headphones. The glance over at Flynn's house is innocuous and nonchalant. He practiced on fifty other houses.

He is nobody.

For a minute after the glance, he digests what he's seen. He replays it over and over in his head. It's a flash frame.

Harry keeps walking downhill to the north. Straight north and then a full circuit of East High School and then into City Park by the lake and back toward her house.

Harry stops at the big bookstore on Colfax. He browses the magazines. He orders a shot of espresso from the coffee counter, drinks it in four slurps.

◆ ◆ ◆

He kills another hour.

He tucks the headphones inside his jacket. They are too big for his pocket, but if he keeps them on his head for the return trip past Flynn's house, he might become memorable. Mary had spotted them, after all. He doesn't want to think about Mary.

The afternoon is dead.

This time Harry will pass Flynn's house from the north, walking uphill.

Harry slouches with a world-weary stoop. He slows. Nobody else is on the sidewalk on his side of the street, but there are people outside Flynn Martin's house.

Glance.

Jesus! It's hard not to linger. He is tempted to stop, turn, and stare. But no.

The glance pulls in all sorts of information. It's like looking at a painting by Hieronymus Bosch. He will return to the image in his mind many times and see new things. The main action involves a tall Black woman coming down the steps to the sidewalk. She is striking, lean and long. Behind him, Harry hears a car door open and the car start. But before that, and behind the woman coming down the steps, is Flynn Martin on the porch with a tall man.

Her father—Michael Martin.

There is something purposeful going on among these three. The more Harry reviews what he's seen, the more he realizes the overriding feeling among them is one of eagerness. And teamwork.

He couldn't hear a thing.

But the sense of it was businesslike. Earnest.

The bus stop is only a few blocks from her house. The same bus stop where he left Flynn's phone, to force her to work for it.

Harry sits down on the bench and waits.

He reviews everything he's seen, everything he's taken in.

It's obvious.

Flynn Martin is not, as he demanded, working alone.

CHAPTER 40
MONDAY

Flynn can't count the number of ways this is a bad idea.

Swintex.

Laura Rojas.

Their thread is thinner than a flea's eyelash.

They have no proof that the wife of Enrique Rojas has returned to the same city she once departed, the city where the family lived when both parents were alive.

What if the Rojas family had been drawn to Ciudad Juárez for the work in the maquiladoras? What if they were from a city or town far to the south? Or anywhere else in Mexico? What if Laura Rojas took the children and went all the way back home instead of back to Juárez?

It's too late now.

Her father sits across the aisle, the tray table down as he works on a crossword. One row up and across, the back of Tamica's head slumps against a window.

◆ ◆ ◆

They take a Lyft from their downtown hotel to the bridge. They set out on foot across the long expanse, pedestrians guided into a long chute like cattle. The temperature is midsixties. The break from Colorado's cold is welcome.

The view down to the right is obscured by a metal fence capped by a high metal awning along the length of the bridge. To their left, a waist-high railing keeps them separated from traffic. Cars inch along as they wait their turn at the security station.

They cross vast acres of concrete, train tracks, and the inert Rio Grande, as brown and creamy as butterscotch pudding.

Walking across is faster. Her father found this tourist-advice tidbit online. Plus, taking a rental car into Mexico comes with all sorts of hassles, including extra insurance.

They are an odd trio. Her tall father, moving gamely. His eyes take in everything. Tamica's too-cool Blackness, seeing everything around her but not making it obvious.

What would Goodman say if he saw this group crossing the bridge from El Paso to Ciudad Juárez?

"Based on *what*?"

She pictures his puzzled, paternal, disbelieving face.

Her father carries nothing. Flynn carries a small generic brown purse, strapped around her neck and shoulder. Tamica totes a large hippie handbag with a subdued paisley print. The bag includes her personal digital camera, the one that records high-quality video. With the giant data chip inside, Tamica says they can shoot for an hour. She has a spare chip, an extra charged battery, and a small wireless audio rig for the camera. She also packed a digital audio recorder as backup.

Tamica has given Flynn's father a quick rundown of the audio recorder's functions, a streamlining step if they find themselves in a tight spot for time or space.

Or security.

Border patrol is a snap. They have their passports. They all tell the same story. This is an excursion into Juárez for lunch and an afternoon look-around. Their ascetic approach to "packing" speeds up the screening.

Stepping foot into Mexico, Flynn imagines the daily horrors of a few years earlier. How did the cops manage to keep track? How did they manage to count? How many murderers got away?

How did the cemeteries keep up?

"Coffee? Sure. I have funerals at ten, eleven thirty, and three; perhaps I can squeeze you in right after lunch?"

Were any of the bodies found *here* by the *farmacia*? Or *there* by the *dentista*? At its nadir, Ciudad Juárez was home to three thousand murders in one year. Almost nine murders *every day*.

Casket makers and tombstone engravers must have recorded banner years. Funeral home income? Off the charts, but likely most bodies did not receive formal burial.

For a serial killer, you couldn't ask for a better environment. You could get your jollies once a week and nobody would have time to connect the dots. Or stop to wonder. But that's not what serial killers want. They seek the limelight. They want attention.

Now Juárez celebrates the relative peace. The fight for control of the supply chain that feeds demand north of the border has cooled. They are down to one or two murders per day.

Reporters who have covered the wars haven't fared much better. More than a hundred reporters have been killed since the turn of the century.

On the other hand, journalists who curry favor with the ruling government are treated well. They are showered with gifts and favors.

Critical writers are "disappeared."

A few hundred yards inside Mexico, Michael opens his Uber app. With Tamica's help, he enters the Spanish address for the Parque Industrial Gema.

Tres personas.

They stand and wait.

"Very close," says Michael.

A minute later, a blue Nissan Pathfinder rounds the corner.

The driver's name is Miguel. Double Michaels up front. Tamica introduces herself from the back seat. Miguel nods in acknowledgment. "*Con mucho gusto,*" he says. His black hair is combed straight back from the top of his high forehead. He has a narrow face and a dark goatee that looks like a permanent fixture. Flynn puts Miguel at twenty-five. He wears a plaid periwinkle shirt, a few buttons open to a hairy chest and gold chain. There's a sparkle in his eyes.

Flynn wonders about all the friends and family he might have known who were killed.

◆ ◆ ◆

Gutted storefronts and oversize gas stations zoom by. How many *dentistas* does Juárez need?

"*Aquí,*" says Miguel.

A one-story building stretches out in both directions. Silver block letters shine in the morning sun: SWINTEX. The building boasts all the personality of government storage. Or barracks.

The lone gap in an iron fence around the perimeter makes room for a narrow entry to a parking lot crammed with vehicles. Cars are parked at odd angles in the broad muddy shoulder of the road too. Miguel pulls into the stubby drive to turn around and get headed back the other way.

"Ask him to wait," says Flynn. "We'll pay twenty dollars, whether it's ten minutes or an hour. Either way."

Tamica negotiates.

Miguel scratches his cheek. "*Espero aquí,*" he says. "*Claro.*"

"I'll wait here too," says Michael.

"Why?"

"You don't need a mob. If Laura is there, she'll feel plenty nervous about two people, let alone three."

◆ ◆ ◆

A petite receptionist behind a high counter greets them with a practiced grin.

The receptionist speaks English and, in fact, lives in El Paso.

"Every day you have to go through security?" says Flynn.

"There are no shortcuts, I'm afraid." Her name is Zoe Fernandez. None of the chitchat warms the ventricles of her palace guard heart.

"I'm a reporter from Denver," says Flynn. "I'm in Juárez looking for a woman named Laura Rojas."

"I'm afraid we don't—"

"I'm sure," says Flynn. "I'm not asking you to take her off her shift and bring her out here. We have some information about her husband's death back in Denver. Perhaps at break. Or lunch."

"She's—"

Fernandez is unprepared.

This is the beauty of in-person approaches. They don't allow time for a PR huddle or recalculating body language.

Flynn waits. Tamica waits.

"This is an unusual request," says Fernandez. She invites them to have a seat, then steps to a door in the corner of the reception room, pushes it open, and disappears. The throbbing clatter of industry leaks into the reception room for a moment and then falls away.

"She's here," whispers Tamica.

Flynn grabs a copy of *Wired* off the coffee table. She crosses her legs. She sits back with a look of indifference. Routine.

Five minutes slip by before the door swings wide. "One moment," says Fernandez, owner of a gaze known to glum security guards the world over. Fernandez sits down and resumes her duties at the desk, only the top of her head visible.

Flynn fights off images of Laura Rojas being escorted out a back door. Swintex doesn't need a worker who attracts trouble.

Five more minutes of pretending to read.

Five more minutes of resisting every instinct to text her father and let him know what is happening, ask if there's a way for him to circle around the back. Watch for windowless black vans speeding away.

Swintex might be watching the two Miguels via security cam . . .

The door swings open again.

The man who steps through is one zillion percent Anglo. He sports thick-frame glasses, a blue button-down shirt, a yellow paisley tie, and a weak comb-over. Gold stud in his left earlobe. He arrives with the grim visage of a surgeon after a failed operation, shaking his head to telegraph the tragic news.

He extends a big hand, which fits his hefty frame. "Ken Davis," he says. No title. None needed. *Bouncer,* thinks Flynn. He reeks of cigarettes. "And I'm sorry. Zoe has already explained, but we are not in the business of delivering messages to employees unless, of course, it's your relative, and even then, an emergency."

"She does work here?" says Flynn.

"No comment," says Davis. "We don't identify details about our staff."

"I respect the policy." Flynn aims for reason. She rehearsed scenarios with Tamica and her father for more than an hour back at the Days Inn. "And I understand it. I think. This is an unusual situation, given how Laura Rojas returned to Mexico. Her husband was murdered."

Flynn waits to see if the information leaves a mark. Davis stands with his hands in front of him. The fingers on one hand tap out a rhythm on the knuckles of the other.

"Perhaps for the same reason—even more so," says Davis. "She does not need to be reminded. Or dragged back in. And, I might point out, she is not alone as a woman or man or son or daughter or brother or sister who is familiar with the word 'murder.' Not in this town."

"I know. Awful. And I'm glad things have gotten better. But Laura might have information that will help determine what happened to her husband. Why he was killed. And—maybe who did it."

"And Swintex can't be in the middle of all that," says Davis. "Again, you know, if she was here. Zoe said you're from Denver?"

"That's right," says Flynn.

"Well then, go Broncos." For the first time, he smiles. "They have to get to the Super Bowl. I mean, wow. I'm from Rapid City, South Dakota. I'm sure you know, but Denver Bronco Country? It's not a place. It's a state of mind."

They find Mexican Miguel standing outside his Pathfinder, two shiny black boots on the asphalt. He smokes a cigarette and listens to a horn-heavy Mexican ballad on the radio.

"*¿Mi padre?*" says Flynn.

Miguel points down and across the road to a pop-up canopy. Flynn makes out her father's lanky frame. He is talking to one lone man seated at a white plastic table.

"Protestors," says Tamica after she and Miguel exchange a few words. "Workers' rights."

That is the father she knows—always drawn to controversy, even if he doesn't speak a lick of Spanish.

An old white sheet dangles from the blue canopy:

Justicia a la Clase Obrera

"A familiar vibe," says Flynn. "Working conditions and pay?"

"'Justice for the working class,'" says Tamica. "Unionizing."

Despite all the cars parked everywhere, the outside of the plant is devoid of humans except for the four organizers under the canopy. The security cameras mounted on the building's exterior are as easy to spot as guard towers at Denver County Jail.

Her father shakes hands with his new friend and starts walking back.

"She's here," says Flynn once he's within earshot.

"I know," says her father. "She'll be out here at lunch break. She's one of the main activists and one of their best recruiters."

Laura Rojas arrives at lunch break in her Swintex worker uniform, a blue sleeveless smock and off-white slacks. She is in a group with three other women. Same uniforms. They all carry lunch bags. Flynn hates herself for picking Rojas out of the quartet, but Laura looks the most alert and aware. She is the youngest too.

"You look familiar," she says to Flynn with a heavy accent.

"I'm a reporter."

Laura's eyes dart back and forth between Flynn and Tamica. Her father has gone back to the truck, to wait with Miguel. Laura's coworkers settle around a table under the canopy. Laura remains in the street, clutching her belongings and food.

"I would like to talk with you," says Flynn.

Laura Rojas's hair is straight and close cropped around a wide face. Her dark eyes are wary.

"You're from—"

"Denver."

"Are you here to talk about workers' rights? About twenty-three dollars a day in wages?"

"No," says Flynn. "It's about Enrique."

Rojas puts her things down on the table. Her compatriots sit on white fold-up chairs, seats no bigger than salad plates. The chair legs sink into the soft dirt of the roadside shoulder.

"We only have a few questions," says Flynn.

"No," says Rojas.

"Maybe we meet after work?"

Perhaps Rojas is putting on a show for the security cams.

"No, *gracias*," says Rojas.

"It's a bit more complicated than Enrique," says Flynn. "So answers to a few questions might help with some bigger issues. And it may help with what happened to your husband."

"*¿Prefieres hablar en espanol?*" says Tamica.

Rojas lets loose with a terabyte of Spanish. Her hands come up. They go down. She points at the factory without looking at it. She points under the canopy at her friends, who sip soup and nibble on hunks of white cheese.

Tamica stares, nods.

"She says her one concern now is workers' rights and better pay for the people who are making millions and millions of dollars in profit for American corporations," says Tamica. "She doesn't want to get tangled in anything to do with the people Enrique ran into, and we wasted our time and she wishes that we have a nice fucking safe journey home."

"That's all?"

"The highlights." Tamica winks.

"Is she living here? In Juárez?" says Flynn.

Rojas understands the question, says a word in Spanish that Flynn doesn't know.

"Nearby," says Tamica.

"I'm wondering why you left Denver," says Flynn. "Out of the blue."

"I wanted to be at home." Rojas is back to her accented English. "Nothing felt right in Denver after Enrique was gone. Nothing."

"But—"

"Nothing. That's all."

"We came a long way," says Flynn.

"Not so far on a jet," says Rojas. "You will be home before our shift ends."

"We will keep your name out of it," says Flynn. "We're here to tell a story, to get to the truth."

Rojas looks down. Does silence equal the sound of a mind changing? A tear shoots from an eyelid down her cheek.

"I have a deal," says Rojas. "I keep to my side of the border, and then there are no troubles. *Lo siento.*"

"We won't use your name," says Flynn. "I swear."

Rojas turns and ducks under the canopy. She sits with her friends at the rickety, off-kilter table. She pours noodle soup into a plastic bowl and eats with a plastic spoon.

◆ ◆ ◆

Flynn walks halfway back to *los dos Migueles*. And stops.

"I'm not giving up," says Flynn.

"Okay," says Tamica. It's the most dubious "okay" ever uttered.

"Follow her home. Get her outside this scene."

"And how are you going to figure out which one of these vehicles is hers when it comes to the end of the workday? What if she carpools? Or takes the bus?"

"I didn't come all this way to find her and then not have the conversation we need to have. She doesn't believe we can protect her identity."

"She might think whoever she is afraid of back in Denver has a long reach."

Flynn glances back to their Uber driver Miguel and the Nissan.

"So she's not going to make it easy," says Tamica. "So what's our move?"

"Think," says Flynn. "We aren't going back without getting what we came for."

CHAPTER 41

The more Harry reviews what he's seen, the more he is able to see one thing.

The Black woman *belonged*.

To the situation.

To Flynn.

To the moment.

There was an air about the trio. A togetherness.

What Harry saw and what he heard, however brief the moment, can be interpreted only as three people working together.

It's made him woozy, almost seasick with confusion.

Pissed off!

How *could* she?

He didn't sleep last night. He tossed and fidgeted.

Now, at work, he wants to rest his head on the desk. As soon as his head hits the gray laminate surface, he'd be gone. Out.

But he doesn't want to draw attention to himself or have anyone ask questions or wonder about his work performance. He goes back over and over what he saw.

Who the hell is the beautiful Black woman? And what the hell is Flynn doing? Does she think she can get away with not going solo?

◆ ◆ ◆

At the library, Harry waits for a turn at a computer. He makes a note of the time on his phone. And gives himself permission to close his eyes.

Harry jolts awake, worried that half an hour has slipped by and he's missed his turn.

He's only been out for six minutes.

He massages his forehead. He rubs the base of his skull, rolls his head around.

He takes his assigned seat at a computer between a fat man who smells like the bathroom at a forgotten bus station and a tall Hispanic teenager with cheap headphones. Machine-gun noise from the military-themed video game leaks from the housing of the kid's dime-store cans. He plays at full volume.

Harry wants to hurl.

Make this quick . . .

Harry pulls up the website for Flynn's station. He does a quick scan of the entire staff—nothing. He finds one Black face, a woman, but it isn't the woman who was with Flynn.

Next, Flynn's Facebook.

He's reviewed plenty of Facebook, X, and even TikTok. It's part of his work. Applicants for the quasi-political jobs, the "limelight crew," as he calls them, require extra time. And thoroughness. With the six-figure income, boys and girls, you can't be too careful. It's stunning how someone's Facebook can vary apples to asparagus from the poised picture of polish he or she presents in person when ties are cinched, shoes are buffed, makeup is fresh. Versus social media, all about dinners littered with wine bottles, every other post about alcohol, and how much he or she insists on strict work-life boundaries.

Flynn isn't much for posting. He's gone through her page before. Harry has a feel for her preferences. She is a minimalist. Mother Mallard's Portable Masterpiece Company or some similar junk. Terry Riley or Philip Glass, for crying out loud. What is the point?

Flynn Martin treats social media as an afterthought. A photo of a river and a mountain. A post about the new Star Wars entry. One about a new restaurant. A shot out on a trail in Central Park, where she's gone for a walk with a friend. Shot of the trail. No friend. No Flynn. Blah, blah, *bland*. Bah, bah, *white sheep*.

Not one selfie.

And *there* . . .

Clutching a "regional Emmy" for the Heartland Chapter for her coverage of a story about water in Colorado, "From the Mountains to the Plains: How the Big Thompson Roars—or Doesn't."

Flynn's caption: *With my best friend and fabulous photographer, photojournalist Tamica Porter, who shot every frame. We wrote this series together. Could not feel more proud.*

The shot was taken post-banquet.

A *photojournalist* . . . !

She has pulled in others.

In violation of every instruction.

And where the hell has she gone?

Harry's temples scream. Giant sharp tongs, like the old-timey ones for toting blocks of ice. He feels as if someone is picking him up from above, the pincers drawing blood. A temple-*ectomy*, perhaps. It might feel good.

He heads back to work.

He feels the tick of the lunch clock. He is overdue. How much time has he spent? Once he jumped to Tamica Porter's Facebook, it became an endless stream of photos and casual selfies and those brilliant white teeth and, in one beach shot from Puerto Vallarta, her trim tummy stretched out like a long chocolate runway between scraps of yellow bikini. The waist on her is like a delightful magic trick, all those endless acres of beautiful Black skin. So many of her posts are about stories she's worked and her view of the world, and Harry feels like he knows Tamica Porter in his bones. She is serious and intelligent and whip smart. And no sign of a steady boyfriend but one of a White girlfriend, and the hug looks way beyond platonic. He spots Tamica's hand around one drink in her entire feed, a shot of her holding a beer at one of the new brewpubs. Harry hates drinkers so much, especially those who lie about their habits, fib about their consumption, pretend they've never been busted for DUI.

It's refreshing to come across someone so wholesome.

And smiling.

But the main thing is Flynn Martin has pulled in a teammate. In fact, two.

She will pay a price for doing so. There is hell to pay. What he doesn't know is whether his plan will change. His whole project. Everything. If he steps on the basement floor, it will be all her fault. If he steps on the basement floor, there is no guarantee.

Of anything.

CHAPTER 42

The scene is one part NASCAR, two parts haboob.

Cars roar out of the lot. Every single make, size, model, shape. New and old. Most as American—that is, Japanese, Korean too—as apple pie. Swirls of dust choke visibility down like a dirty fog.

There are buses, too, as Tamica predicted. Four white school buses, packed to the gills.

If Laura Rojas rides a bus, they're SOL.

Miguel positions his Pathfinder so they can watch from the driver's side and jerk out into the flow of traffic when the time comes.

If it comes.

Miguel has a good view from the driver's side. Flynn sits behind him with a good view too. Tamica sits next to her in the back seat and leans over to try and help. Her father corkscrews around from his perch in the front seat. He doesn't have the best angle.

Their windows are rolled up tight. Dust and pebbles tick off the glass.

Flynn explains her theory. Laura Rojas will have Colorado plates. She wouldn't have had time to switch out Colorado plates for state of Chihuahua license plates. Day trippers are common. Look at Ken Davis and Zoe Fernandez. There will be other out-of-Chihuahua plates. Most will be Texas.

But Flynn Martin doubts that, with kids to settle and reeling from the death of her husband, Laura Rojas has prioritized a trip to Mexico's DMV.

Long shot?

Maybe.

Worth a gamble?

Definitely.

Flynn fears there is a back exit. Or maybe Laura returned to the canopy to pass out flyers, or maybe a meeting of the rabble-rousers is underway. Or maybe she works overtime to grab a few extra pesos.

No, not with kids . . .

They spot plenty of Texas plates.

Three New Mexico.

Everything else Chihuahua.

The rush fades.

The sun fades.

"Hell," says Tamica.

"*Nada*," says Miguel.

Flynn's phone chimes, an email.

"Tip for Flynn."

Flynn feels Tamica interested, leaning in.

Tilts her phone away . . .

> Told you NO HELP.

Types: I am alone.

It's her constant state of existentialism, thinks Flynn. She isn't lying.

The cars cruise, but they are no longer bumper to bumper.

How else to find Laura Rojas? Given Laura's visibility in union politics, maybe she's been quoted in the newspaper. Find the reporter who talked to her, get a cell phone number? Maybe they can find the online white pages for Juárez and start calling every Rojas in a city of 1.2 million.

There.

Green-and-white plates.

On a minivan.

And Laura Rojas, eyes peeled ahead, behind the wheel.

Alone.

Tamica squeals.

Miguel pulls out like a roadside cop after a speeder.

Tamica slaps Flynn's thigh.

"Jesus, you're good," says Tamica.

"Lucky is all," says Flynn.

Laura Rojas heads west. She drives like she's delivering fresh eggs, no cartons. Flynn jots down the license plate. Rojas's gray Dodge Caravan looks almost new.

The traffic thins. The air cools. They climb into the low hills on dirt roads. The housing developments echo suburbs in the United States, minus the curbs, gutters, and fancy lawns. The neighborhoods don't seem like they were glued together.

Flynn's phone chimes again.

> I know you're working with your photographer friend.
> Deal breaker!!!

"Must be important," says Tamica.
"Pain in the ass," says Flynn.
Types back:

No clue what you think you know.

Reply:

I ain't fucking PDQ for nothing.

Miguel keeps a healthy distance from Laura's tail. He is a pro. Or he has watched how it's done on TV. Miguel lets Rojas disappear around the wide curves. Nobody tells Miguel what to do. Flynn turns around in her seat to peek at the lights from the city falling away behind them. She wonders how in the hell PDQ knows she's brought in her father and Tamica, decides to not dwell on that particular issue.

She texts Wyatt to let him know everything is going well and she loves him. Flynn feels suddenly so far away. Wyatt texts back with a few questions. She tells him Mexico is fine and that his grandfather sends his love.

Miguel mutters something. Tamica translates. "People in this neighborhood have maids. And nannies."

The Caravan turns and tips its nose down a stubby driveway. A wide garage swallows it whole with room to spare. The garage door remains up, a soft rectangle of golden light in the gathering dusk.

Miguel slows two houses later.

No game plan . . .

Laura Rojas stands with her back to the road in a huddle of men, maybe six.

The men are chalky and covered in grit. Drywallers. Next to the house where Miguel pulled over, the shell of a new home takes shape.

"Boss?" asks Miguel.

"Stay here." Flynn pops her door. Tamica does the same. "But stay close."

Flynn walks. The night is cool. She reaches the top of Rojas's short driveway and stops.

"*Me seguiste*," says Rojas.

Tamica translates: "You followed me."

"Go away," says Rojas.

"I want to help," says Flynn.

"No," says Rojas. "No trouble. No complications. I told you."

Tamica translates. Flynn wraps her head around the idea of Rojas's Denver neighborhood compared to the new fancy digs.

"I don't need your name," says Flynn. "I need context."

"But you want my name. You have it."

"I won't use it. It's what we do. We protect sources."

How is trust developed, extended, guaranteed in a place with the history of Juárez? And how do you accomplish it in a few minutes across international borders and across the language barrier too?

"You want me to tell you what?"

"How this happened."

"What?"

Rojas gives a signal to the men. The huddle of workers breaks apart. The men trudge past them, talking quietly in Spanish. Engines snap to life—collective throats being cleared among a gaggle of pickup trucks.

"This house. Your car."

Rojas looks down. "Why?"

"Is this Enrique's money?"

"You're going to take it away?"

"I'm not writing a story about you or Enrique. It's about a story he's connected to. And you might know something that would help."

"You're going to put this on TV?" says Rojas.

"I don't have to use your name. Or say anything about where you are now."

"So you tell the whole world?"

"Whose idea was it to return? To come back?"

Rojas holds her gaze, sorts through the variables.

"Whose idea?" says Flynn.

"I met with them."

"Them, who?"

"*Policía.*"

No translation needed.

Rojas purses her lips.

"They came to you?"

"There was another reporter. A newspaper reporter."

"Robbie," says Flynn. "McGrath."

Rojas nods.

"I have children. I have a new start."

"Nothing will happen to you."

In Juárez? Flynn has no reason for certainty.

Flynn's phone chirps with a text alert. She ignores it.

"Enrique earned the money." Rojas's hands start to move. Flynn takes this as a good sign.

"What questions did she ask you? The reporter? Was Enrique working for the police?"

"Enrique was working for his family, to give us a better life."

"But did he have a relationship with the police?"

"That is what Robbie asked," says Rojas. "What she asked about."

"Who told you to leave?"

Laura Rojas puts a finger across her cheekbone, as if to find the button to squelch the surging tears.

"I don't know much."

"Were you *told* to leave?"

"No," says Rojas. "Encouraged."

"Encouraged how?"

Now both eyes flood, but the waterworks don't impair her ability to speak. "Did I do the right thing?"

"I don't know," says Flynn. "What did you do?"

"My name," says Rojas. "You won't use my name?"

"Promise," says Flynn.

"Would you like to come inside? My children are waiting."

"Yes," says Flynn. "Thank you. We have two other people with us. Our driver and . . ."

How would one explain a father's presence?

". . . another reporter who is helping me."

Tamica heads to the Nissan. Her father steps out.

They all follow Rojas down to her house.

Tamica clutches her bag of tricks.

"*Gracias,*" says Flynn. The slope down is steep. "*Muchísimas gracias.*"

At Rojas's front door, Flynn waits. Rojas greets her children, dropping to one knee to receive exuberant hugs. Flynn pushes aside thoughts of Wyatt. Rojas's kids stare at the entourage of invaders.

Flynn checks her phone.

The text is from Goodman:

Your outcast days are over. Call me.

Right when she needs more free time.

Not less.

CHAPTER 43

Harry spots the black sedan and stops. He is half a block away on a path that cuts through Governor's Park. The sedan stands out like an infected pimple on a model's face. It's parked under a streetlight on the stub of Pennsylvania Street that dead-ends in Governor's Park.

He stares at the darkened windows of the car for one full minute before letting his gaze drift. He spots the second, an identical twin dripping with cop essence.

Harry's condo building sits between the two vehicles, but Harry knows the cops could be anywhere in the vicinity.

Or this could be a coincidence.

An acid bile burbles inside. He scolds himself for watching too closely, but it's dark.

Harry is tired, worn out, pissed off.

And now this. Maybe they have cops all over Capitol Hill. Or maybe they think they have zeroed in on something.

But any renewed investigative work in Harry's corner of the Capitol Hill thicket will only be based on the old fucking cases and not the new because, as a plain matter of unvarnished fact, he did not kill Robbie McGrath.

So who stirred the pot? Who prompted a fresh canvass of the area?

Harry has a bad feeling about the answer to those questions.

Or maybe . . .

Jesus.

The cops walk out of the building to the north of Harry's. They look purposeful. One is Black and thin, medium height. He has a bald head like a dark chocolate billiard ball. The second cop is White and female. Younger, slender, short dark hair. She is a full head taller than her partner but listens like an understudy learning a part. Both cops wear dark pants and dark-blue waist-length jackets. They stop at the first car. The Black cop opens the front door like he might be about to climb in, but then they both stand and set about the busy business of cops chatting. No rush. The female leans against the car with her back to Harry.

Harry cuts across Governor's Park so he can come down Pennsylvania Street like he is arriving home, per normal. He hustles without being obvious in case anyone is watching for odd reactions.

But guilty parties—and Harry isn't guilty, at least not for Robbie McGrath—do not strafe a pair of detectives gabbing by their not-so-stealthy unmarked car.

Harry tucks his headphones away. He was planning to finish Mahler's garish Eighth Symphony all the way back to his condo. But now he needs his ears for whatever conversational shrapnel he might glean.

He pretends he is lost in thought. Oblivious.

He will walk as close as he dares. He keeps his gaze focused on a spot six feet in front of his stride, head down.

This isn't like Flynn Martin's place, where he couldn't risk staring. But he can't be obvious. He can't stop and ask how they're doing, what they're up to, *Is there a problem, Officer, in the neighborhood?*

The female cop has her back to Harry but turns at the approaching footsteps or turns because she turns for no reason at all. Even in the forgiving glow of a streetlight, her face reveals more age and experience than Harry had assumed, almost like a magic trick. Harry quickly adds a decade to his original estimate. She isn't a newbie. Her gaze is seasoned and wary.

She looks at him longer than the average person might look. Cops can do that. Maybe they are supposed to do that. Maybe that's how they're trained. Harry and the female cop don't lock gazes. It isn't a stare-down, but it lasts several seconds past a glance.

Harry nods. If one end of the scale is completely ignoring the presence of another human being and the other end of the scale is a protracted genuflection where you don't return to vertical until given permission to do so, Harry's gesture is one baby step in the positive territory from complete disregard. But he communicates respect.

She nods back. She matches his chin bob with one of her own, no smile. She doesn't look like a smiler. She looks like she hasn't smiled in a long time. Has his gesture triggered a basic instinct in another human being, to match signals of acknowledgment? Dogs exchanging sniffs.

Whatever they are discussing stops when she turns. Harry has pierced an invisible bubble of personal space.

Colloquium interruptus.

The Black cop never looks over, but Harry feels the woman's gaze on his back like dual laser beams.

Harry walks. He isn't going to stop and ask, "What's up?" like some dumb hick.

He hears their car door shut, not a slam but close to that level of assertiveness.

Harry hustles through the double-buzzered door of his condo building. He is swift and efficient with the keys for one door and keypad code for the next. He catches a glimpse of the two cops heading his way in the reflection off the second glass door as it opens.

Once the elevator door closes behind him and he is alone, Harry resists every urge to pound the wall. You can never be sure about new video surveillance, anything like that.

The presence of the cops is no *coincidence.*

They are here precisely because of what he's feared.

The new fake case means the cops are mucking around again in their old hunches, their pet theories. They will take their failure off the shelf, blow off the dust, and wonder what they missed.

And he knows exactly who to blame for dragging her ass.

CHAPTER 44

Laura's house is spare and ultra clean. The walls are white and blank. The sensation is unnerving, dreamlike. Flynn and her father sit on a low mauve couch. Tamica takes a side chair closer to Rojas to translate.

In Denver, says Rojas, Enrique worked with a man known as "Captain A." Money was good, then money went dry, then money started to flow again "like water," and then it went all the way dry.

"Bone dry," says Rojas through Tamica.

Enrique Rojas took a job. "Helping." "Moving stuff." "Moving goods."

Cocaine, if Laura Rojas had to guess.

Or heroin. Cheap heroin going north. Enrique was doing an easy job. "Nothing complicated," says Rojas.

Enrique was owed money. He was certain he was being shorted. He wasn't going to sit back and pretend he didn't care. He was not happy about the way he was being treated.

The last Laura Rojas had seen of Enrique was when he headed out on a cool night to go talk with Captain A or the people who worked for Captain A to go get square.

It was a lot of money. Thousands. It was enough for a few months' worth of groceries and rent.

"Enrique knew he was right," says Rojas.

When Enrique's body was found, Laura Rojas spent a week in mourning. Then, a messenger arrived at her door. The messenger said he'd come on behalf of Captain A. The messenger had a deal. He said Enrique had an insurance policy. A good one. Laura Rojas could cash out the policy if she returned to Ciudad Juárez. No questions. No talking to anyone. A new house, and a good near-new minivan, would buy her silence.

Her old job at Swintex waited. All she had to do was go along.

Go along, get along.

Her escort rode with Laura Rojas and her children all the way to the border. He left her at the border, watched her drive across, and said he had tickets to fly home.

"And your escort's name?"

The voice is her father's.

"Carlos," says Laura.

"American guy? Mexican guy?" says her father.

"American," says Laura.

"Was he a cop?" says Flynn.

"I would guess yes. Clean. Almost shiny."

"Age?"

This is her father's witness now.

"Thirty at the oldest."

"Who did he work for?"

"He didn't say much," says Rojas. "He did all the driving. He seemed bored. And angry."

"Angry at who?"

Laura seems to respect Michael Martin's age. Or maleness. Or direct manner. Or all of the above.

"He seemed upset by the whole trip. All the driving."

"But he drove—your minivan."

"I sat in the back and read books with my children. I didn't mind."

"You drove straight through?"

"We stopped somewhere in New Mexico."

"No last name?" says her father.

"No," says Rojas. "He spoke perfect English."

"Good driver?"

"He didn't want to get stopped, that was for sure."

"And?"

"And what?"

"And did you get stopped?"

"Not for speeding," says Rojas.

"For what?"

"For going too slow." Rojas's smile is ever so faint. "They searched the car."

"Did Carlos get a ticket?"

"Yes," says Rojas.

"In what city?" says her father.

"In Vaughn," says Rojas. "In the morning. On the highway outside of town. I always liked Vince Vaughn. The actor. That's how I remembered. Now, I don't like Vaughn. I was so scared."

"But no drugs," says Flynn. "No contraband."

"No," says Rojas. "But I was scared they would want to know more about Carlos and his relationship to us."

"But Carlos got a ticket?"

"Yes," says Rojas. "Not a happy man. He said only a few words the rest of the way to El Paso."

"And then, what? He watched you drive across the border?"

"Yes," says Rojas. "And Captain A too."

"Captain A was there?"

"That's what Carlos said. He said Captain A was watching. It was around the bridge where people cross over. There were many people. We had no idea who was who. Carlos told us to not look around. Captain A flew down, I guess. To make sure."

"To make sure you followed through?" says Flynn.

"Carlos seemed unhappy to see him," says Rojas. "Unhappy that he wasn't trusted to take care of everything."

"Captain A was a cop?" says Flynn.

Rojas's lips go ziplock tight.

"But I don't understand why you had to leave Denver."

Rojas steels herself. "They said it was too dangerous."

"For you?"

Flynn thinks: Or *them*?

"Yes, I think," says Rojas.

"Why would they think you were in danger?"

"I don't know," says Rojas.

"How many times had Enrique met with this reporter?" says her father. "With Robbie McGrath?"

"I don't know," says Rojas. "I only met her once."

If someone in Enrique's network ratted him out for talking to a reporter, Enrique would need to be stopped. And if the reporter knew where his family lived, his family would need to disappear.

"And the union work?" says her father.

"What about it?" says Rojas.

"Why are you doing it?"

"Because I want to help," says Rojas. "You can't sit there and take it."

"And why are you telling us this?" says Flynn.

Laura Rojas thinks for a long time.

"All I can tell you is two things. First, the little people? In both countries? The overlooked? Workers in the maquiladoras? Same as the nobodies from public housing in Denver. We get the short end of every stick. And then we are expected to say thank you. And second, Captain A. Captain A was a cop. I'm sure of it. Something Enrique said. Enrique said Captain A didn't have to worry about the police. You know, *because*. Well, that's not right, is it? No worse than Juárez. Some police learn to look the other way. And when they look the other way, they never look back."

CHAPTER 45

The way Harry keeps his condo 365 days a year is precisely what will make them wonder. Harry needs to present an alternative universe of personal style, not all the way to bachelor slob but more relaxed, more normal.

Harry pulls the rubber drain rack from below the sink, fills it with dishes. He smears a smudge of spaghetti sauce on a plate, leaves it on the counter to dry with a fork. One bottle of fruity IPA goes down the drain; the empty goes on the coffee table. After pulling a few bottles and boxes down from shelves and cupboards, Harry quickly clutters up a kitchen counter that was otherwise showroom ready.

He scatters magazines on the kitchen counter, flips a paperback book on the floor near the couch. He flops a towel over the sink in the bathroom, scatters his toiletries around the counter. He yanks on the bedspread to give it wrinkles. He dumps dirty socks from the hamper on the bedroom floor. He jostles around his music collection, leaves a few CDs open.

He puts Prokofiev on the stereo—that gnarly Piano Concerto No. 3, all the anger and agitation—and an NHL game on the TV for sheer confusion's sake.

◆ ◆ ◆

Harry tugs on jeans—disgustingly common things, an old pair, *Jesus Christ, so plebian.*

And hears the knock.

A knock?

Nobody knocks.

He doesn't even know the sound of knuckles on his door. The impression is more mahogany than bright birch. The door absorbs the percussion, mutes its authority.

Condo buildings prevent random bothering and pestering and pollsters, and even the cup-of-sugar neighbors know condos aren't *that* kind of place unless you run into each other every day in the elevator at the same time and start with the friendly chitchat.

The knock again. Three raps this time, like the first. Unsyncopated. Staccato. Quarter notes.

In a hurry.

Does anyone ever knock once? Is one knock not a knock? Something to be ignored?

Two knocks seem to be the minimum but Harry guesses three is the average, and how often do the knockers go for some happy rhythm to imply the intrusion is nothing of the sort? No cop ever knocks with *bum-buh-da-bum-bum.*

The peephole confirms his fear. The same two. And since police no doubt have special training to sense when someone has approached a closed door from the other side, he swiftly opens it and strikes a civilized, understated smile. He wants to come across as confident but not cheerful, by any means. He wants to project a place between obsequious and aloof, between uber-helpful compliant and slightly annoyed.

She is the first to speak. Detective Diana Amador. Her partner, the bald Black guy, is Detective Rodney Bell.

She asks if they could come in. She calls the shots. It's her eyes that matter. Detective Bell attends to her like a weak-kneed sycophant. He seems nervous, like he is afraid of blurting something out. Will they skip through his apartment or invest themselves in it?

Detective Amador takes the good leather armchair. She sits on the edge like she might spring into action at any moment. Detective Bell takes the smaller accent chair, a tufted turquoise club. He stares at Harry, waits for his partner to start.

Detective Amador gives Harry a look, points at her ear. Harry uses the remote to bring Prokofiev and all his witty dissonances and sly sarcasm down to a volume that will allow for conversation. Harry thinks about giving the pair a brief lecture on the sheer range of Prokofiev's genius. Should he start the schooling with the fact that Prokofiev died on the same day as Joseph Stalin? And that since Sergei Prokofiev lived near Red Square, the throngs mourning Stalin made it impossible to remove Prokofiev's body for three days? Up against the headlines and details of Stalin's death, Prokofiev merited only a brief mention on page 116 of the newspaper.

You pick the wrong day to die after spending your whole life in the arts, and your departure from earth merits a blurb following 115 pages of tribute to a brutal dictator who murdered three million.

Harry wets his lips with a warm tincture of IPA from the empty beer bottle. His mouth tightens. He sits on the couch, leans forward for a moment in a position that assumes this will be jolly quick. The mere presence of two other human beings in his condo, let alone *cops*, changes everything about the space.

They run through the basics, name and age and employer and family. Detective Bell's notebook is so small it looks like he might be scrawling notes on his palm.

When it comes to marital status, Harry tells stories about two near misses, makes it seem as if he is recovering from the heartache. "Meredith was a darling," he says of the first, "but ultimately not a city girl. And Theresa, well, she was a free spirit." He can see both "girlfriends" in his head. "But I'm in a relationship now and, well, who knows?"

Bell makes a note. He alternates his gaze from his partner to his dermatoglyphic whorls.

"How long have you lived here?" says Amador.

"Seventeen years." Harry throws out a number that sounds good. "I lose track, but I think that's right. I can check—"

"That's okay," says Amador. "And again, you work where?"

"I'm a manager in human resources. State of Colorado. Department of Education."

"Downtown?"

"Straight across from the capitol. A fellow public servant."

"For how long?"

Does he sound sporty enough? Carefree enough?

And what is this approach to finding their killer? Their long-ago killer? What nontactical, nonstrategic, nonthoughtful, random wishful thinking is this? What do they hope to spot? Or smell? Or sense?

"Sixteen years. I'm not changing the world or anything, but it is steady—"

"Do you keep to certain routines?" Why doesn't she let him finish? "Belong to any clubs or groups or anything like that? Something for your weeknights?"

"Dates here and there," says Harry. "You know how easy it is nowadays to meet women, I mean. Seriously. Who would have thought? But, yeah, some nights it's me and the television. The budget's not bottomless. Can't go out every night, much as I might like."

They had partially triangulated his home neighborhood back then, thanks to one broken vase and where he had dropped the trash. Did their precious profile indicate something about a city dweller? A denizen of Capitol Hill?

Or had someone seen something he did not know? Was there a shred of something? A witness? From the old days?

Harry flashes on Robert Berdella. After Berdella's first victim went missing, police interviewed him. They bought his explanation that he had not seen the nineteen-year-old since driving him to a dancing contest in a Kansas City suburb. But if they had inspected Berdella's house? The Butcher of Kansas City would never have killed five more.

Detective Amador asks Harry to think back and recall his whereabouts for the prior two weeks. Various nights, various times. Mostly centered around a Tuesday night.

Detective Bell speaks! A throaty baritone, no less. Do they plan on asking if they could search the joint too? They will have to open every book and the back of every drawer, every red tin can of spice, take the bed apart, unzip the covers of couch cushions, et cetera.

"Have to give that some thought," says Harry.

"Take your time."

"Had a date with my new girlfriend." He gives a look like he's straining his brain. "But I'm pretty sure that was the night before the one you're asking about. We went to an art gallery in the Golden Triangle. These blurry weird photographs. Then to dinner at the Cuban restaurant over there. It's like in an old house. Feels like it, at least. Then we grabbed a nightcap and said good night." *And I mugged a bum for the satisfaction right off Colfax.*

"The night before?" says Amador.

Harry stares off like he is concentrating. Prokofiev's quirky phrasings seem harsh and unnecessary. The concerto is working its way to the giant undertow of its heavy denouement. Harry hopes this chitchat interview thing will reach a more abrupt finale.

And, of course, handcuff-free.

"That was the night after," says Harry. "Sorry."

"And by the way," says Amador, "you'd give us the name of your date?"

"Of course," says Harry. "Sure."

"So," says Bell, "think back. Check your calendar, maybe?"

"Well, I don't put social stuff on there. I don't put anything on there," says Harry. "All I've got is work meetings."

Do they know where he's been? It would be sick and twisted to turn up now without an alibi and then they strip his place down to the studs and he gets nailed for the long-ago activity when he has zip-fucking-ola to do with the new one. Maybe they've been watching him all along? Have they pulled security camera footage from outside his building three times a week to watch his comings and goings? Have they put a tracking bug in his briefcase?

A fresh flush of sweat slimes Harry's back. His hackles flare. He kicks himself for underestimating the potential threat.

Flynn . . .

"You can get back to us." Amador pulls a business card from an almost invisible pleated chest pocket. Harry takes it. "Email is fine. Next day or so?"

"Hard to remember," says Harry.

"Understood," says Amador. "But we'll need to know. And the name of your date. Receipts or anything that can confirm your whereabouts."

"Mary Belson," says Harry. With authority. No hesitation. Will they really check on an alibi that makes no difference? "She works in the Department of Revenue."

"Have an address?" Bell again. Three-word statements or questions are his specialty.

"What do they call it? Uptown? I don't have the street number in my head, but it's on Nineteenth Street there. All the new townhomes."

The fresh knock on the door catches Harry like a thunderclap in the middle of a blue-sky day. He startles but covers up by standing like a soldier at surprise inspection. He gives Amador a little hand gesture, requesting permission.

"Please," she says. "Answer it."

Four quick steps, selling the whole carefree schtick. Prokofiev is done.

Maybe so is he?

Behind him he hears the rustle of clothes and the sound of them standing and mumbling. Harry reaches for the door and looks back and, indeed, they are standing and following him as if they are done or perhaps wanting to meet this unexpected visitor or poor lost soul.

How do you get lost in a condo building?

This time, Harry skips the peephole routine. Wouldn't that look suspicious? He swings the door wide.

He is greeted by two enormous human beings. Both men. Both with Schwarzenegger shoulders. Badges, guns, handcuffs, extra bullets, flashlights, nightsticks. The only things missing are hand grenades or antitank missiles you fire off your shoulder.

Amador and Bell are behind Harry. He is the meat in a four-cop sandwich.

"You guys wrapping up?" says one of the new cops.

"Yes," says Harry, turning back around to his own visitors. "Though I don't think you were asking me."

"Yes," says Amador. "As a matter of fact, we were."

The cop who has yet to speak sidesteps past the clusterfuck group hug at the threshold and welcomes himself into Harry's apartment. Amador and Bell step out into the hall. Harry holds the door open with his weight and his back and he stares at the new arrival, who takes in the living room and open kitchen. The new cop gives the walls and ceiling a once-over like a housepainter contemplating a bid. Harry wishes he had put Prokofiev on repeat. These artless cops would never know the difference. But now his condo is deathly quiet, and the new cop will have no idea of Harry's taste and sensibilities.

"Excuse me," says Harry.

The cop is halfway down the hall toward the back, some item of police paraphernalia jingling like the ghost of future jail cells.

"You got a problem with this?" says the cop.

"I think I'm supposed to ask for a warrant."

"So you do have a problem," says the cop. "Why is that?"

"I'm a procedures guy," says Harry. If they get a warrant, he'll have time. If they wave off the legality, it will be hours before they find anything worth a head scratch. But when they do . . . "And my lawyer, well. Would go apeshit."

"You have a lawyer?"

"Yes."

The lie stops the cop in his tracks.

The cop nods. "Procedures," he says. Mocking tone.

"I suppose," says Harry. The three cops in the hall gab among themselves, oblivious.

"You got some embarrassing stuff back there? Or worse?"

"I'm availing myself of my rights." Harry notes the oblong black shape clipped to the officer's chest pocket. "Your body camera isn't on."

"Son of a bitch," says the cop. "How about that?"

"A warrant," says Harry. "If you don't mind."

"Actually." The cop comes back to the door, stands close. "I do mind. If it weren't for procedures, we would have caught this son of a bitch by now."

Harry's mouth goes suddenly sandpaper. His heart flies off on its own whacky beat. He knows what he's going to do when they leave. He's going to make a list of rules. He'll call it the "Prototype Rules." Admitting your mistakes is the first step to getting better, and he needs to admit there are places he screwed up. He should not be here with this oversize cow cop in his face. He'll make a list of rules and then he'll have to figure out a way to hand it down to a worthy successor. They are out there. He knows they're out there. Someone who admires his own work and thinks they can outdo him, hit a higher number.

Harry clears his throat. Says, "I'm sure you'll catch him."

"All with the help of cooperative citizens like yourself," says the cop. "My older sister—the oldest? Oldest of five? Her coworker's sister was PDQ vic number one. Part of the reason I became a cop. People think we forget. We don't."

CHAPTER 46
WEDNESDAY

"You know how dangerous Juárez is? You ever read any Don Winslow?" Goodman leans on Flynn's waist-high office space divider. "What the hell were you doing there?"

"Working on something."

"With Tamica."

"Yes," says Flynn.

"And you can't say what it is."

"It was on my dime," says Flynn. "Does it matter?"

"So? It's not anything for us? At any point down the road? Or did you pick up a freelance gig?"

"Something like that," says Flynn. "And, to answer your question, I don't know."

"You won't need our help? Ever?"

"I didn't say that."

Flynn's computer is remembering its essential functions after days in a coma. A thick syrup of emails cascades down. The "unread" counter hits five hundred, keeps ticking. All urgent. All now! Flynn has already scanned a few on her phone. She will have to go through them all again, to make sure she didn't miss anything.

PDQ?

One long day of *nada*.

Is she in business? Does she want to be?

Has her source dried up? Moved on? Given up on her?

"I finally get you green-lighted to return, and you're in Mexico," says Goodman.

"Was I confined to quarters?"

Hadn't the exile limbo purgatory thing been enough? Was she supposed to wait at the door for the minute her punishment was lifted?

Like a wounded puppy?

Clearing the checkpoint back to American soil was a snap. On foot. They had taken an all-American Uber back to the hotel and downed two rounds of margaritas and one round of beers. Tamica passed around her audio recording, Laura Rojas as clear as NP-*fucking*-R. They had flown back on a midday flight, getting lucky with the rebooking and three open seats. Had Juárez even happened? Laura Rojas seemed, now, as if she lived on another planet. But what company in the United States did not treat its workers like lucky slaves, the same as Swintex? Flynn knows they're out there, hiding in plain sight. It would be hard to compare her own relative professional independence as a television reporter to someone who works in a maquiladora, but the station's top-down white-as-rice power dynamic would be completely familiar to Laura Rojas.

"What story?" says Goodman.

"We're not sure."

"To do with what?" says Goodman. "Generally speaking?"

"Robbie McGrath." Flynn doesn't want to linger on the specifics. "You got Snelling's jets cooled off?"

"He's not a happy camper," says Goodman. "But I told him I needed you back. I put myself on the line. And I got rewarded by finding out you had not only flown the coop, but you'd flown the whole damn farm."

Uttering "sorry" crosses her mind. Flynn can't bring herself to do it. There is something icky and overly paternal about Goodman's company line. She hates Snelling's Wizard of Oz schtick too. The little man making big pronouncements but never seen.

Her cell phone buzzes with an email alert. She ignores it.

"We're here," says Flynn. "Came as fast as the FAA and the airlines allow."

Goodman lays out her assignment. It involves interviewing a state legislator behind a bill that would ban hunting for mountain lions.

"The lawmaker is from Boulder," says Goodman. "Grab him down at the capitol and then find a hunting guide or, you know, anyone opposed. And you better jump on it; half the day is shot."

When Goodman departs, probably happy to be back in charge of Flynn's life, she glances at her phone:

> What are you doing with your photographer? Miss Black America? And with your father? You told them. I know you fucking told them.

CHAPTER 47

The senator proposing the new law wears a skinny blue tie and rumpled suit. He is vegetarian health freak scrawny and equally earnest.

Authority speaks. Authority fixes problems.

"Mountain lion hunters are only after a trophy. They're in it for the photo. You remove a dominant tom or a strong queen, you get orphaned subadults who can't fend for themselves. Disrupts the social structure. That's when you see problems with the interactions with humans."

Flynn sort-of listens. She composes replies to PDQ in her head.

For reaction to the lawmaker, she and Tamica stop at a sporting goods store and interview two guys shopping for rifles. Sharp retorts to the Boulder lawmaker and all the animal rights activists spew forth as easy as pushing a button.

Flynn writes her piece in fifteen minutes. The story is as predictable as assembling a paper doll. Tab B goes into Slot A; Tab D gets folded over and shoved into Slot C.

Tamica edits the piece in another twenty minutes. While Tamica slices and dices, Flynn writes web copy and crafts three social media posts, hits send.

Finally she replies to PDQ.

> Don't know what you saw. What you think you saw. You are jumping to conclusions. Or guessing. Am making progress.

She needs to be more observant in general—who is watching her? Following her?

A lightning reply:

> You are working with them on something.

Flynn:

> I'm always working with my photographer. And my father is one of the best reporters I know.

Reply:

> Bullshit. I know. I can smell it.

Flynn writes a lead-in for her live shot for the five o'clock show. Though she has better things to do, it's good to be back. She paces the sidewalk outside the sporting goods store and practices her stand-up. Tamica fiddles with the backpack phone and light stand.

Flynn needs to stay on Goodman's good side.

For a few weeks, at the least, she will toe the line.

"Great work," says Tamica. They stand in the covered section of the station's parking lot. Flynn offers a quick tight hug. She couldn't have made the trip to Juárez alone. She owes her father too.

"You take care of yourself," says Flynn.

"I always do," says Tamica. "Who is going to find Captain A?"

"We are," says Flynn. "And if I know my father, he's going through DPD rosters right now."

Flynn calls ahead to Max. She drives to Bear Valley listening to talk radio. Broncos ad nauseam. Flynn wonders what a city could be like if it converted all the money and passion it spends on professional sports—tickets, beer, food, parties, everything—into money and passion to support public education.

She switches to *All Things Considered* and wonders how long the show would last if it considered *all* things. Eternity times what?

She pictures Robbie McGrath meeting Laura Rojas in Sun Valley. Flynn pictures the chain of events leading to Laura Rojas and her two children sitting in a car for the long trip out of town with the stranger Carlos behind the wheel. And such a big deal that Captain A had to zip down to El Paso to watch her drive her minivan across the border, as if that made it permanent.

Flynn wonders when she'd been spotted by PDQ. How did he know she was with Tamica and her father? In Sun Valley? In Texas or Mexico? (No chance of that.) Had PDQ come back to the house?

And seen what?

Flynn calls her father, puts him on speaker.

"You sound like you're calling from Helsinki," he says.

"The first syllable is right," she says.

"Traffic?"

"Only as if every other driver in town is headed to the same place as me."

No straight road connects her part of town with the neighborhood where Max lives. The driving route is a series of byzantine jogs. No zip line. Or helicopter service. Or personal drone.

"Are you calling to crack the whip?"

"You think I'm calling to check on your progress? What kind of daughter do you think I am?"

"I think you're my daughter, and that means you're my *kind* of daughter too."

"You're saying I have no choice? That free will means nothing?"

"I'm saying we raised you right."

"You mean, with an edge."

Flynn wouldn't have it any other way.

"Call it anything you want," says Michael. "But let's talk when you fly back from Helsinki. A tin can and some string might work better."

"Wait, wait," says Flynn. "What about Captain A? Or Carlos the nonspeeder?"

"I think I heard the snapping sound of a whip. I'm calling in every favor, every source."

"You got friends in New Mexico?"

"I got friends with access to databases. The speeding ticket should turn up a last name and hometown for Carlos. As for Captain A, it could be a nickname and not a formal rank. With fifteen hundred sworns, you're always going to have the jokesters. 'Captain A' could be as meaningless as 'Captain Fantastic' or 'Captain Jack Sparrow.'"

Negotiating two more days for Wyatt to stay with Max requires all the tact she can muster. Flynn even, *gasp*, flirts. She hints, well, *maybe*. She says El Paso went well. She makes it sound like her trip was easy-breezy. Heck, all the way to carefree.

She agrees to a Budweiser, though the beer underscores her fatigue. They sit at the kitchen table, one side shoved against a wall. A small television on the counter gurgles Fox News. Based on her keen detective skills, dinner was spaghetti. Empty jar of marinara on the counter, colander in the sink, garlic hanging heavy.

Max wears a decade-old forest green T-shirt and a new pair of jeans. The jeans are crisp and dark. They hug him nicely. The omnipresent Ruger in his front pocket has not yet burned in its telltale outline, but the lump is there. She hates that Ruger, the fact that he keeps it around Wyatt. If Max is vertical, he is always carrying. In uniform, he carries two.

She mentions Max's idea of a date, then gives one of those smiles. Max gets the message.

She says that if Wyatt can stay for another two days, it would be tremendous, and three days would be gold.

She needs the time and space. And she wonders if three days is enough time for a contractor to rip out Wyatt's room and build a new one? And of course move the closet to a new location? And make it all look new and different but the same? So Wyatt will never suspect a thing?

Wyatt is right there. He sips ice water from a glass. What kid drinks *water*? He is probably getting more TV time and he probably likes being around his father for longer than a weekend. Wyatt doesn't seem to have a strong opinion one way or the other. Max has discovered another parent at Wyatt's school from Bear Valley, and Max says he might be able to call and set up a carpool trade for the runs to school.

"I saw your story on the mountain lions," says Max, surprising Flynn that he flipped the station off Fox. "Figured you were back."

Flynn chases fatigue to the corner. She says nothing.

"It was an afternoon quickie." Flynn doesn't mind the double entendre. "By the way, any progress?"

The beer tastes like college. She might choke down half. Wyatt stands. He skips down the hall. Flynn doesn't have to wonder about Max's domestic cleanliness. He is fastidious, probably more so than her. But she wonders about the number of women who have inspected the premises with an eye on the same concern. And the ones who didn't care.

"On your pal?"

"Enrique Rojas."

"Not much."

"Name of a responding officer or the investigator assigned to the case?"

"I've got those," says Max. "But we are talking no witnesses. And no physical evidence on Enrique himself. He was beaten. With a bat or something. Skull, ribs. Face."

"Beaten right there?"

"No," says Max. "Security footage from a warehouse camera about a block away shows a van coming up the alley. The van stops. Eight seconds total time it's not moving. When the van rolls on, the body is there. Rewind the footage, the body isn't there."

"License plate?"

"Can't make it out. The angle is too high."

"Make?"

"A Ford Econoline. 2002. Or three. The cargo version, you know, solid side panels. Can't tell the color because it's black-and-white footage. And it's grainy as hell. And one more thing."

"Yes."

Men drop their guards so quickly, Flynn thinks, when they think they're getting some.

"Not about Rojas. About your music. PDQ music."

"I didn't even think you were going to bother."

"Sources." Max grimaces. "I turned it into a conversation, you know."

"And?"

"Same piece each time. Classical. You ever heard of a composer named Holst? *The Planets*?"

"Me?" says Flynn. "I know Mozart, Beethoven, and is it 'Bock' or 'Botch' or 'Baaaach' like you're clearing your throat?"

"Don't know," says Max. "For PDQ, it's Holst. A piece called 'Jupiter.' On headphones. Always on headphones playing off an old-school iPod Nano."

"That's weird." The jolt flashes her chest and races down her arms.

"Yeah," says Max. "I know."

CHAPTER 48

Where the hell has she *gone*?

For a second straight night, Harry does the casual stroll thing past Flynn's house.

Lights off, porch light off.

Dead, dead, dead.

No trick timers to make a ruse out of it, nothing.

Harry doesn't buy Flynn Martin's denial.

In fact, she confirmed she was working with them—*but on something else*? She's been caught but can't admit it. Harry felt her weak grab for an explanation.

It's pure crap and it pisses him off.

Harry takes the 24 north up Josephine Street, gets off at MLK Boulevard.

He waits for the 43, listening to Brahms's Symphony No. 1 in C Minor. The guy spent twenty-one years writing it. Twenty-one! If Johannes Brahms spent more than two decades writing one piece of music, Harry can spend forty-five minutes listening to it and understanding it, appreciating its themes and textures.

Harry loves the thrilling recapitulation of the first movement, the four-bar allegretto played by the clarinet in the third movement, and the gloomy downer of the fourth movement. Nobody can listen to

Brahms's Symphony No. 1 in C Minor and not think of Beethoven's Ninth. Every time Harry hears it, all he can think of is Brahms waking up on some ordinary Tuesday in the mid-nineteenth century during those twenty-one years and thinking, *I've got an idea.*

And writing a couple of notes. A measure.

How do you know when you're done?

Seriously? How?

◆ ◆ ◆

The symphony continues to unspool as he steps off the 43. Tamica Porter's place stands midblock on California Street. You might be able to slide an envelope in the gap between the houses. All Queen Annes.

Tamica's front porch is dark. Her house has the same dead unlit look as Flynn's. He found the address on the website Whitepages. The state pays for a full-blown account. He triangulated the information with a few social media posts around her house to confirm it's hers. Coffee shops in nearby Five Points, photos in the nearby pocket park, moving-in photos that are three years old.

Harry reminds himself to be careful. Tamica is younger. She is taller than Harry. Maybe stronger. All those long bones and limbs. The lucky guys who get to stare down. The lucky guys who get it all with no bikini. Women too? Harry's got no problem with that. Men doing men, women doing women—really, whose business is it? What is it like to sleep with a beautiful Black woman? All that darkness plus one beautiful burst of pink, the prelude to a dream.

And Tamica's too-cool smile. You probably have to fight for that smile, but it would be worth it.

Harry walks three blocks toward downtown. He takes off his new headphones—*velour ear pads!* The sound is exquisite. No leakage. He keeps a mannequin head in his closet to test for leakage. These are Sennheisers. He pulls them down around his neck.

The night is damp and cool. Not much moves in Curtis Park. He takes a right and walks two blocks, circles back.

Tamica's house sits in a dark gap between two alley lights. A waist-high chain fence surrounds her postage-stamp backyard. A butterfly latch holds the back gate in place. Harry pulls his hand up under the sleeve of his coat. He flips the lever.

Two steps lead him to the covered back porch.

The back door is locked.

He peers through the door's big window. No interior lights are on, but a light from California Street, out front, lets Harry see the open main floor.

A back window doesn't budge.

Harry pulls on a pair of blue nitrile gloves. He shoves a hand under the heavy doormat. He feels along the rough wood planks. He squelches a yelp as his hand snags a splinter. The shard jabs straight through his glove like a lance. The splinter dangles from the pad of his palm, right under the pinkie. He bites the splinter with his teeth, his nose getting a full whiff of the sulfuric nitrile. He yanks the splinter out, wipes the glove on his black jeans.

He removes the glove from his uninjured hand, the right, and shoves a finger under the glove on his left hand to check for blood.

His probing digit senses no dampness, but he pulls it out and licks the tip of his index finger, waiting for the telltale taste.

Nothing.

No blood.

And no key.

The window casing? Standing on tiptoes, he reaches the top. His gloved fingertips come away gritty and dirty.

No key.

Above the doorframe? He can't reach the top. It's three inches out of reach.

A big wooden bench is too heavy to drag, but Harry finds a wire milk crate under the bench. He empties it of stiff frozen rags and an empty plastic bottle with a spray nozzle. He flips the crate over and places it on the welcome mat. It wobbles like one of those goddamn half ball balancing things touted as exercise.

He stands in a partial crouch. His knees shake. He gains stability. And reaches up.

The kitchen explodes in light.

The blast catches him flush. It may as well be a howitzer aimed at his chest, his face above the window.

Harry leaps.

The milk crate crashes against the back door with a brutal thump, Harry hoping like hell he doesn't hear the sound of breaking glass.

Harry braces against the fall. His wrist buckles. His ribs howl. He lands half on the porch. His chest and shoulders flop down the two steps. He comes up crawling. There is something really wrong with his left leg.

He hobble-runs.

His right leg drags his left.

He keeps his eye on the butterfly latch. He feels like he's been shoved off a boat a mile from shore and given a minute to swim back to a dot-size campfire. When did the yard get so big?

Harry waits for the prison camp floodlight. Maybe Tamica has guard towers manned with sharpshooters and he missed them on the way in. He hears an involuntary guttural gag from the pain or the panic. Or both.

Harry can't stand without severe pain. His leg burns.

The world slows. He could be breaststroking through a bucket of wet cement.

A blue glove extends in front of his face and it inches toward the butterfly flap on the gate. He hears a squeak as it swings toward him and he drags himself through and rolls into the darkness of the alley. He hears the back door open and a voice:

"Hey, you crackhead motherfuckers, get the hell out of here!"

CHAPTER 49
THURSDAY

"When did this happen?"

Tamica tries for composure.

Flynn hears the concern.

"An hour ago? Two? I'm just so rattled, like I've been assaulted. Sorry to call so late, I just need to hear a friendly voice."

"Are you calling the cops?"

"Around here?" says Tamica. "Full-blown burglaries you gotta wait an hour or two. I think it was kids going for the television or a laptop, and they moved a milk crate as if I keep a hidden key or something."

"You went out there?"

"The back gate was open. So, yeah, I went out there. Closed it. Shined a flashlight under the porch too. About the scariest thing I've ever done."

Flynn scolds herself for not telling Tamica that PDQ is onto their team. Their work. But how the hell would PDQ have known where she lived?

It seems impossible, but so was PDQ's awareness of the comings and goings at her house.

"I'm coming over," says Flynn.

"What?" says Tamica. "I was calling to talk to someone. Believe me, I've got all the inside locks done up right, and I put a chair against the back door by the kitchen."

"Look. I'm alone too."

"Wyatt?"

"The rest of the week, he's at Max's. Is your couch open?"

"Wait a minute," says Tamica. "You said you wanted to come out here and take a look. Okay, fine. But you're doing more than looking."

"You moved the crate?"

"Had to," says Tamica. "Practically tripped over it when I came out here."

"Where does it live?"

"Huh?"

"Where do you keep it?"

"Under the bench. Rags and stuff."

Tamica stands on the porch under a single overhead light, hands stuffed in the pockets of her purple puffer coat. "You're freaking me out."

"I don't mean to," says Flynn.

"You looking for footprints? Fingerprints? I mean, burglaries are like another city tax, right? And they or him didn't get in, so let's call it good and go in and pour a monster glass of wine and find a good documentary to watch."

Flynn waggles the flashlight beam back and forth across the walkway connecting back steps to back alley. She stares at the metal flaps holding the gate in place on either side and wonders if they might have snagged a fingerprint.

It's 3:00 a.m. The city is dead. Sleep is immaterial.

"You ever think about a padlock?" says Flynn.

"Not so much with a fence any five-year-old can vault."

"A dog?"

"On our schedule?"

"You got a point."

"What are you looking for?"

"I don't know."

"How about a glass of Shiraz to ponder it all?" says Tamica.

"I'll be right in."

The back door opens with a squawk. It closes with a clattery thump, its window rattling in the frame.

Flynn squats in Tamica's would-be yard, grass like gnarled feisty knots. The flashlight in her hand is like gripping a dry icicle. Flynn trades hands. Blows air into her frozen fist.

Flynn zaps the beam under the porch. Sad lumber, worn cinder blocks, and a scattering of loose bricks like a contractor's junk pile. She shifts to the other side of the concrete sidewalk and squats again, closer this time to the porch now since she has a rough idea of the flotsam underneath and the fact that no viper sprung at her throat. Flynn sweeps the light wide and under the steps. Her beam catches a thin dark cord. Flynn duckwalks two struts closer. She follows the cord one way, and it ends in a plug. A mini. She follows it the other way, and it connects to a pair of black headphones.

New.

Black.

High end.

Flynn helps herself to a spatula from a glass canister on Tamica's kitchen counter. She scoops the headphones with care and, back inside again, holds her trophy like a dead snake. The long cord dangles to the laces on her Nikes.

Two eyebrows at maximum elevation ask one question.

"Not mine," says Tamica. "Who doesn't go wireless these days? But those are better than the station's. Better than mine when I edit. Damn, those are *nice*. Sennheisers."

"How nice?"

"One model they sell runs about two thousand. Those people want to hear if the drummer inhales during 'Whole Lotta Love.'"

Flynn follows Tamica's instructions and locates an extra-large ziplock bag in a kitchen drawer. She tucks her prize away and closes the seal.

"What are you going to do?" says Tamica.

"With?"

"With the skull candy?"

"Skull candy?"

"The cans. The ear spray."

"Aren't we hip?"

"Well, some of us. What are you going to do?"

"See if there's anything on them."

Tamica pours out two wines, leads Flynn to the couch.

"DNA on a burglary that didn't happen? You'll get results after the first woman steps foot on Mars."

"We'll see," says Flynn.

"Connections." Tamica takes a bite out of her wine. "I better report the noncrime if you're going to turn in evidence on a nonburglary."

"That's okay."

Flynn raises her glass.

"I ain't toasting nothing until you tell me what in the absolute hell is going on," says Tamica.

"What?"

"That wasn't crackheads out there. They would have sold the damn headphones for the cash."

"What?"

"Someone knows something. You know something. Coming in here like Lady Sherlock."

Flynn gulps. Hopes it isn't visible. "I can't tell you."

The last thing Flynn wants to do is give Tamica any reason to feel the way she feels, like finding a backstreet arms dealer and buying the best Glock on the market, permit or no.

"One of those deals," says Flynn.

"Deal me in."

Tamica stares like a bored executioner.

"I can't risk telling you," says Flynn.

"Look," says Tamica. "First, if I've got prowlers and would-be intruders or rapists or something worse coming to *my* house, I better damn well know what's going on. Second, we are friends. If you don't trust me, who do you trust? You can't keep every little damn thing to yourself."

"He'll harm Wyatt," says Flynn. "He knows where my father lives. He knows where I live."

Tamica tips her head back, closes her eyes.

"Lord Almighty," she says. "I may need to start going to church. Again. It's him?"

"I'm in a dicey spot," says Flynn. "He knows everything about me."

"And one coworker, at least," says Tamica. "You know for sure this was him?"

"Yes," says Flynn. "Dead sure. And now you have to keep this to yourself. He's already pissed off."

"So the headphones are his?"

"Unless they were there before tonight and you missed them in broad daylight?"

"I wouldn't have missed those," says Tamica. "So turn 'em in. Must be dripping with DNA."

"Still doesn't find him."

"Cops could pull security footage from all over the place if he came here, to my house. What if he was on a bus tonight? Or light rail? Light rail goes right by, a few blocks away. In Five Points. They have cameras."

"Then the cops will be all over everything I'm doing." Flynn takes a glug of wine. "And some of the stuff he's led me to goes straight back to the cops. You heard about Carlos. And Captain A."

"So you're going to sit on this?"

"If I alert the cops that I'm in touch with him, do you think my boy is safe? My father? My ex?"

"Me?" says Tamica.

"He wants me to get the killing of Robbie McGrath detached from his reputation. His list," says Flynn. "I'm working on that first."

"And letting a killer roam."

"I'm not 'letting' anything. I'm taking it one step at a time. Robbie McGrath was into something, knew something. You heard Laura Rojas."

"Jesus," says Tamica. "You're making me complicit."

"You said you wanted to know," says Flynn.

"But now I don't get a choice." Tamica grabs a throw pillow, hugs it to her chest as if it might double as a bulletproof vest.

"You have a choice," says Flynn. "And if you want me to change my mind, I will. I'll go whatever direction you want to go. But if you stick with my plan for now, you have to make the same choice I'm making—at least for a few more days."

CHAPTER 50

Harry hasn't figured out what precise motion makes his chest feel as if a red-hot poker is wedged between his ribs.

He can sit for an hour without feeling it and then *wham!*

His left wrist throbs. It's puffy. A purple blotch swarms over the joint, ebbing and flowing like the bubbles in a lava lamp.

His left knee balks at weight. He can hobble, but it requires great discipline to fake a regular walk with short-short steps. He practices in his apartment, six steps in one direction. And turn.

He calls in sick. He makes it sound lighthearted. Stupid. Clumsy. He calls it what it was, "a bad tumble." "Mr. Coordinated has struck again." "As soon as I can breathe right, I'll be in." "I'll check in tomorrow, but I might be out a few days. Don't want to frighten the children with the way I look."

If he were getting medical help, his order of priority would be ribs, wrist, knee.

Has he cracked a rib? Two?

There is nothing any doctor would do for cracked ribs. Maybe they are only bruised. He cools his ribs with a gel pack. Duct tape holds it in place. He rotates two gel packs in and out of the freezer. He loses a bit of chest hair to the tape each time. The depilatory burn feels good by comparison with everything else. Maybe Mary would like to come over and yank out the rest of his hair. Maybe she keeps waxing strips.

Maybe her upright wink is shaved. Maybe she knows a way to make torture feel good.

He slept on the couch for an hour here, a few minutes there. He refilled ice bags twice during the night for his wrist.

He blames Flynn Martin for his pain. He blames her for pulling in her father and Tamica Porter—*and then lying about it!*

God only knows how he'll shower. Or dress.

It's a damn good thing the cops didn't come around when he looked like this.

And what if they come back?

How closely are they watching? Plainclothes? Undercover? What if they send a fake applicant to the department to get inside Harry's office?

The biggest problem is the headphones. He didn't notice their disappearance until he found a spot to crouch down and hide by a dumpster in an alley, waiting for the adrenaline jolt to fade. He'd dragged himself all of about a block, and when he sat down on the hard dirt, he noticed that the Sennheisers were gone. He only hopes they fell in the alley behind her house or someplace where they'll be found by a passerby. And not by Tamica Porter.

The next-biggest problem is the late-night decision to hop into a cab. It would have taken all night to "walk" all the way. Hobble. Stagger. Stumble. Totter. He was in no position to sit around and wait for a bus.

He'd seen taxis at the Warwick in the past and had set a course for Eighteenth and Grant, steeling himself for other pedestrians he encountered on the sidewalk, toughing it out to appear normal and upright.

The cabdriver was old. He had a long ponytail. He didn't say much. Harry asked for a ride to an intersection a block from his building. Harry tried to appear as normal as possible. But folding himself into the cab's back seat required blurted yelps of pain. Climbing out produced similar barks of woe. The cabbie would not soon forget the half-disabled passenger who knocked on his window near midnight outside the Warwick Hotel.

The ride lasted four minutes, tops. He paid in cash, so thankful he had enough. A ten covered the ride and a decent tip.

Fuck!

The DNA on the Sennheisers.

The cabbie.

And the mess at Tamica Porter's house.

Maybe . . .

Maybe Tamica will chalk it up to life in the city. Even though Tamica's block is in the revival mode, on the upswing with remodeling and yuppies and coffee shops and all of that, there are plenty of fearless bangers roving around, looking for stuff.

Aren't there?

◆ ◆ ◆

Harry swallows six ibuprofens, two at a time.

It's afternoon. He needs to shake off his ailments. He needs to remember to breathe as if he is sleeping in deep REM.

Bach? Will a few concertos bring him back to a grounded place? He can't bring himself to listen to music. All he can think about is Flynn, Tamica, and Flynn's father. Their collusion is a major blow. It's as bad as it gets.

The library? He has questions to look into. He might access his work databases. If he can imagine moving, he can cab it to the library. But with his injuries he will be too conspicuous. Harry scraped his left cheek too.

The thought of hobbling out of the building, trying to get around? He would be a pitiful sight.

Harry finds a sitting position on the couch that minimizes the flash points around his wounds. He puts the laptop on his thighs. First he opens a new folder in his computer. Names it "Prototype Rules." He right-clicks, scrolls to Properties, clicks the General tab, the Attributes option, checks Hidden, and then hits Apply. He takes a few moments to jot down lessons learned. He can help future others, though he'll need a way to deliver the information to the right hands. He stretches his legs across a brown square ottoman. His knee complains for a moment, then stops bitching.

To do:

Practice walking.

Find a way not to limp.

Get out the old makeup kit.

CHAPTER 51
FRIDAY

If the old lady who fell from the roof serves as an indication, Jerry Damphouse works in District 2, which covers Park Hill.
Old lady?
Sixty-eight?
Flynn scolds herself. Her father is sixty-nine. She doesn't think of him as an *old man*.
Flynn logs in to her email. She cringes at the familiar subject line.

> There is a price to pay for bringing in help. This is precisely the kind of bullshit move I told you not to pull.

And a second email, same subject line, five minutes after the first.

> What were you thinking? Download Confide. It's an app.

And the third, same subject line, one minute after the second:

The pressure is on! They are looking into the old cases. I know this for a fact.

Flynn replies: I am working hard. Making progress.
What she wants to write is: *We have your headphones.*

◆ ◆ ◆

Sometimes the local district police officers, those who don't follow rigid protocol or insist upon clearance from downtown for every public utterance, are inclined to help.

On a good day.

But reporters don't call a cop and ask for an interview. Channels are channels. Chief Wills makes all the decisions about who speaks and what is said. PR dude Dwight Hatcher preps the interview subjects once the green light is given. Every risky line of questioning draws an analysis, no matter how innocuous the questions might appear on the surface.

It wouldn't hurt to reconfirm Jerry Damphouse's assigned district. Flynn calls District 2 and asks for Officer Damphouse.

Whoever answers says she'll check the schedule and puts her on hold.

Flynn hangs up.

◆ ◆ ◆

"Now what?"

Goodman leans over her partition.

"You tell me," says Flynn. "I have plenty of stuff to check."

Start with the cop? Or start with the daughter of the woman who died? With the loose ends waiting to come through on Enrique Rojas, she needs to pick up the other lead from Robbie McGrath's notes, certain as ever she will be shoving her hand down into another bucket of spiders.

"Still on El Paso? This big tip?"

"The tip, yeah." She'd slept at Tamica's for the second night in a row. She wasn't sure Tamica had settled down. Flynn had showered and changed at home and made it to work well before the morning meeting, like the apple-polisher she is not. "There's a woman I need to find. It fits into all of this."

"Feeling solid about it?"

"I'm not feeling solid about anything," says Flynn.

Flynn pulls up the notes and the file on the Margaret Stack story from iNews, the internal system her station uses for content creation and story workflow among reporters and producers. The iNews system amounts to group notes, group writing. Chris Casey did the original story of Margaret Stack's last day. Casey included her daughter's phone and address in the notes file. The bad news is that Margaret's daughter Barbara lives in Golden, a half-hour haul to the west.

"Flynn Martin?" says Barbara. "Been watching you for years. I am so sorry about what happened to you at the . . . at the, you know."

"Thank you," says Flynn.

"How did this come around to you?"

"Long story," says Flynn. "I'd like to see if there's a time I might come out to Golden and we can chat about everything."

"What 'everything'?"

"I'm following up on how the police handled the call."

"Glad to talk," says Barbara. "But I'm not in Golden. I moved back to the city, to Park Hill. My mom's house. It's been in the family for decades."

A break, thinks Flynn. *A gift.*

Her karma might be improving.

Flynn meets Tamica in the station parking lot. The plan is to ride together.

"I'll catch up," says Flynn. "The story will write itself."

"What have you got?"

"The daughter of the woman who fell off her roof," says Flynn. "It's on the way, and then I'll shoot over to Swansea."

"We're already late."

Their assignment, because Goodman wants Flynn to know the beast needs feeding, and that Flynn's issues are secondary, is to cover the protests by residents of the Swansea and Globeville neighborhoods, who believe their neighborhoods have been neglected and exposed to bad air and groundwater pollution. The protest is on behalf of hundreds of homeowners and activists battling a steamroller of progress with a capital *P*.

Power.

Profits.

"Those things never start on time."

"You have to put in an appearance," says Tamica. "Goodman will know."

"I'll get there," says Flynn.

The Stack address is on Forest Parkway, reserved for Park Hill royalty. The house is a broad-shouldered brick beauty. Three fat fairy-tale dormers jut from the high-sloped roof. The front porch looks big enough to sip summer cocktails with a hundred of your closest friends.

Barbara Stack is midforties and trim. All business. Short brown hair, outdoorsy skin, and a necklace with gold geometric tassels. She wears a loose-fitting chestnut pullover with an open neck. Her black jeans look brand new.

Flynn goes through the pleasantries, offers sympathy, and follows Barbara around back, to where her mother fell. The tulip bed is mulchy and fallow in its January garb.

Back inside, they sit on wicker bar chairs at a kitchen counter. Flynn has a good view out over the parkway, framed by the massive porch. She feels time ticking, declines the offer of coffee. Barbara Stack drinks from a Denver Broncos mug.

Really? Is there no escaping . . . ?

"Did you call Robbie McGrath, or did she call you?"

"I called."

"Why?"

"Because no ordinary burglar would have found what these idiots found."

"What do you mean?"

"The crackheads got my mother's laptop. They swiped my mother's Canon—she loved taking pictures of flowers, had a whole Pinterest community. They cleaned out her jewelry, took her iPhone, loose cash from the kitchen. She always had a few twenties lying around. Oh, and pills. Painkillers for her arthritis."

"But," says Flynn.

There is a price to pay for bringing in help.

Flynn shudders. Is she in the right place? Doing the right things? Asking the right questions? This all seems so disconnected.

"But I don't think druggie knuckleheads would have had time to rummage through the desk in her study where she kept, hidden away, a few thousand dollars in cash for emergencies. It's gone. She had another hiding spot upstairs. In her shoe closet. Cleaned out."

"Locks in either spot?"

"No," says Barbara. "They were hiding spots, that's all. One stash behind files in a desk drawer and the other behind her socks and nylons in a small chest."

"And how much upstairs, would you say?"

"At least ten thousand," says Barbara. "I scolded her about keeping it there. But she didn't trust ATMs and didn't like to stand in line at the bank."

"She lived alone?"

"My father died three years ago. But my mother was feisty and fit, and that's probably why she felt she could climb out on the roof."

"Other kids?"

"What do you mean?"

"I mean, do you have other brothers and sisters who would have known about these hiding spots and who were here in the days after she fell? And who would have swiped the cash?"

"I'm an only child," says Barbara.

"So what do you think happened?"

"My mother calls 911. The cop gets here. That's Jerry Damphouse. He finds the house is empty. Does some checking outside, finds her body, and then realizes he's alone."

"Do you know for a fact he was here alone?"

"I pulled his report."

"And?"

"My mother called 911 at 11:15 a.m. She's upstairs when she hears the break-in. She's whispering on the call. I haven't listened to the tape, can't bring myself."

Barbara Stack steels herself. Her voice catches. She fists her breastbone.

"Officer Damphouse arrives at 11:23. In his report, he said he did a quick check of the perimeter, the outside, and didn't see anyone or, at first, find my mom. Hard to believe if his eyes were open at all. Anyway, he has reason to go inside when there's no answer at the door. Threat to life or safety—he doesn't need a warrant. That's all fine. But he doesn't call to report finding her body until 11:50. That's a long, long time to sniff around."

"Any security cameras?"

"Not us," says Barbara. "Footage from a house across the street shows his squad car arriving. Twice you can see his legs moving back and forth outside. Then the other cops show up and the emergency vehicles, et cetera."

"Nothing on the burglars?"

"They came in through the back. Broad daylight. Back door jimmied. They must have thought the house was empty."

"I don't mean to come across as skeptical," says Flynn, "but you're sure there was money in that drawer and in the closet?"

"Milk in the fridge, fresh Jamaican coffee beans in the canister, and piles of cash in those two spots," says Barbara. "My mother would go to the store and buy three tomatoes, take a hundred dollars out as cash back, add it to her stash. She thought we should be doing more doomsday prep, that sort of thing. Halfhearted about it, though. There's a pantry full of soup and canned food in the basement, but that's as far as she got."

"And you told Robbie McGrath all of this too?"

"Right where you are sitting now."

"And she was interested?"

"Very."

And why the heck didn't Robbie publish anything?

The link Flynn needs is between Officer Jerry Damphouse and Sun Valley errand boy Enrique Rojas.

Cop alive, errand boy dead . . .

Robbie dead . . .

"The burglary was mid-April, right?"

"April fifteenth. As if tax day wasn't bad enough to begin with." Barbara pushes back tears. She slumps her head into her hand. "You know, it took some time for me to even recognize everything that the burglars had taken. The obvious things. A day later, I got in a panic about all that cash and couldn't believe when I found it was gone."

"Did you call the cops first, to add the cash to the list of stolen items?"

"Yes," says Barbara. "And I got the equivalent of a big yawn. The detective assigned to the case didn't care at all."

"And the burglars?"

"They never found them. None of the items turned up."

"So how long until you called Robbie McGrath?"

"Maybe two weeks after things settled down."

"So all this happened, talking to Robbie, before the end of the month?"

"Probably by the first week of May," says Barbara. "Or even mid-May by the time she came over to chat and I could show her around. I have it in my calendar."

"Did you hear from her again?"

"Off and on. She would call and let me know that work was progressing. Said she was looking for others with similar complaints."

"And when was the last time you heard from her?"

Barbara takes a moment. "I'd say mid-November. She said she was asking me questions from her draft article, the fact-checking step. She was thorough, I must say. I remember her saying she was going to ruin a whole bunch of Thanksgiving dinners, but the timing couldn't be helped."

"She was ready to publish?"

"That's what she said."

"With your quotes?"

"I wasn't thrilled about hanging my name out there, but yes."

"So you'd give this all to me on camera too?"

Barbara tips her head back, stares at the ceiling. Comes back. "Part of me was a bit relieved. You know, grateful that I wasn't out there in public pointing fingers. But it bugs me. And that was a lot of money. So, yes."

"And what did you think when you heard Robbie McGrath had been murdered?"

"I did what everyone else did," says Barbara. "I checked all the locks on every window and door in this house. That fear came rushing right back, the kind that makes you wonder about every single person you see. Aren't we all counting down now? Another eighteen months, right?"

CHAPTER 52

The microphone is a useless prop. Flynn holds it while the neighborhood activist, a tall Hispanic woman, runs through her talking points. Flynn asks three questions. She missed the main event, but this one-on-one will establish her presence. It's good cover.

It isn't a bad story. A broad swath of poor neighborhoods has taken it on the chin. Zip codes are predictors of health outcomes.

Always.

Tamica shoots a series of neighborhood streetscapes—kids on swings at the local elementary school, a mother washing her front window from the inside, a UPS driver delivering a stack of boxes, a trash truck making the rounds. They stop an older man walking the street and ask for his opinion, but he waves them off, even when Tamica breaks out the Spanish.

Flynn feels eager, anxious, touchy, and nauseous all at the same time.

There is a price to pay for bringing in help.

Flynn follows Tamica to City Hall. They interview the mayor's spokesman outside on the east steps. Flynn writes a four-sentence stand-up on the drive back to Globeville for the live shot. Why is it always the poor neighborhoods that get kicked around?

"Making progress?" says Tamica.

"Something's not adding up."

"Let me know when it starts to compute, because I look forward to sleeping again."

Tamica hunts for a good location that will put the downtown skyscrapers over Flynn's shoulder for the stand-up. Flynn thinks about suggesting no live shot. The anchor can cue the tape. But the station loves live shots no matter how thin the excuse. "Live to be live" is the mantra. Flynn calls her father, offers CliffsNotes version of her conversation with Barbara Stack.

"I don't understand why Robbie McGrath didn't do anything with the story," says Flynn.

"Being thorough," says her father. "She had the luxury of time."

"But it wasn't that complicated. Or intricate."

"Maybe she wanted to see if there was a pattern. One of the worst police corruption rings in the country was right here, back in 1961. Forty-seven cops busted. All involved in a burglary ring. Lining their own pockets, covering it up. National shame. International headlines."

"In that case, Officer Jerry Damphouse should thank his lucky stars," says Flynn. "But how is Jerry Damphouse connected to Enrique Rojas?"

"Do they have to be?"

"Feels like there must be something."

"Will Barbara Stack go on record?"

"Reluctantly," says Flynn. "But she'll do it."

"Then maybe Officer Damphouse will give you the same squirmy look of panic he gave Robbie McGrath. And then you'll know."

Tamica gives a ready sign, two thumbs up.

"Walk in Robbie's footsteps?"

"Not all the way," says her father. "I can't even believe I'm suggesting this. Don't go alone. I mean, McGrath was a lone wolf. And now that I'm thinking of it, you should stay with me or a friend until all this blows over."

"You're scaring me," says Flynn.

"I scare myself," says her father. "One more thing."

"Sure," says Flynn.

"I found Carlos."

"Laura's slow-driving chauffeur?"

"Carlos Herrera. A $250 ticket for reckless driving. I got his address."

"How the hell?"

"I have a new reporter pal in Albuquerque. And I owe him. Big time."

"And?"

"Carlos is a Denver guy."

"Not too surprised about that. Can you text it to me?"

"Sure."

"Gotta go."

"Be careful."

"Okay," says Flynn. "Except if I'm not."

The text comes through while Tamica tweaks the angle on her shot.

The address has a recognizable vibe to it.

Bear Valley.

Where all the good cops live . . .

CHAPTER 53

What it comes down to is soreness.

The painkillers help dull the various stings. After the ibuprofen, he dips into his stash of oxy, a rare treat like a candy bar.

He can, in fact, mimic a normal-looking walk. Maybe not his normal walk. An observer might think he has a corncob shoved up his ass, but he can walk. Part of it is mind over matter, remembering not to cough (so painful). The oxy like magic. The drug reduces his breathing, chills him out.

Harry finds a dark wig, hair an inch over the ears. He finds a pair of eyeglasses, geek-style round John Lennons with a heavy frame and a gray tint. He digs out an old pair of brown chinos, so glad he's maintained discipline around the care and feeding of his nontoned figure. Maybe he is plus ten pounds. Age, hell. Soft in the middle. He is sure there are months off and on where he's been plus ten. A few weeks of vegetables and protein always cure the blob.

He digs out a pair of shoes he can afford to toss, a pair of brown loafers with a monk strap. They are well worn, which will help with the image he desires. Plain, dark-blue sweater and a gray jacket from the back of his closet. The jacket doesn't offer much warmth, but it will have to do.

He hasn't thought any of this would be necessary. Going to all this trouble is due to Flynn's wrong, wrong choice to bring in help. Harry doesn't care what she claims.

He knows.

He will take off the wig and glasses for the trip from his condo and down the elevator and out the door. He will find a dark spot in Cheesman Park to slip them back on.

He grabs a clipboard and a copy of his survey about climate change, so generic it doesn't matter. At the last minute, he recalls the yellow rectangular ID, laminated and pretty, and the blue lanyard from which it dangles.

Harry practices his walk one more time, floating a bit now on the oxy.

It's been a long time since he's donned the ever-popular door-to-door pollster nerd ensemble.

CHAPTER 54

District 2 headquarters sits a few blocks from I-70. The building is surrounded by warehouses and industrial buildings except for a vacant lot to the south. Diagonally across the street, white cabs half fill a lot at the Metro Taxi headquarters, rooftops like shiny cobblestones in the fading dusk.

Flynn parks in a visitor spot at the station, glad she isn't driving a company truck. There is no need to sound alarms.

As she steps out of her car, Flynn is greeted by a familiar, resinous odor. Flynn wonders what it's like for a veteran cop to get a whiff of a thriving marijuana grow and know the old reflexes no longer serve any purpose.

◆ ◆ ◆

The police building is brick and glass with a giant gray slab of steel thrust down the center like an architectural hatchet.

The entryway is sleek. And cold.

The receptionist wears a crisp uniform, fresh out of the box. Her hair is pulled back in a short blond ponytail. She might be old enough to have second teeth. Her tag reads MORRISON. She fluffs the welcome mat the same way she would for a suicide bomber.

"You look familiar."

"Flynn Martin. I'm a reporter."

"And you want to speak to Officer Damphouse because?"

"A detail from a story I'm working on."

"Did you clear it with downtown?"

Good god, how were questions even answered before they invented *channels*?

"You know, it's the fastest kind of question," says Flynn. "I mean quick."

Morrison studies her again with the terrorist once-over.

"You know the media relations office, I'm sure, Miss Martin?"

"I mean, it's not even something I need a quote on or anything; it's fact-checking. Like I said . . ."

Flynn snaps her fingers.

Morrison stares at her computer. Flynn hears a few clicks and steps back, gifting space. And patience. The combo works.

Flynn texts Tamica: **Progress.**

Flynn texts her father: **In his tracks now.**

She checks X, Facebook, and her station's website. Instagram.

Flynn hears a voice coming from the bottom of the Grand Canyon. "Excuse me? Miss Martin?"

Flynn looks up. She'd floated off in a dark fog, the perfect place to appear nonthreatening.

"Yes?" she says.

"Officer Damphouse will be here in five minutes."

Flynn texts her father. Her thumbs work about as well as if they were covered in fat wads of duct tape. It takes her three tries to get three words right.

I'm going in.

Hits send.

CHAPTER 55

"Is your mom or dad home?"

The kid looks a bit worried.

"I need an adult." Harry pulls out the ID, offers a cursory glance. "I'm doing some polling on issues about the environment. You know, climate change. But that's okay."

Harry turns as if he will happily skip along to the next house. *No matter.*

"She's not here. She will be back later."

The kid's words are clean and precise. His speech pattern is adorable.

"Later?" says Harry.

The kid shrugs. "Yes." Clean. Emphasis on the *sss*.

"I am going up this block and back around and almost done for the day." Harry tucks the clipboard in tight to his chest. "Getting dark and all, so—"

"Come back later," says the kid.

"Do you happen to know her views on climate change?"

"Yes."

"I mean, these only take a minute." Harry thumps the clipboard.

The kid steps out on the porch, pulls the door tight behind him.

"Well, more than a *minute*," says Harry. "We'd probably need to go inside."

"Against the rules." The kid reports this as easily as he might say the time.

"Of course," says Harry. "Well, it's getting a bit dim out here and I don't see like I used to."

"My mom knows about climate change," says the kid, sire of all that ripe laundry. "She's a reporter and she talks to all the scientists."

"Oh, really?"

Harry riffles through the pack of sheets in his clipboard. He drops his pen like a klutz, bends to pick it up, and shoves loose with his thumb a photograph of a sad polar bear marooned on an ice floe no bigger than a canoe.

It's the most pathetic he could find. Printed off on a regular sheet of paper, it flutters to the wood floor of the porch like a cartoon leaf floating to earth in a Disney flick. It lands face up. The kid squats down and studies the shot, reaches to grab it.

"What about polar bears?" says Harry.

The kid looks around, like someone might be watching. "I'm the one who knows about polar bears."

CHAPTER 56

Officer Damphouse looks as if he's come from a funeral. One cheek puffs out more than the other. His eyes are sunken and twinkle-proof. He comes through the swinging gate to the civilian side of life.

"You've checked with downtown?" No introductions. No handshake. No half smile. No black coffee. "You know the drill."

"Do you know what I'm here about?"

"Not a clue."

"Did you talk to another reporter recently?"

"What does it matter?"

"I'm putting a few pieces together."

"You know there's a formal process for media requests."

Is his body cam on?

What if?

"It's about Robbie McGrath."

"Even more so."

Damphouse keeps his voice at an even keel.

"What did you two talk about?"

There is a price to pay for bringing in help. What the hell?

"I've been here a long time," says Damphouse. "I paid my dues long enough to earn a spot as technician, then corporal, then sergeant. I took the sergeant test three times before I passed. Took the lieutenant exam twice and bombed, far as I know. The point is, I tried. That was all five years ago. Now I keep my head down. I do what I'm asked. I hope I don't catch a bullet from some druggie skinhead or get in a wreck chasing a drunken speeder."

Flynn says nothing.

"I'm not doing anything now to put my family, my career, or myself in jeopardy when I'm this close. *Soooo* close."

"Then what did you tell Robbie McGrath? I know you walked away from an interview."

"Right. And told her nothing."

"Except then she went from talking to you to getting involved with the story about a guy who got murdered, Enrique Rojas."

"And so?" says Damphouse.

"Enrique Rojas appears to be a nobody, but he had some sort of a connection with the police."

"You've lost me," says Damphouse. "Take your questions downtown."

"So you know who I'm talking about."

Flynn doesn't want to mention about Laura Rojas being ushered back to the border along with a big fat virtual piggy bank stuffed to the snout with large bills.

"I thought I told you, there's nothing in this conversation for me. Nothing."

"I have Barbara Stack on the record. There's a long gap of time between when you arrived at her mother's house, responding to the call on a burglar, and when you called for backup."

Damphouse looks stunned. "Another case of amateurs playing cops."

"What did you tell Robbie McGrath? How did you convince her that you weren't to blame for the cash being cleaned out of the spots where no ordinary burglar would look?"

"Do you know how ridiculous that sounds?" says Damphouse.

"She's on the record. I've seen the spots. You'd needed time to dig around." The more pissed off the look on his face, the more emboldened Flynn feels. "I am doing a story."

"With what?"

"With what she told me. And the fact that it was one of Robbie's last stories. Next to last, in fact."

Damphouse hitches up his belt. Steps back. "Why are reporters always trying to solve the world?"

"Excuse me?" says Flynn.

Officer Damphouse inches back to the gate, back to safety.

"Solve the world?" says Flynn.

"You know what I mean."

"We don't try to *solve* the world." She doesn't raise her voice. She doesn't need MORRISON to get alarmed. "We ask questions, and then let the answers take us where they lead. Sometimes the answers aren't right, though, and the next thing you know, people start lying. Or hiding. Or both. Or worse."

Damphouse raises a hand to say *enough*.

"And sometimes people tell us things, and they sound reasonable. If something screwy is going on, we check it out and that's it. We're in it for the same reason you guys are—to make the city a better place."

Now both hands are up, as if backing away from a crazy lady.

Is he?

"So we ask a few questions. And I happen to think you've got a few answers. You're playing the odds, hoping you can skate through. In the meantime, how many more people are going to die? You're the dead end. The *dead* dead end. The next time PDQ goes to work, go ahead and pat yourself on the back and take some credit for the fact that he's out there and rolling along. I'm running with what Barbara Stack told me, and I've got it all on tape. So you can decide how you want to handle your end when I put in a formal request for a formal interview through formal channels, and then you can explain your formal, careful approach to investigating burglaries and how you could have missed the mother's body in the flower bed for half an hour."

Flynn turns and heads out.

She texts her father: **Butthole kicked. He is not happy.**

Her thumbs are working better.

The reply is quick: a smiley face.

CHAPTER 57

Flynn heads to her father's place, south on York Street past City Park.

And then decides to call instead.

"Don't wait up," says Flynn. On Bluetooth. In her head, she plots a route west on Thirteenth Avenue and then maybe Santa Fe to Hampden and west again. The streets are open. Rush hour has stopped rushing. Lights click green to whisk her along.

"Sounds like you got his attention."

"For sure," says Flynn.

"You're not going down there tonight."

"Where?"

"To knock on the door of Carlos Herrera."

"Maybe," says Flynn. "Or maybe I'm going to Bear Valley to visit my men."

"Wyatt's with Max?"

"Yeah, Max has been a huge help. Can't begin to tell you."

"You need a plan for Carlos."

That's the tricky part. Having kicked one cop's shin, should she whack another's? What if she watches Carlos's front door all night to monitor comings and goings? Jot down license plates? Snap telephotos? That is, if she had a telephoto lens and a camera and knew how to use them.

"Lack of a plan didn't hurt us in Juárez."

"I'd wait for daylight."

"My daylight hours belong to the station—that's the problem."

"If you catch him on the job somewhere, you might run into his pals. Say, Captain A."

"Don't wait up."

"Flynn. C'mon."

"Don't worry. I'll be back soon."

At a stoplight, she finds the number for the newspaper, dials it, and asks for Charlotte Laswell.

"You mean Charlie."

"Yes, Charlie." Flynn's speedometer hits sixty-five on Santa Fe South. The streets are so open she could be leading a presidential motorcade.

"May I tell her who's calling?"

"It's a friend. We're supposed to meet for drinks. I hope she hasn't left yet."

Flynn hears nothing, then a cautious voice: "This is Charlie. Who is this?"

"It's Flynn Martin."

"Oh hi," says Charlie.

"Favor time," says Flynn.

"Fire away."

"I'm wondering if you can go into Robbie's files and pull a copy of a story she was writing?"

"Log-in?"

"I've got her password," says Flynn. "Remember? Withers gave it to me."

"I'd need to check. You know, with Withers or someone."

"I'm looking for one story. I can almost tell you what it says. I'm trying to confirm that she wrote it up."

"I thought you looked in her computer."

"We did," says Flynn. "I feel like we missed something, and I also feel like Robbie must have known how to hide what she was working on. Do you know how to find hidden folders?"

"Hidden folders?"

"Look, I can't give you step by step from memory. I'm driving. But google it. 'Find hidden folders.' Something to do with the View tab and the Search options. I have a hunch she was secretive, wary. You know?"

"I'm pretty new here."

"I'll owe you a favor." Like father . . . "In fact, I'm close to finishing a big story, and what if I called you back about an hour before it airs and I'll give you the heads-up? It could make your name. Might be next week, the week after."

"Four hours." Charlie cuts her off—a tough negotiator.

"Two," says Flynn. "And you can't put anything online until my piece runs."

"How *big* a story?" says Charlie.

"The whole city will stop," says Flynn. "Is that big enough?"

"What was Robbie's password?"

"Takedown123."

CHAPTER 58

"It doesn't seem as if your mom is coming home."

"Well," says the kid. He sets his jaw. Thinks. "Depends on where she ends up. If she is doing a story in Boulder or Colorado Springs, I know she'll be late. Well, *later*."

They are friends now. Harry leans against the kitchen counter. The kid's survey answers show a more liberal bent than Greenpeace and Environmental Defense Fund combined.

"I want to show you a poster display I did about Antarctica," says the kid. "The rate of icebergs calving."

He bounds upstairs in a flash.

The kid's phone sits on the kitchen counter, screen full of peppy icons.

Unlocked . . .

Harry knows he should be going.

Harry wants to leave a mark, a message, a "Tip for Flynn." He wants to scare the living crap out of her.

He wants to make sure she knows he's gotten inside her house again, face to face with her son. It would be so easy, say, to leave him lashed to his bed.

The screams, though. He's unprepared.

Harry is high and woozy from the oxy. He has that fizzy loose sensation of not being able to focus. Struggling with the kid, especially in his wounded state? It takes all his concentration to move in normal fashion, let alone think about an attack.

The kid might be quick.

Or?

CHAPTER 59

At the long light along Hampden at River Point, Flynn types the Herrera address into her phone's map, clicks Directions.

A blue line shoots west. Flynn's stoplight flips green. She glances at the route. The line doubles back on itself, then snakes into a neighborhood south of Bear Creek.

Five minutes away.

Her phone pings with a fresh email.

Flynn glances and drives.

The sender, "Laswell, Charlie."

Subject line: "Here It Is."

The map's cobalt line tugs her west.

Flynn cedes power to the blue dot.

The poor woman had no choice . . . the dot kept taking her!

A green light at Knox Court says, "This way, please."

Didn't Walt Whitman say something about contradictions?

Do I contradict myself?

Very well, then.

It won't hurt to drive to Carlos Herrera's address.

She doesn't have to *do* anything.

The blue line turns north at Wadsworth. The blue dot follows. The line reverses course at the first intersection, and she doubles back to the east on the frontage road, headlights glaring at her from Hampden.

The line heads north at South Ivan Court and then hangs a right down West Floyd Avenue.

Flynn remembers doing a story around here years ago, a search for a missing boy along Bear Creek. The neighborhood is a tight klatch of housing on the city's southwestern edge. The area has a closed-off, smashed-in feeling between the highway and the creek. The street is narrow, parked cars on both sides eating up a portion of the middle. She is glad not to encounter any oncoming tanks.

West Floyd Avenue ends in a cul-de-sac. Flynn pulls to the center of the asphalt circle. Cars line the circumference, no room for a visitor. The blue destination marker announces the finish line somewhere in the thick of a town house complex. Her high beams catch the tan clapboard siding of a two-story building.

Where to park?

She glances in her rearview, thinks about driving back out of this tight spot. A pair of headlights sits frozen in the middle of the street, a block back.

Doesn't move.

The lights stare.

Flynn begins a three-point turn, and on the second tack, in reverse, she glances back. The headlights diminish in a hustle-ass retreat. Her Malibu comes around and she jumps on the accelerator, but not in time to catch her stalker, her mind already racing back across town to District 2 and Officer Jerry Damphouse.

Really?

She's drawn a tail?

Late as always, her heart recognizes the panic and pounds out a fresh rhythm. Her armpits tingle with a stab of sweat.

Flynn comes out to the end of West Floyd Avenue, stops. Her tail has gone *poof* in the night. The driver has skills, that much is clear.

Flynn finds a spot and parks. She opens Charlie Laswell's email. Her hands do that shaky-wobbly thing.

The writing is rough in spots, but all there. Robbie McGrath was known for her clipped, blunt sentences—fact after dry, dry fact. Robbie McGrath left herself a few blank spots filled with question marks. Here and there, a "check this!!" Robbie McGrath had Jerry Damphouse dead to rights. It looks like page one material as far as Flynn Martin is concerned, including Jerry Damphouse's lame denials. But there is no mention of Enrique Rojas or Laura Rojas or Ciudad Juárez. She feels like she's constantly hopping from a boat going one direction to a train going the other.

Flynn stands outside her car in the cool night air. She tips her head back to the dull beams of the citified stars and wonders what the hell she's getting herself into.

CHAPTER 60

Flynn leans on the doorbell and steps back.
Nothing.
She knocks with authority.
And waits. Looks around. Waits.
The door opens with no prequel clattering from the inside, as if he's been standing on the opposite side all along.
"Yes?" He stands back from the door.
"Carlos Herrera?"
"And you are?"
"My name is Flynn Martin."
A light goes off, but it takes its sweet time.
"The reporter."
"You are Carlos Herrera? Officer Herrera?"
"You were the one at the convenience store," he says.
Carlos Herrera is five nine and slight. He has dark eyebrows and slick, short hair. He's wearing a tight blue windbreaker and gray shorts, like a boxer taking a break from the ring.
"True enough." She wants to set an example around honesty. "A sad day for sure. And you are Carlos Herrera?"
Herrera starts to close the door. "Go through downtown," he says. "You know."
"Can I ask you about New Mexico?"

Herrera tries on a puzzled face, but he didn't major in theater. "About *what*?"

"A town called Vaughn, New Mexico."

"I have no idea."

"So I can ask downtown about your trip to Texas? To the border? They can explain it to me?"

Herrera processes his options. "I don't know what you're talking about."

Other than slamming the door like a bad cliché, this claim is the weakest reply at Herrera's disposal.

"Chauffeur business as sideline work?" Flynn has half a notion to look around, see if her tail has resurfaced. She tries not to sound threatening. Or cocksure. "You escorted the wife of Enrique Rojas to the border, with her kids."

"My off-duty time," says Herrera, "is my own."

"True," says Flynn.

"You're married to a cop," says Herrera.

"Was." Cheering erupts from a television inside. Coincidence? "You seem to know a lot about me."

"So you know about our pay."

"Yes, but—"

"This is all none of your business," says Herrera. "And last time I checked, there is no law about taking a weekend drive."

"Who asked you to make the drive?" says Flynn. "Who paid you?"

"Who says I got paid?"

"You were the one who brought up money," says Flynn. "So you did drive her down there?"

"I don't see where you're going with this," says Herrera. "But it was my time. End of story."

"Not quite," says Flynn. "Wives of murder victims don't usually receive such personal attention; do you know what I mean? Do you have a rough idea of how it looks?"

"You'll need to leave," says Herrera.

Flynn recognizes his look, along the lines of *holy fuck*.

She has what she needs, except for an affirmative acknowledgment that he made the trip to Juárez.

"I can tell the whole town about this new service being provided by off-duty police officers," says Flynn. "Is there a number folks can call if they feel like they are in danger and want a safe ride out of town?"

"Jesus," says Herrera.

"Tell me who you were working for," says Flynn, "and maybe I'll keep your name out of it."

"I haven't told you a thing."

"Tell me about Captain A."

Herrera says nothing.

"I will be coming back with a camera. We have copies of your ticket in Vaughn. In New Mexico. We know you were there, and we know where you were heading because I've been to Juárez and I've talked to Laura Rojas. She confirmed you were there. And you confirmed you were there—"

"I confirmed nothing."

"As a matter of fact."

The door closes in her face.

CHAPTER 61

Flynn's Malibu sits like a quirky lowrider with tricked-up hydraulics, so low on one side it almost scrapes the street.

If her tires are clocks, the matching set of four knife gashes are at high noon. Illuminated by her phone's flashlight, the gashes are two inches wide—no simple pocketknife.

Flynn calls AAA first, Max second. She starts her undriveable car for warmth. She figures she is being watched, if not by the tire-slasher and stalker dude with the headlights, then by the big camera in the sky.

Max shows up first, perfunctory hug as greeting.

"Lucky me," says Flynn.

"What were you doing here?"

Max's F-150 idles, blocking the tight street.

"An interview. Chasing down a lead, I guess you'd call it."

"Did Tamica leave?" says Max.

"She wasn't here," says Flynn. "And I didn't need a camera."

"That same story?"

"Yes, that one."

"El Paso, et cetera?"

"Yes." Max doesn't press for details. Yet.

The guy from AAA wiggles her Malibu from its parking spot, rolls it up on a flatbed tow truck, and gives her the address where it's heading. The tire shop, a few blocks south on Federal, opens early.

She'll be back in business by midmorning.
Unless her tail has a stronger message in mind.

◆ ◆ ◆

"I can call you an Uber," says Max.

They wait at a light at Sheridan Boulevard, halfway back to Max's house on the five-minute ride.

"My car is all the way down here," says Flynn. "Can I spend the night? Rather than having to come all the way back?"

"Wyatt," says Max.

"Wyatt what?" says Flynn.

"I dropped him at your place. Two hours ago. Like we agreed. I mean, he'll be okay for an hour or two, but—"

"What?"

Her mind races over an earlier text exchange with Max. She doesn't need to double-check it. She screwed up. Again.

Flynn hits Wyatt's number on speed dial. Her heart races across town. She pictures Wyatt in his room, alone.

Waiting.

Wondering.

"Goes straight to voicemail," says Flynn. "Weird."

"He's fine—"

"I'm trying again."

How had she lost track of the days? Of the plan? She'd gone right past her house two hours ago.

Her phone chimes with a Confide message:

Are you doing anything? Anything at all? Or are you out fucking around? You had your father and Tamica with you in Mexico! And yet you have the sheer gall to claim you were working alone!

"Who was that?" says Max.
"Work stuff," says Flynn.

What the hell do you have to say for yourself?

"Pushy," says Max.
"It's okay." They're parked outside Max's house. "I'm dialing again."
Flynn's phone chimes again. She fights the urge to glance at it.
"Voicemail again," says Flynn. "He doesn't even talk on the phone all that much unless it's you or me. It's all text and messages."
"Somebody is after you," says Max.
"I need to go home," says Flynn.
"Now?"
"Yes."
"He's probably switched his phone off. Or left it in another room."
Flynn decides she can give one calm answer. She can't guarantee a semblance of sanity for answers number two, three, or twenty. "He never turns his phone off. And he never forgets where it is."
"We can try again in ten minutes."
"And I'll keep trying," says Flynn, "all the way back."
"Now?"
Flynn glances at the latest:

You are worthless to me. But, as you know, I know where you live.

She hits redial on Wyatt's number.
"Hi, this is Wyatt, leave a message . . ."

CHAPTER 62

Max drives with a bit of mustard.

Flynn hits redial, hits redial, hits redial . . .

Halfway back, Max worms his way into the silence. "I don't get the full-on alarm here."

Flynn wipes a tear in the dark.

◆ ◆ ◆

Max stops in front of her house. The dread in Flynn's gut matches the sensation in her head.

She unlocks the front door, steps inside her own goddamn house like she is the late-night burglar. Her heart lets her know it does not approve.

Kitchen light, on.

Front hallway light, on.

TV room light, on.

The back door is locked, but Flynn steps outside for a moment to study the yard and stare at the garage.

All dark.

Upstairs, dark. Flynn whacks every light switch, checks every room. Closet doors fly open with ferocity. "Wyatt?" She hears the crack of fear in her voice.

From Wyatt's bedroom window, she spots Max by the door to the garage. The interior light of the garage flashes on, flashes off.

Back downstairs, no note, no message.

No Wyatt.

Out front on the porch and then sidewalk, looking up and down.

Out back in the yard for a more careful walk-around and then the alley, looking up and down.

◆ ◆ ◆

"Did you come in with him?" says Flynn.

"What difference does that make?" says Max.

"Did you?"

"I watched him unlock the door from the street, saw him go inside. He waved goodbye. Like a hundred times before."

"You didn't see anything unusual?"

"We wouldn't be here if I did," says Max. They stand in the kitchen. "Why the freak-out? Maybe one of his friends invited him over. Riley or Hayley or Andrew."

"Riley and Hayley live way down by the school. I doubt he'd walk that far. At night," says Flynn. "And Andrew gets dropped off from Washington Park."

"But try Riley and Hayley."

"I'm not even sure I've got their numbers. Or know their last names," says Flynn. "I think I'd recognize Riley's house, but—"

"I've got them," says Max.

Max finds Riley's parents in his contacts. Flynn heads to the bathroom, tucked off the back by the sunroom. She plunks herself down on the toilet lid. She hears Max's muffled voice, opens Confide.

What did you do with Wyatt? Where is he?

Hits send.

Watches her hands shake.
Feels her body convulse.
Leans forward, puts her head between her legs.
Hears a beep.

So I have your attention?

Where is he?

You want to confess now? About Mexico? About your HELPERS??

Flynn mutters, "Fuck you."

I can have the cops here in two seconds. They will pick up your givomh . . . erase . . . fucjing . . . erase . . . fucking trail.

Flynn waits.
"You okay in there? Riley's folks haven't seen him," says Max.
"I'll be there in a second."
"I'll try Hayley."

I'll take your son in exchange for you breaking our deal.

Where the hell IS HE??

I'm finding other help.

There is something weird about Robbie McGrath. How she died. Where the hell is my boy?

Last I saw he was fine.

Don't play games.

I'm not. Did you check everything? Every detail? There is no chance of a spot-on match. Zero. Zero. Fucking zero.

I am sure that's true.

What had she done? She'd engaged with a monster. She thought she could tangle with PDQ. She thought she could get all the good shit she needed from him without provoking the bad.

This is not a game to me. I am being smeared. Someone is taking advantage of me by spreading a vicious lie. Your job is simple. Prove it's a lie! If you have made progress as you claim, and think you know where to strike, then you have to go with a battering ram and all the authority bestowed on reporters by the great gods of journalism and you've got to bash their doors all the fucking way down. Your boy is fine. He thinks he found a new soul mate.

Don't you dare touch him.

Then you need to get cracking!

I've come so far.

Not far enough.

Tomorrow is a big day. I went all the way to Mexico to chase a lead. For you. For this.

And you took a fucking team.

How the hell does he know that?
Flynn has one need.

Send my boy home and tomorrow will be a big day.

I don't deal in tomorrows. What, people don't answer questions after the sun goes down? You have one horrific death dragging you down. Do you need another?

Send my boy home.

You are not in charge. I can find a better reporter. Can you find a better son?

"Jesus, Flynn, you okay?"
Max, outside the door.
"Give me a sec," she says.
"Hayley too. They haven't seen him."
Flynn flushes the toilet. And shouts over the whirling: "Maybe he walked to my dad's?" She hears him step away from the door.

Need time.

A tear splashes on her phone. The hand holding the phone won't hold still.

You don't want to get beat on this story, do you?

I won't be.

You want redemption, right?

May as well play along . . .

Yes.

Then get busy.

My son!

Check every detail. What doesn't match?

My son!

He's fine. He's got a hamburger and fries. He seems fine.

He doesn't eat red meat!

You do know that human beings sometimes say one thing and do another. Don't you?

CHAPTER 63

Wyatt eats his fries one by one.

He picks up the end of each french fry, puts the tip between his teeth, and nibbles it down like a cartoon rabbit.

He munches all his fries first and then sets about lathering the inside of his hamburger with ketchup before taking a bite, putting the sandwich back down on the plate to chew. He is a methodical eater. He chews like a nutritionist's dream.

Niko's is medium busy. Harry's view is to the side and from the rear of the kid, who sits at a two-top facing the front door. Harry scrunches into the corner of a booth off to the side. He keeps his head down. He messages back and forth with Flynn like a goddamn teenager. He nibbles at the Athenian, a big Greek salad with oodles of kalamata olives and fat hunks of white feta.

Harry got lucky. After the painful and arduous walk back from Cheesman, he made two passes past Flynn's house. On the second pass he saw the kid come out and start walking. Wyatt was an easy tail. When the kid reached Niko's, Harry waited five minutes and then followed him in.

The kid must have decided he didn't want to be alone without his phone, must have decided the man with the survey questions was a bit odd or too creepy and opted to wait for Mom by getting his own dinner.

The only question now is when the boy might decide to head home.

Harry flags his waitress, the same one who checks on Wyatt, for his check. Harry pays in cash. He tucks an additional five-dollar bill under his water glass.

He wants to be ready outside in case an opportunity presents itself. Harry stands, wincing. He forgot to not put pressure on his bad wrist. A shot of pain flares from his knee, meniscus and ligaments throbbing and pissed off at having to work. Harry grunts. It comes out louder than he wants. The first step is a doozy, like his leg has fallen asleep. He isn't sure if his right foot is on the ground. He totters, bumps an empty table next to him. The table rocks and comes back. Harry catches it, but not before both place settings slide off on their matching napkins and crash to the floor. Somewhere behind him, Harry hears a gasp.

"You okay, hon?" says his waitress. She holds a coffeepot in one grip, two dirty plates in the other. "You okay?"

"Yeah," says Harry. Grimaces. "Fine."

"Be careful," she says.

Harry says nothing, tries another step.

Better.

He needs to get outside, get his joints moving. What he needs is a bag of ice the size of Greenland.

Harry feels eyes in the restaurant gunning him down. They think he's a homeless bum who wandered into the Palace Arms at the Brown and ordered the prix fixe. Harry steadies himself on the seatback of a booth.

"Harry?" A woman's voice. "Is that you?"

Without thinking, Harry looks around.

"Mary Belson." Harry has no idea why he says the surname out loud. She sits with friends in a booth.

"What are you doing way over here? And are you okay?" says Mary.

"Yeah," says Harry. He releases his grip from the booth so he doesn't look helpless. "Slipped and fell like the uncoordinated geek that I am."

"Barely recognized you without the headphones," says Mary. "They're like your personal electronic plumage, did you know that?"

"Oh, sheesh," says Harry. "Well. I didn't realize they were a fixture."

He teeters. Prickles fire in his leg. Harry turns himself sideways. He backs up a step so he isn't right on top of them.

Mary is one of four women. They are a wild variety of ages and types.

"These are my friends Martha, Heidi, and Colleen."

Head-nods. Harry doesn't have time for greetings. Knows he's supposed to flash his talent at chat.

Mary stands, puts a soft clamp on his forearm, and guides him to the door, which is two doors with a crammed purgatory vestibule holding cell before freedom.

"You look like you could use a friend," says Mary. They are alone in the antechamber, like a vacuum. "You sure you're okay? What *are* you doing way over here?"

"A favorite place." Harry glances around. The kid zips his jacket, straps on his backpack. "The Greek food."

"I'm so sorry about the other night." She half whispers it, gives him a naughty smile.

"Sure," says Harry.

He should apologize for his immature exit.

The kid is moving.

Harry will need to move for the kid to get around them to the actual front door.

Or Mary will have to move. "I'll email you or something."

"Okay." Mary flashes her perfect teeth. Her eyes brighten. "And if you don't, I will."

Harry turns his back to the approaching kid, pulls Mary with him to one side of the chamber to create a path for Wyatt Martin to scooch around. The last thing he wants to do is do-si-do with the kid. He's removed the disguise since the encounter at Flynn's house, but still.

"Look, I'm sorry too." The kid walks around them. Coats brush. "I would welcome the chance to, what do they say these days, reboot?"

"Good," says Mary. "I'm so glad we ran into each other."

"Feel so silly about the fall," says Harry.

"Take care of yourself."

Mary turns, leaves him standing in no-man's-land.

Harry buttons his coat. He shoves his hands in his coat pockets. His right hand is wrapped around the battered carcass of the kid's phone. He puts his head down as if he is walking out into a howling blizzard.

He stands on the sidewalk in the night.

No kid.

No nobody.

A No. 10 bus pulls away from a stop across the street, heading west. The next one won't be along for another thirty minutes.

The world is pissing on his play.

CHAPTER 64

"You're not telling me everything."

They are back in the kitchen, the mill-around zone. The stand-and-fret place. Max leans back on the counter, arms folded. Every few minutes, he paces a small circle. Flynn's path slashes diagonally back and forth, each turnaround point ending with a good glare-down of the front door or the back.

"I'm going out," says Flynn. "Walk the streets, walk the alleys. What would it take to get the police here? Alert them?"

"A call," says Max.

"They'd come?"

Does she want them?

The dirty rotten police questions will pool at her feet like a rancid swamp.

One time Flynn Martin ignored what the cops were telling her and got a hostage killed.

But wait! Another time she had a solid connection to a serial killer but thought she'd keep it all to herself, let the whole city squirm in terror while she figured it out.

"Officially or unofficially?" says Max.

"Either way."

"All depends on who is calling. The circumstances. All of that."

"What would they do?"

"Alert the system, keep an eye out, poke around. They will ask you and me a bunch of questions about tonight, everything we're doing. And by the way, your dad is heading over."

Max's cool is hard to take. Harder to fathom. Maybe he thinks it's worth a missing son to find out what's going on.

"So do you want to spit it out now?" says Max.

"I can't."

"You keep things to yourself way too much."

"It's complicated."

"What isn't?"

"I want to go out looking."

"He's either where he went to or he's in between on his way back," says Max.

"You seem so sure."

"I know it hasn't been that long. It feels that way to us, but not really."

"The cops won't care?"

"A few hours of a missing kid? Ho-hum."

"So you're not worried?"

"Worried, of course. My hunch is there's a logical explanation. Plus, he's a smart kid. But if you want, I'll put in the call? Make it a cop thing."

Wyatt's disappearance could make the 10:00 p.m. news, let alone every phone in the state signed up for emergency alerts. If the cops reach a "reasonable" conclusion that Wyatt was abducted, they could issue an Amber Alert. Flynn knows the criteria. Knows the kind of detail she'll have to reveal to convince the cops they need to do everything. Knows she'll be dragging cops to the basement to show them the blanket bundle and what's hidden inside. Knows she'll be showing them text scrolls on Confide. Knows she'll be drawn and quartered. Pilloried. Vilified. Castigated.

Ridiculed.

And it's not the kind of attention she needs.

But what Wyatt desperately does need.

Does she have a choice?

"Get them here," says Flynn.

"Okay," says Max, showing her his phone like it's her last chance to change her mind. "They might be able to find out more about whatever is so 'complicated.' Because they will ask what's been unusual or out of the ordinary, and I will be obligated to say you're working on a story or something that you'd—"

The front door opens. Flynn's heart leaps. She'd been caught at the far end of her circuit farthest from the front door.

Turns.

"Hey there," says her father. "Look at who I bumped into on the way over."

CHAPTER 65

Harry chooses the dark side of every street. He zigzags south of Cheesman Park. His knee barks. His wrist throbs. Should he ask strangers if they're packing oxy? He stops every now and then to rest. He stops every now and then to message Flynn, but she has stopped replying. Harry wants something tangible, to prove her progress.
But . . . Mary.
Mary. Mary. Mary. Mary. *Fucking* Mary. Why?
Mary is a problem.
A big fat problem.
Bumping into Mary is Flynn's fault because it all goes back to Flynn Martin pulling in others.
Of all the joints between Uptown and LoDo and Capitol Hill and Congress Park, why? He didn't need the encounter or her outright forgiveness, as if he can erase from his memory the way she floated her dark overtures. As if he can forget what she *really* wants to do. As if he can go out on another vanilla date and have a vanilla time.
Harry hobbles. A side-to-side gait takes pressure off his knee. The quasi-limp forces his left hip to move funny and now it's complaining too. His motion lacks efficient forward progress. He moves down the long straightaway of the Seventh Avenue Parkway, dreams of oxy tugging him along like the mirage of a shimmering oasis.

CHAPTER 66

"Where were you?" says Flynn.

"At Niko's."

"You took yourself to Niko's?"

Trying not to sound angry . . .

Trying not to alarm Max . . .

"You weren't home and, well—" Wyatt pauses. He looks at Max. "I lost my phone. I got scared."

"I can't imagine you losing your phone," says Flynn. They took a few minutes for hugs, for making Wyatt a cup of hot chocolate, for agreeing the crisis is over. "That would be like losing your pants. It's attached to you twenty-four seven."

Wyatt offers a wan smile. "It was here. And then I ran upstairs because there was this man and I needed to get something—"

Wyatt hits full stop. Tears overflow their banks. His chin quivers.

"What? For who?" Max, with a streak of admonishment at the ready. He has helped himself to a beer. He sits down next to his boy. "Did someone come to the door?"

"A man." Wyatt wipes his cheeks on his shirtsleeves.

"A man?" says Flynn.

Random men roaming the streets isn't a thing, but it happens. Nonprofit do-gooders, Mormon youths, door hangers for window cleaning, trash haulers.

"A guy asking questions," says Wyatt. "Taking a survey."

"A survey about?"

"Climate change," says Wyatt. "I liked him at first, but he was kind of strange."

"Strange how?" says Max.

"Well, he took my phone. It was right there." Wyatt points to a nothing spot on the counter. "He had a clipboard."

He read Wyatt's texts when I was in Mexico . . .

He probably made note of all Wyatt's contacts . . .

Family and friends . . .

"You let him in the house?" says Max. "Haven't we talked about that?"

"I wasn't going to at first. I wasn't."

"You think he took your phone?" says Max.

"I snuck a picture of him. But of course it was on my phone."

"So you were worried," says Max.

"He stayed so long," says Wyatt. "Talking and talking. That's when I ran upstairs. I was trying to figure out what to do. Then I heard the front door close."

"What did you eat?"

Max might think she is changing the subject, taking the pressure off, but it's the last question she wants to ask.

"Cheeseburger." Wyatt cries a quiet tear. "I know, I know. But every once in a while. And fries."

"Can we find your phone?" says Michael. He digs his cell phone from his jacket. "I can't remember if I set up one of those apps to track phones or not. Flynn?"

"You've got it, Mom!" Excitement oozes from every pore. "And I'm on your list. Of course."

Flynn hands her phone over. Wyatt's right thumb flashes, in fix-it mode.

Even if a magical dot materializes, she doubts Wyatt's phone will be with *him*.

Why is she secretly hoping there is nothing?

Because she wants this day to end? Because she fears the person who might be holding the dot? Because she wants to sort this all out one step at a time and not take a shortcut to the finish?

Wyatt frowns. "Maybe he's got it turned off," he says. "We can check again later. You've got a bunch of messages, Mom. A *bunch*."

"Every day," says Flynn. "Welcome to my life."

"I mean, they are flying in," says Wyatt.

Max leans in for a look.

"They flock together. Mostly junk," says Flynn.

What she needs now is for Max to decide to drift home, resume routine. She had a vague idea to take Wyatt to a hotel in Cherry Creek, sheets with thread counts in the thousands. They will build a dark cave of bedding and pillows, secure the door with dead bolts and chain locks, and post two beefy doormen with assault rifles in the hall.

"You're using one of those encrypting apps?" says Max. "The messages don't save? Scan once and done?"

"Yes," says Flynn. She holds out her hand. Wyatt slaps the phone in her palm. "Someone thinks they are special."

"My work here is done," says Michael. "Thanks for the evening stroll."

"I'm going that way," says Max. "I'll drop you off."

"It's okay," says her father. "Exercise. You know what they say."

"No," says Flynn. "Take the ride. I'd feel better. It is getting late. Please."

There must be something in her look because her father doesn't argue.

◆ ◆ ◆

Wyatt says good night, gives hugs she doesn't want to end, says he's sorry, runs upstairs.

Flynn walks Max to his car. She peers up and down the street for goofballs and oddballs. Nothing. Nobody. A mild breeze puffs with the reeking rendering from the dog food plant by I-70, an anachronistic odor in a city working so hard to be clean and spiffy.

"It's time," says Max.

Her father climbs in the car, pulls the door shut. Max comes around to the driver's side.

She gives him a full tight hug.

"Time for?"

"Time for you to tell me everything that's going on."

"I can't."

"You think you can't."

"No, I really . . ."

"You're worried about Wyatt because someone is coming after you based on this tip? Your story? Something to do with PDQ."

"I'm worried because my boy didn't answer his phone," says Flynn. "And it turned out I had reason to be worried because not only was he not home, but a stranger was in the house."

"You want to keep spinning the world on your fingertip? Like nobody else is even around?" Max's voice holds steady, but the intensity is unmistakable. "Do you have any ability to know when you're in too deep?"

Flynn pauses. She wants to appear thoughtful and appreciative. She wants to not let Max see the sting of his indictment. "I wish I could take the offer. But it's too risky."

"You're going to need help—at some point."

"You have something," says Flynn.

"What do you mean?"

"You're trying to get permission to tell me something."

"It might not be much," says Max.

"I'd be glad to decide what it's worth."

"I'm not telling you shit or Shinola unless you tell me everything."

"Dad's waiting," says Flynn. "And how do I know you have something good?"

"It's gold."

"Where does it lead?"

"If I tell you that, I don't get what I want."

Max's capabilities as an assayer are top notch. He knows what constitutes shiny stuff to a reporter.

"Tell me," he says. "Bring me in."

"What if I look like a fool?"

The relief from Wyatt being home wells up inside her.

Maybe it's time.

"Try me," says Max.

"I can tell my ex," says Flynn. "I can't tell the cop."

"I don't know the difference," says Max. "I'm not two people."

"No?"

"Well, am I talking to my ex or a reporter? Where does one stop and the other start? Some switch I don't know?"

Flynn walks a small circle, tips her head back.

"I want you to keep this to yourself," says Flynn. "Until it's time. When it's time, we'll call in the cavalry, okay?"

"Okay."

"Deal?"

"Jesus, Flynn, come on. You want a handshake? Blood?"

"Maybe both," says Flynn. "But if I'm laying everything out, Dad needs to hear this too."

CHAPTER 67

Wyatt is lying on his side, tucked under the blankets. It's strange to see him with a book and not flipping through his phone.

"We'll get you a new one." She sits on the bed, pats his legs through layers of blankets. "No more strangers in the house. Ever."

"Never," says Wyatt. "In a million years."

"How about a million billion?"

"Even then." His lower lip curls out. His eyes mist.

Wyatt puts his book down on the floor with the care of an antiquarian. He rolls on his back and puts his hands behind his head.

"Sounds like they came back inside," says Wyatt.

"I have to go over a few things with them—it's no big deal," says Flynn. Only the most difficult information she might ever lay out for anyone. "Your job is to go to sleep. We know you're sorry."

"One thing."

"What's that?"

"This is kind of weird."

"What?"

"The guy who I talked to? The guy asking questions? He had these strange shoes, with these funny-looking straps over the top. And buckles."

"He did?" says Flynn. "Buckles?"

"Loafers," says Wyatt. "You know, no laces. And these straps. Like decorations."

"Monk straps," says Flynn. "The monks preferred them to sandals when they kneeled down to pray, protected the tops of their feet."

"At Niko's, there was this guy talking to a woman near the front door, and I had to kind of go around him and I looked down—it was the same pair of shoes."

"Coincidence?"

"Not the same *kind*," says Wyatt. "The same pair."

"But it wasn't him?"

The hamburger . . .

The fries . . .

"Same height, but no glasses. His hair was different. But the shoes."

An electric tingle buzzes Flynn's arms. "Did you see him before you stood up? Was he with anyone?"

Wyatt thinks. "I didn't notice, no."

"He didn't follow you out?"

"I don't think so." Wyatt looks worried.

"Coincidence," says Flynn, sure it's not. "It's like when you learn a new word and then you see that word in three different places within a day. You wouldn't have noticed the second pair of shoes if you hadn't focused on the first."

"You think so?"

"I think you need a good night's sleep," says Flynn. "So do I."

CHAPTER 68
MONDAY

Dr. Russell Malik's head is hairless, save for a well-groomed mustache.

The skin wraps itself like a pink balloon on his bright dome, except for three corduroy ribs of skin on the back of his neck.

His eyes spark blue under square black glasses. He is a cool, low-key guy. When you oversee a few thousand autopsies each year and grow comfortable around defense attorneys who are ripping you to shreds in court, an excited but defrocked television reporter isn't going to rankle your nerves.

Malik, chief forensic pathologist for the medical examiner's office, agreed to the in-person chat but cautioned that he wouldn't say much and that he might be in mourning if the Broncos lose their playoff game. Fortunately, forty-some overpriced athletes had gone out and won the game in Kansas City, meaning that a few million regular ordinary working joes can all walk a bit taller on this brisk Monday morning.

"Ultimately, of course, you need the chief medical examiner," says Malik. He is accompanied by a boyish man with surfer good looks wearing ocean blue doctor's scrubs. Malik's suit could pass for accountant or lawyer. They are both unfazed by the morning chill. "You know how this works."

"It's not a big deal to confirm for me that the ME is having another look into Robbie McGrath's murder."

Malik grins. Flynn waits.

"The chief is a good evaluator of what is a big deal," says Malik. "And he's not beholden to the conclusions of others."

"Is it the ME himself who is raising questions or one of the staff?"

"I don't know where you got your information," says Malik. "But, again, Dr. Coates responds to all media inquiries."

"And he is where?"

"At a conference in San Diego."

After the rocky night with Wyatt's agonizing disappearance, the tense but civilized conversation with Max and her father had lasted until 1:00 a.m., including Max passing along the tip that the ME's office is "concerned" and is doubling back over everything.

Making waves.

Having Wyatt in the same four walls, asleep, required that Max keep his voice down. A good thing. She tried to get them both to see every minute since the death of Debbie Ernst and the day things went bonkers haywire at the convenience store with the asshole Alfredo Sanchez.

At the end of her long and detailed walk-through, Max agreed to see if he could dig up the current assignment for Carlos Herrera as well as any known associates on the force and the names of his superiors. Max also agreed to poke around for a cop who went by the nickname of Captain A. And find a cell phone number for Jerry Damphouse.

Flynn then spent the weekend focused on Wyatt time and ignoring all the Broncos hype, with the lone exception of bugging Chris Casey for Dr. Malik's cell phone number.

"But you've been asking questions?" says Flynn. "You saw something, something not matching the others?"

"I can say 'No comment' a different way, if you'd like," says Malik.

Flynn lets the pause linger. Tamica stands over her right shoulder, camera rolling.

Malik clears his throat. He gives a nearly imperceptible shrug in the direction of his surfer-doctor cohort, turns back to Flynn.

"There appear to be some discrepancies."

People can't stand silence. Camera on? Mouths must move. Quiet is the most powerful word vacuum on earth.

"To do with?"

"I can't be specific. But I don't see the harm in confirming that we are asking questions."

"External wounds?"

"I can't say."

"The . . . *staging*?"

"I can't go into details."

"So more than one detail? More than one discrepancy?"

"I didn't say that."

"There is no question *how* she died, is there?"

"No, but in cases like this, it's important to analyze all the details, so we know—and so everybody knows—what we're dealing with."

Malik's accomplice leans in. He whispers something in a cupped hand by Malik's shiny ear.

The ME shop in Denver is known for the quality of its doctor-level forensic pathologists. They work alongside the police forensic teams at key crime scenes. Flynn has always wondered how you can hang out with so many dead bodies every day, weighing organs and checking stomach contents, without wondering how your own body will look when your turn comes.

"That's all," says Malik.

"But you believe the PDQ pattern doesn't hold?"

"We have questions," says Malik.

"What prompted the reconsideration?"

Tamica brings her camera down to hip level.

"Is that off?" Malik head-bobs to Tamica's gear.

"Yes," says Tamica.

"Not fake off? Not pretend off?"

"*Off*," says Tamica.

"We have a good relationship with DPD," says Malik. "Rock solid. But it wasn't our department that jumped to the PDQ conclusion. You know, at the outset."

"What's different?" says Flynn.

"We're reviewing the old cases. And the new one."

"If it is a new one."

"If it's from the same perpetrator. It's definitely a new case."

"Right," says Flynn. "So is it the method of killing?"

"I've said enough."

"Wait."

After Wyatt had gone to sleep, Flynn slipped down to the basement. She took out the bundle of bedding and the doll and the headphones and the music gizmo. She made a precise list of everything she could name, right down to the color of the iPod Nano (lime), its capacity (ten GB), the "Jupiter" piece (performed by the London Philharmonic, conducted by Adrian Boult; no other tune loaded on the device), and everything about the doll too. She confirmed online that it was an original American Girl made by Pleasant Company, based on the stamp on the back of the doll's neck, before the company was bought by Mattel. The doll was a Molly.

"Do you only look at the body or do you look at everything?" says Flynn.

"We look at anything that's relevant."

"Was there an error in, perhaps, the staging?"

Malik stares.

"We're off the record," says Flynn. "I can't use this. I only need to know if I'm getting warm. I heard PDQ's victims were listening to music on an MP3 player, one of those iPod things, when their bodies were found. Classical music. Holst. 'Jupiter.'"

"Everybody knows you are married to a cop," says Malik. "You know everyone knows that, right?"

"And I don't take advantage of that fact," says Flynn. "I have my own sources."

"Then keep digging."

"In the same hole?"

Malik turns to go, backpedals a few steps: "Until you hear your spade go *clink*."

CHAPTER 69

"How did you know to ask the question?" says Goodman.

"*That's* all you care about?"

"Well, it's a damn good get. How did you?"

"Sources."

They had watched the tape three times, then listened to the last off-the-record bit, high-def audio on Flynn's phone. Malik didn't ask if her phone was recording, did he? They wouldn't blindside Malik by airing the phone recording, but Flynn wanted Goodman to hear it.

"The ME is going to come unglued—one of his crew stepping out of line. Cops will go berserk," says Goodman. "And the music?"

"Holst was a big deal to PDQ."

Tamica sits at the editing controls in the screening room. Her last shot is frozen on the screen. It shows Malik, back turned, walking away. Tamica had fired up her camera for the visual as soon as Malik and his whisperer had turned tail.

"Maybe Malik sees things differently than Coates," says Goodman. "Maybe there's a fight going on inside the coroner's shop. Or maybe he's after airtime."

"Does it sound that way to you? His squabble is with the cops."

"You've tried to reach Coates?"

"No," says Flynn.

"Give him a chance. It's standard procedure."

"It's a story right there," says Flynn. "Even if Coates doesn't respond."

"And did you get a reaction from the police?"

"Don't tell me you're going to hold the piece for that."

"It will take two minutes," says Goodman. "Close the loop. Otherwise, tomorrow's paper will run with the cops rebutting this puppy."

"You're not going to air this until I get a response?"

"One step at a time."

"But *will* you?"

"Nobody is beating you or us on this story. And it would get lost in all the Broncos coverage anyway."

"Isn't that something you could fix? You know, set priorities? Help this whole city recalibrate its freaking priorities?"

Goodman ignores her fantasy. "See if DPD will bite. Even if Hatcher won't engage, or if he gives you a blanket assertion that the ME's staff is off base, you can paraphrase him on the set. Flynn?" Goodman leans back in the producer's throne, one step up on a platform behind where Flynn and Tamica sit in the editing bay. "Does this all connect with Mexico?"

Flynn turns in her chair to face him.

"It's all balled up," says Tamica.

"What she said," says Flynn.

"How?"

"It's information from the same source, which, in this case, appears reliable."

"Somebody on the inside?"

Easy questions require no dodge. "Very much," says Flynn.

"You wouldn't have gone to Juárez or buttonholed Malik without this source, correct?"

She can't describe it in a way that will make sense. Or tempt Goodman to call in a buzzing swarm of cops.

"The answer to your question is yes, the same source. And then following the leads."

"It's good," says Tamica. "High-grade stuff."

"We're close," says Flynn. "Or closer. We could run Malik solo today and follow up with Coates and the DPD when we get them."

"No," says Goodman. "The whole story in one piece."

"They can stall me. Us. Everyone."

"I'm fully aware," says Goodman. "But you don't want the cops to have another reason to keep you on their shit list. Do you?"

CHAPTER 70

Flynn leaves a message with Barry Coates's assistant.

Urgent, et cetera.

As soon as possible, et cetera.

Next, Flynn thinks of a half dozen sources who might have Barry Coates's cell number in their possession, including two of his suburban counterparts. One is long retired. The other is on vacation. Flynn spreads messages around town like confetti sprayed from a speeding helicopter.

Next, Dwight Hatcher.

"The ME is a separate operation," says Hatcher. "And they do great work."

"Is that the official statement?"

"Trying to make sure you haven't forgot how the agencies operate, that's all."

"First, I haven't been gone that long, and second, it's not every day that your chief comes out and sets everyone's hair on fire with a claim that a serial killer is back in business after being gone for a decade and a half," says Flynn. "I need an official statement from someone about your degree of certainty about the claim that Robbie McGrath's murder was the work of PDQ. Along with some comment that affirms the match between Robbie and the other three—Berns, Pedigo, and Schultz."

"Okay," says Hatcher.

"Okay—who am I going to interview?"

"No, I meant 'okay,' like I heard your question."

"And?"

"And I'll get back to you."

"Today?"

"Long shot," says Hatcher.

"You can say anything. Dump a whole big bucket of whitewash right on my head." Flynn wants this package on the air, for her own sanity and as a sedative for PDQ. "You can say anything. Any. Thing."

"I'm not used to having reporters draft my talking points," says Hatcher. "But no thanks. We'll get you something."

"When?"

"Can't say."

◆ ◆ ◆

Flynn drives home.

She holds out hope for getting the story on air if Coates suddenly calls from San Diego.

Or she can suggest to Goodman that she talked to Hatcher and it's clear the cops are dragging their bureaucratic asses to screw everything up. Maybe that will be enough.

She calls Max and gets his voicemail. She leaves him a message of effusive thanks. She can almost imagine thanking him with something special.

Almost.

◆ ◆ ◆

Flynn finds her father at her dining room table, looking through old newspaper stories about PDQ.

"We need the link between Jerry Damphouse and everyone around the Enrique Rojas story, like this Captain A," says Flynn.

"Like I said the other night, call Damphouse back," says her father. "Do what Robbie McGrath was getting ready to do. If you press the same button, you might get the same reaction."

"I don't think he'll answer my call," says Flynn. "He was one torqued-off cop."

"He has no choice but to talk with you again," says her father. "He'll want to know if you've made any progress. Hell, you might be calling to let him know his name is going to be splattered all over the news."

"Which is an option," says Flynn. Again, though, Goodman will insist on an official reaction.

She tells her father the basics of the Dr. Malik interview and shares her frustration with Goodman's insistence on a formal comment from DPD.

"He's doing the right thing," says Michael. "This way, you'll get the whole story and let viewers make up their minds. One day, not a big deal."

"To you."

"Nobody is going to beat you on Dr. Malik."

"Don't agree with my boss," says Flynn. "That makes you an accomplice in my purgatorial nowheresville."

"I thought you were back in the grind," says her father.

"I'm back," says Flynn. "But I'm so low on the totem pole you can only see the top of my head."

"What can I do to help?"

Flynn thinks.

"Two things."

"Shoot."

"Ask Judy Hayes if she's ever heard of Captain A."

"You want me to call her?"

"Yes. Max is poking around, but Judy Hayes might have the magic touch."

"After that warm reception at the newspaper?"

"You are old pals," says Flynn. "Play that up. Scribblers-in-arms. Do you have leverage?"

Her father twirls his phone in his hand. "I have desperation."

Michael calls. Waits. Waits some more. Puts the call on speaker. Introduces himself to someone who finally answers. Asks to be patched through to Judy Hayes. Asks Hayes if she has heard of a Captain A.

"Nope."

"Could you ask someone who might know?"

"Nope."

"I know it's not precisely in your job description," says Michael, "but neither was my going to bat for you with management at the end of your ninety-day trial period. You do recall that you were on the bubble. Back when the newspaper had a line of reporters out the door, looking for work? We had worked together on the story about the state representative caught in the motel room on East Colfax with an underage boy? I saw your potential even though the city editor at the time was not a fan of your, shall we say, rather gruff style."

Michael Martin lets that sink in. Flynn pumps a fist in the air, loving it when her father plays hardball.

"Oh," says Hayes.

"I'm glad you remember," he says. "Yes, the union has been very good to you, hasn't it? The pension is not what we hoped it would be back in the glory days, but it's something."

Her father listens, makes the flapping-mouth mime with his spare hand.

"So, yes, Captain A. Get me that name and we will be square."

Her father clicks the phone off, sets it down. "She has a good memory," he says. "Bit prickly around the edges, though."

Between Max and Judy Hayes, thinks Flynn, something has to turn up. "Kind of late in the day for it, but have you had lunch?"

"After two o'clock," says her father, "any meal is considered dinner to those of us in the senior set."

Flynn works on a cheeseburger, picks at the fries. Her father dives into a Greek salad, the Athenian. Niko's is sleepy. Flynn fights off daydream images of Wyatt eating alone.

Or PDQ watching.

"Is the evening staff on yet?"

"Some of us," says their waitress.

"Were you working last Friday evening?"

The waitress is as round as the beaker of coffee in her grip.

"Nope, why?"

"I'm looking for one of the waitstaff who might have been here that night. My son was alone and he, well, encountered someone. I'm afraid it's a bit of a long story. You don't, by any chance, use closed-circuit TV?"

Niko's manager, Thaddeus, is burly and polite. He understands the nature of Flynn's request, doesn't balk. He leads Flynn and her father to a back office. Thaddeus toggles a switch near his computer. He says something about the Broncos, then drops the subject when Flynn and her father don't engage. The monitor jumps to a grid with four rectangular views—live action. The pictures are sharp. Three cameras cover the interior. A fourth captures the patio tables on the sidewalk.

"All the video is stored now in the cloud," says Thaddeus. "I forget how many terabytes we have with our account, but we keep footage for a month or so, and then it's gone forever. At least, that's what they want you to believe. Is this for a story, Miss Martin?"

"Maybe," she says. "I didn't know you knew my name."

"Of course." Thaddeus grins. "I've been here twenty years next month. I watch the news. You work for my favorite station."

"Well, okay then," says Flynn.

"Where are people going to get the news if we don't have newspapers? Or news? Or people asking questions? And this is Michael Martin, of course." Thaddeus gives her father a multiple-pump handshake. "I miss your column."

Thaddeus pulls up a dashboard for the camera system. Flynn steels herself. What might hurt more? Watching her boy eat alone or watching her boy in the same space as *him*?

"Friday—what time?"

"Seven-ish," says Flynn.

Video in all four grids zips along in sync. The video is in color with remarkable detail. The light in the restaurant ebbs and flows as the January sun coughs up its meager offerings. And then fades. At full dark, Thaddeus slows to double speed. Flynn gasps when Wyatt walks through the door and helps himself to a table.

"My son," says Flynn. "Can we isolate that camera? And freeze it there?"

A waitress stands by Wyatt's table. Only half the tables have customers, but none are singletons.

"Okay, double speed," says Flynn.

She watches Wyatt wait. And squirm. And look around.

After a few minutes at double speed, a man enters. Alone. Flynn puts up her hand like she's stopping traffic. Thaddeus hits pause as if he's worked in television news edit bays all his life.

"Holy shit," says her father.

The angle is from the back of the restaurant, up high.

The man wears a gray jacket. His head is down. He's alone.

"Him?" says Thaddeus.

"Yes." Flynn is sure. *Him.* "Is he a regular?"

"The waitstaff would know better than me," says Thaddeus, "but I don't think so."

"Looks so ordinary," says her father.

"Real time," says Flynn.

Thaddeus releases the video.

The man makes his way to a booth. He orders. He keeps his head down like a recluse who is not used to public spaces. He focuses on something in his lap, which Flynn knows is his phone.

"Who is he?" says Thaddeus.

"Someone who came to our house when Wyatt was home alone." Flynn wants to crawl through time and the video monitor, yank her son out of there. "Someone who got inside with Wyatt."

"But your boy doesn't seem to recognize him," says Thaddeus.

"We think he was wearing something different," says Flynn.

"A disguise?" says Thaddeus.

"Yes."

"Bad man," says Thaddeus.

"If he pays with a credit card?" says her father.

"That would help," says Thaddeus.

"Good idea," says Flynn. "But he won't."

Wyatt's cheeseburger arrives. The man tucks himself into the corner of his booth like he's highly contagious.

"The waitress who is serving him?" says Flynn.

"Elizabeth," says Thaddeus. "One of our veterans."

They watch and stare. The basic tableau doesn't change for ten long minutes.

The man pays in cash.

"Too bad," says her father.

Wyatt is finishing, but the man stands and appears to lurch and stumble. And rights himself.

PDQ—first to leave?

"Maybe he wanted to be outside and waiting when Wyatt walked home."

Her father answers the question Flynn was thinking.

"Wait!" says Flynn. Again, the stop sign. Again, Thaddeus hits pause. "One of those women . . ."

One of the women from a nearby booth suddenly stands. She looks like she's come from work. Pencil skirt and a matching long-sleeve turtleneck with some sort of floral-print wrap around her shoulders. Her hair is short. The woman grabs PD-fucking-Q by the forearm. She is happy to see him, which doesn't seem possible.

The man turns. The man keeps his head down, but it's the best angle yet of his weak jaw and high forehead. The man's look is generic to the core.

"Okay." Flynn gives a finger roll in the air.

Thaddeus lets the video go.

PDQ and the woman dance their way awkwardly into the vestibule. And chat.

Wyatt stands to go, pulls on his jacket, and heads for the front door. The man and the woman maneuver a bit to make room for Wyatt. If any of the other three women who remain seated know the man, they don't let on.

"The woman?" says Flynn.

"We'll ask Elizabeth," says Thaddeus. "I don't know her, but Elizabeth might."

"Now?" says Flynn. "And can I get a screen capture? The side view of him?"

"Not regulars," says Elizabeth, "but I've seen them before."

"Four checks or—?" says Thaddeus. "Do you remember?"

"Friday was a long time ago," says Elizabeth.

Flynn waits.

Elizabeth thinks.

"Cash," she says. "They only had appetizers and hot drinks, if I remember. Tea, no booze. One of them paid for the whole thing with two twenties. I remember a comment from one of them about when you use cash, you spend less, which I believe is a true fact."

Elizabeth gives a shrug, unaware that her version of events shatters all of Flynn's hopes.

CHAPTER 71
TUESDAY

Mary on email.

Flynn on Confide.

Harry can't see straight, can't focus.

He doesn't like distractions. He likes to work at work.

Today, he needs to stay seated as much as possible to not draw attention to his wounds. Jennifer and Sandy have already fawned over his odd gait. They want to fetch him pho from the place next door at lunch. *Gawd,* he hates pho and all its messy pretensions. They ask what painkillers he's taking. Now *that* is hilarious. If they only knew he is floating on a cloud.

Somewhere, he lost most of the weekend. Monday wasn't a whole lot better. Lost to the ether. Oxy always makes him feel like he is sitting by a warm fire in a cozy mountain cabin.

At work, he likes to show his dedication and attention to detail. There is plenty to do. The testing department's director slot is open. Jennifer Hills wants him to gather employee feedback on how the "Walking Buddy" program is working. The budget office needs an entry-level analyst. The federal program folks are looking for someone to work with migrant education. There are applications to certify, backgrounds to check.

But.

Flynn: I am waiting on one more shoe to drop. Today. I have a top official asking questions about Robbie. He is on the record. Story should run tonight.

Reply: So? You've betrayed me. And my name is still out there.

Mary: The movie was fine, thanks.

Reply: Want to do something tonight or anytime this week?

Flynn: Starting to crack open, I am sure of it. Worked a lot this weekend.

Reply: YOU pulled in help. That is a problem I will address.

Mary: Busy week. I'm afraid not.

Reply: Aw, come on.

He has plans for Mary. Harry imagines what she will think at the pinprick injection, the slow fade from daylight.

And how guilty Flynn will feel for not obeying his instructions.

Will she put two and two together? The parallel with her other big fat screwup? Will she finally recognize her down-deep character flaw?

But can he?

PDQ is gone, right?

Although wouldn't it be something if he helped disprove Robbie McGrath was the work of PDQ one day and the actual PDQ returned the very next?

DPD's collective head would spin like the green-faced girl in *The Exorcist*.

Flynn: Watch tonight. Not sure yet if 5, 6, or 10. Waiting on a DPD response.

Reply: DPD. So good at what they do.

Mary: Crazy schedule right now; sorry.

Reply: I don't believe you.

Flynn: Stay the fuck away from my boy.

Reply: Oh, so you're feeling better.

Over his shoulder, a work voice pokes through the warm bubble. Jennifer.

"Harry?" she says.

He suddenly realizes it isn't the first time she's uttered his name.

"Sorry," he says, turning. He plops the phone on his desk with a clatter. "Sorry."

"Federal Programs needs those background checks done. For the migrant office?"

Give him a week, Harry thinks, and he could find a reason to disqualify every single applicant.

"Close of business, maybe sooner."

"Thanks," says Jennifer. "You okay? You look like you walked out of a sauna. But it's like chilly in here."

"I'm fine." Harry wriggles his shoulders as if working out a kink. "I promise."

Mary: Just the way it goes.

Reply: When? Next week?

He doesn't want to sneak into her house. He wants her to hold the door open, let him in.

He will be her last visitor.

Mary: I'll let you know.

He makes her wait a full five minutes. Then: I'd be interested in a reboot, whatever you call it. Start again?

CHAPTER 72

"A *statement*?" says Flynn.

"You want it or not?" says Hatcher.

"I have Dr. Malik on camera."

"And you'll have our statement to read."

"You made me wait for a statement? Nothing on camera?"

Hatcher says nothing.

"Okay, Jesus. Lay it on me."

"I'll zap it to you right now," says Hatcher.

Flynn hits refresh on her email.

She speed-mumbles it back to Hatcher: "The Denver Police Department works in close collaboration with the medical examiner's office on hundreds of cases every year. We respect the competency and professionalism of Dr. Barry Coates and his staff. Our investigation is continuing and we will follow the facts wherever they lead, including the opinions and insights of the experienced staff at the medical examiner's office."

"Utter BS," she says.

"Thank you," says Hatcher. "Thank you very much."

◆ ◆ ◆

"Good," says Goodman. "We'll run it as breaking news on the six and recap it on the ten, including anything else new. How about Coates, did you reach him?"

"Hasn't returned my calls," says Flynn.

"Okay, finish the edit on Malik, and then we'll need you on a live shot in Larimer Square for the six."

"Wait." Flynn gets a bad feeling. "Larimer Square? And no live shot for the Malik piece?"

"Big rally for the Broncos. They're closing the whole street. Bands and cheerleaders."

"The freaking *Broncos*?"

"Did you know they won?"

"I heard something. I think. Was that the sporting contest with those athletes who bash around on the field, all risking CTE? The game that devours the first half of our so-called news show after every game they play?"

Flynn wants to call Max, see what he might have found. She wants to manage the edit of the Malik story. She wants to hang around the newsroom and bask in the delicious anticipation of releasing a big story. It will look utterly ridiculous, to the average viewer, for her to be popping DPD's big balloon one minute and then plastering on one of those fake live-shot smiles the next in a sea of Broncomania.

"I know, it's not your thing. But consider it a chance to show your versatility," says Goodman. "Smile into the camera and say things like, 'Wow, look at this crowd.'"

◆ ◆ ◆

Flynn pulls up Confide.

> Okay, it will be on the six and again on the 10.

> Better be good.

> It is.

And then?

Then the chips fall where they may.

Meaning?

Trust me.

And right now?

Wait.

I don't like waiting.

And don't think less of me if you see me doing unrelated stories.

I already think less of you. Much less. Like what?

This Broncos rally.

Short straw, eh?

Not my thing.

I will watch.

◆ ◆ ◆

Flynn taps in Jerry Damphouse's cell, number courtesy of a text from Max.
    Thinking, this time, she will pour honey.
    Not vinegar.

She gets his voicemail. She says the nicest things she can say. She talks about the bigger picture. She tells him she is going down to cover the Broncos rally and asks if she might call him after.

Can they meet?

Can they start again?

CHAPTER 73

A throng of blue and orange jams Larimer Square, sidewalk to sidewalk and gill to gill. A stage blocks off the intersection at Fourteenth Street.

House of Pain follows Guns N' Roses and then, of course, Queen. "We Are the Champions." Loud enough for a stadium, let alone a closed-in city block.

No, Flynn wants to say, *the fans are not the champions. You're* fans. *Can we have accuracy in our stadium anthems, please?*

Maybe there should be a follow-up song, "We Are the Fans of the Champions."

Flynn wants to hurl.

"Welcome to the Jungle."

Fun and games *blah-buh-dee-blah.*

Beer slops out of giant plastic cups. Street vendors sell hot dogs with steaming piles of sauerkraut. Faces painted blue or orange or both. Cheerleaders onstage twirl silver pom-poms like balls of Christmas tinsel, skinny bare midriffs in defiance of the cold. Bright-white fringy chaps like they've climbed down off a merry-go-round plastic bronco, certainly no flesh-and-bone horse. Flynn inhales a blast of marijuana with a top note of patchouli.

Tamica waits with the gear two storefronts from the stage.

"Holy crap," says Flynn. "Bore me to pieces."

Tamica stifles a fake yawn.

The music stops. The cheerleaders switch to random-pose mode. Faux cheeriness, impossibly perfect hair. Pom-poms shake. John Elway, player turned team executive, climbs eight steps at the side of the stage. The throng erupts. The live video on giant screens flanking the stage zooms in on Elway's aw-shucks grin.

Flynn checks her cell phone while Elway talks. Twelve minutes until her live shot. She jots down a few notes. All she has to do is remember a few key words.

Frenzy.
Anticipation.
Bedlam.
Broncos.
Elway.
And remember to smile.

Flynn scans the screaming mush of orange and blue. One man stands on the perimeter of the media zone. He wears a black jacket with the collar up. Not a Bronco-tribe bit on him. He looks plain and unimportant out of uniform. He looks, more than anything, defeated.

Flynn nods. She tucks her cell phone in a pocket. She holds up ten fingers and then five more.

CHAPTER 74

Harry hides in the crowd like a grain of sand blowing across the Sahara.

His face carries the team colors. The bridge of his nose serves as the dividing line between the two. The face paint makeover is the result of a well-spent fifteen bucks at a makeshift booth a block back. Mary Belson wouldn't recognize him, even if he had his tongue down her throat.

The crowd stews in a sea of frothy fanatic frenzy. Loudspeakers blare cheesy classic rock that is repetitive and painful, the PA speakers in overdrive.

Harry works his way to the front. He focuses on the stage and the dancing cheerleaders in white Western getups, complete with chaps and fringe, tummies showing. *Yeehaw.*

Harry shoulders his way toward a spot where TV cameras are gathered. Comfort in numbers. He moves slowly. He isn't feeling any pain. It's like a ghost pain. It could come screaming back any minute if the oxy wears off.

"Go Broncos," he says. "Go Broncos." He needs a drink in his hand if he's going to fit in. That's okay. Harry doesn't drink, but he has that foggy, loose sensation from the drug. He keeps his head down, uses his shoulder like the bow of a ship breaking ice.

"Go Broncos" works the same as "excuse me."

Harry stands ten feet from Flynn Fucking Martin. The television crews work side by side in a bubble of space created by a half circle of orange plastic barrels. Flynn Martin is the closest of the three reporters to Harry. With Flynn is the elegant and inscrutable Tamica Porter. They both look glum and disinterested.

Flynn checks her hair in a pocket mirror. She rehearses. Black jeans, running shoes, and an oversize, loose-fitting blue station jacket with the logo, all topped off with a Broncos cap. She looks slight, smaller than he imagined, as if she could be snapped in two without much trouble.

"Goodman?" says Flynn.

Harry could reach out and grab her by the nape—which she might deserve, given what she's done.

Flynn presses her unused ear with a finger, stares at her shoes.

"Get me Goodman," she says.

Flynn Martin stares at some nut in an orange wig, who holds his beer high and roars, "*Hell yeah, Broncos!*" Harry raises his fist in solidarity, pumps it twice.

"Goodman?" says Flynn. "You said three minutes till you come to me?" She waits.

"Okay," she says.

Elway ends with a hoarse "Go Broncos!" shout. The music cranks. "Crazy Train."

Ozzy and oxy a tidy mix, but Harry feels the decline of civilization in the first juvenile moments—the shout, the vibraslap, the rudimentary guitar. Sophistication on the run, elegance in hiding. Holst would hurl.

Flynn puts her back to the stage. She walks in Harry's direction, leans against an orange barrel.

"Can you hear me now? Is that better?"

She listens.

"The coroner called? Got it."

More listening.

"I'll be right back."

More listening.

"Mayor is there too? Okay, it's a party."

She hangs up, but, Harry thinks, nobody *hangs up*. She punches her phone. Taps a couple of buttons, puts it back to her ear.

"Dad—?"

The crowd erupts, together, as one giant lung. For ten seconds, Harry can't hear a thing.

"—so I'm going to meet him after this, and I thought someone should know."

Flynn listens a moment, says "Thank you," snaps her phone shut, and gives a thumbs-up to Tamica.

Tamica hands Flynn a wireless microphone. A roar rises from the crowd. Players ascend to the stage.

Flynn says, "Yes, we are live here in Larimer Square, where it is bedlam and you can feel the anticipation from the crowd for this weekend's big game. If the crowd on game day has a tenth of the energy of this crowd, then the outcome of the game is no longer in doubt—they may as well go ahead and declare the winner right now. We talked to a few fans as things were getting revved up. Let's take a listen . . ."

Harry worms his way out of the crowd, no "Go Broncos" pleasantries paving the way this time.

Dad on the phone? Tamica right there like family?

There are going to be repercussions.

CHAPTER 75

"So, that was a few of the thousands of fans who are packed into Larimer Square here tonight, and, well, it was hard to find anything other than enthusiastic predictions for a big Broncos W this weekend."

Flynn fakes sincerity with the best of them. Happiness too.

"Did I say 'hard to find'? Impossible to find. Lots more music down here tonight and a few more pep rally speakers from what I'm told, but no doubt the party will continue long into the night. Back to you all in the studio, and if you're asking me anything, believe me, I can't hear you."

Flynn hopes she is on camera. Her earpiece is useless. Tamica gives the universal throat-slash motion with an index finger.

They are done.

And out.

◆ ◆ ◆

Flynn looks back at the spot where Jerry Damphouse had been standing.

Flynn knifes her way out of the horde. She scans the crowd, plunges her way to relative freedom outside the crush of bodies toward Fourteenth Street, behind the stage and away from the mayhem and the insanity.

Her phone buzzes.

Goodman.

"Barry Coates got off his airplane and came straight to the station," says Goodman. "He wants to talk with you twenty minutes ago."

"Is the piece airing?" says Flynn. If so, the anchor should be about to do his lead-in. *That Flynn Martin, she can cover pep rallies and break stories about police investigations . . .*

"We're going with it," says Goodman. "But we told Coates we will update the ten if needed."

"His mood?" says Flynn.

"Low boil," says Goodman. "Seething."

"I'll be back as soon as I can get out of this crazy crowd."

Flynn checks her texts—one from Damphouse.

I'm straight down Larimer Street by the creek.

Why the hell didn't he wait? The word "trap" crosses Flynn's mind, but there are enough people coming and going that the location seems like a poor choice for an assault.

Or murder.

Flynn has one thing going for her—she is another reporter.

Robbie McGrath and then Flynn Martin, back to back?

Wouldn't look good.

At least her father knows the names behind the ringleaders of whatever conspiracy she is attempting to kick in the collective gonads. After her funeral, maybe he can pick up the pieces?

Maybe?

Larimer Street crosses Cherry Creek before it reaches westbound Speer. She crosses Speer at the light, feels a buzz in her hands, ignores it.

Jerry Damphouse stands back from the sidewalk in a triangle of filler grass between the Speer Boulevard arteries. She puts up a finger as she approaches but keeps her distance and calls Charlie Laswell. In two minutes flat, Flynn recaps the basics.

"Promises kept," says Laswell. "Holy crap."

"I'm afraid I haven't given you as much lead time as I said I would," says Flynn.

"It's okay," says Laswell.

◆ ◆ ◆

"Didn't care for the show?" says Flynn.

"Quieter here," says Damphouse.

She goes for a handshake. He takes it. "What can you tell me?"

"You called the meeting." Damphouse looks more relaxed. "Something about a new approach?"

"I'm only interested in one thing," says Flynn. "What you told Robbie McGrath. Did you give her something better so she wouldn't write about what she'd found out about you? Better than the story about the money and things missing from Margaret Stack's house?"

Damphouse looks less imposing out of his uniform.

"Did you kill Debbie Ernst?"

Damphouse holds Flynn's stare.

It has been—*what*—several whole hours that she hasn't thought about the misery from the Pump 'N Go?

For the rest of her life, will anyone be able to drag her around by the nose through a mere mention of the dead woman's name?

"Of course I didn't kill her."

"Then imagine the same amount of certainty when I tell you I had nothing to do with the missing cash," says Damphouse. "So let's start right there and get that cleared up."

"Okay," says Flynn.

"I didn't touch a thing," says Damphouse. "And I got no idea who did. I have theories, maybe, but I'm in no position to do squat about them."

"But Robbie McGrath didn't believe you?"

"She was going to fucking run with her story."

"Or claimed she was?" says Flynn.

"She read me sections of the story she was getting ready to publish. I would have been toast. My word against the Stack family? Does anyone believe cops anymore?"

"So you traded."

"Wait," says Damphouse. "Do you believe me now?"

"My deal with Deborah Ernst was on tape for the whole world to see." Even hearing the name come out of her own mouth makes Flynn hesitate. Her throat catches. "The whole world knows I didn't pull the trigger."

"Yeah, but did you kill her? How's your guilt factor?"

"Different thing."

Flynn's phone buzzes, the message variety.

"Don't let me keep you from your busy world," says Damphouse.

Flynn glances at her phone—Confide.

You seemed to be enjoying that whole scene down there too much. Mayor too? Okay, it's a party.

Flynn stares at the screen.

Mayor too? Okay, it's a party.

Her words.

From her mouth—*on a phone call.*

The only way PDQ heard them was if he was on the perimeter of the space cleared for the media. He could have reached out and grabbed her. What? Twenty minutes ago?

Flynn does a slow look-around, fights off a queasy wobble.

"Expecting someone?" says Damphouse.

Traffic. Pedestrians. The glow of light from the rally at the square. The muffled echo of the booming PA.

"Well?" says Damphouse.

"I was supposed to meet some other people, back at the station. But then for a second there I thought I got my signals crossed."

"You okay?"

"For now," says Flynn.

"In a rush?"

"I have people waiting, but they'll manage. Why?"

"Isn't this what you want?" says Damphouse.

"I want what you gave Robbie McGrath. You had an agreement?"

"Nothing on paper," says Damphouse. "But we understood each other."

Flynn pictures the scene back at the station, with Goodman chatting up Dr. Barry Coates. She imagines the mayor and his entourage tapping their feet. Mayors and patience are not an item.

Flynn tries not to picture which goofball in the crowd behind her had been PDQ.

"I want to be clear on the terms," says Damphouse.

"The Stack story is bogus. Got it."

"I am not making the same deal I did with Robbie McGrath."

"All right, then. What's next? What can you tell me?"

"This time it's mostly show," says Damphouse. "And only a bit of tell."

"We're going somewhere?" says Flynn.

"Yep."

Again, her phone jumps.

I have decided your punishment for involving others.

Flynn glances at her watch, apologizes to Damphouse for taking a moment to text.

Replies: Everything changes when my piece runs.

"Are we going far?" says Flynn. The words come out dry and hacked, her throat as supple as plywood.

"Not far."

"How far?"

"A spot in North Denver. Ten minutes up, ten minutes there, ten minutes back."

"Just you and me?"

Damphouse looks around. "See anyone else?"

"My car is parked clear on the other side—"

"And I got my car right here." He head-bobs to a spot behind her. "We could be halfway there by now if we stopped talking about it."

CHAPTER 76

The idea is rich. He can't shake it. What if, as a theoretical "for instance," the Denver Police Department finally holds another big fucking deal news conference about who was really behind the murder of Robbie McGrath, and, say, a body turns up a few hours later, this time with the whole scene executed to PDQ-absolute-delicious-verifiable perfection?

What if?

Evening news conference by the cops?

A body found the next morning.

Morning news conference by the cops?

A body found by dusk.

It would be an uppercut to the police chief's jaw, teeth splattering like a cartoon fistfight.

Like sunshine in the park flipped to a howling hailing horrible thunderstorm with no warning.

Like the hands chasing each other in Variation 23 of Goldberg, which happens to be playing in his head, courtesy of Trevor Pinnock.

Every once in a great while, Harry gives the harpsichord another chance. Pinnock isn't bad. The harpsichord is like a banjo or an accordion. Or harmonica. A tincture as good as a gallon. Harry is always growing, however, always open to new ways of thinking. This harpsichord? An irritating noise, to be sure, but it doesn't distract from his enjoyment.

Maybe the oxy helps.

Oxy and harpsichord—like a fat funky blunt and the Grateful Dead.

Harry pours himself an E&J XO. It's a bit early for brandy. But Harry doesn't drink. He only sips.

He took a taxi from the stupid Broncos rally to a Mexican restaurant near his condo. He'd walked from there, proud of his ridiculous Broncos face paint. He had hoped to run into somebody he recognized from his building—by the mailboxes, in the elevator, in the hall—but it didn't happen.

Brandy.

Oxy.

And the six o'clock news with Flynn Martin's "big news."

What a combination.

CHAPTER 77

Officer Jerry Damphouse drives a black Dodge Durango with a black camper shell. The vehicle rides high like a monster truck. Flynn has the sensation that they could drive up over the cars ahead and squash them, if needed, during a zombie apocalypse.

Flynn glances at her phone to check the time. Her piece has run. A quick glance at her email proves it. The first email's subject line is NICE JOB. The second, WHOA. The third, I KNEW IT.

The earthquake is rumbling. Judy Hayes should be making calls to chase a television reporter. For once! The nationals. *The New York Times*? Maybe the mayor and Dr. Barry Coates watched the piece from the comfort of the reception area at her station's office. Maybe they watched from the comfort of a more appropriate location, like Snelling's well-leathered office.

Flynn feels a desperate urge to text Max, but she doesn't want to appear nervous. Or clichéd.

And what does PDQ think?

Confide wakes with an answer:

Big build up for little delivery. You didn't exactly take me off the hook.

"So—what kind of a place are you going to show me?"

No Lie Lasts Forever

She should be making conversation, right? The decent thing to do?

"You'll see," says Damphouse.

"You ever hear of a cop who goes by the nickname 'Captain A'?"

"You're married to a cop, aren't you?"

"Was."

"Why don't you ask him?"

"I did," says Flynn. "That's why I'm asking you."

"DPD is a big place," says Damphouse.

"But only a dozen or so captains? Fifteen?"

"Yeah, but there's Captain America and there was Captain James T. Kirk and Captain Morgan," says Damphouse. "Captain Kangaroo. Could be anyone's nickname. Why?"

"Name I ran across," says Flynn.

"Trying to figure out what Robbie McGrath was working on," says Damphouse.

"Yes."

"And?"

They are northbound on Pecos Street. They cross over I-70 and plunge back into the quiet neighborhoods of North Denver. There isn't much city left.

"And a bunch of names came up, but a guy named Captain A seemed to be helping some people."

"What people?"

"The widow of a young man named Enrique Rojas, for one. Captain A helped the widow and her two kids get out of town, back to Mexico, after he was murdered."

"How is that helping?"

"Captain A was helping himself," says Flynn. "A reporter had come around, and Captain A and his group or whatever didn't want anyone to find out what Enrique Rojas was doing before he was killed."

"Is that right?" Damphouse's tone is singsong, too easy. "The widow was dangerous?"

"To him," says Flynn. "He was afraid she would talk, so he cut her a deal. But there was no Captain A connected with whatever you showed Robbie McGrath. And with what you're about to show me. At least, I think."

"Nicknames," says Damphouse. "Throw ten guys who have never met into a locked room, and half of them will have nicknames within twenty minutes. That bonding bullshit, you know? Defines the club."

"So the answer is no?"

"Like I said," says Damphouse.

Flynn texts Max:

North Denver. 56th and Pecos. I've got problems.

Damphouse jerks to a stop. "You're worse than a teenager." He laughs.

"My life." Flynn hits send on the message. "I can't even remember how we communicated before these, can you?"

A text from Goodman:

Where the hell are you?

Damphouse kills the engine. He unsnaps his seat belt, pops his door, climbs out, and leaves her sitting in the dark.

Flynn follows, the Durango's bank vault door unimpressed with her upper body strength. Damphouse parks half off the shoulder. She lands with a stumble. The ground falls away, and she hangs on to the swinging door to remain upright, then staggers around to the front, feeling out of sorts.

Goodman:

What the hell?

"What the hell," says Flynn. "Where are we?"

A sheet of city lights shoots north. Power lines and two giant transmission towers and their steel gray lattice dominate the foreground. Red taillights and white headlights on I-76 in the far distance. The fixed white noise hum familiar to every city on earth.

Damphouse crosses the road. He stands in front of a small suffering house that has lost all its mojo. Plywood covers the windows as if a cat 5 hurricane is bearing down. The mini porch sags. A wonky sidewalk leads the way to the door's dilapidated stoop. A faint glow seeps through the cracks around the door, but Flynn has a hard time believing the place is wired for electricity.

Damphouse stands in the gap of a waist-high metal fence.

"Here?" says Flynn. "Inside?"

"Well, yeah."

"It's safe?"

The code violation enforcement team could hit their monthly quota for tickets after a two-minute walk-around.

"You asked for it, here's your big fat lead."

Goodman:

Let us know you're okay.

"Jesus," says Damphouse. "So popular."

"Nature of my business."

Flynn sends Goodman an anxious sweating emoji face.

"I assume there's some sort of illegal stuff going down out of this house, and all I have to do is come back and wait around, see who is coming and going and then take it from there, right?"

"There's more than that," says Damphouse. "I could have given you the address and left it at that. Give me five minutes. Ten at the most."

"You gave Robbie McGrath something juicy, and she backed off your—situation. Whatever it was," says Flynn. "We'll call it a 'situation.'"

But you're not going to help me figure it out right now, and besides, I've got something going on back at the station."

Someone steps up behind her. A large hand clamps her bicep.

Her thoughts run to the dark side of the moon. And back.

"I know," says Damphouse. "When it rains it floods. Your lucky day. I called a meeting."

CHAPTER 78

One thing Harry has going for him is all the traffic in and out of Mary's place. All the Tinder traffic. By now, the neighbors must be rolling their eyes.

One problem, however, is what happened at Niko's. What did Mary say after sitting back down with her three movie pals?

Did she mention she knew him through work?

Not ideal.

And if the cops come around for another chat?

Yes, he knew her.

Yes, he'd been to her place.

They had a few dates, so what?

Harry wasn't one of the men slipping in and out of her bed in the Tinder revolving door of random lust and the casual hookup. *She even told me she used Tinder!*

With Mary, he took the traditional approach—traditional dinners, traditional date fodder like the art gallery.

Harry needs to work on his alibi. He needs to cleanse his apartment of questionable stuff. Will they question his music collection, the fascination with deaf composers? Not only Beethoven (so obvious!) but Draeseke and Holzbauer and Smetana too? What about his headphones? Why so many? Should he edit down to one pair (it might kill him) for appearance's sake?

Harry's colorful Broncos face remains. Two hours have passed since Flynn Martin dropped her so-called bomb of a story. It's good work, but she would have been nowhere without his guidance.

Harry checks online. The story is having the desired effect—creating a stir, and now *The Denver Post* and the other TV stations will run their versions and the pressure will rise. Who *really* killed Robbie McGrath?

◆ ◆ ◆

Harry pours himself a stiff E&J XO in his favorite heavy tumbler. He sits by the window and watches the comings and goings around Governor's Park. He picks Bedřich Smetana's lovely String Quartet in E Minor, the youthful enthusiasm Harry knows from the opening, the Allegro vivo appassionato. Lots, in fact, of appassionato. The piece's title is *From My Life*. It is autobiography, in less than thirty minutes, put to sound. It is utter honesty, pure heart, and it is loaded with detail. Sublime.

Harry knows what's coming, the piercing shriek of the violin that screams to the world how Smetana felt about his terrible case of tinnitus and the slow closing-in of the world of sound.

For now, Harry lets the violin dance and play.

PDQ, now in the process of being "cleared" of Robbie McGrath, is under no obligation to adhere to the old pattern of fifteen years ago. It isn't like there is a pledge form out there for serial killers. It isn't like there are rules. It's okay to adjust.

He reminds himself to add a few thoughts to "Prototype Rules." About flexibility. Adaptation. Going with the flow.

◆ ◆ ◆

Tonight, the law enforcement folks are figuring out their next move. The mayor too. How quickly will they side with the questions and doubt of Dr. Russell Malik? They might need to hold a news conference pronto and get behind Malik—or brush his claims aside.

If they back Malik, it might happen quickly.

When that happens, he needs to be ready because . . .

Wham!

If Harry is going to pull the pin on his surprise, it needs to happen fast. The faster, the better.

CHAPTER 79

Inside feels chillier than outside. A lamp sits on two stacked milk crates next to a lumpy sagging couch. An eclectic group of chairs, two of them functional thanks to duct tape, sit in a semicircle facing the couch. A quarter sheet of plywood serves as a coffee table. A dull stench like long-dead rodents sends a hand to cover her mouth and nose.

Carlos Herrera sits on the couch. Next to him is a man Flynn has never met. His sheer bulk is impressive. He might be fat, but it's more about the space he displaces and his relative mass next to Herrera. The weak light catches a cheek and its craggy surface.

"Phone," says Herrera. He stands, hand outstretched.

Flynn clenches the phone in her fist. She shoves both hands in the pockets of her jacket and pulls her arms close to her body.

"Let's have it," says Damphouse.

Flynn stares at her escort traitor. The hand around her bicep squeezes all the way to bone. Keeps squeezing. Flynn doubles over at the waist in a tight ball. Damphouse yanks on her arm, and it comes flailing out and the phone goes flying. Flynn gasps and falls, her knees stinging on the bare wood floor.

The phone lands near an open doorway that leads to a back room, maybe the kitchen. The phone lands upright. For a moment it issues a defiant glow. It blurts out the arrival of yet another text. The reply to the alert is the heel of Herrera's cowboy boot.

Flynn stands, not of her own accord.

"What the hell?" she says. "I get to see everything Robbie McGrath got to see."

"Who?"

This question comes from the man Flynn doesn't know.

"Robbie—"

"Do we know any Robbie somebody?"

Bruiser stands as he says this. He comes between Flynn and the pathetic wattage from the lamp. She puts him at six feet and an easy 250.

"Robbie who?" says Damphouse.

"No clue." Herrera shrugs.

"And here I assumed you gave up another scandal, a better one, to protect your own name," says Flynn.

"I thought we had an agreement."

"Until I knew you were part of this," says Flynn.

"What is 'this'?" says Bruiser.

With Damphouse and Herrera both being cops, Bruiser's profession isn't in question. Flynn's nose for a cop is as good as a chef's at picking out garlic. It's something about the haircuts and the eyes. The entitlement.

"That's what I'd like to know." Flynn stands, wobbling. She feels like she's been battered by a gauntlet. She counts her options for escape. She gets as high as zero.

"Oh, Robbie McGrath," says Bruiser. "Well, we have no idea about Robbie McGrath. She was killed by PDQ, as the entire city is fully aware."

"No," says Flynn. "She wasn't."

Bruiser straps on a puzzled face, so lame it wouldn't pass the audition for community theater. "How can you be so sure?"

"Sources," says Flynn. "Good ones. Robbie McGrath found your dirty show, and she was close to writing it all up."

"Oh really?" says Herrera.

"Maybe there's no television here or Wi-Fi or even indoor plumbing, but in fact tonight the ME came out on the news and said the same thing. Robbie McGrath was not killed by PDQ. On the surface it might have looked okay, but too many details were, you know, off. Which means the search is wide open."

Bruiser rolls his eyes. "You don't say."

"Yep," says Flynn.

"But it seems as if the assumption about PDQ is something you've been operating on for some time."

"Really?" Flynn matches Bruiser's bullshit-level fake sincerity. Given a nanosecond outside, she could hurl.

"We have sources too," says Damphouse. "Eyes. Ears. Friends."

Flynn's first chat with Damphouse was when? She couldn't keep track of the days. How quickly had Damphouse alerted his cronies that there was another reporter sniffing down the same trail as Robbie McGrath?

Or had they heard something earlier, based on her trip to El Paso and Juárez?

Or . . . Max?

"And so?" says Flynn.

"And so we know you have been knocking on doors, poking around across the border." Bruiser paces a circle. "By the way, we got news from Juárez. The deal on the house for Laura Rojas? Fell through. I guess she's back to figuring out where to live and how to make ends meet. All that unionizing work, you know? The bosses frown, as you might imagine. All they need is a small reason to show you the door. So many others waiting for the work. Right? Rough country, tough times."

Bruiser looks at Herrera for acknowledgment, as if the lone Hispanic in the room is an expert on news from border country.

"Definitely not the land of opportunity," says Herrera. "Unlike this one."

Flynn pictures Laura and her kids wandering in an unforgiving city, shudders at the thought.

Damphouse blocks the front door, behind Flynn. Herrera stands by the scrap metal corpse that was once her phone.

The longer she keeps the trio talking, the better. The longer they stay in this awful spot, nasty as it is, the better.

Flynn fears Damphouse the least in terms of size and age.

"Your problem," says Flynn, "is how are you going to explain another reporter—so soon?"

"No idea what you're talking about," says Bruiser.

Stay relaxed . . .

Surprise is key . . .

Except she feels so small. And so surrounded.

"What's your point?" says Herrera.

"That if you all seem worried," says Flynn, "it confirms there's a problem."

"With?" says Bruiser.

"With PDQ. With Robbie McGrath's murder."

"And they think people will believe your stories?" says Bruiser. Matter of fact. "After that horrible mess *you* made? The innocent, sweet college girl?"

"Did you ever think, What if you'd taken the cops' advice?" says Damphouse. "That Deborah Ernst might still be here? Have you thought about that a few times?"

She steps to Damphouse like they're old friends. "Like I said downtown—"

She jabs Damphouse in the eyes with two stiff fingers. He bleats. He is going down when her foot comes up and she catches him flush in the balls. His gasp switches to a cry like a desperate beggar. Damphouse thuds to the floor, grabs himself.

In the blur of movement, her heart sprinting, a black holster flashes. She spots the grip of a dark handgun on Damphouse's hip. Damphouse writhes on the floor, spews something unintelligible.

She squats by him, unsnaps the holster, and Flynn feels hands—too many to count.

On her leg. Shoulder. A clamp on her neck like a cold vise. One of them has her by the ankles, the other by the wrists.

The room spins like a busted ride at a cut-rate carnival.

Down is up. She corkscrews midair. Her last thoughts are a quick note of regret to Wyatt and that the landing is really going to hurt.

CHAPTER 80

Flynn wakes to muffled sounds. She feels tape on her face, the way it grabs when she moves her mouth, even to grunt.

Flynn's head pounds. Her wrists are bound. Flynn strains at the binding until she is sure she's drawn blood.

She's on her side, legs tucked up. She can't separate her ankles. She can't stretch her legs all the way without hitting the end of whatever box or coffin contains her. Her head touches the other. She writhes and wriggles. She leans up but her head bonks the top. Her hip bone burns. Flynn taps the box with her feet. Then jabs. The sound is hollow and plastic.

Muffled sounds of male voices in short, sharp barks. An engine rumbles to life. Flynn's box shakes with a mechanical purr.

Flynn pictures an abandoned gravel pit in the windblown hills of Wyoming. She imagines the waste lagoon of a hog farm on the eastern plains of Colorado or a mothballed mine shaft in the mountains. Cops must know best about disposing of bodies in better ways than two-bit murderers.

Flynn fights self-pity. Every time she thinks about her own stupidity, she tells her brain to go fuck itself. She has to think of something before her body is dumped in some never-to-be-disclosed location.

CHAPTER 81

"Harry? Jesus, what are you doing?"

"Is it late?"

The oxy bubble! He feels bulletproof.

"I was going to bed."

Harry has changed again, scrubbed his face of all the orange and blue crap. He rode the 0 back up Broadway, hoofed it to Mary's door.

"I came to apologize," says Harry. "I know it's late. Well, I didn't know it was that late."

Mary looks—*what*? Exasperated?

"Holy hell. I was so worried about you when I saw you at Niko's," says Mary. "You did not look yourself—at all."

They're inside by the shoe-drop mat. How did he forget the whole slippery socks thing? How? Maybe he'd whack her in the head with the heel of his Florsheim cap-toe oxfords.

"Really?" says Harry. "I wanted to apologize. It was one of those strange moments. My head was in another place. I was thinking so hard about something else. I don't know."

Mary stares at his shoes. Harry kicks them off.

"When in Rome," he says.

"I see you've got the headphones."

Smetana. He wonders if he listened to a piece a hundred times in a row, if he'd hear something new each time. With Smetana, maybe. *From My Life* will be his soundtrack now.

Now and forever.

"Yes," says Harry.

"Yes, what?"

"I'd love a drink."

"Well, I didn't—"

"I know. A quick one."

"Really quick?" says Mary.

"So quick."

Mary wears a gathered robe of some vintage. A bit of cleavage. He will soon see it all.

Bare feet—flash of red toenails. What if she's already *entertained*? What if No. 1 recently departed? What if No. 1 left the sheets a mess? Wet? Sticky? What if she isn't interested?

Fuck it.

"Wine?" says Mary.

"If it's not too fussy," says Harry. "Do you have any brandy?"

"Armagnac."

"Even better." Harry stands by the kitchen counter. No sign of dirty glasses. No sign of a predecessor. "A quick sploosh to toast. Shall we toast to clearing the air? What are you drinking?"

"I'll join you," says Mary. "You going to take off the headphones?"

Harry puts the headphones on the counter. They clink glasses.

"Okay." Harry raises his glass. For getting a late-night knock on her door, Mary appears, in a word, *game*. She's a live wire. But she suffers, down deep. Everyone suffers. Everyone needs to appreciate their everyday suffering. Get in touch with it. "Here's my apology. I'm sorry. I've been difficult. I'm here to start fresh. I'm up for anything. I promise not to be so opinionated. I promise not to do anything, well, *weird*. I promise not to make you feel uncomfortable."

Mary laughs. It's a sweet laugh, even cute and kind. It's the laugh of a college girl saying *I'm easier than you think*. "Apology accepted," says Mary. "And I can see the look in your eye."

"Look?" says Harry, playing along. "What?"

"You want to cut to the chase."

"Who, me?"

"What you could use is a long massage, Harry. Deep tissue, long and hard."

"Well," says Harry. "Then how about a go?"

"Just like that?" says Mary. "Three minutes after you're in the door?"

"Cutting to the chase," says Harry. "Your words. Part of the apology. Part of the whole package."

"Jesus." Mary looks at him hard. "It's not leap and go."

"But we know each other. We can finish our drink, watch something first? I think the best thing to do is get past all the awkward stuff. Clear the decks. I'm totally normal except maybe how much I love classical music. Did you know Bedřich Smetana wanted to compose like Mozart, but his father didn't see a career in music for his son? Can you imagine what our world would be like if more fathers and mothers steered their offspring toward the arts?"

"Who the hell is Bedřich—" She tries to pronounce the last name, gives up. "You're an odd one, you do know that?"

"Maybe a bit," says Harry. "Aren't we all?"

"Well, then, I'm sorry too," says Mary. "Come on. Bring your glass. I'd hate to see the Armagnac go to waste."

CHAPTER 82

Flynn braces herself so her body doesn't bang around during the hard stops. She flops and turns like a dying fish in the bottom of a boat. In her mind, it's the Durango. No highway. All stop and go, go and stop. Flynn whacks the side of the box with her legs.

Whack.
Thump.
Whack.

Her wrists remain bound, but her struggle with the tape has yielded an inch of give. She claws at any crevice where she can feel a perch. Her fingers probe a gap in the plastic box. The feisty edge tears at her skin. She feels above her and finds the three-fingers-wide opening on the security cover, her roof. Flynn scooches it forward. The material retracts onto its spool. Flynn guides it back with care so it doesn't snap or make a sound.

She is inside the camper shell.

Streetlights.

A gift.

Flynn stays low. She keeps up with the kicking and grunting routine as cover to suggest nothing has changed. With the light, she sees the edge of the duct tape around her ankles. She times her shouts and cries to cover the work of yanking at the tape. She throws a tantrum for the last bit, then calms down with a resigned soft sob. Sounds of a helpless victim, conceding to her pathetic fate.

Flynn peels the tape from her mouth. She takes in a slow suck of fresh air. She saws the tape around her wrists on the plastic edge. Her hands come free.

The SUV slows. Flynn gropes behind the panel. The viscera behind the plastic cover are a confusing mess of boxes and metal. She grabs at everything. Anything. She reaches high under the panel, pulling on random stuff.

The SUV stops. The rear window above her releases with a subdued *whump*. A trickle of cool air settles on her sweaty face.

A door opens—the overhead light snaps on. And off. A second door. Light again. And off. A dark silhouette flashes to her right—and one to her left.

Voices. Flynn crawls to the shadow of her compartment, hoping like hell it isn't time for Bruiser and Herrera to check their cargo. A conversation outside her rear window spits voices, no words.

Flynn waits. She puts her head down, curls up.

Headlights close in behind.

A shard of streetlight catches the handle of something tucked into a slot, off to a side of her rolling cell. She wraps a hand around it and gives it a tug. Her fingers trace a handle to its business end, a square-edged shovel. She pulls it close to her body like a lover. She curls her body around her treasure in case of a random flashlight. If one of them opens the back door to inspect, she will plant the shovel between the eyes of one captor. Two if she has time.

Flynn's heart whacks the floor of her box. She lifts her head. She puts an eye in the corner of the window.

Busted old van.

Solid side panels, light colored.

Standing by the front door of the van, a massive silhouette from the van's headlights.

Dwight Hatcher.

Talking with Bruiser and Herrera. Damphouse, she expects, is writhing back in the shit shack on the floor.

Hatcher stares at his phone. He hands Bruiser something. Bruiser and Herrera climb in the van and pull out. The van's beams flood Flynn's compartment with light, but not before Flynn drops down flush to the bed of the camper shell.

Flynn curls in a ball in the darkest shadow.

The front door opens and then snaps shut.

Flynn pushes open the back of the camper shell window, vaults herself sideways over the tailgate. One hand grips the shovel, and it follows her up and over, metal on metal.

CHAPTER 83

The only thing to catch her is gritty asphalt. She skids and scrambles for the side of the road.

Runs.

Flynn focuses on house lights across a dark patch of park, willing her legs to pump in an unfamiliar way.

Behind her, a car door slams.

The sound is unmistakable.

And so much closer than she thinks possible, given her head start.

Flynn holds the shovel close to her chest. She makes a sound like she's exhausted. Done.

She staggers. She gives the heavy breathing a bit of extra drama. It doesn't take much.

Flynn stops.

And turns.

"Motherfucker," she snarls.

Hatcher is a black hulking shadow against a black sky in a dark park. A voice. A shape.

"You're coming with me."

"Captain A, I presume?"

"Come on now," says Hatcher.

"You were there way back. First time around with PDQ."

"Damn right."

"And not happy when they shut things down?"

He jerks in a breath, lets out a long sigh. "We almost had him. A day away. Right on his tail."

"You got involved with those dirty cops Robbie McGrath was after? Covering for them? And when Robbie comes poking around, you think maybe you can prove your point, stage a scene, force them to go after PDQ again?"

Hatcher's feet scuffle in the grass. His clothes rustle. Blackness. Darkness. He sniffles. Black shape. Black shadow.

"You're annoying, Flynn Martin."

"But you rushed, didn't you?" says Flynn.

"Fuck you," says Hatcher.

"You rushed on the music," says Flynn. "You didn't think anyone would notice. Or maybe you didn't think anyone had *ever* noticed. PDQ? He used one version of 'Jupiter.' Every time. Same song, same version. *London*, you motherfucker." The words come easy. Half guess, but it makes sense now too. "A conductor named Boult. London Philharmonic. It mattered to PDQ, but it didn't matter to you."

"Nosy reporter cunt."

The voice gives her a spot. Flynn plants one foot. She grips the shovel like a baseball bat. She swings, guess-aiming for his legs. She hears the *whoosh*. The blade lands with a satisfying crack. Metal on bone. The blow rattles her hands. The black shape falls with an agonizing groan. Flynn tosses the shovel at the heap.

And runs.

CHAPTER 84

Mary's upstairs room is warm. Her bed is expansive. Mary places herself on the side of the mattress by the lamp where she might read a book, as if they are to only use a small section for whatever is to come.

She pulls a condom from a drawer in a side table. How many times has she made *that* move? She rips the package for him, takes it out. She holds it for him, the squishy disk like a priest's wafer. An offering.

Harry doesn't mind.

Tonight, he is the new lucky enthusiastic boyfriend.

No weirdness.

Smile, compliment, lick, enjoy, show patience, no rush, keep your head down.

Literally!

Enjoy.

Vanilla sex isn't bad. It ends at the same finish line.

Harry is inside her. He compliments her shape. Her breasts, in fact, are full and beautiful. She looks longer in bed, sleeker and more youthful. Gazelle. Lioness. Animal. She is comfortable nude, relaxed about it all. Experienced. Her confidence speaks volumes. It's enticing. She likes anticipation too. She smells of rose and lavender.

Harry leans up. She reaches a hand down to feel around. He pulls out over her protestations and slides down to use his mouth and tongue. He wants to see Mary lose control. He grabs her hand and puts it back on herself so she can touch the right spots the right way. He watches for a bit and kisses around, then moves in and does his level best to be the giver.

Mary plunges her head under a pillow. Gasps.

Harry takes it as encouragement to continue doing what he's doing, and he vows the patience of Job in his oxy bubble in Mary's bed in a moment he's been thinking about for a long time and here he is, now, right now, right now, savoring her.

Tomorrow, she'll learn that Beethoven and Shostakovich are side by side, that for every Ode to Joy there has to be a String Quartet No. 8 in C Minor.

One defines the other.

Tonight is about the reset. It's about getting Harry's foot in the door.

PDQ is ready.

He has been waiting in the wings, staring at the main action, for too long.

Mary's breaths are short. Her amygdala is shutting down, her hippocampus too. In order to come, she needs to give over to the pleasure centers in her brain. In order to come, she needs to let her guard down.

All the way.

Tomorrow, given what Harry is about to do now, her guard will never go up.

Until . . .

◆ ◆ ◆

"I know," says Harry.

They are *lingering*. She has one leg covered, one leg exposed. Harry leans his head on a hand. She sits up with her back on a bundle of pillows.

"You *found* her?"

"It wasn't that far from the bar to our place," says Harry. "One bar in town. I mean, there weren't that many options unless she bailed and went into Brush or Fort Morgan to drink. I had a bad feeling."

Mary looks on the verge of crying.

"And you knew, immediately?"

"The car was a mess," says Harry. "There was no way someone could have survived."

"But you went right up to it?"

Harry pauses.

"It wasn't like a thing you decide to do or not do."

"You knew you'd see your mother—dead?"

"And part of me knew it would be over."

"For her?"

"Well, yes, the agony for her. The miserable situation she was in. But over for me too. She stood up to him," says Harry. "That is, occasionally. But more often than not, she would play music, this certain piece of music, and pretend she couldn't hear. But she could hear. Every single blow."

Harry loves the effect the story has on women. Having the story is worth enduring what he endured. Almost. At some point or another, all the women hear the story. Sympathy 101.

Harry is a man of wealth and taste. Except for, well, this one thing.

Three of the women who heard it weren't conscious when he went through the story, but he told them anyway.

With Mary, he is doing things out of order.

CHAPTER 85

Flynn leans on the ringer. Duct tape dangles from her wrist like streamers. She waits a full quarter second, then raps on the security door as insurance, bloodied hand smearing the glass.

Flynn scans behind her, across a strip of park, and gets her bearings, the northern edge of Sloan Lake. West Denver.

Flynn's hand stings. Blood trickles down her calf from the scrape on her knee. Flynn knocks again. The door opens.

The look on the man's face tells her all she needs to know.

"Help." Thumb to ear, pinkie to mouth. "It's urgent."

"You okay?"

The words come muffled through the security door. The man is older and slight.

"I'm a reporter with—"

"I know." A key clacks as it spins, then the outer door is ajar, the most welcome gesture of trust ever extended in her direction. "I know who you are. What the hell happened?"

Flynn steps inside.

"The phone," she says, "as fast as possible."

CHAPTER 86
WEDNESDAY

Jennifer Hills rarely stops to chat before dropping things off in her office. This time, she asks about his bumps and bruises, but he downplays everything. No big deal.

"But the police?" she says. "Claiming at first it was PDQ and now? Did you see the late-night news?"

"What? No."

Playing clueless.

"The police chief and the mayor say they are taking another look. The ME's claim and all that. *Jesus.*"

"So if it's not PDQ, isn't that better?"

"Good god, no. Not if there's someone else who knows what PDQ did. And could pull it off? Like PDQ cloned himself or trained somebody else? How's that *better*?"

"I hadn't looked at it from that angle," says Harry. "I assumed it was good news, perhaps, that he hadn't resurfaced. I mean, maybe he did die in a car crash or something before anybody could put two and two together, you know? And so then that would mean the cops had to look for someone who had access to all the details, who thought they could stage something. You know? It would limit the search."

"I don't know." Hills has a wonderful husky voice. Inscrutable eyes. "To me it feels like a double sort of extra-nightmarish hell."

Sandy Ingalls, when she arrives late for work and going on about the parking woes out there, agrees with her boss. The chat is Harry's worst nightmare. Ingalls goes on. And on. Harry wants to tap his wrist and say, *Look at the time, look at the time.*

After Sandy Ingalls settles in at her cubicle, Harry pulls up the newspaper website. Reporter Judy Hayes, a name Harry has been following for years, takes a cautious approach about the new information. Hayes credits Flynn's station for the late-night comments from the police chief and also for the interview with some bigwig in the ME's office.

But there it is: "Police sources say that the ME's questions have shifted and broadened their investigation. Their initial assumption about PDQ's involvement has been downgraded as they reconsider the evidence in a new light."

There it is.

There it fucking is.

He will, he supposes, give Flynn Martin an ounce of credit. One point. Maybe two.

Harry works for twenty minutes. He goes through the motions, makes the regular sounds, does the regular things, makes the regular comments. Asks Sandy for this file, gives her back that file. Tells Jennifer Hills about a problem he found with an applicant for a position in special education.

Then, he texts Mary:

Thank you for opening your door. Thank you for the reset.

I slept like a baby. What time did you leave?

Around 3. Ubered home.

He had walked the whole way. He hadn't slept since dozing, for an hour, in Mary's bed.

And now?

At work. You?

I couldn't move this morning. I'm taking a day. Don't tell anyone. I could drag myself to work, but I feel so . . . satiated, I guess. Relaxed.

At some point, Harry fetched a second round of Armagnac. Was that after? While they were lingering? He can't remember all the things he said, but he knows he sounded earnest and heartfelt. No music nerd stuff, nothing like that. She had so many questions about Harry's mother. And Harry's mother's sad death. She was good at empathy. Or maybe it was the real thing.

Sorry if I cost you a day.

Small price to pay.

And a smiley face.

I was wondering if I could buy you a proper dinner tonight or perhaps, if you're staying in, I can bring food over?

Two nights in a row?

Not being pushy, I hope. Doesn't sound like you had other plans.

Well, no.

Okay, then, what time?

Harry applies himself. He puts in a busy morning. Focused, or makes it look that way. Inside, he's all teenage giddy.

When Jennifer opens her Tupperware tub of tuna for lunch, Harry walks down the marble staircase to the lobby and pulls up Confide.

You done good.

Feeling better?

Much. This Hatcher guy?

One of the homicide boys back then. He was chasing you.

He failed.

Claimed he was right on your tail.

Obviously not!

Behind the scenes, the cops are even more emphatic. They know now Robbie wasn't yours.

Really?

Guaranteed. You'll see.

It's been a long road.

What do you mean?

Life owes me a break, don't you think?

On what basis?

Everything.

Such as?

You know what a scherzo is?

Musical term.

It means joke, a humorous bit. A playful interlude before all the minor chord misery. My early days? No scherzo. Just dad and his fist. Mom and her glass.

So what you did was all justified?

Mom tried, you know? But she couldn't stand up to him. And then she was gone. She went through the windshield, you know? Head and shoulders. No seat belt. We lived out in the country. A short drive from the bar, but you don't have to be going fast to do some serious damage. I only hope she didn't feel much pain.

Colorado?

Nice try.

So you worked those issues out? By killing?

I'm better. That's all. And now it's back to normal. Getting there, anyway.

You're fooling yourself. You think you've changed.

Don't do that. Fifteen years of squeaky clean.

That stunt with my boy. INVADING my house. You haven't changed.

Fuck you.

That's not transformation.

Fifteen years!

Of not lighting the powder keg. But it's still there.

I am a functioning, normal, every-day member of society!

You expect society to shrug and say "There, there, no worries?" Every child who grows up in an imperfect family gets to hurt others? Gets a pass?

He BEAT THE HELL OUT OF ME! She IGNORED IT!

And you were helpless?

It was relentless. Do you get that?

I get that life isn't fair.

Yes, YOU should know. I hope your reputation is restored.

Don't worry about me.

If you insist.

You need to turn yourself in.

Now you've gone crazy.

Better for you.

I've told you. I got better. On my own.

The publicity has given them time to look at the evidence again. Plus, you made some mistakes.

Harry wants to jump through the phone. He was so close during the Broncos rally. He could have snapped her twiggy pretentious pompous entitled neck.

Says you.

I'm telling you it would be easier if you came in, put an end to it. No more looking over your shoulder. Wondering.

You got one albatross dangling from your neck. Deborah Ernst. Her dead body will look like a baby hummingbird compared to the bloody monster that will dangle next to it.

I'm giving you facts.

And the FACT that you told others gave me an idea. You'll get all the credit.

I did everything you asked.

Except... GO IT ALONE.

Harry closes Confide, deletes the app.

CHAPTER 87

Flynn waits for a reply.

She types: Turn yourself in.

She wants the last word, even if he never sees it. In the remote chance that Confide's messages are, in fact, stored on some ultra-secret cloud high in some digital stratosphere, at least she has urged Mr. PDQ Asswipe to do the right thing.

Inside, Flynn trembles. The exchange proves her point—his volatility is right there. All you have to do is scratch it.

If the investigators ever come around, if the good police find a reason to think she needs investigating, at least she has created a bit of a so-called record. And she managed to prod Harry into spilling his guts.

And if it *was* Colorado, how many drunk women plowed into a tree and killed themselves, what, twenty-five years ago? Thirty?

How hard will it be to develop a list?

Flynn puts her new phone down on her desk. Her fingers function on her right hand, but the left palm is wrapped in gauze from bracing herself against the fall and skidding on the mean pavement. Her left knee sports a cousin wound and companion bandage. Her flying squirrel routine would draw a six, at best, from a friendly judge.

All things considered, the bodily damage is minimal.

◆ ◆ ◆

The last twelve hours are a fuzzy, woozy hodgepodge blur.

Three hours of police investigation at the scene, dominated by a dozen or more squad cars, an equal number of unmarked vehicles, and an ambulance. The cluster of cop cars turned night to noon. Dwight Hatcher was carted off to the hospital with a fractured leg.

Officer Jerry Damphouse, she found out from Max, had rammed his SUV into the base of the overpass where Hampden crosses Federal. Cops estimated his impact speed at eighty miles an hour. Four other cars wrecked as they avoided Damphouse's manic path, but nobody else was seriously injured. The site of his suicidal wreck is fifteen miles from the dilapidated house in North Denver, so he apparently took his time to work up the courage.

Bruiser was Captain Vic Akin. He'd been arrested by state troopers, thanks to her description of the Ford Econoline, as he fled west on I-70. Flynn had no doubt it was the van on the videotape when Enrique Rojas's body was dumped in the alley. Herrera was with Akin. They were both in jail now.

Flynn's rolling cell was a second pickup with a camper shell. Ownership and registration are being sorted out.

Based on Flynn's description and location, the cops have gone to the sad house on Fifty-Sixth Avenue to secure it for evidence.

The sheer scale of the police activity on the north side of Sloan Lake meant overnight crews from all the media outlets got footage of lights flashing and police officers milling about. But reporters had a hard time piecing together the bigger-picture story. Something about dirty cops. At first, Damphouse's suicide looked unrelated. The cops were saying even less than what Dwight Hatcher might normally relay, which wasn't much.

Flynn's station carried the general facts on the morning news, but so far there has been no mention of her involvement. *Good.* When she made calls from the random house at Sloan Lake, she first called 911, then her father, and then Goodman. Both Michael and Goodman were awake—and worried. Max, after finding the doleful cop lair in North

Denver and calling for help, had stayed with Wyatt, who had been in an anxious mood all night after her phone gave up the ghost under Herrera's boot. Goodman and her father came to the scene at Sloan Lake.

Flynn is sure she explained all the events and all her decisions and how she ended up driving to North Denver with Officer Jerry Damphouse 895 times. At a minimum. Some explanations were in excruciating slow motion. Others were given a *Reader's Digest* touch.

The only detail she will not reveal, of course, is one.

Her father delivered her back to her Malibu, parked downtown. On top of everything else, she had to follow him back to his condo with a giant GO BRONCOS! scrawled in red lipstick on her passenger-side window.

There was no way she was sleeping alone. She drank a 4:00 a.m. beer, dozed off and on for two hours, drove home to get a fresh set of clothes, showered at her father's, drove to a phone store on Colfax Avenue, and waited a torturous hour while the sales dude pulled all her data from the cloud, restored all her apps. Adrenaline and fatigue battled for supremacy.

At work, Goodman gave her the full-court press. He pulled in Tamica to bolster his case, but Tamica took Flynn's side and urged the station to trust its team. Chris Casey was dispatched for the follow-up on the Damphouse suicide and the arrests of the three police officers. There was a brief discussion about whether or not to include the kidnapping of reporter Flynn Martin—and her escape—in her own station's coverage. Flynn had seen more than a few of the Sloan Lake lookie-loos with their cell phones out, taking video. She is being plastered, she is sure, across all social media. As soon as the police step forward with their recap, her name will be entangled in the whole mess.

It's inevitable.

The only way to control the story is to own the story.

Flynn's questioner this time is Sara Cornette. Flynn wonders how things would have turned out for Debbie Ernst and all of them, Jerry Damphouse, too, if the vacation schedules had put Sara Cornette on Aruba during a different week.

Tamica stands behind the camera. Sara Cornette sits behind the lights in the simple interview set in the cold studio. And Flynn answers every question in sober, calm, matter-of-fact detail.

The only detail she will not reveal, of course, is one.

"So who suggested following Robbie McGrath's work?"

Cornette has no list of questions. Flynn tells the whole story about Damphouse and going for the ride to North Denver. Flynn sinks into a trance, searches for a calm space. Goodman listens, off to the side. Tamica stands behind the camera. The only thing Flynn will keep to herself, for now, is her source.

"The idea grew out of a discussion with my father," says Flynn. The statement holds a kernel of truth. "And it seemed logical, to see where Robbie had been working. I was following a thread, like any other story."

"When did you realize that PDQ was, I guess, being framed?"

Flynn thinks back through the blur of days.

"I'm not sure." PDQ will see this. That's a given. "It was a gradual kind of thing. I had a coach helping me step by step. My father, Michael Martin. When it comes to journalistic credibility in this city, a name many know."

"When did you realize you were chasing police officers? Corrupt police officers?"

"Well," says Flynn, "whenever it was, it was much too late."

"Let me get this straight," says Tamica. The long interview with Cornette is over. Good luck, thinks Flynn, in finding the best few minutes to use on air. "You want to screen the footage from the Broncos rally?"

"He was there," says Flynn.

CHAPTER 88

"Now it's time."

Max has that look.

It isn't only the look. It's his whole damn grounded self. Always so sure. It's the solid register to his voice, the cadence to his words. He knows not to plead.

Flynn says nothing.

And doesn't say no.

"It will come out," says Max.

"Are you sure?"

"Another one of your fellow reporters will dig it up."

"Nobody knows except Dad. You. Tamica. And me."

They stand in the parking lot outside the station. It's midafternoon.

"For now, nobody else knows," says Max. "But you'd be in a stronger position for your own personal PR if you go to them, lay it out."

"Them?" says Flynn.

Max nods.

"So this is the cop talking," says Flynn.

"I don't get this thing where you think I'm two different people."

"I wouldn't have much to give the cops if I did talk to them," says Flynn. "He's used every encrypted trick to communicate."

"You don't know what you have," says Max.

Flynn can't tell him about the blurry side-angle-view screen-capture shot from Niko's. She can't tell him about the much better picture of him in goofy Bronco face paint. He was so close he could have tapped her on the shoulder.

"Give me a day," says Flynn.

"Why?"

"Let this settle down. Catch my breath."

"Every hour matters," says Max.

"He's been gone for fifteen years," says Flynn. "He's not going to resurface now—he wanted his name cleared for Robbie McGrath, and that's what he got. A day isn't going to matter."

"You need to tell me how or why you're so sure of that fact."

"Because I know why he wanted me to help him," says Flynn. "He wants to go back to his hole. He feeds off the pride of avoiding capture all these years."

"You have no idea how they can pluck DNA out of thin, nothing air. If you have anything he might have touched—anything he might have brushed up against—it might be enough for them to get that first scrap of information about this asshole. Think of the families out there. Waiting."

"Jesus," says Flynn. "No pressure."

"I'm laying it out. How's it going to look?"

What does she have left to prove?

What?

"You're right," says Flynn. "But—one day. Okay? I want to give Wyatt a hug he'll never forget. I want to buy my father dinner. I want to find a way to thank you."

She also feels an urge to press harder about identifications from the quartet of women at Niko's. If there is a way to nail down an ID on one of them, it might lead to the one who knows PDQ.

"You're taking a big risk," says Max.

"One more thing," says Flynn. "Captain A—Dwight Hatcher. Any idea how he got that name?"

Max grimaces. "When DPD turned down the heat on the PDQ work way back when, Dwight Hatcher became known for his explosive tirades. They suspended him without pay for eight weeks. Anger management program too. Somewhere in there, the Captain Asshole name was born. When he came back, they assigned him to vice, and he figured the whole system was corrupt, so he settled in with some bad apples and found a way to make up for his lost pay. By then, the nickname had stuck."

"And he kept his ties with Akin and that bunch even after being reassigned to communications?"

"Yeah," says Max. "He had his own secret tap and crooked money flowing. Ties that bind."

CHAPTER 89

"You're back," says Elizabeth. "Table for one?"

"Not today," says Flynn. Niko's is slow before the evening rush. Elizabeth stacks silverware roll-ups in a plastic bin. "I was hoping to catch you."

"Okay." Elizabeth looks cautious. Worried.

"It's about that same group of customers."

"What?"

"Is there anything else about them that might help us figure out a name for any one of them? One would help."

"I mean, I don't know."

On the way to Niko's, Flynn weighed the pros and cons of coming all the way clean to the cops about PDQ, like Max wants. Spill all. Her interview with Sara Cornette was, of course, incomplete. It's due to air on the five, the six, and the ten—tomorrow. The station wants a day to get the town pumped to see Flynn Martin tell all. Tell *most*.

But when the whole story comes out, what will her life look like after the city learns she was working with PDQ? Who will savage her decision-making *then*?

"It's such a blur in here, you know? Sometimes you go table to table and you're a robot. The key to good customer service is—"

Elizabeth stops. Stares at her feet. Comes back.

"Wait," she says. "One of them had a nice camera on the table. I asked about it because I fiddle a bit with photography. Anyway, I asked her about the camera, and it turns out she's a street photographer. Artsy stuff. And she said her daughter had picked up photography from her and had 'blown up.' Of all things. They were all on their way to see her daughter's show at a gallery downtown."

Flynn rubs her cheek. Thinks. "Unfortunately, that doesn't really narrow it down."

"I know." Elizabeth is ready. "But I remember the woman said her daughter had been featured in that arts weekly. *Westword*? She was heading to New York for a big show. So later I went online and looked, and when I saw the name, it lined up. Emily Berns."

"With a *u* or an *e*? B-e-r-n-s?"

PDQ Victim No. 3 was Berns. The last one. The drugstore cashier. Hearing the name gives her a shudder, but it has to be the universe stirring up random shit.

"Why?" says Elizabeth. "With an *e*, I believe."

"Very strange," says Flynn.

"How so?"

"I'll know soon enough if it's a random coincidence," says Flynn. Sure, the city has been refocused on PDQ, but most people don't walk around knowing the spellings of the surnames of his three victims.

"The show is at the Rive Gauche," says Elizabeth. "I didn't think there was much of a 'Rive' around here to have a 'Gauche,' unless you count Cherry Creek. But there you go."

CHAPTER 90

Flynn wasn't wrong when she mentioned all the looking-over-the-shoulder stuff.

That zinger hangs around like a gloomy cloud.

But . . .

Normal is.

Normal does.

Normal comments.

Normal interactions.

Steady.

He pulls out his best earbuds, cues up *Liebesträume* by Liszt, but he can't connect. Not now. Not today. Who knows that Franz Liszt's father was a buddy of Beethoven's? And Haydn's?

Harry wants the music to obliterate his thought process, to scoop him up in its soul and whisk him away.

But Liszt fails.

Next, Schubert.

Harry feels a special kinship with the easygoing tunesmith for one major reason. Schubert knew the internal burn of mercury thanks to the pills he took to treat his syphilis. The pills killed him at such a tender age.

But Schubert is too wimpy. All Harry can picture is Schubert cowering in Beethoven's shadow, so in awe of the master that he avoided greeting him on the streets of Vienna.

At work, Harry checks the news stations online. The coverage features a cop Harry has never seen before explaining that the police chief has ordered a full internal investigation. There is a booking photo of a cop named Vic Akin, another booking photo of a cop named Carlos Herrera, lots of mentions of Dwight Hatcher (five photos of him over the years, from early days as a cop to PR honcho), and footage of a mangled SUV so embedded in a bridge abutment that it looks as if it's been through a junkyard crusher.

There is a photograph of an officer in uniform, smiling. The smiling cop was the guy behind the wheel of the speeding SUV and, clearly, part of the dark cop gang. Reporters commandeered a small park near Sloan Lake to show where a kidnapping of a fellow reporter had come to an end. In daytime, however, there is nothing to see. The gist of things isn't hard to pick up. Drug smuggling. Fake undercover "investigations." And *The Denver Post* featured a prominent story by the one and only Judy Hayes that runs through Dwight Hatcher's previous assignment as a homicide detective and a key member of the PDQ "war room" from way back when (*What a joke, what a waste of time and money!*).

Flynn's station promises that Flynn Martin will tell the "full story" at five.

Ha! PDQ laughs at that one.

Not hardly.

Harry knows far too much about Flynn's son, Flynn's father, and Flynn's favorite camerawoman for her to breathe a word.

That unsettled feeling.

It is familiar and yet odd at the same time.

Is it that hyperawareness coming back?

Is he already committed?

If Harry is forced to testify, under oath, he'd answer *yes*.

Harry packs his briefcase for the trip home. He is the last to leave.

The night is just beginning.

CHAPTER 91

Flynn finds Rive Gauche three blocks south of the DPD headquarters. Flynn can only begin to imagine the political infighting and bureaucratic snarling inside the massive building as the cops try to regain the public trust, but however they decide to go about restoring their reputation, it's going to be a long, long road.

The gallery is a converted Victorian house, most of the main floor gutted for one big open space.

The receptionist is close to six feet tall, with Little Orphan Annie hair and oversize orange-rimmed glasses.

"In fact," she says, "Emily was here a few minutes ago."

"Really?" says Flynn.

"That U-Haul van out front is hers. She went out for coffee but shouldn't be but a minute or two."

Flynn waits on the creaky wood porch. In a minute, Emily Berns crosses the street, heading back. She is short and sullen. Spiky-angry hair. A silver nose ring. She is accompanied by a young man with waist-long dreadlocks. They cradle giant to-go cups. Emily wears a baggy dark-green jacket, fashion by army surplus. The boyfriend, tufts of a starter beard on an underslung chin, wears a dark hoodie sweatshirt with a Metro State University logo.

At first, Emily Berns thinks the news station wants to do a story on her work and the big show in New York. Flynn sets her straight, but doesn't want to raise suspicions by bringing up the fact that she shares a name with one of PDQ's victims.

"My mother?" Emily scrunches her face.

"I'm looking for a friend of your mother's. Your mother and three of her friends came to your show."

When was it? Flynn has no idea. She can't do the math.

"Right," says Emily.

"Do you know her friends?"

"Well, I met them. But I don't *know* them."

"Is your mother—reachable?"

Flynn waves her phone as a prop.

"You want my mother's phone number?"

"That's the idea," says Flynn. "You could call her and explain it first, if you want."

"You're a TV reporter?" says Emily.

Flynn nods. Isn't her station's jacket enough? Corporate emblem as good as a sheriff's badge?

The boyfriend half smiles. "She was the one at the gas station." He says it like Flynn is an exhibit in a quirky roadside museum, *Reporters Who Fucked Up.*

Flynn wishes she'd brought Tamica. Or Max. She stares at Emily, ignores the boy.

"Can you at least say what this is about?"

The boyfriend's eyes are stoner glazed. "Reporters," he says as a one-word self-fulfilling indictment and conviction.

"It's important," says Flynn.

"Can you say what it is?" says Emily.

"I'm going to make you an offer. I have a good friend who recently left my station. A reporter. She moved to New York two months ago, big contract with a network affiliate. She loves art and she loves photography. You get your mom on the phone, and I'll make a call to her and she can do a feature. Put you on the map."

Emily's eyes light up. Flynn shoots a quick glance at the boyfriend, who looks like he's sucking on a sour pickle. "What's your cell number?" says Emily. "I'll text you all my mom's contact info."

Flynn gives her the number.

"And text me all the details of your show. Gallery, date it opens, all that good stuff—address and everything. Shoot me your bio, a headshot, and maybe a statement of work too. I'll forward it to my friend, and you can expect a call."

The lie comes easy, but the trade-off seems justified.

"Okay," says Emily. "Deal. What's your reporter friend's name—the New York reporter?"

"Hey," says the boyfriend. "I'm sorry."

"Stuff it," says Flynn.

"Your friend?" says Emily. "What's her name?"

"Send me your mom's info and I'll text it back," says Flynn. "Everything."

CHAPTER 92

Flynn drives a block, stops. Her heart feels like the edges of an egg on a too-hot pan, fluttering and bubbling. She wills Martha Berns to answer.

It works.

Flynn introduces herself. Martha sounds patient, thanks Flynn for the compliment on her daughter's artistic success.

"My friends?" she says.

"A group of four the other night when you went to the gallery? Stopped to eat at Niko's first?"

"What's this about?"

Like daughter, like mother.

"Do you recall a moment at Niko's when one of the four in your group spotted someone—someone she recognized?"

Martha lets the question settle. "Yes," she says. "I do."

"Which one of your friends?"

"Is she in trouble or something?"

"Not at all."

"And you're a reporter."

"Yes." Why does affirming that label feel like a confession?

"But I've got no proof of that."

"I suppose you don't. A matter of trust, I guess. Are you paying attention to what's going on in the city?"

"Well, sure."

"Do you watch the news? Or read the paper?"

"Kind of. Sort of."

Mentioning PDQ might be too alarmist. "There is this story breaking now about this ring of corruption in the police department."

"Right," says Martha. "What about you give me your number, and I'll call her and discuss it? Privacy and all."

"It's urgent."

"Like *now* urgent?"

"Yes," says Flynn. "Like yesterday."

CHAPTER 93

How now, Gustav Holst?

Would Harry even be in this moment if it wasn't for "Jupiter, the Bringer of Jollity"?

What if Gustav Holst had not become a composer? If the neuritis in Holst's arm prevented him from playing piano?

Hmmm?

What then?

"What if" is a pointless road.

What Harry has already accomplished is a feat.

Skill, courage.

Endurance.

Patience.

He's got them all.

Okay, maybe not perfection. He's made some mistakes. He should add "humility" to his list of positive traits because he certainly hasn't been perfect.

And now he can make them look like utter fools.

Again.

◆ ◆ ◆

Inventory time:

1. iPod Nano.

His last one.

2. "Jupiter, the Bringer of Jollity" loaded on it. Adrian Boult, of course.

Harry hears those trumpets, drained of bombast and in balance with the strings and the other winds.

3. Headphones. Cheapies from Walgreens.

The point, of course, is the tableau. She won't be listening because she will be dead.

4. Syringe with four-inch needle.

It's been a long time since Harry has practiced puncturing the tympanic membrane, but there isn't much to it. Once she's unconscious.

5. Nitrile gloves.

6. Harry's Personal Surveillance Identity Prosthetic, a realistic mask that carries the image of the most generic White American guy ever born. It looks like any other human being (and not a mask), other than the eyes.

It's the best $200 Harry ever spent. He likes wearing it around the condo. Sometimes he catches himself off guard.

7. Mercury.

Harry's remaining two ounces of the quicksilver wonder remind him of all the time spent cruising estate sales looking for antique jelly thermometers, the occasional old-school thermostat too.

8. Fentanyl.

During his three-year run, Harry found what he needed on the streets. He knew the edgier spots of town. It wasn't hard. It was a matter of going in firm and clear. Years later, when he saw a story about how easy it was to order Chinese fentanyl online, he thought it wouldn't be a bad idea to have a supply on hand in case his downstairs brain started acting up again. So he had a small batch shipped to his work address. Piece of cake.

9. Burner shoes.

What else?

10. Cable ties. Eighteen-inchers. Black.

The idea of this timing concept is exquisite. How can it get any better? And he has already scoped her place. What an advantage!

He'll be apologetic.

Maybe share a drink or two. Maybe he'll fuck her again, first. Could he? No.

Obvious issues with that if there is fresh . . . *whatever.*

With the mask and gloves, there will be no exposed skin. He will be in. He will be out.

Or maybe he'll wait a bit.

Make it normal at first.

Maybe he'll play bartender and crush a few oxy tabs in her tumbler to get the party started.

You want it rough? Okay, let's give it a go.

Then the stinging jab of fentanyl.

Then, he'll roll her on her side and perforate one eardrum. Always the left.

Then, the mercury.

Harry lays out his supplies in a black messenger bag and sets the bag by the front door.

CHAPTER 94

Flynn stares at her phone. She isn't texting and driving. Or talking and driving.

She is staring and driving.

Unless the phone rings and prompts a welcome detour, there is only one person she wants to see.

Well, there are two people, but Wyatt is clear across town in Bear Valley.

◆ ◆ ◆

January haze cloaks Cheesman Park. Damp sheets of mist settle on every surface. Night chews up day, swallows it whole.

Flynn parks her Malibu on the street. She checks her voicemail to make sure no calls snuck through during her staring contest with the obstinate, mind-of-its-own device. The voicemail queue sits empty. She walks across the street to her father's condominium, then worries the cell signal might not penetrate the concrete-and-steel structure during the brief elevator ride to her father's floor.

Flynn waves off her father's offer of beer and vittles. She accepts coffee. She won't sleep for a week, at least, even with a dinner plate full of melatonin nibbles.

Her father listens with the patience of a statue. Flynn holds up her phone to show him the last defiant hurdle and asks if he has a

Glock handy so she can threaten the phone until it burps up a call from Martha or her friend.

"What's going to happen then?" says her father.

"Then this woman from the restaurant gives me his name."

"And then?"

"And then we have the name."

They sit at the table by the picture window. An occasional jogger trudges through the gloom below.

"And you want to do this all on your own because why?"

"Because he's mine," says Flynn.

"Yours?"

Her father has that look, which isn't "a look" at all. It's pure inscrutability. The less he appears to judge, the more he judges.

"What is this, cognitive therapy?" she says.

"You must have a plan."

"I want his name first—and maybe where he works. Or lives."

"And Max?"

Max means all the cops.

"What about *Max*?"

"You have to ask yourself, Why don't you want his help? That is, *their* help?"

"You're sticking up for the police?"

"Most of them are good people—top to bottom. And you don't want to go toe to toe with PDQ. So pull them in," says her father.

"He came into my *house*." Flynn stands. She flashes back on the doll, the chair in the closet, the terrifying roller-coaster ride when he pretended to have kidnapped Wyatt. "I want his name. I want to get his name and hand it to the cops, at least. Signed, sealed, done, delivered."

Her father moves about as much as the stone pavilion at the top of the rise across the park. "What are you trying to justify?"

"Nothing," says Flynn. "Except maybe that my instincts don't suck."

"Okay, then. Wrap your instincts around the idea of pointing a finger at a guy who has done a bang-up job of protecting his identity for more than fifteen years. And wrap your instincts around the public reaction when they find out you've been sitting on something that could have saved them all a week or two of dread. Pure dread."

"Well, you know—"

Flynn's phone chirps. The caller is unidentified.

"Think about it," says her father.

CHAPTER 95

"I know it's an odd question," says Flynn.

"Martha says you wanted to know the name of the guy we ran into. In the restaurant?"

"Exactly."

Flynn expects her to spit it out.

"Yes, but—Flynn Martin?"

"Yes?"

"You were involved in that incident."

"Yes, that was me."

"One of my best friends was that young woman's teacher at Regis." The woman, so far, has only identified herself as Mary. "She's having trouble sleeping. She can't stop thinking about how it all happened. And now you want me to spit out the name of a friend, a friend who has every right to privacy, to someone I don't know? I mean, I don't even know it's you, other than your say-so. And if I could verify it, I'm not sure it's any of your business."

The words sting. Flynn says nothing.

"I mean, the whole city knows what you've done here in the past day or so," says Mary. "But you're going against one of my fundamental personal codes here. I work in human resources."

"For?"

"Again," says Mary. "That's a personal question. But I will tell you I work for the state. So I'm a public employee. And I feel a bit responsible about that fact."

"Is that where you met him, by any chance? At work?"

The pause is enough. "Yes," she says.

"In your same agency? Or department?"

Can't Mary hear the edge in Flynn's voice?

"No," says Mary.

"Then, another?"

"A reasonable deduction," says Mary. "But I'm not playing twenty questions. Do you want me to text him or call him, tell him who is asking and let him decide?"

"No," says Flynn. "In fact, that might backfire in a way you don't want to know."

"Then tell me everything," says Mary. "You don't think I can handle it? Is that it? The folks in HR, you know, we know that people are complicated. Layered. They are not everything they seem at first. That's a given."

"This is complicated," says Flynn.

What can she offer? What can she trade? How can she get through?

"I've got time," says Mary.

"He'll never know I got his name from you. I protect my sources."

"I'm sure you do," says Mary. "Except I will have broken my promise to myself, to protect the privacy of others. Everyone I work with. Everyone I know."

"This is not a routine thing," says Flynn. All she has is Mary's first name and telephone number. How many state agencies are there with an HR department, and how many have an up-to-date website listing their HR department employees? Maybe Max can turn the telephone number into a street address if it comes to that. "I would say 'urgent,' but that doesn't feel like a word that even begins to touch the level of immediacy or alarm."

"Then call the police," says Mary. "He's coming over in a bit. I will definitely tell him we had a chat, and I'll tell him to give you a call."

"He's coming *there*?"

The pause is protracted. Flynn waits.

"You are worrying me now," she says. "Something in your voice."

"Make sure that door stays locked," says Flynn. "Look, this is no longer a reporter talking. This is a woman. And we're woman to woman, okay, person to person. Pretend for one moment a good friend is warning you. Someone you truly trust. Your principles are all wonderful and I respect them to the red-hot center of my journalistic core, but don't do anything to let him think you're there. Leave every light the way it is—off or on. Stay out of sight. And tell me your name and where you live. If you think I'm wrong about the stakes, once this is over, I'll quit my job."

Flynn gives her space. And time. Seconds like minutes.

"I have my rules," says Mary. "My standards."

"Me too," says Flynn.

"I try to live by mine."

"Reporters make mistakes. It happens."

"You weren't *reporting* when Deborah Ernst lost her life. You were doing something else."

"I was trying my best," says Flynn. "I was trying to help. I was doing as I was asked. And it was the last place I wanted to be. Same as now, trying to get through to someone who doesn't know me on the telephone. Trying to help."

"I'll give it some thought."

"Does he seem normal to you? All the way normal?"

"What is normal?" says Mary. "Never ask someone who works in human resources to answer *that* question."

CHAPTER 96

The evening is slick and chilly. The sky oozes moisture. Harry walks east five blocks, south five blocks, west five blocks, and comes back around to Mary's place. He floats in the dappled oxy mist.

Mozart's *Jupiter* Symphony soars on his headphones, the shimmering violins like a warm rain.

He need not worry. He can justify every stray fingerprint—they'd been dating.

For crying out loud.

From across the street, he stares at Mary's front door. He stares at the window upstairs. He pictures himself the night before, inside her place. He remembers how she tasted, how she squirmed.

Harry stares at the door.

And the window.

It's time.

He texts Mary.

There in a few.

Waits.

Sorry, Harry. I need a raincheck. Sorry if you've already headed this way.

So damn fickle!

I got a place all picked out.

A raincheck is fucked.
Now that he's all primed.

Another night.

Please?

I'm "pleasing" you back. Let's not rush.

What? Why? I'm almost there. One drink. I want to see you.

Like I said . . .

I know now how good you are for me.

You're jumping to conclusions. This is what I meant by taking it slow.

Since the other night, I feel like it's a new Chapter for me. Sorry to be so blunt.

This is what I meant.

You tame me, center me. It's like you know how to make the world stop spinning.

It hasn't. I need a night.

One drink?

One drink leads to another and then, you know.

Swear to the drink only.

I need alone time. Please don't push.

What's changed?

I brought you something. A small token of appreciation.

Waiting.
Waiting.

Jesus, Harry. Pushy isn't a good look. Go find a bar. I'll text you in about an hour. I need to pull myself together.

A bar? He doesn't hang out in *bars*.

CHAPTER 97

Harry squats in the shadows. He digs into his bag. He waits for a moment with no passersby.

He slips on his mask.

All he needs is the initial pause, that's all.

Why is she stalling?

◆ ◆ ◆

Harry knocks on her door.

Waits.

Rings the bell.

Waits.

The games!

Knocks.

The door opens.

"Fuck off," says Mary. Agitated. Frazzled. "I have pepper spray. Read the sign—no solicitors. *Go!*"

Harry listens to his own breath. She's never seen this face before. It's the face of bland, generic, and everyday White. Later, she might realize that if she'd looked closely, she could see it wasn't real, that the cheek skin and the nose skin and the chin skin didn't move the way they should. The skin lacks suppleness. Humanity.

Harry says nothing. He cocks his head like a robin listening for a worm.

"Please—" he says. "I only need a minute."

Harry pushes the door back with authority.

She stumbles back. Gasps. Trips a bit on her precious parking lot for shoes, keeps her balance.

Harry slams the door behind him.

She screams, a quick blurt.

He catches her by the opening to the kitchen.

Oxy buries the aches. Adderall jacks him up, counterpunches the drowsies. He is riding a poor man's speedball.

He gets an arm around her neck.

She twists and wriggles away. She's strong up top.

She scrambles over the couch, heads to the back door.

Another scream.

He is right behind her, catches her around the waist this time, and scoops her up and he flashes back on all the other times, the delicious burst of adrenaline.

Harry gasps for air, drops her on the couch.

He falls on top of her.

And her flailing fists.

His bag too far out of reach . . .

Motherfuck.

"Harry, please," says Mary. "Is this a joke? A fantasy?"

"Who is Harry?" The last guy she will ever see is the man in the mask. Generic Dude. "You been seeing someone else?"

"Harry, let's talk."

"Who. The. Fuck. Is. Harry?"

Harry's lips scrape her whistle-clean ear as he says it. She smells like cedar and patchouli. What is she hiding?

How long will it take to reach for the bag? And come back?

She squirms. She rolls over, face down. She bucks and squirms with her hips. Maybe he should fuck her first.

Give her hope.

"Harry . . ."

"One more mention of Harry and I'll smack your pretty little face."

A cell phone buzzes.

The phone sits on the edge of the glass coffee table, smack by the engraved snake munching its own tail. The electronic gizmo vibrates, and for a moment Harry thinks it's the snake that's rattling, because the snake slithers up and shakes its head at Harry and then settles back down, eyes like red-hot daggers.

Harry sucks in a breath, recoils.

The cell vibrates angrily.

"Who the hell is that, little missy? Maybe that's Harry calling?"

Right in her woodsy-smelling ear.

Again the insistent buzzing rattle.

The snake curls off the table like a cobra, stares at him for a long minute, settles back.

Harry's whole head is warm. The mask itches. His chest thumps.

Again, the buzz.

It's out of reach.

"Somebody wants you bad," he says.

Harry stretches to reach the thing, to shut it up or throw it through a window. He has to reach past the snake.

He eases his pressure on Mary to reach the damn thing.

He grabs the phone, flips it over.

"Hello?"

He answers in a high-pitched falsetto.

Hears nothing.

Again, "Hello?"

Same falsetto.

"Who is this?"

Recognizes the voice.

Cannot believe it.

Little Miss Star Reporter.

Why the fuck—?

A kick catches him flush in the face.

Harry falls in a heap by the coffee table. The phone skitters away.

Harry lays prone on the floor. His jaw aches. Mary's pale fingers grab the silver phone. He's within striking distance of that goddamn snake. He hears her.

"Help. Yes, help. Come now. Police too, police yes. Now, now, now."

Harry wants to curl up under the table and go to sleep. His head spits sizzling flames of sweat. The flames will light the house on fire. The fire will consume Mary and her house and he will slip out the back door unscathed and . . .

No.

He struggles to his knees, to his feet. Wobbles. Staggers. Whacks his shin hard on the coffee table. Harry grabs the table by the snake and throws the glass over and it shatters with a happy crash.

Then, quiet.

Where is Mary?

Where has she gone?

Harry slips off his mask, grabs his bag.

Outside, the night air smacks his face. It's cool and refreshing.

CHAPTER 98

Mary's house is empty, but the upended coffee table and shattered glass say it all.

No blood.

No body.

Thirty-three minutes since Mary answered the phone. Since, finally, she offered up his name.

Harry Kugel.

Flynn finds Mary's number in recents, hits it again.

No answer.

Back outside, the sidewalks are slick. Noisy weeknight drinkers escape from upscale bars. If Harry Kugel is smart, he'll slip into one of the busy joints and hide in a back booth, then slink down a sewer grate at closing time and leave himself to the hungry winter rats.

But PDQ isn't smart.

Only lucky.

How else to explain his sloppy aborted break-in at Tamica's? Or his plan now to go after someone in his own circle? Maybe one of his few friends? Harry has been lucky since the beginning.

Max texts:

Five minutes out.

Flynn sends a thumbs-up, but five minutes is an eternity.

She needs a direction to head. The one-way street in front of Mary's house is blocked with squad cars. Lights flash, radios chatter, orders are barked.

Flynn calls Mary again, no answer. Flynn answers twenty questions from one detective. Answers most of the same questions from another. She is vague about the degree of communication she's had with PDQ. She boils it down to "a tip." *A tip* led her to Niko's. *A tip* led her to the female foursome. *A tip* led her to Rive Gauche, and then she got Mary Belson's name and number from one of Mary Belson's friends in that group and Flynn tries to stay patient and answer the questions, but her mind races off down the streets.

He is moving now, jumping from shadow to shadow in the night in hopes of making it back to his lair and closing the door and resuming life as an ordinary dude.

But it's all over except for the capture, except the worst thing will be for Harry Kugel to pull a Jerry Damphouse. He doesn't deserve to take the easy path off this planet. He needs to stand for his horrid, hideous past.

◆ ◆ ◆

Flynn stands in the cool night air. She wants to move. Cops fan out in all directions. She wants to help. She has the shape in mind. His general size. She compiles images from Niko's and the football rally footage in her head.

◆ ◆ ◆

It's doubtful the cops got it wrong back then, about PDQ living on the south flank of Capitol Hill. If PDQ is heading home, he will head south on a side street like Pearl or Pennsylvania or the alleys in between, dodging streetlights.

Flynn heads south. On foot. Texts Max:

Heading south on Pearl.

The reply comes in a flash.

Leave the search to the cops.

Flynn slows at Pearl and Seventeenth. She waits for a burst of traffic flying out of downtown. Texts Tamica:

Follow me? Come to me? Urgent. 17th and Pearl.

A sleek black unmarked sedan pulls to the curb where she stands.

Max climbs out of the passenger's side. With him, two plainclothes cops. One is Wade. White. The other, Cornelius. Black. Set jaws. Shoulders for toting around grand pianos.

"You sure?" says Max.

"About what?"

"That he headed this way?"

"Following my gut," says Flynn. "Where's Wyatt?"

"With a neighbor. He's fine."

Flynn leads. Cornelius matches her pace on the opposite sidewalk. Wade hugs the shadows in the street by the parked cars, a few paces behind. Max stays on Flynn's shoulder, jostling her a bit as they move. She doesn't mind.

Sixteenth Avenue.

Colfax Avenue, under the shadow of the basilica.

Nothing.

They leave the traffic-laden Colfax behind and slip into the quieter residential streets—an urban hodgepodge of houses and small apartment buildings. Their strides are double a normal pace.

"We got his home address. South of the Governor's Mansion."

"What?"

"We have cops covering every angle around Governor's Park. The only thing is if he's smart enough to not go home. Then it could be a very long night."

At Tenth, Flynn glances left, glances right—

There.

Headphones.

Dark coat.

The flat lump of a messenger's bag strapped to his back.

"Fucking right there," whispers Flynn.

Max sees him, signals to Wade and Cornelius.

"Straight into the park by the Governor's Mansion," she says. "Pennsylvania dead-ends right there."

CHAPTER 99

Footfalls spank the wet, slick road. Wade runs five paces in front, striding on the balls of his feet. Cornelius scampers west to follow PDQ down Pennsylvania, creating a seal in case PDQ turns around.

Max and Flynn follow Wade. Their triangle moves down the center of Pearl Street. Flynn jogs.

A hefty black gun materializes in Wade's grip.

They cross a traffic-free Eighth Avenue, Flynn insisting they walk across at a normal heading-home-from-the-bars pace in case PDQ crosses at the same time.

Nothing.

They run south on Pearl, a massive old mansion as cover on their right. They follow a driveway where it cuts between two big houses and then the stub of a road tapered down to a sidewalk that pulls them to the heart of Governor's Park. To their right, Pennsylvania dead-ends inside the park.

Flynn's internal clock says they have a minute's lead at most. "Guns away. Now." Staging is everything.

Flynn peers out between the narrow crack of light between the bulwark torsos of Max and Wade, the cops facing her.

"Pretend we're friends. We're having a laugh. I'll start." Flynn ups the volume of her voice, gives it a weird lilting drawl.

"Aw, you guys. You make me laugh. You want to hit one more bar?"

"Well, sure." Max, stiff as an undertaker. Or the undertaker's client.

"Looser," whispers Flynn. "We're like half-drunk."

Wade bellows with authority into the night, wolf teeth flashing. "Oh yeah. That's for sure." He laughs again, whacks Max's back. Flynn laughs to add a female trill to the beefy chorus, and Max offers an awkward chortle.

And PDQ strolls out of the darkness.

The same gait.

The same grim bearing.

Straight back.

And the headphones.

He won't even hear their irrelevant theater.

"He's coming," she whispers. "But he's got the headphones. He's not going to hear us. Fifty yards out. Don't turn around."

PDQ is out of the direct beam from the last streetlight and back into the shadows. He prefers the street to the sidewalk. The thick ear cups of his fat headphones make for a distinctive silhouette.

"So close," she says.

A car door slams in the distance. A helicopter buzzes overhead—and keeps going. An orange tabby leaps from the shadows of a parked car and sprints through a pool of light. Flynn glances at the canopy of trees overhead. Even with her escorts and all the weaponry around, she feels very much alone.

"Don't wait too long," says Max.

Wade reaches into his jacket.

"Three," says Flynn.

The street dead-ends at a curb. PDQ has four strides of street left.

"Two," says Flynn.

PDQ stops.

For no reason.

Ten feet away.

He stares at the huddle in front of him. He pushes his headphones back over his head. He pulls his bag around to the front of his chest, reaches inside.

Wade pulls out his gun, starts to turn.

"Don't," says Flynn.

Harry stands and stares.

He knows.

"Fuck," whispers Flynn.

Wade turns, gun drawn. Max matches him, gun drawn.

Flynn steps around Max and walks into the light, off to the side of the two cops.

"Oh my," says Harry Kugel. Unimpressed. He stands dead center in a wash of overhead light.

Tinny violins bleat from the headphones.

"More Holst?" says Flynn.

Harry takes in the scene. "If you can't tell Mozart from Holst, why are you even alive?"

His entire countenance is bland. Oval face, a high forehead, shortish hair, and inset eyes. He is compact, shorter than she'd imagined.

Harry Kugel holds a syringe. The needle glints in the streetlight. "Don't even think about coming closer," he says. "And you know, I haven't done anything. Oh, I suppose you could get me for buying synthetic fentanyl. Yep, this shit comes from China through Canada. Or maybe it comes from Mexico on the same shipments of heroin and cocaine being smuggled with the help of dirty Denver police. From Juárez, perhaps?"

Harry holds it so the needle points up.

"I mix my own," says Harry. "And this particular batch has a kick about a hundred times what you might get from a teaspoon of street-grade heroin. I'd give you thirty seconds."

"Emily," says Flynn. "Emily. Karen and Amy."

"Years ago," says Harry. "Years and years ago. And I've gotten better. All on my own. I didn't need one dime of public money to get fixed. Think about that. You could spend more to park your car downtown for thirty minutes than it cost the taxpayers—nothing—to fix me. And I'm good. All good. Not only that, I did this city a favor. By stepping forward, by letting the world know Robbie McGrath wasn't me. Think about it. Think about all the hundreds and maybe thousands of lives that would have been ruined by the vile street dealers who knew they didn't need to worry about the police coming around? Have you thought about that? In the big equation in the sky?"

"Emily," says Flynn. "Karen and Amy. Their families."

Harry closes his eyes as if summoning patience.

"How are you feeling these days, Miss Flynn?"

"Better than you, I'm sure."

"Feeling better than after your snafu with the hostages at the gas station?"

"Drop the needle," says Max.

"No," says Harry Kugel. "You put the guns down. Both of you. Or I kill myself."

"You don't want that," says Flynn.

"No, *you* don't want that," says Harry. "For me, not so bad. I've had issues, as I've explained. My father, you know, all the beatings. My mother. You know, my mother's accident. Leaving me exposed, you know. Vulnerable. How do you think all that's going to play? It's been hard keeping it all together. But I did it. On my own. Again, credit where credit is due, okay? But it's not easy. Carrying all this around. And if I put this needle in my thigh, all the long suffering will be over. And you? You get nothing."

Behind Harry . . .

Flynn tries like hell not to shift her focus . . .

Cornelius.

Moving.

Stepping.

Harry Kugel's tinny-cup Mozart climbs toward a crescendo.

Harry turns.

"Jesus," says Harry. "They're everywhere."

"Watching your apartment too," says Max. "There's nowhere to go."

"Then all I have to do is wait for you to shoot. That'll look good, a man armed with a syringe. Shot to pieces."

Harry turns to Cornelius, shows him the needle. "Why don't you come around and join your two friends over here?"

Cornelius looks at Max. Max nods.

"But," says Harry. "First. Put your gun down on the ground right there. Leave it. And same for you, Max McKenna and your friend there, big White cop."

Flynn imagines a well-aimed bullet, a wing shot or a wound.

Cornelius circles around to the side, keeps his gun.

"This isn't going anywhere," says Flynn.

"I don't see guns on the ground," says Harry.

"It's not going to happen," says Max.

"Do you really want the world to know that I was your source? How do you think it's going to look when the city knows you were protecting me? That you sat on that information for a long, long time? Even after you discovered that I had been in your home and sat in your son's room—for hours?"

Flynn turns to Max as if considering the question. She spots the outline of the Ruger in Max's front pocket. One more gun won't change the equation.

Flynn takes three steps forward, Max and Wade behind her. Cornelius is at three o'clock in the corner of her eye.

"Fentanyl," says Harry, showing her the stick.

"If my source doesn't mind being outed," says Flynn, "I drag them into the limelight whenever they're willing. Even the assholes."

Harry flinches. "I'm a good person." He has a hard time spitting it out. Each word a struggle.

"Is that why you were planning to kill Mary Belson?" says Flynn.

"Not true," says Harry.

"Then show us the bag. What's in there? Your special gloves. Holst on an iPod. Adrian Boult, right? Extra set of earbuds. Care to show us?"

"My favorite music," says Harry. "And if it's illegal to carry an iPod, I was unaware."

Flynn takes another step. There's a faint sparkle in his eyes. *He's loving this.* His eyebrows are reddish, faint.

"There will be no confusion," says Flynn. "Nobody on your jury will have a hard time wondering why you had those things in your bag. But there's also Emily, Karen, and Amy. You don't get to walk away."

"Fifteen years!" says Harry.

"Doesn't matter."

"Fifteen years," says Harry. "I've hurt nobody."

"Don't worry. You'll go down in history as someone who got away with it for a very long time," says Flynn. "Won't you want to read about yourself? How well you maintained a life for all that time? Hidden in plain sight? Won't the stories be, you know, flattering?"

Harry looks down, takes a moment, looks back. *A flicker of a smile?*

"Bit of a legend," says Flynn. "History making, I'd say. National news, Harry. National fucking news. Someday, someone will ask to interview you. Maybe do a book."

She is close enough to see it but doubts anyone else does. Harry stands taller. His chest puffs.

She sees the crack of a grin.

"Well," he says. A whisper.

Behind Harry, Flynn catches movement.

The motion is vague, blurred, and off center.

"Fifteen years. Worked hard. Hurt—" Harry's voice cracks. He points the syringe at her. "Hurt nobody."

The blur starts to Harry's left. It's at head level. It's silver, aluminum, and thick. Harry senses something and begins to duck, but not fast enough. The blur catches Harry flush.

Harry grunts hard. He drops in a heap.

The syringe flies up, spins, and drops. The tube rattles, plastic on concrete. Before the syringe comes to a stop, Max and his two cops are huddled over Harry Kugel's inert form.

Tamica stands there, tripod baseball bat in her grip. She exhales and takes a knee, lets her head slump down. "Holy crap," she says.

CHAPTER 100
THURSDAY

Snyder, Colorado, sits on the north side of the South Platte River, six miles up the road from Brush. Flynn wonders, in morbid fashion, if she might find the tree where Harry Kugel's mother died.

And what about Harry's father? Is he around? Will he be lucid? Grumpy? A hater of city folk? Based on Harry's tale, it's easy to imagine a door being slammed in her face. She's familiar with the sound and fury involved.

A crack of orange lights the eastern horizon. The dull strip of color looks as if someone has walked out to the edge of the field, put up a long low fence, and painted it pumpkin. On this winter day, the sun will reveal itself as a tease and then spend the next eight hours behind a thick ceiling of inscrutable gray.

Tamica parks on Fisher Avenue. She peers down stubby Third Street. The street dead-ends in a fallow field. One small house on each side. A black Lab with a graying snout strikes a sphinx pose in the middle of the street, ignoring the morning cold. The old dog stares at the new arrivals. Friend or foe?

The upcoming live shot from Harry Kugel's hometown is thanks to Max. All the reporters are clamoring around Governor's Park, the hospital, or DPD HQ. Which probably stands for "hellish quarters."

Reporters don't know about Mary's townhome. Or anything about her. Again Max came through with the back-channel story. Mary had run from her house. She was scared and had a hard time forming words but found someone to call the police as well. She'd been taken to the hospital and checked out. Her bruises would heal, Flynn thinks, but the terror of realizing who she'd been dating and the close encounter with his barbarity might never find a salve.

Flynn Martin is the only reporter who knows PDQ's full, real name. Police said they wouldn't release it until a news conference later in the morning, time TBA.

Flynn, in fact, plans to utter Harry Kugel's full name for the first time on the live shot, with Snyder as backdrop. Her station has preempted all programming and gone into round-the-clock coverage. The arrest is an all-hands-on-deck story. The coverage this time has a more relaxed quality to it. Metro Denver breathes a sigh of relief.

◆ ◆ ◆

So does Flynn.

But not for the obvious reasons.

It was refreshing to hear Goodman's praise. Nothing over the top, of course, but praise nonetheless. Yes, an actual compliment. Lightning fast, but there it was. "Excellent work."

She knows not to take it to the bank. She is only as good as her next story.

What stuck to her ribs were the words from Max. He was so tender she barely recognized him. He stood close all night, except twice when various investigators insisted on alone time with her. Max had his own statements to give, reports to write. But Max watched out for her as the pieces were sorted out. The mayor, the governor, and members of the city council and top brass from the city and a swarm of media made the scene one of chaos and turmoil.

But when Max came through with Harry Kugel's hometown and the street address where he grew up, he said he wanted to ask her a question. They were standing near the SUV that Tamica would drive on the sprint to Snyder. They were equal parts whipped and raring to go.

Max asked for even more of a "moment."

They walked without saying a word to a bench in Governor's Park, outside the main hubbub. Flynn could have easily stretched out on the unforgiving metal. Her body would have collapsed as if the frozen metal slats were goose down.

Max pulled her in for a seated sideways hug. Flynn barely recognized this guy with the attentive side.

"Okay," said Flynn. She tapped his chest, gave his cheek a quick kiss. "I'm fine."

"I'm not." Max put his right thumb and his right index finger over his closed eyes. She felt his chest shudder. "Jesus, that could have gone wrong about 1.5 million ways."

"But it didn't," said Flynn.

"I was so close to putting a bullet in his chest," said Max.

"But you didn't," said Flynn.

"Because you were in my shot."

Flynn didn't want to linger on the topic. She had recapped everything for the cops. Ad nauseam. She told Max she had to get going, urged him to be there to take Wyatt to school. She wanted Wyatt to hear the news from his dad.

Thinking about Wyatt was what did it. Sorrow and relief welled in her chest like a carbonated bubble the size of a basketball. She wanted to hug Wyatt until her arms dropped off from squeezing. But why not the same feeling about the guy sitting next to her? Where would she be without his help?

"Soon," said Flynn.

"Soon what?"

She heard a crack in his voice, a softness.

"I'm not looking for cheesy closure or any of that."

"We made a pretty good team," said Max. "At least, as soon as you let me in."

"There you go," said Flynn. "Exactly what I don't want to do, recap everything. Not now. And by the way, was that a dig?"

"Only if you let it be," said Max. "There is some value in teamwork. I know now why you did what you did. And I'm impressed."

"You're recapping," said Flynn.

"And you're doing the whole island thing—even now."

"The island thing? And do we have to do this now?"

"No," said Max. "I want to make one point."

"Make it quick."

"Your instincts are good. And you need to let others care for you, you know? It wouldn't hurt."

They had left at 6:00 a.m. after hours of questions from the cops. Tamica chugged an energy drink, Flynn sipped coffee and, for a few blissful minutes, napped.

Seventy minutes and ninety miles later, the dirt-street town of Snyder. Not a skyscraper in sight. Or cop. Or reporter.

"How specific a shot do we want?" says Tamica.

Flynn stares at her phone. Goodman messaged her earlier with a photo from Harry Kugel's senior year at Brush High School. Harry's teenage look was long hair and a pinched smile.

"You mean, are we going to shoot video of the actual house? Like maybe we should confirm it first?"

Flynn thinks about the island where she works, the island of *how* she works.

Of Max's critique.

Let somebody care for her?

"Exactly," says Tamica.

The house is listed to Richard Kugel.

Goodman texts:

How soon?

Setting up. Give us five. Nobody beating us on this one.

ASAP.

How about a little slack around here?

Have you been busy or something?

Tamica unloads gear. The morning chill is bracing, assertive, and damp. They are downhill and downriver from Denver, where cold air comes to pool. Flynn scrolls her phone for developments from the competition. She jots notes for her stand-up. What is there to say?
Harry Kugel grew up here.
Harry Kugel's very troubled upbringing started here.
Harry Kugel went to high school down the road in Brush.
Harry Kugel broke into my house . . .
Someday, it will all come out. Won't it?

They plan to poke around town later, see if they can find anyone who knew Harry back in high school and who might say that they could spot an evil streak way back when. Maybe a former teacher at the high school.

"You going down there?" says Tamica.

"I'm surprised there are no cops at the house."

"Maybe the cops have already come and gone."

"Does that even seem likely?" says Flynn.

"Maybe there's no big fat rush," says Tamica. "Not like anything is going to change."

The it's-all-over feeling is hard to ignore.

"Stay here," says Flynn. "But why don't you get a shot of me walking to the house? See if you can get an angle that shows the front door, but, you know, don't make it look too obvious that you're rolling?"

◆ ◆ ◆

The house sits back from Third Street. Lazy smoke snakes up from the chimney. The gray plume pancakes against the overhead inversion. The air smells like sweet burning wood and cow pasture, a fine noncity aroma with a definite appeal. Real. A medium-size barn sits behind the house in the murky morning.

Flynn climbs five steps to the wide wraparound porch. Wood planks wheeze. Squeaky-clean windows reveal a golden glow inside the house, but Flynn keeps her eyes front and center.

Why so nervous?

How many times has she knocked cold on someone's door? A thousand?

She taps a gold fox-head door knocker with her left hand. Three beats. She tucks her wounded hand with the gauze bandage in her pocket.

The door opens wide.

"Good morning."

The man is medium height. Seventy-plus. White, thin hair. Thick glasses. Slightly stooped. He wears gray Carhartts like he's about ready to head out for chores—or maybe he's already been.

"Good morning." Flynn catches a whiff of coffee. And bacon. Glorious bacon. "I'm a reporter from Denver, and I'd like to ask you a few questions."

The look on the man's face is pure confusion. "Thought maybe I'd won a prize or something. We enter those sweepstakes things, you know. We saw your truck down the way, and they always bring a television crew, you know?"

"No," says Flynn. "I'm afraid not. Are you Richard Kugel?"

"Far as I know."

"This is about your son, Harry."

"Harry? Oh my."

The look on his face is alarm or excitement. Flynn can't be sure. Richard turns and takes a few steps back inside the house, waves Flynn inside. "Alice!" he shouts.

To Flynn's right is a room converted to a cozy library, floor-to-ceiling books and two brown leather chairs. To her left, an old rustic dining table set. Simple and inviting. A carafe of orange juice. A giant pepper grinder. Two teal place mats. Behind the table, another wall of shelves, this one devoted to family photos and knickknacks. Dead center in the wall, a clockwork orrery on a round base. Earth is painted lilac, the only planet given a shade other than dull copper. Jupiter is ginormous.

"Alice? Your wife?"

"There better not be another Alice in the house," says Richard. "Forty-five years together last month."

"Forty-five years?" says Flynn. "Wait—you didn't lose your wife in an accident?"

"What?" Richard Kugel frowns. "What are you talking about?"

A woman makes her way through a swinging door where, no doubt, they store secrets about frying perfect bacon. The woman is fit and trim, a bit sprightlier than Richard. She wears a bright-red apron over blue jeans and a thick brown sweater. Her toffee hair is clipped short. Tidy. Efficient. Sleek. Hearty.

"What is it?" she says. "Something wrong?"

"It's about Harry," says Richard. "And maybe that you had an accident?"

"Harry?" says Alice.

"The police haven't contacted you yet?" says Flynn.

"Police?" says Richard. "What about?"

"There was no accident years ago? Drunk driving?"

"Drunk driving?"

"You've been married all along?"

"Saint Mary's Catholic Church, downtown Brush," says Richard. "I don't get what this is all about."

"We lost contact years ago." Alice looks worried. "Harry stopped all communication. We tried and tried, but after a certain point, it was all one way."

Flynn shakes her head. Wrong house? Wrong Harry? Wrong what? "He said he lost his mother in a drunk driving accident."

"I have one glass of brandy every year on Christmas Eve," says Alice. "A ritual. And it's a pinch of drink. One bottle lasts us years. And years."

"Your son said—" This will be an even more challenging detail to utter. "Harry said he was punished as a child?"

Punished is the mildest word she can conjure.

"*Whupped*, you mean?" says Richard.

"Oh my," says Alice. "He never touched them. *We* never touched Harry or any of them—he's got three brothers, all good kids. We've got eight grandchildren too."

"You talked to Harry?" Richard Kugel seems excited.

"Yes," says Flynn. "I've talked to Harry."

Alice pauses, glances a question at her husband.

"We have plenty of eggs and a whole pot of coffee. Come in and tell us what you know. Your friend up the street, too, the one pretending she's not taking pictures with that fancy camera? Tell her to come on down here and get warm, have some breakfast. Tell us what you know. But keep in mind, Harry was always a very good liar. What's he done now?"

ACKNOWLEDGMENTS

Thank you to Jessica Tribble Wells and everyone at Thomas & Mercer. Thanks to my diligent, supportive literary agent, Josh Getzler. Thanks to Danielle Burby for her early interest and enthusiasm as well. (This novel probably wouldn't have happened without Danielle.) Also thanks to Kevin Smith for finding dozens of inspired ways to make this story better and to copyeditor Bill Siever and proofreader Elyse Lyon for their meticulous efforts and significant improvements. Heartfelt thanks to veteran Denver reporter and anchor Kelly Werthmann for answering my many questions about television news reporting today.

ABOUT THE AUTHOR

Photo © 2019 Tom Sandner

The son of two librarians, Mark Stevens was raised in Lincoln, Massachusetts, and has worked as a reporter, as a national television news producer, and in public relations. *The Fireballer* (Lake Union, 2023) was named Best Baseball Novel by *Twin Bill* literary magazine and named a Best Baseball Book of the Year by *Spitball Magazine*. His novel *Antler Dust* was a *Denver Post* bestseller in 2007 and 2009. *Buried by the Roan*, *Trapline*, and *Lake of Fire* were all finalists for the Colorado Book Award (2012, 2015, and 2016, respectively), which *Trapline* won. *Trapline* also won the Colorado Authors League Award for Best Genre Fiction.

Stevens's short stories have been published in *Ellery Queen Mystery Magazine*, *Mystery Tribune*, and *Denver Noir* (Akashic Books). In both 2016 and 2023, Stevens was named Rocky Mountain Fiction Writers'

Writer of the Year. He hosts a regular podcast for Rocky Mountain Fiction Writers and has served as president of the Rocky Mountain chapter for Mystery Writers of America. Stevens also writes book reviews, which you can find at https://markhstevens.wordpress.com. He currently lives in Mancos, Colorado.